ALSO BY

HANNAH LYNN

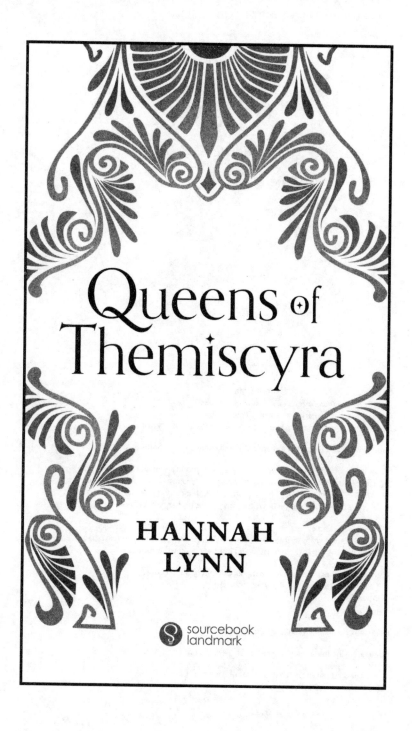

Queens of Themiscyra

HANNAH LYNN

sourcebook landmark

TO STEPHIE AND LAURA,
WARRIOR WOMEN

Copyright © 2022, 2024 by Hannah Lynn
Cover and internal design © 2024 by Sourcebooks
Cover design by The Books Covered Team
Cover images © 13Imagery/Shutterstock, letovsegda/Shutterstock

Sourcebooks and the colophon are registered trademarks of Sourcebooks.

Published by Sourcebooks Landmark, an imprint of Sourcebooks
P.O. Box 4410, Naperville, Illinois 60567-4410
(630) 961-3900
sourcebooks.com

Originally published in 2022 by Hannah Lynn.

Cataloging-in-Publication Data is on file with the Library of Congress.

Printed and bound in the United States of America.
LSC 10 9 8 7 6 5 4 3 2 1

PART I

ONE

HER BLADE WHISTLED THROUGH THE AIR, SURE AND UNWAV-
ering, first through the warrior's leather armor, then
through the soft flesh of his belly. A spray of blood arced
upward as he toppled from his horse. Already racing away, Hippolyte
paid him no mind. Her mare's hooves churned the dry earth beneath
them, sending up clouds of dust as the queen locked her aim on her
next victim. Within moments, he too lay face down in the dirt.

From all around came the clang of metal—swords against
shields, arrowheads against breastplates—and the stench of blood,
bitter and cloying, hung densely in the arid air. The aroma was one
she knew well. One of battle. Of sweat and pain. Burning skin under
the glare of Helios's sun, of horses slick with perspiration. But above
all else, it was the scent of victory.

Their adversaries, who only an hour ago had been screaming in rage
and fervor, were now crying in fear, begging for mercy, choking as they
drowned in their own blood. If they were fortunate, her women would
offer them a swift death. Flies had already arrived in droves, settling on
open wounds, buzzing around the corpses already graying in the dirt.

By the time the last scream had faded, and the sun had reached its zenith, the earth was crimson with the blood of the fallen.

Hippolyte cast her gaze across the scene. These were young men. Some barely in their teens. It was a weak king who thought to send such boys to face them.

"Back home to Pontus and Themiscyra, my queen?"

Hippolyte turned to face Penthesilea. Her sister sat upright upon her horse, her embroidered tunic, leather trousers, and boots—the traditional warriors' garb—possibly even more stained with the colors of battle than Hippolyte's own. The princess's bow was stowed in a sling on her back, the elegant weapon with its double curve, smaller than those their enemies favored. Smaller than those that littered the ground around them.

The bow had been carved, planed, and strung by Penthesilea's own hand. Wood and bone, shaved off in the finest of slivers, imperceptible to some, yet enough to shift the weapon's balance and ensure the truest of flights. Hippolyte could not imagine how many arrows had been loosed from it that day, how many bronze tips had met their target, piercing hearts or skulls. Penthesilea's arrows did not miss.

"Back home to Themiscyra, sister," the queen replied. "Although first we must collect our payment."

It was a handsome settlement; the best they had received in months. The bulk was in metals—gold, iron, bronze—that would be hammered out or melted down, but there were other items, too. There were jewels, both raw stones and those already cut and polished. There was pottery. There was even a lyre, and although she did not play herself, Hippolyte knew many of the women would strike a fine tune from it.

Within the city walls, the king had thanked them profusely,

bowing low to the ground in the awkward, angular movements of one unaccustomed to such humility, even less so toward women. Hippolyte was almost as uncomfortable with the display as he was. Afterward, settled into a more reposeful posture, he asked if they wished to stay the night. Most kings prayed she would refuse and offered only out of courtesy, and this was the case today. She could not help but note the flash of relief dart across his face when she declined his offer and found herself feeling a pang of sympathy for the man. This was unlikely to be the last battle they fought for him.

Their saddlebags full and their horses rested, they began the ride east, back to the region of Pontus and their citadel home, Themiscyra.

The journey to the edge of the Black Sea would take two days at a leisurely pace. If needed, they could ride at a gallop and without stopping unless unavoidable—that was the way they had ridden to reach here—but the women and the horses had earned a little respite.

Blue skies, scattered with feather-like clouds that hovered motionless in the still air, stretched above them as they rode. On a clear day like today, from its southernmost point, they could see all of Anatolia. To the north, beyond the Sea of Marmara, was Thrace, and west, across the Aegean, lay Thessaly and Athens. They had traveled to these places, and further still. They had traveled to Thebes and the Peloponnese, called to fight for kings who might otherwise have lost their lands. Called to rain their arrows on armies with whom they had no quarrel. And paid handsomely for it. Sometimes the battles would come one after another, and they would race from one belea-guered land to the next, always ready, always victorious. But for now, they were headed home to rest, basking in the scent of the ferns that littered the hillsides around them.

Women chattered as they rode. There was always a rush that came after battle. The adrenaline that had lent them such force and ferocity now drew words from their lips as quickly as the blood had spilled from their enemies. Such exuberant conversation between her women might endure for miles, over plains and through valleys, across rivers and around grand lakes. Yet inevitably, at some point before the sun set on that first day after a battle, the quiet would descend. The quiet in which they recalled those they had lost. Those that had been granted the most honorable of deaths. A warrior's death. An Amazon's death.

"Four women made their first kill today."

It was Antiope who spoke to the queen through the quiet. "Four who can ride with us to the Gargareans next spring."

"That is good news. I will meet with them personally upon our arrival home."

Shortly after midday, they halted at a shallow lake that had survived the droughts of summer. Shingle stones shimmered beneath the surface as the women knelt to wash the blood and grime from their skin and watched as swirls of red eddied from their palms.

While Hippolyte and her sisters considered Themiscyra their home, this was not the case for all Amazons. Certainly, many dwelled within the citadel walls, with the protection and luxuries provided by so many warriors living in close proximity, but there were those who found such a life constrictive and claustrophobic. These nomads spent their time away from the battles wandering the steppes and camping out beneath the stars. They hunted with bow or spear, preferring to make small fires and pick the meat from the bones of the birds and beasts they had caught alone, rather than with the company of the other women. They craved solidarity, returning to join the rest of the warriors only on those occasions that required them to do so. At festivals, or to fight, or to embark upon the annual springtime trek south to the Gargareans. There was no enmity between the two groups of women. The queen had no preference in how the women lived and did not judge one way of life more favorably than another. Each woman could choose to spend her days in the manner in which she found the greatest delight, and each woman would therefore fight for it with the strongest fire.

By the time they had pitched their bivouacs, the sun had long since sunk below the horizon, and streams of stars glimmered above them. A chorus of cicadas hummed and buzzed, a complement to the chatter of the women. Lying with her back on the grass, her sword by her side, Hippolyte listened. This was her favorite time to learn—the night after a battle had been fought and won. The women would regale their comrades with stories of their opponents: how they fought, how close they came to striking them down. The maneuvers they had mastered and those that had nearly lost them their life. The queen would seal it all away in the back of her mind, ensuring they would not make the same mistakes again.

They had lost a dozen women that day. Nothing when set against the hundreds their opponents had suffered, but more than was acceptable. They had brought the bodies with them, wrapped tightly in linen to be returned to their homes in Pontus. They would perform a proper burial there, committing the women to the land with their weapons and horses and all the honor they deserved.

Next time, Hippolyte told herself as the fire sizzled and spat, she would not lose any. And she would offer a greater sacrifice to her father. Her father. Her immortal father. Ares, the God of War.

———

On the second day, the sky had brightened to the point of brilliance, Helios's glow so radiant they were forced to pull their hats lower on their heads and squint so tightly their eyes were barely open. The grass they trudged was short, brittle, and brown, and the horses flicked their tails, agitated by a heat that caused the flies to buzz in swarms and their coats to darken with sweat. Spring was a swift season in these parts, with lush green turning dusty and arid almost overnight. Heat rippled from the ground, blurring the air immediately above it. This part of the journey would end soon enough, though. The further northwest they traveled, the cooler it would become. And by nightfall, Pontus, and perhaps even Themiscyra, would be in view.

Hippolyte considered the harshness of life in a place such as this, for there could be little to hunt, nothing to fish, and no prospect of farming such lands. She had seen mules, gray and hunched, long eyelashes drooped and blinking, but no horses. The leaves were already browning on what few trees there were, their brittle twigs too weak to bear the meanest of fruit.

As was often the way when she passed through such lands, Hippolyte thanked the gods for all they had been given in Pontus and Themiscyra and vowed once again to present a sacrifice to her father upon her arrival home.

Hour after hour they rode, without stopping, even when the sun reached its apex. There was nowhere to stop, no shade to be found at this time of day. On they rode, until clouds began to form above them. Thick and white, like freshly plucked down, these clouds cast thin shadows on the earth. Small at first, they ripened as she watched. Swelling with water, their bases glimmering with gray as they muted the sun's rage.

There would be rain soon, Hippolyte thought, staring at those clouds. Strong, refreshing rain that would fall in great sheets bridging the void between sky and earth. This was the rain she had raced as a child, the rain she had lifted her head to greet, the rain she had let flow across her face, its very coolness replenishing her. Her memory stirred with moments from her childhood, she and Penthesilea riding out for days, living only on the rabbits that they caught or the berries they could forage. These were the days before Ares had chosen her ahead of her sister to rule the Amazons, despite Hippolyte not being the oldest. Only once had Hippolyte succeeded in drawing blood against Penthesilea. A nick. Nothing more. But that had been enough for Ares to name her queen.

But now she dwelled on the times before that, when they would train and spar and ride from dawn until dusk unburdened by the cares of leadership. They spent their time learning about their land. Practicing on horseback those acrobatics that would one day be put to the test in battle. But this had been one of their favorite games: to watch clouds thicken, to stand completely motionless beneath them. There they would wait while the clouds grew grayer and grayer until they had swollen so fat they could no longer contain all the moisture within them. At that point, the instant when the clouds cracked apart and unleashed their downpour, the girls would squeeze their horses and fly in an attempt to outride the rain.

Sometimes they made it. Sometimes they would reach shelter before the storm met them, or else keep riding at such pace that the clouds in time would lose their weight and have nothing left to drown them with. But more often than not they ended the game drenched. Soaked to the skin by the downpour. Hair plastered to their heads; their horses sodden from ear to hoof. And they would laugh as the icy water ran down their spines. Afterward they would build a fire and dry their leathers before riding back to Themiscyra and their mother to continue their training.

Noting again how the clouds were burgeoning above them, Hippolyte signaled to the women to pick up their pace. Squeezing her thighs around her bay mare, she urged it to a soft canter, and then faster still until she was galloping. Slicing through the grass.

The air drew through her hair like a comb as she closed her eyes and lifted her head to the sky. Not even the thrill of a battle could compare to this, to the thunder of hooves rumbling through the earth beneath them and the cold blast of air needling her skin with pleasure. The laughter of the women as they rode was more melodious than any lyre. More tuneful than any flute. All were now following her lead. Galloping as if their very lives depended on it.

A glance behind her brought a smile to her lips. Several of the women were taking advantage of the opportunity to practice their horseback combat positioning, twisting to face behind them or else balancing on their knees as their horses sprinted across the ground, their feet barely grazing the short stubble beneath their hooves. Some, Hippolyte saw, were grieving, remembering those who had been lost, all daughters, sisters, mothers. She would let the mourners ride out first next battle. Let them drown their pain in the blood of others.

As they approached the coast, the storm broke. Rather than the downpour she had hoped for, it fell in a mist. A light shower that formed perfect droplets on her skin and clothes before evaporating into nothing.

It was here, where the foaming waves crashed against jagged cliff edges, that the horses picked up the scent of home. Their pace quickened without instruction from their riders. Their nostrils flared as they turned in unison like a flock of birds, the pull of home upon them, the certainty that there was nowhere else on earth quite like it.

The citadel of Themiscyra had been built on the steppes of Pontus, with views out over the Black Sea. The land that surrounded them was an oasis, regardless of the time of year. It did not suffer droughts or floods. Their animals did not get plagued by mites or vermin, and the forests that filled the far regions to the east were as bountiful as the sea to the north. Birds, rabbits, wild pigs, and mouflon made their homes above and below the ground, their songs and snuffles providing choruses day and night, their tracks weaving among the thick layers of foliage that made a bed of the forest floor. Had they chosen to do so, the two thousand strong Amazon women might have picked a different-colored fruit for every day of the week, although no food was ever more satisfying than the food that came from a hunt. They would hunt that evening, Hippolyte thought to herself as she rode ahead of her sisters and the women. A good hunt to celebrate their victory and to find an adequate sacrifice. They would need to salt and dry more meat, too. Preparing for the long trips that might await them.

The queen's mind was so lost in her home and the future that it took her a moment to spy the flash of light on the peak of a hill several miles to the east. And even when she did see it, within a blink she had disregarded it as if it were some trick of the evening light, like rays reflecting off a puddle, or light caught on the sheen of iridescent wings. Small lakes and tributaries littered the land, though generally at lower levels than this. Birds, however, could be found everywhere. It was likely to be a bird.

"My queen." Antiope had sped from behind to catch her. "Did you see that? Did you see that light?"

"I did." Hippolyte was about to dismiss any concerns her younger sister might have had when the light flared again, directed straight toward them. Her heart quickened. It was no accident. It was a sure and certain signal, a flash of polished brass. One of the many mirrors placed along the tops of the steppes so that the women could signal each other. But the pattern of flashes was one they had never used before—one they had never had cause to use before.

It was well known, throughout Anatolia and the whole of Greece, that if men or women were in need of the services of the Amazons, the women would hear of it one way or another, but it would always be their decision as to who they aided. Sometimes money played a part, but often it was the righteousness of the cause that made the choice for them. Never did anyone other than the Amazons themselves set foot on the silver sands of their beaches or ride the dense forests to reach the steppes of their home. To do so would certainly bring about an intruder's demise. But in spite of this, the sequence of flashes came for a third time, and it could mean only one thing.

Outsiders had come to Themiscyra.

TWO

IT MUST BE A MISTAKE," ANTIOPE SAID. "AN ACCIDENT. A SHIP that has gotten lost, perhaps?"

There was no fear in her voice, only confusion. Confusion Hippolyte could feel herself. The single short, fleeting flashes of light had each lasted the same duration and had come consecutively, with no pauses between them. It was the sign that a boat was approaching from the Black Sea and encroaching upon their land. But for someone to land on their shores deliberately would be an act of war. A war that they would undoubtedly lose. There were only two possibilities: either this ship had lost its way or its sailors had lost their minds. Whichever the situation, she would not waste time wondering.

With a whip of her hands, she dug her heels into her horse's side. Raising the reins, she pushed her body forward into its withers. The animal knew the movement well. Within two strides, it was galloping forward, its rear legs sweeping back and forth in unison as its hooves skimmed the earth, Hippolyte's hair pushed back and away from her face by the force of the wind.

"Your zoster?" Penthesilea called to the queen as she quickened her pace and galloped alongside her. "We must prepare to fight. We must prepare for war."

Always the fight was at the front of Penthesilea's mind. The kill. The glory. It was true, there had been competitiveness between the pair. The desire to shine brightest in their father's eyes. But out of all her sisters and the women she fought with, there was no one that Hippolyte would rather have beside her in a battle. No one as fearless when faced with the gleam of a thousand swords. No one whose hand or mind were quicker. Her ax, her bow, her spear, whatever the weapon, if it were wielded by Penthesilea, it would not falter or miss. She was the warrior of all warriors.

"I have the zoster here." Hippolyte replied. The horse maintained its speed as the queen leaned to one side, slipping her hand into the satchel that was strapped fast to the saddle. A saddle stitched by her women, filled with wool and horsehair to soften the long rides. From out of the satchel, she pulled a large belt, which, with only one hand now on the reins, she fixed around her waist.

The leather zoster, which held her sword and knives, was reinforced with bronze and gold plaques and shone with a soft luster, reflecting all the light that fell on them. Etched into it were patterns so intricate and delicate it was obvious to all who saw it that it was the work of the gods. Despite its metal plates, it was supple between her fingers, and its shape had molded to her body over the years of wear.

The gift had been handed to her from her father, Ares, on the day she had been crowned Queen of the Amazons. His acknowledgment of her strength and leadership of the women. It had cemented her position as ruler and served as a physical reminder of the ichor that ran through her veins. In every battle since receiving the gift, she had worn the zoster without fail. Now she sometimes felt her women fought for the belt as keenly as they fought for her. For it displayed the truth: that each of them was blessed by Ares, and his hand would see their fates remained strong.

Hippolyte spoke to only her three sisters, who now rode alongside her, Antiope and Penthesilea to her left side, her youngest sister, Melanippe, to the right. "Signal the women to stay back. This may yet be a misunderstanding. I do not wish for bloodshed unless it is necessary."

"They have come to Themiscyra. They must pay the price they deserve." Eagerness for battle rang out in Penthesilea's voice.

"They will, if it is deserved. We do not condemn simple mistakes, though. There may well be an innocent explanation for this."

"I should return to the citadel. I should head to the children. See that they are protected," Melanippe said. She was by far the youngest, barely old enough to battle when Hippolyte had been crowned queen. Her hair was the fairest of them all, but her skin the darkest. Her almond eyes, while the same shape as her sister, had a unique wideness to them. A youthfulness, almost an innocence. This was the first time that Melanippe had come to battle since the birth of her twin daughters the previous spring. She had been eager to return to the field, to feel the weight of her sword in her hand again, to feel that cut of a breastbone beneath her blade, and Hippolyte had welcomed her back to the fray. However, now she could see the pressure this absence had placed on her, which was only heightened by their current situation.

"Plenty of women remained in Themiscyra. Over half our numbers. They will have protected them. You will stay with me. I wish for all the daughters of Ares to ride in together."

"As you wish, my queen." Melanippe dipped her head slightly as she rode forward. There would be no discussion on the matter. The queen had spoken.

No more conversation followed. No more words passed their lips other than to spur their steeds. The distant sweeping sounds of the sea were drowned out by the hammering of the horses' hooves, the heaving of the riders' breath barely muffling the drumming of their hearts. The light on the steppes flashed only once more. The women upon the hill would have noted that the army had changed its speed and would know their signal had been received. They, too, would be arming themselves now, preparing for whatever was to come.

Led by the queen, the warriors took a weaving path up the steppes. It was not the fastest route back, but it allowed them sight of the sea below, and what they lost in time they would gain in knowledge of these intruders. As the sea came into view, Hippolyte pulled on the reins of her mare, easing it into a slow canter before drawing it to a halt. Her heart pounded as she checked the zoster around her waist and observed the scene below.

The water was choppy, surging with frothy whitecaps that were broken by the wind before sinking back into the swell ready to rise again. Above them swilled dark clouds, their edges tinted with violet. Clouds that threatened a storm but were scudding fast across the sky. Experience told Hippolyte they would pass the mountains before the rains broke. Normally the queen might lose herself in such a view— the perfect backdrop against which to ponder battle plans for the future. But today her gaze held fast on the ship.

The Amazon women rarely traveled by sea if it were avoidable. Their horses could take them any place they wished to go, often faster and without the fear that Poseidon, or some other jealous god, might turn his wrath in their direction and impede their journey. As such, she did not have an intricate knowledge of sea vessels, could not expatiate upon them in the way she might upon horses or weapons or the way a bivouac of leather pelts can be assembled to withstand any terrain or weather. Still, she knew enough about water vessels to know that what she was viewing was a trireme. And a trireme was a ship of war. If the men on board came to shore, it would be a fight on their sands.

With three rows of oars and brass plates that shone a burnished orange in the muted evening sun, the ship's mainsail slapped back and forth in the wind, its percussion fighting for dominance amongst squalls of seagulls and the crashing of the waves. Hippolyte felt each smack of fabric as if it were a hand against her skin. An echo of the thudding within her bones. This was no lost vessel. No merchant been blown off course by a storm. These were rich men. Powerful men. And powerful people knew exactly where Themiscyra was.

They had dropped anchor a fair way from the shore, perhaps suspecting the sharp coral and rocks that hid beneath the surface close to land. Perhaps they had chosen the distance, knowing that they were beyond the reach of the women's venom-tipped arrows. The specifics didn't matter. They were too close by at least a hundred miles.

The queen strained her eyes, trying to see more. At such a distance she could make out no details to identify the vessel's origin, but she knew around two hundred men could fit aboard such a ship. Perhaps three hundred. It was a fact that caused her confusion, rather than distress.

In some battles, such a number might suffice for victory, yet what were three hundred men against the two thousand women of the Amazon army? Her women could kill them all with their arrows before they set a single foot upon the sand. And if it came to it, they would. But surely the intruders knew this. Perhaps if they had come as a fleet, a hundred such vessels, outnumbering the Amazons ten or twenty to one, they might stand a chance. But one ship. What could possibly be the purpose, unless every person aboard wished for a swift death?

"There, have you seen it? They are coming to shore."

Just as Penthesilea spoke, the queen's eyes fell upon another vessel in the water. It had been dropped on the far side of the trireme and only now was coming into view. It was a small smudge. A dark shadow amongst waves, little more than a blot beside the trireme, though recognizable still as a small rowing boat.

"That cannot hold more than a dozen men at most," Hippolyte said, her horse fighting against her hold as she held her there. Had she dropped the reins, it would likely have run straight to its stable without pause. But she held it there, watching as the small vessel drew closer. A dozen men, perhaps, but from the way their vessel raced forward, oars plowing through the water, they were strong.

"What can they be thinking?" Penthesilea asked. "This cannot be an attack, can it?"

"We rule nothing out," Hippolyte replied. "Keep your arrows at hand. It will not be long now. Men have come."

THREE

S UNLIGHT FRACTURED ON THE WAVES AND DANCED IN THE
evening air. The two parties arrived on the beach at much the
same time. Hippolyte and her army galloped through the long
stalks of bindweed and saltwort, flattening the plants to the sand as
the horses barreled over the dunes, snorting from the pace at which
they had been forced to go.

The rowing boat had maintained a strong speed to the shore,
and a quiet chant from the men aboard now reached the women's
ears. Ten men. That was all. They were close enough now that the
queen could count the individual figures. Could see each of them,
clad in armor, weapons in their hands. Ten men. Ten more than had
ever set foot on their land before.

Three hundred of her women were already waiting, women who
had not been needed at the last battle or who had stayed behind to
tend the children. This was a duty, necessary to safeguard the future
of them all, although many women would admit it was not their
preferred way to spend their time. The days and nights were long,
and the cries of young children did not set a heart pounding the

way the cries of war did. Those women who had waited were ripe for a fight. Primed. Prepared. Hippolyte could see it in the way they gripped their weapons. She could see it, raw and smoldering in their eyes. They were itching to spill blood. Their arrows and spears were raised, their armor fastened, their steeds straining on their reins. One exchanged a glance with the queen and dropped her chin. *The children are safe*, the look said. Hippolyte responded with a single nod. *They will stay that way.*

The other women fell into line without a word. Five deep and four hundred abreast, they formed an unassailable wall of warriors. A wall though which none would pass. Her horse snorted, the young mare foaming at the bit, its breath forming clouds in the air. With her shoulders back and bow in her hand, Hippolyte rode to the front of the women, her sisters remaining close behind. Any man who faced a daughter of Ares knew his end would be swift, but one who faced all four? They would soon find out.

All eyes locked on the queen awaiting her command. She galloped the length of her women, allowing the mare's head to flick back and her legs to kick out, before she turned in a tight circle and rode back the way she had come, stirring up the sand and sending a spray of dust into the air. The briny aroma of the sea held domain among the air's scents, but within it swirled nuances found only in Pontus. The tang of chokecherry and wood sorrel. The sweetness of pine and hornbeam. Aromas she would recognize no matter how long she was parted from them, just as she would recognize the slopes of the steppes or the vastness of the sky. This was her land, given to her by the God of War, and she would defend it with her life.

Before the watchful eyes of her women, and the men on the boat, she drew to a halt in line with the vessel and parallel to the shore-line, where the sand altered from dark to light and only the thinnest blanket of water rose over her horse's hooves. The boat was now mere yards away. The men were no longer chanting.

"Hold your arrows."

She projected her voice, but not for the benefit of her women. Rarely did she need to give battle speeches anymore. Her women had trained since birth, held spears in their hands when most their age would have been holding wooden toys. They required no urging to fulfill the task into which they had been born. She projected her words so that the men in the approaching vessel could be under no illusion as to who was in charge. One word from her, and fifteen hundred arrows would rain down on them. A hail of brass and wood from which the only escape would be death.

She moved to face the water. The men had jumped from the boat and were waist-deep in the waves. All of the men who had disembarked were of impressive stature, but it was the one at the front who drew the women's gaze. His shoulders were almost as broad as the oars in his bore were long, and his arms as thick as a horse's neck. Saltwater spray glistened like the stars in his hair, which fell in waves beneath his shoulders, and his face was framed by a tightly curled beard. His figure alone was imposing, but his garb even more so. For over his head hung the skin of lion.

"Heracles." Hippolyte had never set eyes on the demigod before, but the warrior's reputation preceded him. As, she assumed, did hers.

"Queen Hippolyte," he responded. The queen stiffened. So, he did know who she was, which meant his arrival was no accident. Penthesilea was right. They had come for war. Hippolyte enunciated her next words clearly.

"Given that you know who it is that you address, I would advise you to step no further. You will not find anything here, other than a brief ending."

Heracles the demigod. Heracles the son of Zeus. Heracles, soon to be killed by the Amazon queen Hippolyte.

His lips pursed in a slow chewing action, and though he did not step closer, he did not appear concerned by her words. Simply contemplative. His men, however, had concern writ large across their features. Some were dark-haired and dark-skinned, some fairer and with skin bordering on chalk white. They had been handpicked to join him on this expedition, no doubt for their skills with a blade. Every one of them bore scars upon his arms and torso. Some of the lines were faded, almost lost in the ripple of muscle, but others were fresher. Pink and angry. All of them had seen fights before this one. They did not cower, but their eyes showed hesitation. They knew that this fight would be their last.

There was man among the remaining nine that drew her attention almost as keenly as did Heracles. He was the next largest, the sinews in his arms and legs bulging, and other than Heracles himself, was the only man viewing the scene with anything other than trepidation. His hair glowed a deep burnished blond, and rather than scanning the lines of warriors like his companions, his eyes were locked on her. When at last he noticed that she had caught him watching her, she could have sworn those same eyes glimmered and a pink hue flushed his cheeks.

"Believe me, I mean you no disrespect," Heracles spoke, her attention returned to him. "I understand what I have done in arriving here, but here is the only place that I will find what I seek." His eyes fluttered momentarily downward, shifting his line of sight to her belt. It was the minutest of motions, no doubt imperceptible to any without her level of observation. But to her it conveyed the reason for his arrival. Without breaking his gaze, she rested one palm on the central brass plate of her zoster.

"I have not come seeking bloodshed," he said, his palms raised up in a gesture of peace. "Perhaps we could have a conversation."

"I believe we are conversing, are we not?"

"I was hoping for a little more privacy, as welcoming as this reception is." His eyes twinkled, and the corners of his mouth twisted upward into the slightest of smiles, but it did not fix in place. Instead, he dipped his head. "There are matters of some discretion I would like to discuss with you."

How would the scene unfurl should she refuse him this? This was her constant action, the endless scroll that rolled out in her mind, scanning through every possible outcome. Each move she made on the battlefield was wrought with instinct, but she had never confused instinct with haste. Every action had a consequence, and with each strike of her blade, she knew exactly what those consequences would be. She knew her next move. How many arrows remained in her quiver. How many strides her horse would take to reach the next opponent. She knew where her nearest woman was, where her furthest woman was. Each of her actions bore repercussions for her and for those around her. Repercussions that could stretch out in time and space, could affect them all for seconds or for years. And this situation was no different.

From somewhere in the back of her ranks, a horse whinnied, impatient as it awaited her response. But the horse would have to wait, and so would Heracles. For though her mind was settled, she wished to delay him. To draw the moment out. To prove who held the upper hand. Yes, she could end him now. A single gesture, imperceptible to him and the others, would see her sister Penthesilea send an arrow straight through his sternum. The rest of his men would fall in moments, dead before they even knew they were under attack. With that she could leave the bodies to the sea. A job done. It was an option. It was, she thought, the option her women expected her to choose.

Behind her she could sense their collective thoughts, a cloak of apprehension falling around them. Would she do it? Would she send the order? She was within her rights to do so, and none of the women would think any less of her for it; the men, after all, were trespassing. But that was not the queen she wished to be. That was not the leader she aspired to be for her women. Or the leader Ares had chosen.

Beside her came the shifting of sand as Penthesilea broke her line and moved closer to the queen, her fingers still firmly on her arrow, her eyes fixed on the target before her.

"I do not trust him," she whispered to her sister. "He is a killer."

"We are all killers here," Hippolyte reminded her. "It is not the *what we are*, but the *why* that matters."

She could feel her sister's frustrations spilling out through the air toward her, charging it with tension as if she were Zeus himself.

"You cannot let him walk upon our sands. Surely you will not?"

"I can and will do as I believe is right," Hippolyte said without emotion.

Her eyes once again moved away from Heracles and this time fell upon the trireme. The boat swayed back and forth, clicking and clanking with the rhythm of the waves. One ship. Two hundred men. They could end it all so quickly. But how many more would follow? A boat that impressive had great funds behind it. Thebes, perhaps? Or Corinth? Either way, if blood was spilled that evening, she knew it would not be the last, and their homeland, their sanctuary, might suffer a war that lasted generations. Her mother had fought to keep these lands free from the bloody fists of men. That would not change under her ruling.

"My women will take your boat," she said finally. "If you step on this sand, it is by my ruling only, and it will be by my ruling that you are allowed to leave."

"I understand," Heracles replied and nodded to his men at the same moment Hippolyte signaled to her women. As the men, still waist-deep in the water, backed away from the small vessel, four women rode into the waves, which broke into white froth on their horses' legs. Only one woman dismounted, passing her reins across as she waded deeper, carrying a rope, which she swiftly tied around the boat. The other women were there simply to keep their arrows targeted on the men, who were now closer to Heracles, their eyes constantly moving as they tried to anticipate from which way an arrow might come. Only the blond-haired one seemed free from fear. His eyes were rooted on the queen fixed with a look of complete fascination. It was not the first time she had drawn such gazes, and she paid it no mind.

As the woman dragged the boat up onto the sand, Hippolyte nodded to Heracles.

"You will follow me. Your men go with my women."

"As you wish."

"And one wrong move will be your last."

What followed took place so quickly that even later she could barely recall how it had begun. Her attention was still on Heracles, in his lion's garb. Penthesilea's arrow had not moved a hair's breadth, but Melanippe and Antiope had now shifted back, casting orders to the women behind them. Hippolyte did not think her attention had faltered for as much as a heartbeat, and believed that her vision encompassed all she needed to see. But the scream that shot through the air told her otherwise.

One of her women was in the water, fallen on her knees, mouth aghast and arms flailing, mere feet from Heracles's men. She picked herself up, hair dripping wet, eyes white with shock.

"He has come to kidnap you, my queen. I heard it myself. Heracles has come to kidnap our queen!"

FOUR

THE ARROWS RAINED DOWN, A HAILSTORM OF COPPER AND
snake's venom. Arrows she knew would not miss. One
strike, and the venom would infiltrate the blood and render
Heracles paralyzed and dead within a moment. They whipped
through the air, a swarm of locusts ready to devour whatever they
landed upon. But Heracles barely had to twist his body to deflect the
strikes, sending the lethal arrows straight into the water. Hippolyte's
sights never faltered as she pulled an arrow straight from her quiver
and shot it directly at his heart. Throughout, Heracles remained tall
and unflinching, striding forward. Not a single arrow pierced the
garb, let alone the man it covered.

"He wears the Nemean lion skin." Antiope's explanation was
voiced at the same moment the realization struck the queen. "No
blade or arrow will pierce it."

The Nemean lion. Over the many years she had heard tell of
Heracles's disposal of the animal, the beast that had plagued the men
and women of Nemea in the Argolis. But she had not thought the
task was truly possible.

To wear such a hide upon his back, he must have torn it from the flesh of the lion itself. Yet no mortal weapon could penetrate the skin that covered the creature—not even a weapon cast by an Amazon. For it to be on the back of this man meant that he had not only strength but wiles, too. But how he had managed to kill the creature, unfathomable as it might be, mattered not to her. She would rip the skin from his body and plow the spear through his heart if she had to, war or not be damned.

"Enough of this. I will wrap my hands around his throat and kill him that way," Penthesilea responded, bounding from her horse in a single swoop. Hippolyte reached for her spear and jumped to the ground after her sister. With Penthesilea by her side, she raced outward, toward the sea, but Heracles seemed not to notice. Instead, he turned a circle in the water, smashing the waves upward with his hands, oblivious to the warriors crashing through toward him, spears ready to slit his throat.

"Show yourself!" he screamed. Veins, furious and thick, pulsed across his forehead and down his neck as the sodden lion skin dripped with water. "Show yourself!" he cried again. Hippolyte paused, confused by his actions. His attention was no longer on the queen or her zoster. It seemed nowhere and everywhere at once. His eyes darted from side to side, an angry snarl upon his lips. From all the tales the queen had heard of the hero, she had expected someone rational, levelheaded. Someone with the intelligence and inventiveness necessary to remove the impenetrable skin of the Nemean lion. But the ravings of this man suggested he had lost his grasp on reality.

"I know you are here! I know that this is your doing!"

For a second his eyes caught sight of Hippolyte, and yet he made no movement to lunge for her or her zoster. Rather, he had slowed his violent motions and, still turning in a circle, offered his impervious back to her.

Was it an act? Surely it must be. Some ruse to feign insanity and throw them off guard. But his men were not raising their spears to fight. If anything, they seemed fearful. Concerned for their leader, although they made no move to help him. They barely moved at all.

"Stop now or we will burn your ship and your men to ashes!" Hippolyte shouted against the whirring winds. "We will burn your ship!"

At her words, fifteen hundred lights went up behind her. A cascade of bright fluttering orange that spread from one end of the beach to the other. Fifteen hundred arrows lit and burning bright, ready to fly to both the small boat and the trireme simultaneously. They would answer her call without hesitation.

The hero Heracles stopped, stunned at the sight, almost as if he had forgotten the women were even present.

Hippolyte spoke again. "This is your last chance, Heracles. Turn around now or every one of your men will die." Emphasizing her point, Hippolyte turned and trained one of her own arrows on the blond-haired companion. His eyes widened. He was one of the youngest among the group. And a fool if he thought he could best the Amazons. She felt no pity. She had killed younger, though possibly not as foolish.

Soaked to the skin, Heracles moved to take a step forward, but Hippolyte pulled tighter on her bow. The hero bowed, bending at the knee. His skin flushed from red to white. Sweat dripped from his forehead, pooling on his temples and running down to his jaw, and it took several moments before he regained his composure enough to speak.

"I apologize, my queen. Sincerely. What you saw…what I said….I come only for the belt. Please let me take it, and none shall come to harm. Not my warriors or yours. I do not wish for bloodshed."

"You declared war when you set your anchor in our waters. When you defiled our lands."

"Perhaps that is so, but that does not change the fact that my sole purpose is the belt. My intent is not death, merely the belt." He enunciated his words with such force that spittle mingled with the sea spray. His eyes, once good-natured, were blackened.

"I do not trust your intent," she replied.

A snarl escaped his lips. "You cannot believe that I am here to take you. If I had wanted you dead, I would have reached your shores by now. I would have come here with a thousand men. Surely you can see that? This is her doing. She is the one casting doubt in your mind before I have even spoken my piece."

The queen frowned, confused by his choice of wording.

"*She?* Am I supposed to know to which woman you refer?"

"The woman whose voice told you I was here to take you. The one who screamed. Find her. Find that woman. It will prove everything."

Hippolyte stepped forward, mere feet from Heracles now, pulling her elbow back and increasing the tension in her bow so that it quivered in her hand. A lesser bowman would not have had the strength to hold it at such a point, yet for her it was as natural as breathing. The tension in the string at one with the muscles in her arms.

"You are giving orders to me, on my lands, that you have desecrated?" Hippolyte's voice was calm, belying her words. "You do not order a queen, boy." From behind her an arrow flew. She did not see whence it came, but she knew the act was deliberate. Amazon women did not fire arrows by accident, and certainly not with such perfect aim. It hit the lion skin square on Heracles shoulder. At that speed, it should have bored a hole straight through the flesh. Instead, the metal crumpled as if it were nothing more than a reed, and dropped harmlessly into the water to be lost in the swell. Heracles wiped at his shoulder as a horse would whip its tail at a fly, and when he looked back to the queen, the blackness had gone from his eyes, to be replaced by a desperate pleading.

"I am not ordering you; I am asking you. Find that woman. The one who said I had come to steal you. Find her and you will see that I only come in peace. I come only for the zoster." And then after a pause, perhaps because the word was not one he spoke often and therefore took more time to compose, he added, "Please."

Behind them the arrows were still lit. The flaming tips flickering orange, illuminating the women's eyes as if they were wolves circling prey. Penthesilea stood behind the queen in the water while her other two sisters remained mounted on the sands. This could easily be a ploy. A way to delay her, to stretch out time. Perhaps there were another hundred ships on their way. It was not beyond the realms of possibility.

But even as these thoughts formed, she found herself absorbed by the glimmer that shone deep within his eyes. Anger, hope. Desperation. There were women on guard on the steppes with a view out over all of Anatolia and the sea. They would signal if there were other ships drawing close. And with their arrows already poised, they would not be so foolish as to let anyone leave the triremes again.

"Bring her," she said to her sister.

Penthesilea stiffened. Her eyes conveying her distrust of the men. The fact that she had managed to keep her arrow in its bow this long was close to a miracle, and even when she turned from her, Hippolyte could feel the burn of her sister's glare. Still, she would never contest Hippolyte's will in public and hesitated only momentarily before turning to the women.

"Who was it? Who heard the men speak? Come here now."

Stepping closer still to Heracles, but keeping him in her vision, Hippolyte cast her gaze up and down the row of warriors. She saw her women's focus waver. They, too, loosened their gaze on the warrior as they waited to see who would step forward. A moment passed, then another. Silence swirled around them, tense and tangible. Buzzing with anticipation. Still, nothing, bar the chorus of cicadas and the crash of the waves. Hippolyte shifted her stance in the water, bringing the tip of her arrow up against Heracles's neck and simultaneously casting her focus to her people.

"Step forward. I need to hear your words. I need to know who spoke. There is no reprimand for keeping your queen safe, you know that."

Every horse remained fixed in its place. Every woman waiting.

"I assume your women do not normally disobey your orders, Queen Hippolyte?"

She pushed the arrow tip deeper against his neck. She could feel the force of the lion skin, pushing back against it. She would not reach his flesh, she knew, but her intention was clear.

"My women follow every word I give."

"I do not doubt that. So where is she?"

Unease trembled through the queen. Was it one of his men? Did he have the women? He must have. It was the only explanation—and yet the nine young men remained unmoved. Perhaps another man lay hidden in the boat? Perhaps one had swum ashore? But the women had pulled in the boat to land already They would have seen someone lying in wait.

"Please, Queen Hippolyte. It is her. She is the one who has come to cast torment on me. As she has done my whole life through."

"Who? Of whom do you speak?" Her legs were growing numb from the cold water. One way or another, she would need to end this soon.

"It is Hera. It is the wife of Zeus. Please, my queen. Please let me explain."

FIVE

THEY MARCHED THE MEN UP FROM THE BEACH TO THE limestone city walls, the women on horseback, the men struggling to keep pace in their sodden sandals on the soft grass. To their credit, they did not utter a word of complaint. Although, Hippolyte thought, it was possible that this had more to do with the arrows trained on their hearts than with any stoicism on their part. The city was built on the highest of the steppes, with far-reaching views from the towers placed equidistant, overlooking the sea to the north and land to the east, west, and south. The sand-colored citadel walls were lower than most she had encountered on her travels, but here there was little need for protection. Before today, none beside her women and her father had even set foot inside them. The idea of any person making it close enough to breach them uninvited was simply unthinkable.

Nonetheless, there was something to be said for arriving home after a battle. Even the relief of reaching Pontus's steppes did not compare to the sense of comfort that arose when they finally crossed through their city walls and breathed in the air of home. Air filled with laughter of their women. Of the smelting heat of metal forges and the rugged stones beneath their feet, stones that had been set there by her mother and her mother's women. There were no battles here. No fights or blood loss. This was home.

As they rode through the north gate, Hippolyte dismounted and left her horse to one of her women to lead.

"It is this way," she began, but before she had even taken a step from the horses, she found her route blocked. Penthesilea's face was one of thunder.

"Hippolyte?" Her voice was a low hiss. Threatening. Her glare unfaltering. The queen ran her tongue over her teeth, casting her eye at the men, several of who were now shivering violently behind them. Still, she knew there was no escaping her sister. If she did not deal with Penthesilea's doubts now, then her wrath would simmer and her temper might fray and bring war upon them all.

"We should have left them on the shore. We could have listened to them on the steppes. Why here? Why our home? By the love of Aphrodite and honor of our father, why would you allow them into our home?"

Hippolyte allowed her breath to settle before she spoke. Losing her temper with Penthesilea only ever made matters worse—a lesson she had learned as a child.

"Think rationally, sister. He will not lie to us in our home. He will not risk starting a fight when he is aware that we have him surrounded at every point. Besides, if we do want to end him, we need to remove that lion skin. And that will be far easier done when he is relaxed, plied with wine, made comfortable in the home of women, do you not think?" She watched the thoughts settle in her sister's mind. The contemplation whirring behind her eyes. The air hissed as she drew in a long breath through her nose.

"This is wrong. You are defiling our home. And I do not trust them."

"Neither do I, sister. Neither do I."

Although she prided herself on being above such petty matters, Hippolyte found herself wondering what Heracles and his men made of her home. The buildings certainly lacked the grandeur of those she so frequently passed on her travels. They did not entertain and had not succumbed to the Hellenic notion that opulence was something to be admired, and as a result, the layout of the citadel was ruled, like everything else in their lives, by practicalities. There were no cyclopean palaces, with great colonnades and open atriums, although their arenas were sizable and their largest dining hall could hold every woman in the citadel. But for the most part, their buildings were small plain structures built from densely packed yellow-gray stones that were found in abundance near the cliff faces. The alleyways that ran between the buildings were wide enough for two horses to pass astride, with the stables and armory central. There were no large archways or grand gates, although simplicity did not mean they were without luxuries.

Food was not the only commodity they possessed in abundance. The women had more than their fair share of gemstones and jewels, given as payment and worn with pride. Stone or copper bathtubs could be found in almost all the homes, together with an abundance of oils and flowers that scented the water with a thick fog. But these were not a sign of vanity or frivolity. Like everything in Themiscyra, they had a purpose. The oil from a yarrow root would ease the inflammation from swollen joints. Tension and stiff muscles could be ameliorated with juniper and helichrysum, and even the aroma of clove oil could lessen pain, although not as effectively as when applied topically. The oils and herbs available in the bathrooms of Themiscyra would put any great palace to shame.

Not that she was intending on offering Heracles a soak in one of her tubs.

Still silent, they weaved up through the stone pathways of the city. In normal times, the laughter of children would be the dominant sound here, but this evening there was no laughter at all.

Step by step, they disappeared deeper into the warren of homes and workshops. From their dwindling pace and unfocused gazes, she could tell that Heracles and his men wanted to stop. To gawk or gape or ask questions. But these men were not here to observe or learn about their way of life. They were here so she could decide what to do with them, and slowly, they made their way toward the central building.

Palace.

Palace was the word she had most often heard with respect to the residences of kings and queens, but it did not seem appropriate here. No marble lined their floors, and the cobbled stones that made their walls were no different than those that lined the stables. The food they ate was set on no grander platters than those used in homes nearer the gates of the citadel. Besides, palaces were inhabited and controlled by kings, and the queens that resided in them were nothing more than puppets. Less even than that. Women with the sole purpose of providing an heir to the king. They did not rule. They did not lead. They were not queens in the way Hippolyte was a queen.

"Are you sure you want to do this, sister?" Penthesilea whispered to the queen as they reached the palace steps. "It is not too late. We can end them now. End them here. The gods will grant us mercy. They came to us."

"This way will be best, sister," Hippolyte said gently, brushing her sister's hand with the tips of her fingers before turning to

Heracles. She tilted her chin upward, commanding the attention of the men as she spoke.

"You understand that when you leave here it will in the vein of friendship or else not at all?" she said to him.

"I am confident it will be the former," Heracles said, his face void of the merest hint of a smile.

The queen and her sisters led the men through the weaving corridors, their footsteps echoing against the slate floor tiles, aromas of charring meat floating around them. Her stomach growled in response. Normally a feast would have been prepared for their return from battle. When their bodies had been cleaned and their injuries tended, they would indulge in the spoils of the hunts that had taken place in their absence. Deer, wild boar, rabbits. Flesh so tender it would fall from the bone, fat crisp and juicy. Enough substance to satiate them after such exertion. Enough flavor to ensure that when they closed their eyes, their senses were as satisfied as their stomachs. But Heracles and his ship had put paid to their usual traditions, and tonight would no doubt be a far smaller affair. Still, the clattering of pots and pans drifted through from the kitchens, and she hoped that soon there would be food to eat. They had taken the men into their homes, now; they would need to feed them, too.

By Greek tradition, men and women would reside in different rooms. They would each have their own space in which they could gather and talk of such matters as they saw fit. Typically, the women would use these spaces to weave on their looms, to practice their instruments, to discuss whatever it was that women were not able to discuss near the prying ears of men. And the men, she assumed, discussed things that they considered too crude or else too consequential for the ears of women. But Hippolyte and her women were not Greek; they were Amazons. Every crevice of the city and the lands around it, from the shore of the sea and the banks of the river to the crumbling cliff faces and lush grasslands beyond, was a sanctuary for women. Every action was of consequence to them. Every decision made for them. As such, no insecurity fluttered through the queen as she led the men through the innermost parts of the citadel and into one of the courtyards.

It was the smallest of the three courtyards and offered no view, lacking the light necessary to make it feel truly hospitable. Shadows overlapped more shadows and kept the area cool while a wind funneled in, scattering the leaves from the few trees that grew spindly in pots and bringing with it the undertone of manure from the stables. It was a space rarely used. An added quiet corner where the women occasionally sought privacy, although it was most often frequented by young girls who awoke in the night with the desire to practice their sword skills without the need to go too far away from their chambers.

A chill trailed down her spine as she entered.

"Please, take a seat," she said, indicating the gray stone benches that were placed around the edge of the space.

The men did as instructed, and when each of them was seated, the sisters drew back, taking their own places. There were other women waiting in the corridors. Women who would be ready and in place before the men even had time to draw a sword, should they need to. It was not that Hippolyte did not have faith in the power of *xenia*, the undisputed tradition that a guest might never do harm to their host. It just always paid to be sure.

"So, you have our undivided attention," she said, leaning forward in her seat. "Tell me why you think the Goddess Hera is so intent on your demise that she would come to Pontus and masquerade as one of my women to bring it about?"

Her question was met with a pause, then Heracles pushed back his shoulders. Not so much as to give him an air of arrogance, just enough to assert himself and lend weight to the words that were to come.

"I am the son of Zeus," he said.

The queen stifled a smile.

"I hardly think you are the only one to hold that title," she replied. "From what I have heard, your father has quite the eye for mortal women."

A small smile tilted the corner of Heracles's mouth.

"Yes, it is true. My father's gaze often strays from Olympus and, unfortunately, his wife. And while the blood that flows in me has gifted me in ways most men could only dream, I have endured, and continue to endure that which few others could withstand. Due to her."

It was clear he had avoided saying her name deliberately, as if the mere producing of such consonants would be as ashes upon his tongue.

"You are not the only bastard child of Zeus. Why has she chosen you as the target of her wrath? You must have provoked her anger in some way."

Heracles scowled. "If I have, then it was an action that took place in my mother's womb, for since the day of my birth, and even before, she has continually never ceased in her attempts to rob me of my life. When she failed to prevent my birth, she sent vipers into my crib."

Hippolyte felt her eyebrows rise. "How did you survive?"

"The same way I have survived everything she has thrown at me. By sheer strength and courage. But every attempt that I have foiled has only seen her more determined to end my life. And when she knew she could not beat me by hurting me, she sought out other, crueler ways to destroy me. For is not in our own deaths that we are left to face the worst torment a man can know. It is in the deaths of others. It is in the deaths of those we love."

He paused again. The air had changed. A glacial chill wrapped around his words and all the words he had left unspoken.

"She killed your child?"

It was Melanippe who spoke. Her voice was more delicate than the queen's. More lilting and higher in pitch and, mostly likely, fuller of compassion, too. As such Heracles tilted his head and frowned a little as if he had forgotten she was there. Or that any of them were there at all. A breath later, and he shook the moment away.

"I only wish that were so. I wish that she had killed them, for at least, if it had been her hands that wrestled the breath from their lungs, I would have grounds for vengeance. But what she did was worse than that. She clouded my mind. Cast me into an insanity so that I could not even tell you my own name, far less know my wife and child. I believed they were monsters. I saw them as monsters set on the destruction of my family. And so, I did what any father would do if they believed their family was at risk. I believed I was protecting them."

His eyes were glazed with tears as silence descended upon the courtyard. The breeze that usually swept through the space had been replaced by a stagnant stillness, and at the same time a lump had become lodged in the bottom of the queen's throat. She was a hardened woman who had brought about more deaths in her life than entire armies. And still this act was beyond anything she could fathom. Swallowing hard, she forced the lump back down to the pit of her stomach before she spoke.

"You killed your children and your wife?"

The dip of his chin was the only answer she needed.

"Strangled them with my bare hands, as if they were nothing more than serpents. By the time the madness had subsided, they were lifeless on the ground by my feet, and there was nothing I could do. I have been seeking redemption since."

"Can one?" Penthesilea spoke from beside the queen. "Can one gain redemption for killing a loved one?"

From anyone else, this might have sounded like an insult. A comment spoken purely to anger the warrior. But Hippolyte knew her sister as well as she knew her own mind and understood that the words had come from a place of genuine curiosity. Thankfully, if Heracles had been insulted by the question, he did not show it.

"I visited the Oracle of Delphi. I knelt before the Pythia and breathed in her incense. I wept on her floor. Wept more tears than I knew a man could weep. It was she who told me what I must do to gain forgiveness from the gods for my actions. It was she who told me that it was only King Eurystheus that could grant my purification. That I could gain my atonement in service to him. All my labors, all that I have endured, are at his whim."

"And he is the one who sent you here?"

For the first time, Heracles stumbled on his words. A light cough crackled from his throat. Seeing his discomfort, Hippolyte signaled to one of the women, who brought a jug of water and a cup, which she handed to him. His met her eyes as he gestured his thanks with a tip of his head.

"His daughter, King Eurystheus's daughter, Admete, has one desire: that belt that you wear. She wishes to possess it, and as such I have been sent to retrieve it." He placed his cup on the seat beside him and locked his eyes with her. Before that moment, the only occasions on which she had fixed her gaze on a man so intently had been on the battlefield, in the moments before she would strip that man of his life. In those moments, she knew every thought that stirred behind their condemned pupils. She knew what the men were thinking. How they were praying to every god they could name that by some miracle they might be spared the fatal blow, even as they knew in their heart of hearts that they would not be. But here, now, with her sisters beside her and Heracles's men waiting with their breaths held quivering in their lungs, she sensed it was he that was reading her, and not the other way around.

"Queen Hippolyte, we are both warriors. We understand that in any battle there must be losses in order for there to be a victor. I ask this only because there is no other choice."

The slightest of quivers unhitched his voice, and the queen felt her chest tighten with compassion for the man and the pained loneliness she could see engulfing him. They were demigods, the pair of them. Ichor ran in their veins, but that was where the similarities ended. She had grown up to be the pride of her father, his gifts bestowed to the point of indulgence upon her.

"This daughter of Eurystheus, Admete, what does she want with my zoster? Is she a warrior?"

Heracles's laugh was so sudden and brusque that Melanippe jolted beside her. "No. Just a spoiled princess who I think believes that, if she possesses the prized piece of the Amazon queen, then she will be delivered her strength and fortitude, not to mention her respect. And I am happy to let her believe that. My part will be done by the time she realizes she is the same sniveling little girl she was without it, and I will be one step closer to my redemption. That is my only wish for the belt. I hope you believe me. I have no personal desire for it, just as I have no desire to hurt you or any of your women."

As a new quiet fell, Hippolyte studied the man, taking her time to scrutinize the knots in his brow and the feathered lines of his sun-weathered skin. It was not only a matter of whether or not she believed him. The zoster had been gifted her by Ares. What did it mean if she could give it away so willingly?

"What will happen if I say no?" she asked, her hands resting on her knees. Her body relaxed, although she already knew the answer.

"I cannot leave Themiscyra without that belt," Heracles said, plainly and without emotion. "And I cannot be killed while I wear this skin, which I have no intention of removing, in any situation."

He was not a man who skirted the issues at hand, and she admired that, even though she was still undecided as to how she should react. Her choices were limited, but there were still choices. As a queen, it was always her job to find them.

"In that case," she said, rising to her feet. "Consider this a gift, from the Queen of the Amazons, to her first—and I hope only—guests here in Themiscyra." As her fingers found the buckle on her belt, she watched as Heracles buried his head in his hands, and a sound akin to weeping was muffled by his palms. The queen removed the zoster, a lightness and emptiness resting on her stomach. She pushed the sensation away and presented the belt to Heracles. His eyes lingered on the metal plates. His lips opened, although no words fell from them. Within the courtyard, something new had fallen. An exchange like no other before had taken place, and it was the blond-haired man beside Heracles who acknowledged this. With a coy smile on his lips, he said, "This sounds like a reason to celebrate."

SIX

THE AMAZONS FOUND NO PLEASURE OVERINDULGING IN WINE. The throbbing head and clouded thoughts that afflicted them after such rash revelries dulled their instincts and weakened their aim. Instead, when struck with the desire for deeper relaxation, they threw leaves and seeds on the fire. Deep green and pungent, the plants and seeds they selected would pop and fizz in the flames. The fumes they emitted swirled in mists so intoxicating that the women's minds expanded beyond all comprehension. They would see an entire world in the reflection of a raindrop or hear an entire melody, harmonized at counterpoint from a single unpitched note. They would dance until the morning rays bleached the moon from the sky and their feet were black with ash from the embers. They would sing and sway and cast all the bloodshed and loss from the battles aside. And afterward, they would sleep. They slept late into the day and would rise again, clearheaded and ready to train. But antics such as these, which lowered their inhibitions, were not called for that night, and instead they moved from the small courtyard to one of the dining halls and settled on a feast of venison.

"This feels wrong. We are giving them our food. Acting as if they are our guests, when they have stolen from us."

Hippolyte and Penthesilea had taken a seat in the furthest corner of the hall. Penthesilea sipped wine from her cup while eyeing the men with distrust.

"They have stolen nothing. I gave him the zoster, as you know."

Hippolyte had known this moment would come, that Penthesilea would question her decision to offer Heracles the belt. Antiope and Melanippe might have also disagreed with her action—every woman in Themiscyra could have disagreed—but it would only ever be Penthesilea who voiced her concerns. And no matter how fearless the queen was when chasing down warriors with spears, the same could not be said for those occasions when she was forced to face her sister's wrath. She had ensured she remained in motion all evening, flitting around on the balls of her feet with the agility of a young woman sparring in the arena. One moment she was checking in with the new mothers on how the children had been in their absence, the next she was ensuring the men's wine was flowing and that beds had been found for them for the night in the most secure of locations. But she knew such ruses could not last all night, and now, as a lyre plucked melodically to the intense hammering of a drum, she had given in and stood still long enough for Penthesilea to accost her.

"It was as good as stolen," Penthesilea said again. "A gift from our father, and you gave it to him, because he threatened to have killed you otherwise."

"You would rather I let him follow through on such a threat?"

"You think he would have stood a chance?" Penthesilea hissed her outrage, her words spat into her sister's ear. "There is not a man on this earth who can strike you or me, if we care to defend ourselves."

She had been the same since she was a child. Tempestuous.

Impulsive. But also, truthful. For all her battles, the only wounds that had ever been inflicted on Penthesilea had been those on her pride—like when Antiope fired off a shot before her or Melanippe's horse scattered dust in the eyes of hers—and moments like this were so few, Hippolyte could count them on a single hand.

"What you have said is true," the queen replied, softly. "And no mortal man can defeat us, but he is not a man. He is a demigod. And his father is Zeus. If the rumors are true, he has suckled at the breast of Hera herself. We are not immortal, Penthesilea, and the zoster is merely an object. It is a gift, yes, and treasured one, indeed, but it wields no power. It is nothing without us behind it. Tomorrow they will be on their way, and our lives will return to normal. *Xenia* is sacred, sister. A guest cannot harm their host without enticing the wrath of Zeus himself, you know that. We are safer with them in our home than anywhere else."

"The sooner they are gone, the better."

Silence followed as Penthesilea took another large gulp from her cup while the queen cast her gaze across the room. Large wooden tables had been laid with silver platters, laden with venison. Ten more guests added little to the size of their people, but its effect on the way they engaged with one another was incalculable. The women were not deceived by the wiles of these men, nor were they impressed or intimidated by them. Whatever rumors echoed across the waters, the Amazons held no hatred for men. Every year they took to the beds of Gargareans and enjoyed laughter and smoke and nights filled with fighting and copulation. Some of her women had formed bonds with these men—based not merely on how readily they gave them daughters, but also on their conversation and the enjoyment they found in each other's bodies—and would spend their time with the same man year after year. Others preferred to experience different men. Different bodies. But the women trusted the Gargareans. They had an arrangement as old as the warriors themselves.

But these ten guests were not Gargarean and had brought with them into the citadel an air of uncertainty and distrust that they had undoubtedly earned. As such, the women's voices were tight. The laughter that usually echoed freely through the hall was clipped and harsh.

As she scanned the seats, Hippolyte's sights fell upon the man who had caught her attention on the shore, and her skin prickled as she noticed once again that his attention was solely on her. Without the water flattening his hair, it was thicker than it had seemed, although his gaze remained as penetrating as it had been.

"He has not taken his eyes off you all night," Penthesilea said, following the queen's eyes. "I do not like it."

"You fear he will try to kidnap me, still? I have told you already, we are safe with them here."

"I do not know what it is I fear, but there is something about him that unnerves me. More than Heracles, even. Did you hear his name?"

"I do not believe it did."

"Then I shall go and find it out."

The Amazon had taken barely three strides from her sister, when, for the first time since the food had been placed before them, the young man rose to his feet. He timed his steps flawlessly, gliding between the chairs and tables and past Penthesilea, and then, without once breaking his gaze, he strode directly to Hippolyte and stretched out his hand.

The outstretched hand. It was a simple greeting that the queen had seen frequently during her travels. Several men had attempted to greet her in such a manner—those who had not bowed in humble deference or simply retreated into themselves, desperate to stem the trembling that overcame them when faced with the Amazon queen.

More often, though, she had observed that men used this exchange to greet one another. But she was not a man, and she was not Grecian, and so she left his gesture there, hovering in the air between them.

A hint of pink rose in the young man's cheeks as he lowered his hand.

"I wished to introduce myself. I am Theseus, son of Aegeus, King of Athens. It is a great honor to meet you, Queen Hippolyte."

"So much of an honor that your friend threatened to shed blood on our shores."

It was Penthesilea that spoke from behind him. Clearly, she would not allow her sister to be accosted in a such a manner, and Hippolyte felt a twinge of humor at her sister's protectiveness. She needed no protection. None of them did. But it was the strength of this bond that kept them all safe on the battlefield. Theseus turned, observed Penthesilea briefly, then returned his attention to Hippolyte.

"I understand the manner in which Heracles expressed himself may have come across as impertinent. I apologize for my friend. And I am grateful that, in your wisdom, you have seen fit to come to the satisfactory agreement, which I know was his aim."

Once again, it was Penthesilea who answered. She had shifted herself and was now positioned to the side of Theseus, as if trying to form a barrier between the young man and the queen.

"The arrangement is only satisfactory to you," she spat. "For it only serves you and your cousin. I struggle to see what we have gained from this, other than a smaller portion of meat to eat at dinner tonight."

A small smile twitched on Theseus's lips. "I am sorry that you see it in such a manner. Tell me, my queen, do you feel the same as your warrior here?"

His attention was back on her again. She could see the deep hazel tones of his eye, glinting in the soft light of the oil lamps.

They had the same stirring as the ocean, she thought. A restlessness beneath them, perhaps. A desire to prove himself. That was it.

"I am more than a warrior, boy." Penthesilea snarled at the insult. "I am Penthesilea, daughter of Ares, God of War. Princess of the Amazons. And it will serve you well to remember that."

For all her words and bravado, not to mention a reputation that Theseus would undoubtedly know as well as that of the queen, he paid Penthesilea no mind. His eyes remained locked solely on Hippolyte. Flecked with tinctures of amber, she noted. His breaths were slow, his expression calm and considered as he awaited her answer.

"I suspect that only time will tell," she said. Then she turned to Penthesilea and added, "Sister, why do you not go and see if any of our other guests need their goblets filled? I would hate for them to think of us as poor hosts."

She could almost hear the hissing rise from her sister. *Pouring drinks.* She had given a slave's job to a princess, to the daughter of a god, and no doubt she would pay the price with Penthesilea's mood later. But she knew she there would be no disagreement now. Not in front of others, and the more so before strangers. And so Penthesilea strode across the hall to where Heracles and the rest of his men were sitting at a long table. One of the men was talking in an animated fashion, waving his hands high above his head, his fist clenched as if holding an imaginary dagger, and his eyes wide. The women gazed on impassively, unimpressed by whatever tale this man was regaling them with. She was not the only one who saw this.

"It would appear that our hosts are not awed with tales of war," Theseus said.

"Why would they need tales? Unlike your women, we are well-versed in the nature of war. Each woman at that table has ended more lives than your entire party."

"I do not doubt it. I suspect it is you that should be telling us the tales."

"Without question."

The two remained silent for a moment. The man at the table was growing less animated, although he had not yet abandoned his story entirely, now leaning forward, making claws of his hands, as if transforming himself into the image of a giant beast.

"May I ask you a question?" Theseus said. His eyes narrowed on her, although there was barely a crease on his skin. His hands, Hippolyte suspected, would be as smooth and soft as those of the princesses at the palaces she fought for.

"Possibly, although I may choose not to answer it."

"I understand." He paused and hesitated before speaking again. "Do you find it difficult ruling alone?"

"You mean, can I rule without a king?" Laughter burst from her throat, laced with a bitterness she made no attempt to suppress.

"That is not what I said."

"No, but it is certainly what you implied, with little subtlety."

"No, it was not implied, either." His voice had heated a fraction. "You have misconstrued my meaning." There was a terseness to his voice that bordered on petulance and caused an unusual heat to rise in Hippolyte.

"I, the queen, have misconstrued what you have said to me in my own home?"

"Yes, I am sorry, but you have."

Unaware that she was doing such a thing, Hippolyte could feel her back teeth grinding against one another. *Xenia*, she reminded herself, went both ways. A guest could not hurt the host, but in the same manner, all guests inside her home were safe, unless they wished to bring the wrath of Zeus upon them. And yet Theseus showed not the hint of embarrassment, or even resentment at his words. Instead, he seemed to be struggling to hold his own emotions in check. Keeping his own anger at bay. Why he should display such indignation when it was he who had insulted Hippolyte was beyond her comprehension.

"I did not mention a king," he spoke slowly. "It was you that brought that word into our discussion. I merely mentioned ruling alone. My father is a king, as I have already said. King of Athens. He, too, rules alone. It is hard for him at times, bearing the pressure of a kingdom."

"He has advisers, surely?" Hippolyte asked, unwilling to release the ire that he had fixed within her.

"Yes, of course. Although I do not believe he always trusts their judgment quite as keenly as he should."

"Then I struggle to believe it would be any different if he had a wife. After all, from what I know of your lands, if the king does not believe a group of educated men, leaders in their fields who have been appointed to guide him, I feel it is unlikely that he would act on the advice of a woman who has been placed by his side for the sole purpose of opening her legs and providing him a child. Assuming, that is, she is not trained in the strategy of war. But then, you would never permit your women of Athens to do that, would you? To train? To learn? To fight? Your comment was pointless, no doubt intended to invoke some emotional response in me. If your father is lonely, Theseus, I suspect that this loneliness is of his own choosing."

The ease with which she found herself riled and spitting words like venom from her lips surprised Hippolyte. Such a temperament was not uncommon in Penthesilea or Antiope, but she failed to recall an occasion on which she herself had so readily succumbed to anger, especially as she struggled to justify her indignation. Perhaps it was the stress of the day, for it had been an arduous afternoon. And they had left early the previous morning with little sleep after the fight. Given her obvious irritation, she expected Theseus to apologize or at least to show a little deference or humility. But humility did not appear to be an attribute that Theseus possessed in abundance.

"So I take it you are not ready to accept a marriage proposal this evening?" he asked.

For a moment, a stunned silence filled the air. A stunned silence in which all of the other sounds of the room sank away from her. And then, in an instant, the queen threw her head back and laughed. It was not a laugh like the one she had given earlier; there was no bitterness or resentment within it. For what he had asked was truly amusing— remarkably so. If nothing else, Theseus had a sense of humor. He had broken the binds of tension that had momentarily shackled them and released it a manner that brought her genuine amusement.

"What would I gain from a marriage? I have no desire to extend my lands, and we have everything we need just here. And I have even less desire to become a trophy for some egotistical king who hides in his tent and feeds his gout with wine and red meat while men die for him. To be used solely for my womb while my husband keeps whores beneath my bedsheets."

"You have a poor view of kings."

"I have met many. I consider it fair."

Theseus pressed his lips together. *How old was he?* she wondered. The stubble on his chin was soft and downy. Still thin and patchy in places, and his skin as unweathered as a fresh egg. Twenty? Perhaps younger still. The hope in his eyes gave her cause to wonder how many wars he had seen, if any. He shifted back, perching himself on the edge of one of the tables.

"But it would not need to be like that, do you not see? Marriage can be a partnership. *We* could be a partnership. Imagine. Two great leaders, both gifted by the gods. What a force we would be. What a force our children would be. Warriors, unlike anything the world has ever known. Just imagine it."

The energy that rose from him was infectious, and the peridot hues that now shone in his eyes were almost mesmerizing.

"I think we may have indulged you with too much wine," she said. "You have lost your sense."

"My cup has been filled only with water, for today I wished for a clear head. Tell me, Queen Hippolyte, will you think on it at least? Would you consider becoming my wife? Hippolyte, Queen of Athens. It has rather a nice ring to it, would you not say?"

———

The next morning, the women and men returned to the shore. Four women carried the rowing boat back as they walked over the sand dunes to the water, the vessel propped on their shoulders as effortlessly as if it were a bound lamb. Behind them, eight of Heracles's men chewed on the bark of a ginger root, in an attempt to abate the sickness they had inflicted upon themselves with too much wine. More than once, one of them lost his footing and slid downward, and Hippolyte watched as smirks flitted across the faces of her women. Only Heracles and Theseus were clear-eyed and sure-footed. Heracles had even gone so far as to remove the lion's garb on the walk down to the water's edge. A grand gesture indeed.

At the shore the waves crashed, and the morning scent of mist still lingered as the last of the dawn clouds fled toward the horizon.

"Thank you again," Heracles said. He stood ankle-deep in the water. The queen and her sisters had made the short journey bareback on their horses, which stood in the same formation as they had the evening before, her sisters bracing her sides, bows in their hands. This time, however, the arrows remained in their quivers. "This gift will not be forgotten."

"And I wish you luck with your labors. May the gods be on your side."

"It would be helpful," Heracles chuckled, before offering another small half bow and retreating deeper into the waters, where he helped his sluggish men to push the boat out. As they waded deep enough to climb aboard, Theseus remained on the shore, hanging back until enough distance had been placed between the boat and him that they could no longer hear his companions' voices on the water. At this point, he approached the queen. She did not walk away or dismiss him. She wished to speak to him alone, as well as to hear what he had to say.

"Sisters, the women need to start their training for the day. We lost enough time yesterday. Please take them over to the plains."

The three young women exchanged a glance, in full view of the queen.

"I will be fine," she said, with certainty. "Unless you do not trust my ability to handle myself with one young man?" Nothing more was said. The three sisters dug in and turned their horses in so tight a circle that they carved trenches in the sand as they moved. They would not go far. Hippolyte knew that, after all that had transpired the previous day, Penthesilea would no more let her sister out of her sight than she would turn her back on her while they sparred. The thought made her smile. Whatever rivalry plagued the sisters, it was far surpassed by their loyalty to one another.

"You will need to swim to catch your boat," Hippolyte said, looking down from her horse at Theseus.

"It will be a journey I can manage. It would not be entirely untrue to say that water runs in my veins." He stopped and grinned, and once again, Hippolyte found herself wondering about his age. Eighteen? Nineteen? Old enough to think he was a man and still oblivious to the burdens that fell on one who was truly accountable for their actions.

After a moment, he started speaking again.

"My proposal to you last night. I wished to give it context."

"Beyond your insanity?"

His laugh was gentle. Endearing.

"Perhaps some insanity does indeed play a part. I will not deny that. The way I feel here, on this beach with you, unable to touch you, that alone is enough to drive a man to madness."

These were not the words the queen had expected to hear, but she did not stop him. It was not the first time a man had offered her his hand. And she doubted it would be last. Instead, she remained silent and allowed Theseus to continue. "What I told you about my father, ruling on his own, it is true, but it was not always this way. Before I returned to him, he had a wife, Medea. Her wiles might have been the death of me, and my father. And because of her I am fearful. I am fearful that the same fate may befall me. That I might be deceived. Athens is a new city, still learning its ways. But it will not always be that way. One day it will great. The greatest in all of Greece. For anyone to marry me, would be to their family's advantage."

"Then you are lucky, for you will have the pick of every noble-woman that Greece has to offer."

"But that is not what I want. I do not want my marriage to be based on a strategic advantage to someone or some other family. I want a queen who will help me rule. Who can form strategies with me. Who will stand beside me. I want you, Hippolyte. I need you.

There is no one else on earth who can be my queen. There is no one who would be a greater queen than you."

As Hippolyte looked down at the boy, she felt the swell of warmth within him. Despite his youth and his obvious rashness, he was right. There was no one who would be a greater queen than her, for she was already the greatest.

"Your offer is endearing. Flattering. And I hope that one day you will find the queen you seek," she said, gently. There was nothing more she could add.

Theseus took her refusal with grace, bowing low to the ground, before rising again and placing his hand against the flanks of her horse. His fingertips were only inches from her knee, and Hippolyte could feel a hum, a heat flowing from him into her.

"I will be back for you, my queen. And I know you will say yes to my proposal then," he said.

This time he did not wait for a response. Whipping his hand from the horse, he fixed his hazel eyes on her once more, before turning and sprinting into the sea. Lifting his arms above his head, he leaped into a dive, plunging under the water. As he disappeared into the surf, Hippolyte felt a surge of fear, for the waves had grown in the moments since the boat had rowed from the shore, and a gray swell rose and sank around him. A moment passed, and still he had not emerged. *Had he drowned?* she wondered. Had his proposal been his undoing?

She urged her horse forward and into the surf. And then there, in the distance, she saw him, far further out than she would have thought a man could swim in such a short time, already closing in on the small boat. As his arms rose above his head for a second time and he dived back down, Hippolyte found herself compelled to watch the figure in the deep, and wondering whether there might be truth about the water in his veins after all.

PART II

SEVEN

FOR THE AMAZONS, TIME MOVED WITH A SENSE OF CERTAINTY. There were the regularities. The predictability that came with the changing of the seasons and the wax and wane of the moon, as sure as the flowering of buds in spring and the lengthening of the days as Helios's sun garnered its summer strength. All time flowed seamlessly, its subjects swept into the future like the waters of a river swept into the sea.

And yet, like those waters, it was the unknown, the unpredictability that made the years so alluring. One day the sea might be as calm as a cup of water. So still that a swallow's reflection could dance on the surface, dipping in and out of clouds in perfect symmetry with the world above. And the next day, all that could be gone, and in its place violent, white-crested waves, which rose like mountains toward the clouds, crashing and thunderous, spurred by the wrath of the gods and driving those same swallows flocking inland in hope of shelter. Such were the lives of the Amazons. Sometimes weeks passed without a battle. Sometimes it could be longer still. They would remain in Pontus, would wander on the steppes rehearsing drills to perfect their sword skills, skills they would perform before one another in the arena of Themiscyra. They would salt their meats and train the children. They would mend their weapons, hammer their half-moon shields and breastplates, the copper emerging from the flames with the oil-slick colors of heat still swirling on their surface. They would strengthen their armor still more with further sheets of copper and brass, the luxury of time allowing them to chisel patterns or motifs on their surfaces—the same patterns and motifs that they would ink into their own skin, on their hands and forearms and biceps.

Some days, when the water was still enough, they would take out boats, only onto the shallow reef, but deep enough that the fish they caught could feed fifty of them and still leave flesh to cure. Then they would spend their evenings talking, laughing, and reminiscing over the battles they had won, and placing wagers on who would be the next narcissistic king to seek their services. And yet even within their screams of laughter were the memories of other screams, the screams of pain and fear.

During the course of her reign, they had fought so many battles the queen could not count them all. Battles on green pastures where the bodies lay hidden in the grasses, flowers wilted by the blood spilled on them. Battles on arid plains where not a scrap of grass grew and the women used cloth to shield their eyes from the sand, fighting as if they were blinded and guiding themselves to the kill by the sounds of their enemies' breath. They had fought battles that lasted mere hours, sometimes less, and those that lasted long enough for the moon to wax and wane above them. And they had lost women. Many good women who had been granted the most honorable death there was. For only deaths in battle were lauded by the Amazons.

Yet even amongst the deaths, there were births, and within the walls of Themiscyra, the sounds of children grew stronger and more vibrant. Their training grounds were full from dawn to dusk with young girls wielding first wooden swords and then metal ones, and riding bareback on horses they had raised as foals. They tamed birds, learned to swim in the waters, and brought down does for meals to feed them all. Antiope was the strongest teacher among them. The one with the patience to correct their drills and form, to guide their hands, and to amend their postures so that they might kneel and stand on their horses without risk of falling.

But that morning, a little over six years after Heracles's visit to their lands, it was Hippolyte who watching the young girls practice their mounts and dismounts in the fields. She had brought a small bowl of olives and rested them on the stump beside her while she observed. The hum of insects sounded all around with sweet scents of mintleaf and lemon balm thick in the midmorning sun. One of Antiope's daughters, Echephyle, had caught her attention. At nine years old, her niece's skills at riding were equal to many of those old enough to ride out to battle, although her knife and bow work required attention. Even if these areas were to improve at the same rate as her other skills, she would not allow Echephyle to fight in a battle just yet. Two or three years more, and then she would be ready. In battle, each Amazon had to hold her own, or she would die. There was no alternative. Perhaps the girl would survive an early battle or two, but it was not a risk the queen was willing to take.

For now, Echephyle was kneeling bareback on a mare, her balance not quite steady enough to make the transition to her feet. Each time she tried, one of her feet would slip, and she would slide off to the side, grabbing the horse's mane just above its withers and pulling herself back onto her knees before she slammed against the ground. Hippolyte could recall the girl's younger years, how desperate she had been to ride even before she could stand, and how, when she had learned to walk, she often wandered away from the women who nursed her only to be found in the stables or watching the adults spar in the arena. *Was Echephyle a future leader?* Hippolyte wondered. There was something about her. A tenacity and fierceness that shone, even amongst her most dedicated peers. Would she be the next to command as Queen of the Amazons? It was not a thought Hippolyte ever dwelled on for long—were anything to happen to her, Penthesilea would take up the mantle without question—but she could not help wondering from time to time. For, as she had said to her sister the night the men had arrived on their shores, they were not invincible, and Heracles was not the only demigod wishing to earn a hero's name. With her eyes still on Echephyle, Hippolyte picked an olive from the small bowl and chewed slowly, savoring the saltiness, when the sound of footsteps approached from behind. A heaviness weighed deep in her, yet she refused to alter her gaze. Even when Penthesilea appeared at her side, she maintained her attention on the girl.

"Why are you still here?" Penthesilea's voice was taut. Frustrated. "Everyone is preparing to leave."

Everyone rarely meant quite so many. For the last week, the nomads had been arriving in Themiscyra. Slowly at first and then in greater and greater numbers, they massed outside the walls of the citadel, ready to move out with the other women the moment the day arrived.

Hippolyte spat the stone from the olive into her hand before tossing it to the ground beside her.

"I will not be traveling with you this year."

"Why not?" Penthesilea's voice pitched higher.

"You know why."

Even without turning her gaze, Hippolyte could feel her sister stiffening beside her. For a moment they stood in silence, their gazes lost toward Echephyle on her horse. Perhaps coming here this morning had not been the wisest of decisions, but given that every Amazon of childbearing ability was preparing for her journey to the distant mountain ridge that lay between their lands and those of the Gargareans, there were few places in which she might seek refuge from the loneliness of truth.

"The gods will have their reasons, sister," Penthesilea said softly. "You must believe in them."

"I do. I understand that truth. I accept it, and I am at peace with it. But there is still no reason for me to travel with you. Not when I cannot bear a child."

There it was. She had spoken the truth out loud. She was the queen of the most powerful women on the earth. Ichor of the gods flowed in her veins. On a battlefield, she was omnipotent. She was undefeated. Every challenge that life had thrown at her, she had met with a spear in her hand, ready to attack and conquer. Everything, until this.

"That is not true. You can bear children. You have born a child," Penthesilea told her.

"One child. One boy. A decade ago now."

"You have not lain with the right man. That is all. You should lie with Siranos. For the last four years he has provided daughters for both Iole and Kepes. And two sons with other women, too. Or there is Ouras. He has fathered several of Antiope's and Melanippe's daughters."

"Last year I lay with them both. And a dozen other warriors of strong seed besides. Every night I spent with a different man. It is not the man's seed that is the issue."

Silence swept in on a breeze, encircling the women and trapping them with their thoughts and the words they had spoken. As sisters, they usually spoke with such ease. After all, they had been together since before their memories were anything more than passing clouds. But now, no words could fill this unease. No solace could be found in the truth that surrounded them.

"Sister, you need to go," Hippolyte said, shattering the silence like the ice broken on a water trough. "I am at peace with this. This is the will of the gods. They will grant me a child, a daughter, when the time is right. And I will be ready and willing. But it is not this time."

"How do you know if you will not come with us?"

"I know, trust me. Please, sister, do not press this."

"But what will you do? You cannot think to stay here all this time on your own."

"I will hardly be alone. Do not worry about me, sister. I have plenty to keep me busy."

Penthesilea's face remained folded with creases of concern, and her voice dropped to a near whisper.

"We will be gone for two moons," she said. "We have never been apart for this long."

Hippolyte could not help but smile at the childlike tone of her sister's voice. This, from the fiercest of her warriors.

"Well, for two months, you get to be in charge of the women. Think of it as training, for the future."

She anticipated excitement at this suggestion, yet Penthesilea's solemnity remained.

"That day will not come. I will protect you with my own life, you know that. Not that you need protecting."

"No, you are right, I do not. What I need is more daughters. More children to make the Amazons strong. Now, go." Hippolyte drew her sister in for an embrace. "And enjoy yourself. You have taken gifts for the men? And offerings for the gods to give upon your arrival?"

"I have."

The embraced again, the leather of her sister's tunic pressed hard against Hippolyte's chest.

"We will be back in two moons," she said.

"Ride safe, my sister."

"I always do."

Despite the great departure from Themiscyra that day, there were still many women that remained. Alongside those who were too young, there were the nursing mothers—mainly those women who fallen pregnant during the last two visits to the Gargareans, but also those remained in that role, as the Goddess Leto had seen fit to bless them with an abundance of milk. There were those who had not yet killed in battle—true virgins by the ways of the Amazons, and not yet able to attend the two-month gathering. There were those that were past their child-rearing days, or had lost the ability through fighting or some other manner. There were also those still injured from the more recent round of battles. Those whose bodies, while still fit to carry a child, would not benefit from the long journey, and thus remained behind to rest and recover and regain the strength in their muscles and the skills with their weapons that injury and time away from training had taken from them.

On that first day, Hippolyte stayed in the same place, watching the young girls ride, although after Echephyle failed to master the same skill after several attempts, the queen abandoned the role of passive observer and went up to the girl to offer guidance.

"You are trying to lift yourself from here," she said, knocking her knees. "You need to focus your strength here and here." She tapped her stomach and toes. The young girl nodded silently, keen to absorb all the guidance the queen could offer her. "And kick the horse into a canter. You should be one with your beast. If she is moving faster, you will move faster, too." She slapped the mare on the thigh.

"Go, let me see it."

While Echephyle did not succeed on her next attempt, by the time the sun had begun its afternoon descent, she had mastered the skill not only at a canter but at a gallop, too.

A feeling of pride warmed the queen as she left Echephyle to tend to her horse and headed back up to the citadel. Maybe this was her purpose. As a queen, she should be a mother to all of her people. Perhaps that was why the gods had withheld her own daughter from her for so long.

The next day, she followed the same loose schedule. She woke before dawn to watch the sunrise from the steppes, then headed down to help the girls with their drills. In the afternoon she found herself addressing simple chores that often got neglected when the prospect of a fight awaited.

Four days after the women's departure, Hippolyte used the time to assess her armory. Her kingdom came with so many responsibilities that it was the simple tasks that were often neglected, the sharpening of swords and the restitching of the leather on quivers where it had come undone with time. It was true there were women who could do this for her, women who were probably more skilled at such tasks than she was, but how could she lead people in all areas of their lives if she did not at least partake in their duties?

Slowly she ran the whetstone over the edge of the metal, starting at the hilt. The low familiar resonance was as comforting to her as the scent of leather and wax polish. Her hand followed one long strike down to the very tip, before she returned to the hilt and rubbed the metal down again and again, the blade growing smoother and gleaming brighter with every stroke. It was more than a mere aesthetic improvement. A blunt blade cost both time and energy, either of which could mean loss of life. All of her women took pride in this task, but today she took even longer than normal, laboring over each stroke, watching her reflection grow clearer as her hand moved up and down the blade. With her sword now gleaming, her image curved across its surface, she was reaching for a dagger when the sound of approaching footsteps stopped her.

The woman who had sought her out went by the name of Glaukia. An older woman who seemed at first rather plain to look at. People were drawn to her by her eyes, their hue the most vivid of blues. At that moment she was dressed for riding but not war: leather trousers, a leather top. Sturdy boots of leather and felt, embroidered and with colored beads sewn along the scalloped edge. She wore no helmet and had no weapons strapped to her belt. And yet her cheeks displayed all the flush of a woman going to war.

"What is it?" Hippolyte said, standing as she spoke and picking up the sword she had just sharpened.

The woman's jaw was locked, but it was her hands that drew the queen's attention. They were stained with a deep purple. She must have been collecting herbs, the vital ingredients for remedies and salves, which grew only on the higher peaks that commanded views across the Black Sea. She had come some distance to reach the queen.

"There is another boat," she said.

"Another boat?"

"It has dropped anchor and it is still a way away. Not close enough to reach us by arrow, but there is something else."

"What? What else is it?" The queen was already moving as she spoke, racing from the building and through the citadel, Glaukia not just keeping pace but leading her on. Her women were four days' ride away now. If they were to battle, it would be the young and old who would be forced to defend the citadel. She grabbed her horse, following Glaukia up the steppes to one of their lookout points.

When she reached the crest of the hill, the old woman stopped her horse, pointed out to sea, and spoke. "Do you see it?" she asked. "There is something else. There is a creature. A creature, and it is swimming to our shore."

EIGHT

S HADES OF DEEP BLUE INTERLACED WITH BANDS OF BRILLIANT
white as the waves rolled back and forth, dimming then brightening as wisps of clouds bowled across the sky. Such a perpetual motion made it difficult for the queen to lock her sights on any
object, particularly one that was itself moving—disappearing under
the surface for far longer than any human might keep their breath
held—and reappearing each time closer and closer to the shore. They
had raced to one of the highest points in the citadel, the north tower,
which looked over the sea and offered all the view she needed.

The boat, she could see, was not the same as the one that had
come before. Far smaller and further from the shore than the trireme
had been. Merely a blot on the horizon.

"It could just be passing through. Boats pass at that distance,"
Hippolyte said, searching for the shape amongst the waves that had
once again evaded her view.

"That's what I thought at first," Glaukia replied. "But I first spotted
it when I was gathering herbs yesterday, and it hasn't moved. Why would
it remain in such a place? And what is that creature? I thought perhaps a

seal, or a dolphin, but why would it be alone in such a manner? Surely if it were injured, it would make for deeper water?"

It was a question the queen had no answer for, and was about to say so when the creature once again broke from the waves. Its body arched forward, long arms sweeping up and over its head before it dove back beneath the water. There was barely time to register that it had appeared before it was gone again, leaving her heart racing at the brief sight.

"Was that a man?" Glaukia squinted. "What man moves like that?"

"We must hasten to the beach. Now."

Hippolyte went on horseback, her bow nocked and ready in her fingers with extra arrows in her quiver, despite the fact that the stitching was still incomplete along the top. By the time they had reached the sand dunes, there was no mistaking it. It was a man, and the only place from which he might have swum was the small boat out at sea. How was it possible he could survive such a swim with such a deep swell? Almost every year, one young girl or another would be tricked by the glassy stillness of a calm day and wade out into the waves only to forget the current lurking hidden beneath the surface, ready to rip her from their footing and drag her under. Yet this man swam as if he were a creature of the sea, unconcerned with currents or rips that carried people out to their death. But why?

"Should we shoot him, now?" Glaukia's fingers were ready on her bow. Her hands were weathered, liver-spotted, and deeply wrinkled, but her grasp was unwavering, without so much as a tremble to it. More women had joined them. Most were older warriors, too old to bear fruit from a trip to the Gargareans, but Hippolyte knew that whatever state their wombs might be in, their shooting would be clean. These women could fight.

"It is one man. We should find out what he has come for."

"He has invaded our lands. That is enough."

"He has no protection."

Protection. Hippolyte knew what the old woman was saying. There was no lion's garb across this man's back. Whoever he was, he was unlikely to be the hero Heracles who had arrived uninvited on their shores all those years before. Soon the figure was in the shallow water; rising, he stood proud, his feet on the sea floor. His blond hair was darkened by the water. His stubble was coarser and had grown denser in the years since his last visit, yet even from the distance, she thought she could see a glimmer of mischief in his eyes.

His face broke into a wide smile.

"Lower your weapons," Hippolyte said.

The women looked at her with disbelief, their bowstrings still taut and trembling with force, their arrows ready to fly from between their fingertips.

"Lower them," she said again.

She took three steps forward, not so far as to reach the water, but close enough to separate her from the group. Theseus strode waist-deep in the waves, now, his torso glistening with beads of saltwater. He had gotten bigger, too, she thought. Taller, broader. He must have been younger than she had imagined the first time they had met, for now he approached her a full-grown man.

"Do you not recall what happened the last time you set foot on these shores?" she asked, knowing he was within earshot.

Theseus's smile widened. It was not the same boyish grin he had worn before. There was a depth to it now. A maturity.

"I believe I proposed marriage and you turned me down."

"I was referring to the fact that I threatened to kill you all should you return."

His smile tightened a little, curling upward on the corners of his lips.

"I seem to have forgotten that part. I came purely for the first. Has it been long enough? Have you had time to consider what an extraordinary partnership we would make?"

Hippolyte did not know whether she should laugh at the man or shoot an arrow through him. Both options had their appeal.

"If that is why you have come, then you should turn around and swim back to your men."

He was only knee-deep in the shallower water and mere yards away from her, when, for the first time since she had spotted him out at sea, he paused and rested his hands upon his knees. Then he waited, prolonging the moment before he spoke. His chest rose and fell in long labored breaths that boarded on the theatrical.

"It is quite a long trip. I am not sure I would manage to swim all the way back without a little rest first."

The queen offered her most lingering glower before she spoke.

"We have a fishing boat you can use. You can row, I assume?"

"And if I say that I do not wish to go, then what?"

There was so much confidence in his voice. So much arrogance it was laughable.

There was not a scrap of clothing on his body, and his thighs were rippled with muscle, forming deep gullies for the water to run down. Hippolyte forced her eyes to his face, where the smirk he failed to suppress was enough for her to flex the string on her bow even further.

"If you do not leave our lands, then you will find yourself facing a fight you will not win."

"Is that so? Perhaps you should send the rest of your women away, I would hate for them to see you embarrassed."

Again, that same overconfidence. The way his shoulders lowered, his hand casually combing through his sodden hair. He might have been walking through an agora, a marketplace, inspecting ceramics or bartering down the price of wine.

"I am afraid you must have swallowed too much seawater. Even fully armed, you would not stand a chance. And here you stand without a scrap of clothing, let alone a weapon."

"Then it will be all the more humiliating for you when you are forced to yield."

There was so much taunt in his voice. So much play. Had Penthesilea been present, her arrow would have already pierced his heart. But her sisters were not here, and they would be enjoying their own entertainment—not entirely dissimilar in form—already.

Her arrow flew through the air, but she tempered its release, knowing it would not hit with deadly force, and Theseus, playing his part, clasped the arrow as it struck. He fell back and disappeared beneath the waves. Hippolyte cast aside her bow and drew her dagger; then, against her better judgment, she waded into the water. From below the water, she immediately felt the pull against her legs. She dug her heels deep into the seabed, but the sand slid from under her. Using the momentum to her advantage, she allowed herself to fall, but lifted her legs, clamping them around Theseus's waist. From there, she flipped her body over, pinning him to the ground. As the latest wave fled back to the sea, it revealed Theseus trapped between her thighs as she sat astride him, her dagger at his throat. He let out a deep groan.

While the water lapped over them, he did not fight to topple her again, though she knew he could, his affinity with the water lending him an unnatural advantage, even in his current predicament. He did not move at all, but remained motionless, and naked between her thighs. The cold of the water was like cool balm against the heat of their flesh, both flushed pink, their pulses pounding.

"I think it is time you sent the women away, don't you?" he said.

———

Under Hippolyte's orders, the women returned to their tasks. She did not wait, did not care to seek out a chamber or a bed; she simply took Theseus there in the water. This was what he had come here for. She had seen it from that first glint in his eye as he waded to her. And she would not disappoint. Her exposed flesh was taut with muscles that lined her abdomen and thickened on her thighs. Very different from the frail, feeble bodies of the Grecian women.

For all that Theseus's body was now that of a man, his eyes still widened as he cupped her breasts in his hands, a moan escaping his mouth before he hesitantly wrapped his lips around her nipple, as if this were his first time with a woman. Yet when he entered her, pushing himself as deep into her as he could, it was she who raised her voice in groans of pleasure.

Her blade remained within reach, but she did not move for it. Not until after their bodies had shuddered with pleasure. Only then did she reach for it, before brushing the sand from her body.

Foam rolled up toward her, thin and transparent, then fell back into the deeper waters ready to surge and break again. And each retreat brought with it that gentle sucking sound, like a slow inhalation of the sea.

"Water?" she offered, holding her flask out toward Theseus.

Still as naked as he had been upon his arrival, he rose from the sea, his eyes lingering on her as if simply to look was to graze upon her body.

"Thank you."

Taking the flask, he tipped it up to his lips, then drank until it was empty before handing it back to her.

"Your sisters, I take it they have gone to visit the Gargareans?" Theseus took a seat on the sand.

Hippolyte failed to conceal her surprise.

"I am aware of your traditions."

"So, you were hoping to find Themiscyra abandoned? To pillage our unprotected lands?" She sniffed, and searched his face, ready to continue. But instead of the humiliation she expected to find there, Theseus looked hurt by the accusation.

"No. Hippolyte, believe me, I am not here to trick you. I was fully aware you had not traveled with your women. I came for you and to reiterate my intentions."

"Your intentions for marriage?"

She struggled to maintain a look of determination as she spoke. The anger that had been close to boiling just moments ago had dissipated entirely, and once again her head flew back in laughter at the suggestion.

"You cannot possibly want me as a wife! I am not like your Greek women, you realize that. I am not placid, agreeable, mute, not content to spend all day lounging slothfully in the heat, eating grapes and figs and drinking more wine than might be socially acceptable. That is not a life I have any desire for."

"Then it will not be the life you have. Nothing needs to change. You can live as you do here. Free to ride and fish—"

"And fight?"

"If you so wish." His eyes drifted away from her to his boat, now smudged into a smear by the glare of sunlight. "One day Athens will be the most formidable kingdom Greece has ever known. Sparta, Corinth, Mycenae, all will pale in comparison to our strength, our numbers, our beauty. We will be the pinnacle of civilization, art, education, politics. No other place will compare."

He bore the physical shape of a man, certainly, but as he spoke, Hippolyte could see the old childlike hope still burning deep within him. Dreams of Athens's renown. Dreams of arriving at Themiscyra and convincing the Amazon queen to become his wife. The naivete was absurd. And yet she found herself drawn to him. Drawn to his guilelessness and virility.

"If you are so confident in all of this, you do not need me by your side to make it happen. I am sure that whoever you choose as your queen will consider herself fortunate." Hippolyte's clothes were now fixed to her body, her skin dry. There was no need for either of them to remain where they were any longer. But when she examined his face once more, she found his forehead furrowed, eyes wide and pleading.

"I need you," he said, his tone childlike again, bewildered by her rejection. The expression remained on his face for a moment, and then, in a movement barely visible to the eye, his frown was gone, and his hand had reached around from beside him, grasping for the queen herself. Sweeping backward, Hippolyte danced on the sand, snatching the dagger from her belt, and pressing it into his neck, the tension of his skin yielding beneath its point.

"It would pay to remember who you address." Her eyes bore into him. What was it about this man who had come to her shore, and the depths she saw written behind his irises? He did not fear what she might do to him. He did not believe that this was to be his end, and at the same time, his expression displayed the briefest flicker of remorse. With a dip of his chin, Theseus shuffled back in the sand, his eyes still fixed on hers.

"I apologize. Truly, I have no desire to offend you. But I will not apologize for coming here, or for the reason I have come. You must see this. You must feel this. Hippolyte, my queen! I have seen things since you and I last met. I have visited places both terrible and wonderful. I have encountered the best and the worst of both gods and mortals, and I have changed. But despite these trials, despite how much of me has altered, my feelings for you have remained constant. Seeing you there, as I approached the shore, it was as if my heart had taken wings inside my chest. My very body has no purpose unless it is to stand beside yours. Of all the women, of all the men and gods, please believe me, there is no one else I would take as my queen. I would rather rule on my own, as my father now does, than endure life with someone other than you."

"Then perhaps that is what you should do."

"Or perhaps you should consider that my offer is genuine?"

His lips parted in a sigh, and he turned his gaze to the horizon as if searching for something beyond the realms of sight. Time had passed, more time than she had realized. The sky had taken on a deeper tone, folding crimson and magenta, and the sun was sinking, luminous, into the horizon.

"I would prefer not to swim back to the boat at such a time," he said. "Who knows what manner of creature waits in rest for darkness to fall?"

Hippolyte continued to stare at the setting sun, disquiet churning through her.

"You can stay the night on the shore, then."

NINE

THAT NIGHT SHE FOUND HERSELF UNABLE TO SLEEP, AWARE that beyond the citadel walls, Theseus was sleeping in the moonlight. She had set her women to guard him from the lookouts of their towers with instructions to shoot should he advance from the sand to the dunes, and while she trusted the women with her life, more than once she rose to the window, intent on gazing out on the shimmering shores and searching for his silhouette, only to force herself away before she glimpsed his figure. It was her women he wanted, she told herself repeatedly. With the strength of the Amazons on Athens's side, his kingdom would be invincible. She could fathom no other purpose for his marriage proposal. But the Amazons were not for sale. And if he was expecting her to bear him a child, he would find himself bitterly disappointed. For if she were capable of such a thing, she would not be here at all, but away with her sisters. The next time she spoke to him, she thought, she would make it even clearer that his presence was unwelcome. There was no purpose to his loitering, other than to incur a wrath he would never cease to regret.

When dawn splintered its light across the skies of Pontus, severing the darkness with shards of white, she rode bareback to the shore where she found him the shallows. A large fish flapped hopelessly in his hands, its iridescent scales a lustrous green.

"You have come in time for breakfast," Theseus told her, wading up to the shoreline, adjusting his hold to grasp the fish by its tail so that it hung down by his thigh, still flapping, its mouth wide and gulping. "Shall we move to the dunes? It will be easier to prepare a fire there."

"You should have left by now."

He halted and cast his eyes upward toward Themiscyra. The distant hum of women and children floated to them. Given the absence of so many, the children had taken to the arena and were creating enough noise for an entire army. In that moment Hippolyte found herself lost in the sounds. The sweet tones and timbres like a pattern of glissandi on the breeze. And for a moment, she felt herself grateful that she had stayed, rather than traveling with her sisters as their queen. It was right, she thought, that she should experience all aspects of her women's lives. She found herself lost in contemplation, wondering which other elements of daily existence she had missed in her role as queen, when Theseus spoke again.

"Are you aware that in some cultures, under some laws, the very act we performed on this beach last night would be enough for us to be considered married?"

Hippolyte laughed, the sounds of the children forgotten. "In that case, you should know that I am married many times over."

She studied his face, expecting to see a reciprocal laughter, but instead his features tightened.

"Hippolyte, do you not think it is the gods' gift to us that has drawn me toward this land at the very time your sisters are absent?

Do you not think it was fate that you were spared at Heracles's visit?"

"Spared?"

A torrent of anger flowed through her veins, and she could not have kept the fury from her voice had she wished to. Yet rather than blink in fear, Theseus's eyes only glittered. He was provoking her. Deliberately enraging her.

"Why did you come here, my queen? You could have dispatched any woman to send me on my way. You alone returned."

"I came to ensure you left."

"I do not believe that is the truth. I believe you came because you want me. You feel this burning as fiercely as I do."

"The only thing that will burn is your ship."

She took a step toward him, drawing her sword as she moved. Her pulse drummed wildly, building through her ribs and throat as she raised her blade, yet he made no move to attack her, or even to defend himself. Rather he remained perfectly still, the fish's movement now feeble in his grasp.

"Could we not skip this part? We both know how it will end." His smile sat easy on his lips, and the fury within her deepened further.

"Is that so?"

Lunging forward, the queen lifted her sword to the point beneath his neck where his collarbones met. With the slightest pressure, she drew it down in a vertical line that bisected his chest, stopping at his navel. Blood seeped from his skin, pooling into tiny beads like morning mist on a spider's web. Still, he remained unflinching.

"So, this is what you want? You want to die by my hand, without even defending yourself?" she spat.

He took a small step toward her, the pressure on the sword's tip increasing as he pressed himself against it. His breath came deep and labored.

"No, that is not what I want. But I give you the choice, my queen. You will always have the choice."

Time slowed as she recalled all the other men she had taken. All the Gargareans who had fought her until their lips were bloody and their bodies bruised, and only then, as they continued to fight on through swollen eyes and broken fingers, did she sometimes permit them to join her in her bed. And here was Theseus. Simply waiting. For what? For her to change her mind. To push him to the sand and take him again as she had done the day before.

Once the thought had entered her mind, it took root.

Yes, that was what he wanted, and was it not what she wanted, too? As he had told her, she might have sent any of her women down to dispose of him or send him on his way. Instead, she had come herself, and come alone.

She dropped her sword and kicked him to the ground, watching him wince as the salt bit at the cut on his chest.

"Since you are here, it seems wrong not to make some use of you," she said, still holding the sword as she straddled him. "But do not disappoint me, or I will end you."

"I was born to serve you, my queen. That I promise."

———

By the time they had satisfied themselves with each other's bodies, the sun had risen and was casting golden rays across their skin.

The queen rose quickly to her feet, gathering her clothes as they rocked gently in the waves. The cut on Theseus's chest was already beginning to heal, a thin crust forming on the incision. Had he really doubted that she would kill him? If so, he was the first man to have done so. And the first to have survived her in such a manner.

Noticing her watching, Theseus rose.

"Would it be impertinent to ask the queen for some breakfast?" he said. "The fish I caught has been lost, I'm afraid, and I expect our activities will ensure that its companions will keep their distance for some time." As he spoke, she found herself noting the curve of his mouth. The way his tongue darted in and out, adding a sheen to his lips. "I did not bring any of my weapons to hunt and would hate to wander your lands unchaperoned."

"You should return. Your ship awaits you."

"I will, of course, but perhaps one meal together. Would that be possible? Just a single meal. After all, I have been in the walls of your citadel before. You know that, by Zeus's ruling, I would never do you or any of your women harm."

"And you know that you do not have the strength to do me or my women harm."

There was no humor in her voice, nothing but an angry glare, but Theseus smiled at her response as if she had made some coquettish remark. "So one meal together, then?"

Her horse ambled behind her as they walked up over the dunes. Through the long brittle grasses and across onto the shorter green plains that lead up to the citadel they went. Here, the aroma changed, the scent of damp, fertile earth and fresh water seeping in beneath the sea air, hinting at the lushness that Themiscyra held.

His stride mirrored hers at every step, his arms swinging in the same rhythm as her own.

Wordlessly, they began the gradual ascent to the steps of her home. This was not a pace at which the queen was accustomed to walking. The soles of her feet rolled slowly across the earth before picking up again for each new step. Her knees lifted only slightly, her toes brushing the blades of grass beneath them. This was the walk of someone defying time, although whether she was delaying what was to come, or luxuriating in the present moment, she did not know.

No words had passed between the pair since they had begun their walk, but the air around them was heavy with noise. The chorus of birds so dense that a man could lose a lifetime identifying their songs and, from the distance, the clanging of hammer against rock. During the wetter months, the rumbling of the Terme River would become a roar as it raced out toward sea; now it was little more than a gurgle.

Hippolyte's eyes remained forward, away from Theseus; she knew that merely to look at him would cause her body to surge with uncertainty. By contrast, his gaze had not left her, both earlier on the beach and even now, as they walked. These were not fleeting glances, the quick looks one might cast across a battlefield to locate sisters or enemies. These were lingering stares that burrowed into her, that insisted upon reading her, upon learning her and what she wanted. And with every look he cast, the heat in her chest intensified and spread further.

"The women here, they built all of this?" Theseus asked, speaking for the first time as they entered the citadel walls.

"Who else?" she asked. "We are only women."

"You really do not have men to attend to any of your needs?"

She heard the chuckle break in her throat.

"What needs do you think we might have that we would not be able to attend to ourselves?" she said.

To her side, almost lost in shadow, she noted the eyes turned in their direction. Only Glaukia approached the pair, though, her fingers gripping the knife at her side.

"My queen," she said.

The women would have seen her, Hippolyte knew, this morning and the night before. They would have seen both the fighting and the copulation that followed. And they would talk of neither. Still, Hippolyte paused for a moment.

"Glaukia, please bring some food to my chamber," she said. "You can leave it outside the door."

She did not wait for the older woman's acknowledgment before pressing on toward the palace, Theseus at her heels.

Silence cocooned the pair. The alleyways between the houses were wide enough for horses to ride two abreast, but now they seemed to have grown narrow, pushing his body close to hers.

No. She chastised herself for these absurd thoughts. She had taken plenty of men in her time, and even on the first occasion with the Gargareans, she had remained more levelheaded than she was now. Besides, she had already taken this man.

But, she thought, that had been different. Yes, there had been enjoyment with the Gargareans, but the purpose of their acts was always clear: to increase the population, to produce strong and capable heirs. This act, by contrast, served no purpose other than to satiate a hunger that was burning within her. An itch that had started the moment she had seen him dive through the waters and had intensified with every step they had taken.

"Your chamber?" Theseus spoke as the entered the shadows of the courtyard. "Do you traditionally dine in there?" His voice had changed. Tightened. He was nervous, she realized, and found comfort in the thought. Men were supposed to be scared in her presence.

"Come," she said, taking his hand for the first time as she led him to the chamber.

The warm musty aromas of home were a stark contrast to the

saltiness of Theseus's skin. Stepping toward him, she pressed her chest against his, inhaling deeply. *Did he always smell so intensely of the sea?* she wondered. Moving back again, she traced a finger across the light hair on his arms, still dusted with tiny salt crystals, and then across his chest to the line she had put there. She should have made it deeper, she thought. She should have ensured it would scar.

His skin was softer than that of the Gargareans, and no matter how his stubble had grown, he was still young compared to her. His pulse quickened, a remorseless thud she could feel through their shared skin as she pressed her hand against him.

"I thought we were to dine, now?" Theseus said, his eyes running up and down her body as she began to undress.

"Food will take some time. We will need to find a way to occupy ourselves until then."

Pushing him down on the mattress, she took him again.

TEN

THE AIR IN THE ROOM WAS THICK WITH THE SCENTS OF THEIR tangled bodies. The tang of salt that had clung so densely to him had become diluted and musky, as his damp skin glistened in the silvery light. Dawn was once again upon them. The solo melody of the first blackbird had grown quickly to a chorus of trills and cadenzas. Furs from the bed were draped across the slate floors, tossed aside as the heat had taken them.

It would have been wiser to have slept, Hippolyte thought briefly as the crowing of a cockerel broke through the mingled birdsong. She had tasks to do. Chores that had been neglected from the day before and women to attend to. They had not left the room from the moment they had entered, save to fetch water and yet more food—a small bowl of peaches and a large pomegranate, pulled open, red seeds bursting from within.

Surely, she thought, this hunger that drove them to feast upon one another would eventually expire. Surely, like flames that burned so fervently they consumed all they might feed upon, this passion, too, would suffocate and die. Surely, she would tire of the taste of his mouth and the arch of his hips. Or would this yearning be replaced by exhaustion, for at some point they would have to rest from one another's touch? Whatever tasks awaited her, she thought, they could be postponed a little longer. After all, she was supposed to be away with her sisters and the other women. Each of them would now be performing the same act as she and Theseus had been engaged in all night, and much of the day before. A ritual that, rather than growing mundane and predictable, became more intense with every repetition.

Now they had moved to the floor, insulated from its cold by the fur pelts they had previously discarded, her legs wrapped around him as she pulled him as deep inside her as any man had gone before. But for all the majesty of his body, it was his face that she found irresistible during these acts, in the rare moments in which she had been able to focus enough to watch him. No man with whom she had lain had made any attempt to learn what might bring her satisfaction. Until now. Until Theseus.

He had wanted to know what it was she did to bring her body to climax, so that he might recreate it. Enhance it. And when he flipped her body over and pressed her into the ground, running his fingers up the inside of her thigh, she learned that pleasure was the sole purpose of this act, and in such moments, it was hard to deny the words he had spoken. Perhaps it was true. Perhaps this union had, indeed, been ordained by the gods.

Beneath her, she could feel Theseus's thrusts begin to quicken. She pushed harder against him, against this motion now so familiar to her. She drew her hips down, arching her back until his convulsions were so intense he could no longer keep it within him. With a gasp and release, his body shook again, before all the muscles from his jaw to his toes relaxed beneath her. Sweat dripped down his temples as he groaned and moved to raise himself from the floor. But Hippolyte pushed him back down, the heel of her palm against his chest, holding him pinned to the ground.

When the waves of pleasure finally flooded through her, they came in a surge. Waves that crashed within her one after another, her body shaking, limbs tensing and splaying in involuntary spasm, her nails digging into his chest as she bit down on her lip so forcefully she drew blood. When the waves subsided, she felt her heart pound more fiercely than when first blood was spilled on the battlefield.

"I did not know that women could experience such a response," Theseus said, the whites of his eyes shining with awe.

"That does not surprise me," the queen replied.

During the night, the oil lamps had guttered and threatened to extinguish, and so Hippolyte had taken a tallow candle from a chest and lit that instead. The aroma was harsher, more pungent, but she had little time to think or care about that in the moment. Time spent seeking oil would have meant less time with Theseus tending to her, and given how brief this encounter was to be, that time was not something she was willing to sacrifice. Now, however, in the mugginess of the room, she regretted that decision. With the flames extinguished, the bitter wax had pooled on the stone, while tendrils of sooty smoke had marked the walls, the pungent scent lingering.

"You know that you have ruined me," he told her. He lay on his back, staring up at the ceiling. His chest rose and fell with his breath, the delicate fuzz of hair upon it highlighted by the flaxen glow that glinted through the windows in spears and points of light. "I am ruined. How can I leave this room, knowing that I will never experience pleasure like that outside of it?"

"There is still time for more pleasure," the queen insisted, rolling over and propping herself up on her elbow. Her comment induced a laugh from Theseus. It was a light laugh, higher in pitch than she would have expected. More childlike. Wishing to hear such laughter again, she ran her finger along his collarbone, then moved it down slightly and over the ridge of the mark she had left on him the day before. It would fade quickly, she thought again. Like memories of this encounter. "My sisters are not returning anytime soon. We can enjoy this a little while longer."

Lifting his hand, he covered his mouth and stifled a yawn. His skin displayed more scars than she had expected. They were not as great in number as those on the Gargareans, or on the majority of her women. But some of them were deep. Blades had cut through the flesh, not merely the skin. One began above his sternum, fading almost to silver, and she found her fingers drawing a line across it to his ribs. With his yawn complete, a smile replaced it.

"I may need a moment or two longer," he said, taking her hand and twisting it around so that he might kiss her knuckles. "And some water, too? I can fetch it if you tell me where to go?"

Tension flickered through her. Tension that he registered with a smile. "I understand. Believe me, my queen, I have not come here to invade your home. I am more than content to invade your bed. If it makes you happy, you could blindfold me while you are gone, so that I cannot look outside and see more than you wish me to?"

Did he speak in jest? she wondered. The words might be construed as such, but a sincerity glinted behind his eyes.

"It is fine. I will fetch us both a jug."

She rose and moved to the doorway, her naked body reflecting the sunlight like newly polished bronze. Was it prideful to enjoy Theseus's gaze on her quite so much? Her body was magnificent; she knew this without question. Every day its strength increased. And never once had she taken all it did for granted.

Outside the room, the queen found the silence disconcerting. Another plate of food had been placed outside her chamber for them, but she had not known of its arrival, and now it was crawling with ants bearing as much of the fruit flesh and meat on their bodies as they could manage. Picking it up from the ground, Hippolyte moved through the corridors.

A bowl of hardboiled eggs had been set beside the stove; their mottled shells still warm to the touch. She plucked four, along with a handful of ripe purple plums, and placed them on a fresh silver tray with a jug of water and two cups. But even as she lifted the tray from the table, she paused. Was this the woman she wished to show herself to be? Was this the woman she wished to show Theseus? A serving woman? She had no concerns about carrying food to her sisters, or the other women, for that matter, but they had never sought her for a wife. They had never proposed marriage. They had never seen her as anything but their queen. She glanced at the food on the tray, and decided she was too hungry to consider such nuances. A host always served her guest. That was point upon which *xenia* turned. Although the service she had rendered Theseus had perhaps gone a little further than that dictated by the usual standards of hospitality.

When she returned to the room, Theseus had repositioned himself on the bed. He took a cup from her hand, which she filled from the jug, and drank hungrily. Taking the jug and filling his cup immediately, he drained it a second time. His thirst sated, he placed the cup on the ground and took an egg, rolling the smooth oval between his palms until the shell was nothing more than miniature tiles of mosaic. He peeled them away, leaving only the pure white flesh. Hippolyte found herself watching him intently. The way the white of the egg yielded under the pressure of his teeth. The way he used the back of his hand to wipe his mouth. Such typically human actions. And yet, there was something so fluid about his movements. She had considered this already, more than once during the night, and before that, when she had watched him swim to the shore amid the crashing waves, when she had listened to his comments about their first meeting.

"You know I have been with many men?" Her voiced splintered the silence around them. Theseus's hand paused, hovering above the bowl where the remaining three eggs and plums were piled. His eyes narrowed.

"I do, though I am not sure why you would bring this matter to my attention. Perhaps your aim is to flatter me? Perhaps you wish to tell me that which I already know, that my skills far surpass any that you have experienced before?"

There it was again, that coy smile, and Hippolyte found herself wanting to press her hand against his cheek. To frame his face and hold that moment for just a second longer. There was something so attractive about the arrogance of youth. Something she had never fully appreciated. The infectious optimism that came from someone with no responsibilities other than to gain a name for themselves.

"You were not like any other man," she said, slowly. "I know of your father, King Aegeus, but what of your mother? Was she a mortal?"

He pressed his lips together. "She was. She is."

"Then you are fully mortal." She could not hide the surprise in her voice. It was a thought that had been playing keenly on her mind since he had seen him swim to the shore. It did not seem an action that a mortal could undertake. But if both his parents were mortal, then he must simply be blessed by the gods, rather than kin to them. His smile twisted slightly, before his lips pressed ever tighter together into a thin line.

"My parentage is perhaps not as straightforward as many," he said. "But I would like to tell you, if you are willing to hear?"

Her gaze fixed on his hazel eyes, the green in his irises so bright they shone against the black of his pupils. There was no stirring behind them now. None that she could see. Just a man, truthful in what he wanted to tell her.

"I would like to hear that very much," she said.

With the eggshell discarded, he took a plum. His teeth pierced the skin as he pulled away a piece of flesh and chewed slowly.

"May I?" he asked, gesturing with his hand toward the window. "I will understand if you do not wish me to see your lands."

"I think I can allow you a view of the window," she said, "given what else you have cast your eyes across over the last day. I believe that if the gods or my women were to find me at fault, whatever sins I might commit have already been committed."

She expected a return of his smile, the boyish grin she had already grown to like. Or perhaps even a witty retort. But instead he pushed himself away from the bed and crossed the room to the window. His movement created a draft, the absence of his body from her bed a chill that she had not anticipated. She reached down and lifted one of the furs from the ground, the thick fibers oily and smooth beneath her fingers. Pulling the pelt up and around her knees, she drew in the scent of leather and tannin.

Theseus was standing at the window, looking out across the steppes, his silhouette a black void cut from the world beyond her chamber. From this point, he could see it all, the rolling green of the steppes and the vast waters of the sea, iridescent as the moon on a clear night.

"My parentage," Theseus began, "is unlike that of any man that walks the earth, or that has walked it before."

ELEVEN

H E CONTINUED TO STAND BY THE WINDOW, FEET FLAT
against the slate floor. The same pale silvery sun that
illuminated the lines of Theseus's torso brought forth the
scents from the warming earth. Lavender, honeysuckles, rosehips,
and elder swam around them. Hints of herbs, of wide thyme and the
rosemary that grew in the gardens, mingled with the pungent under-
tones of the horses. Every day the aroma in Themiscyra was slightly
different, its character formed not just by the warmth of the sun, or
the flowers that were in season, but by the direction of the breeze and
the moisture that had fallen that night or risen from the earth as dew.

Whether flavored with sweetness or acridity, under normal
circumstances, Hippolyte could sense the day beyond her chamber
by the scent alone. She could tell whether a storm approached
from beyond the horizon, or whether clear skies would last until
nightfall. Yet this morning it was the aroma of Theseus himself that
overwhelmed her. Peppery and musk-laden, it unraveled in the stone
walls and on the fibers of the furs on which she lay. His scent masked
all others, on her pillow and on her body. Never had she thought so

deeply about the aromas of the men with whom she lay. And never before had she wanted to hold them for just a little longer against her skin.

He had finished the plum, had licked from his lips the last of the juices and the sweetness that dripped downward to his chin. Even then, he licked each of his fingers, extending the moment before he drew his gaze from the window and back to Hippolyte. She was waiting for this, she realized. It was possible she had been waiting for it before he had even mentioned it. How was it that she could feel herself so drawn to a man?

"You do not know about my father. About how I came to be his child, the heir to Athens."

He spoke as if he were stating a fact, rather than asking a question, although the heavy pause that rested at the end of his sentence told Hippolyte she needed to affirm it.

"No. The first I knew of you being heir to Athens was when you told me. I make it my business to stay out of politics. It makes it harder to fight for something if you believe the other party is right."

She offered a short laugh after her words, although there was no humor in it. It was all too easy to be drawn into the beliefs and disputes of others. Lines in the sand blurred and shifted the more she heard, and the harder it became to see the right place to stand or swing her sword. And so, with the occasional rare exceptions, she had made it her rule that the right people to fight for were those who offered the most gold. It was far simpler that way.

"I understand," Theseus said. He cast another gaze out of the window before crossing to the bed, lowering himself beside her, but ensured a space a finger's width remained between them. Her thighs were so close to his. It would be easy to distract him from his story. To straddle him as she had straddled him so many times that night.

To press her lips against his and feel him swell beneath her. Yet she restrained herself.

From outside came the early clamor of the day. The whinny of the horses, the thumps and chatter of women about their work. And then a whistling. Melodic, only without a melody. A call—once, and then again, its shrillness increasing with every repetition. Theseus's attention momentarily flickered. One of the girls was training a hawk, teaching it to read the tone of its mistress's call and the lift of her hand. Teaching it to hunt for her. To fight. Hippolyte wondered if perhaps he might ask about it, but instead, his posture altered, and Hippolyte knew he wished to tell her the story.

To tell her his story.

"I was not raised in Athens," he began, "but Troezen. I assume you have heard of it?"

Hippolyte nodded. "Vaguely. It is not a place we have been called to."

His eyes remained lost, drifting away from her. Even through the darkest part of night, his eyes had been locked tightly on her, as if the mere act of blinking might have caused her to disappear forever. Now, it was if there were a cloak between them. A shroud that he had placed there so that he would not be distracted from his thoughts.

"My father was childless. He had taken a wife, very young, who proved unable to give him an heir. Understandably, this was a torment to him, as it would be for any king, but he married again, this time hopeful that a child, a son, would soon be born to his house. But alas, this second wife died of a fever, leaving him once again child-less. By this time my father was not a young man anymore, and a king without a child, well—all our times are finite—but for a man in his position, he knew rivals would be challenging for his crown if he could not produce a son. And so he visited the oracle in Delphi."

Delphi was a place that Hippolyte knew keenly, if only from rumors and stories told by the men she had helped win wars for. The Delphic temples to Apollo were said to be the greatest in Greece, and the lushness of the grass and the abundance of fruit trees the envy of the world. Of course, the men who said such things had never set foot in Pontus, though she did not say such a thing to Theseus.

"My father gave his offering to Apollo," he continued. "It was more than generous, and fitting for a man of his standing. But the Pythia gave him only a riddle in response."

"A riddle?"

"She told him not to unstop the wineskin's neck." There was a bitterness to his voice. Hippolyte ruminated over the words. To her, it sounded an unnecessary warning, as if the oracle was suggesting the king was at risk of losing himself in the endless lassitude that wine provided. But drunkenness was a habit for the lower classes. For servants and slaves. Surely not for a king. "He was, as you can imagine, distraught at this," Theseus continued. "Condescension from the oracle was the last thing he expected, especially for a man with such judicious drinking habits. He felt as though he had exhausted his final hope. He had expected the Pythia to offer him salvation, to tell him the manner in which he might produce an heir. Considering his journey wasted, he took his time returning to Athens, and stopped to visit a friend on the way. A friend who was wise in the mannerisms of the Pythia, King Pittheus."

"In Troezen." Despite Hippolyte's insistence that she did not observe politics, she was not entirely ignorant of the mighty events and rules of the world. She was a ruler herself, a powerful one, and an ear to the ground was essential if she were to ensure she was ready and waiting, knowing when and where she could be called upon.

"Indeed. In Troezen." Theseus hesitated. One slow breath, one long inhalation and exhalation, punctuated his story.

"While there, the king plied my father with wine. A man in his position would not normally drink to such excess, as I am sure you can imagine. He is not one of those kings. Not in normal circumstances. But he was suffering. He was lost. With the wine in his veins and his inhibitions lowered, he took to my mother's bed. Aethra. King Pittheus's daughter."

As he spoke, Hippolyte continued to listen attentively, but a seed of disappointment had been planted by this latest statement. Given the story of his father thus far, she struggled to see how Theseus's lineage differed from that of thousands across the world; conceptions that occurred after wine lowered inhibitions to the point of recklessness. It was hardly the making of a hero.

"My mother conceived that night," Theseus said. "Although she cannot say for certain whether it is Aegeus or Poseidon who is my father."

"Poseidon?"

"Yes." Another pause broke his tale. A pause in which she watched his eyelids blink and his lips flutter until they landed upon the next word. "When my father was finished with my mother, he fell into a deep slumber. A stupor, I suppose. She, in contrast, found herself unable to sleep, and drawn by some inexplicable yearning, left the palace grounds to wander down to the shore. It was there that he saw her. Seduced her."

"Poseidon?"

"God of the Sea. She walked into the water and lay with him there while the waves raged around them, on the very same night she had lain with my father—with the man the world knows as my father. They stayed together until the first rays of sunlight splintered the horizon, their bodies entwined, before he disappeared. There is no way of knowing whose blood runs in my veins. No way to be certain. Though there is little doubt, as you have seen, that I have an affinity with the water. Once that is beyond the talents of a mortal."

For the first time since he had begun to speak, he looked at the queen, his eyes holding fast on hers as he awaited her reaction. He had told her the truth, and now he wanted to see how she valued that truth. He knew the story of his conception was one she had not heard before. Gods and mortals, of course. That was almost commonplace. But this...this quandary he found himself in, was most certainly intriguing.

"Does your father, King Aegeus that is, does he know of this situation?"

Theseus smiled, although his eyes did not convey the cynicism she had anticipated.

"I am my father's son. I brought him tokens that he had placed in safekeeping for me to retrieve and return to him when I was capable. I rid him of his witch of a wife, Medea, the vile sorceress who murdered her own sons and would have killed me, too, if my father had not been blessed with so keen an eye. And I will rule Athens when he is gone. I am his son. I am both their sons."

There was a finality to his words now. A self-assuredness that Hippolyte had seen before, in her own father. In the gods. *Had Theseus shared this story with other women*, she wondered, *who he had taken to bed?* It was certainly a tale that would draw their attention, and yet there was something about the unease with which he had spoken. The way he had refused to look at her. His halting for breaths, his pauses to consider his words, until his final, confident declaration. No, she did not believe this was something he had shared with many others, if any. She felt something had changed between the pair of them—like the moment a tide reaches its highest point and must be drawn back to the ocean, or the single point in the sky that separates the evening sun from the setting one. The hairs on her arms prickled, and she opened her mouth to speak. But before a word had escaped her lips, Theseus spoke once again.

"I know it may be impertinent, but I was hoping for some fresh air. Although perhaps away from the water. A wander around your garden, perhaps? Before we return to your bed."

The queen twisted her lips, pinching in on her cheeks.

"What makes you think I will let you return to my bed?" she asked. There was no hiding his smile now, as deep a smirk as he had dared show her.

"It is nearly two moons until your sisters return, is it not?"

TWELVE

WHATEVER DUTIES AND TASKS SHE HAD INTENDED ON completing during her sisters' absence were quickly forgotten. The queen now woke and slept not in accordance with the circadian rhythms of the day, but as dictated by her whims. Some nights, sleep was neglected entirely, and it would be as if her body and his had fused together, sweat pouring down their spines as she carved half-moon crevices into his skin with her nails. Other times the urge would strike in the morning as she observed the pale light glimmering off his skin. With the chorus of larks, the queen would find her hands wandering across his body, urging him to wake and to tend to her again.

But there was more than merely sex between them.

They fought. Every day they fought. With no weapons of his own, she allowed him the use of hers. Arrows, blades, whatever tastes he had that day. His strength was admirable, although he was a man who suited the brute power best wielded through an ax or a club. His skill at times was clumsy and his mind easily distracted. A single suggestive look could be enough to beguile him, and give her all the opportunity she needed to disarm him. Had they faced one another in the heat of battle, with death as the final outcome, she suspected his lack of focus would be his undoing.

"If we were to fight in the seas, I would most certainly win," he told her more than once.

"And have you experienced many battles at sea?" she would reply.

They had been riding together, too, another skill at which Theseus lacked finesse. He could mount a horse easily enough, given his height, but once upon it, he would bounce and jolt. All the creature's grace fell from it with this mass of a man astride it. His figure, which cut through the water with such fluidity, was ungainly and misshapen the instant he sat upon a horse. All hard angles and jerking movements. Hippolyte found herself obliged to change his steeds each time he rode, for fear the horse would get used to such a heavy hand. Thankfully, with practice, he had improved to the point that she no longer feared for her horses' spines when they journeyed.

Some days, they traveled out toward the river, taking the paths on the edge of the marshes, where the seabirds would stand long-legged and whittle out grubs and insects from the mud beneath them. Some days they returned to the sea, and Hippolyte would watch as Theseus dived beneath the waves, reappearing with his hair stuck to his face, the water weaving down his cheeks. Occasionally she joined him, paddling until the water reached her knees, but always armed and always alert.

More and more, Hippolyte found her mind tending to thoughts of her sisters, and of Penthesilea in particular. She knew she would disapprove of this arrangement. It would not be the queen's use of Theseus that would anger her sister, for she had been known to take other men besides the Gargareans for pleasure. But Penthesilea would resent and be wary of his presence in Themiscyra, and of the time the queen labored with him.

As the weeks passed, the women who remained became known to him, and he knew many of them by name, too, though he never spoke to them directly. At least in that sense he showed wisdom. He would dip his head slightly, avoiding eye contact as they walked together through the citadel walls, acting as if he were deaf to the whispers that followed them.

A little over half a moon into his sojourn, they found themselves strolling through a garden just beyond the walls. The queen did not concern herself with the gardens in general, being more interested in the horses and their weapons, but that did not mean she underestimated the value of the plants that grew on their land. They, too, were gifts from the gods to strengthen and aid. And while flora of all use and variety grew throughout Themiscyra, it was in this small area of land, situated southwest of the citadel and thus protected from the harshest winds that blew off the sea, that some of the women—those who dealt most with injured—had cultivated crops of the most useful specimens. Between battles and training, these women pruned leaves and plucked weeds and grasses. They snapped off dried flower heads and gathered seedpods, storing them, then sprinkling them back on the earth when the seasons changed, or else grinding them for tonics to ease pain or swellings. Such was the dedication of the Amazons, that on the hottest days of the year, when the sun would blaze like a furnace on their backs, they would gather water from the river and douse the plants until the soil turned the deep dark brown of a walnut shell and worms wriggled to the surface.

In return, the garden provided them with an abundance. The berry from the elder tree could be used to produce a syrup for coughs, or else dried and smoked for the purpose of relaxation. Sweet woodruff was stored with their clothes to repel inspects and moths that might otherwise settle there. The women could prepare a sleeping draft from valerian root, and the leaf from lemon verbena might ease the inflammation around a wound or reduce a fever from infection. As much as the queen would have liked to believe there was no problem that could not be solved with her sword or her sister's arrow, she knew that was not the truth, and on more than one occasion, she herself had been a grateful recipient of the garden's bounty. However, she had never looked upon it with such awe as Theseus did as they weaved between the beds.

"And what is this?" he asked, pinching a stem of pink flower, its densely packed petals surrounding the delicate yellow strings within the center.

"That is a peony." Hippolyte found herself laughing as she spoke. This was not the sort of question she was accustomed to receiving. Women might ask her how to feather an arrow so that it could slice through the air with barely a whistle, or how to hold a horse without reins so that they could stand and fire a bow. Theseus seemed not to know the rules that came with her role as queen, and this brought with it a new sense of freedom.

"What do you use it for?" he asked.

"It can provide a draft that will ease pain."

"And this?"

"That is aloe. The sap eases burned skin," she added, anticipating his next question.

"And that one?"

"That is valerian."

He nodded, as if he knew its use. His eyes roved from one plant to the next, always asking names and correlating remedies. For over an hour, he was entertained in such a manner before they bathed together in the fresh running water of the river, then returned to feast in the citadel.

"Why is your ship still here?" Hippolyte asked one day, when he had been with her for a little past three weeks. They had ridden out to one of the higher steppes and were lying together in the grass. The sweet smell of pine needles and burning cedar swirled around them. "They cannot believe you are still alive."

Theseus rolled over onto into his stomach and took her hands in his. "I told them that I would return within two full moons. If I have not returned by then, they will leave."

"Two moons." The length of time her sisters would be gone. When Theseus had arrived on her shore, a point that distant had felt almost unfathomable. Now, nearly half that time had already passed.

"Is it too much to hope you will have considered my proposal?" he asked, sitting up to view her more clearly. "You have had time with me; you understand my thinking. You can see that I am a man of my word, and Hippolyte, I know now, more than ever, that you are destined to be my queen."

Every time he returned to this theme, it was as if he lessened in age by a decade. In the moment of each proposal, she saw him as young boy who did not understand why he could not go to fight with his father or brothers. A child playing with a wooden sword, unable to swing, yet still pleading for a sharper blade. The circumstances of his conception might have been unusual, but during these moments she saw the brazen arrogance of a Grecian prince. The assumption that he could have whatever thing he desired. But she was not his for the taking.

"This time..." Hippolyte said, considering her words carefully before she spoke. "This time together is something I am unlikely to forget. Perhaps next year, when my sisters leave again, you could return? You could take a wife, and we could enjoy each other's company whenever the opportunity arose for us."

She pressed her hand against his chest. To her, it seemed the most alluring of possibilities. She could never be queen in a place such as Athens, yet it was true, she and Theseus had formed a bond, the likes of which she had never formed with any man or woman. A match of minds and bodies, of wits, and almost of strength. But however appealing the idea was to her, Theseus did not appear to share her sentiment. He pushed her hand away from him.

"Is that the type of man you think I am? The type of king that I would be? That I could take a woman as my wife and behave in such a manner? Do you really think so little of me?"

He was on his feet, lifting the waterskin from the ground. Confused, Hippolyte rose slowly.

"I do not understand why you have taken such offense to this. Is it not what most kings do? Keep their queens for their children, and their concubines for their bed?"

"You consider yourself a concubine, now?"

"No, I simply consider myself free from your deluded rules of decency."

"So now I am deluded." Theseus had turned red in the face, the temper glowing on his skin. "And next you will consider yourself above love, too, I suppose."

It was not the first time he had uttered the word to her, although until now it had been spoken in jest, or lightheadedness, in the moment before he climaxed, so focused on their bodies that his mind failed to conceive the weight of the words rolling from his tongue. "I love you, Hippolyte," he said. "You must know that. With all my heart, I love you."

"Theseus, please. You embarrass yourself."

"Because I have fallen in love with you? That is why?"

"I do not have a place for love in my life."

His fists were balled at his side, his jaw clicking with tension.

"I do not believe you. I see you when you are sleeping. I see you, eyes closed, smile on your lips. Ares's blood may flow in your veins, but so does Otrera's. You are half human, as am I, and you are capable of love."

"You are telling me what I am capable of?"

Hippolyte rose to her feet. She had been wearing a small dagger strapped to her thigh, out of habit, but also for use, to be thrown to catch rabbits, or to cut away small branches. But this was the first time she had reached for it in the pretense of an earnest fight. "You should watch your tongue if you wish to leave here with it. Or at all, for that matter."

"You would stop me leaving?"

"I believe I told you when you first came here that if you stepped on my shores again it would be the last time." They were moving in circles together now. Hippolyte's weight shifted onto her back foot, weighing up her balance as she locked her eyes on her opponent.

"It is a little late to be recalling that promise, is it not?"

"I believe I decide what happens on my own land, do you not?"

They had sparred often, daily since his arrival, but always as a dance. A prelude to what would follow.

Now, Hippolyte found her desire was to hurt him.

She struck on her first lunge, the dagger slicing a diagonal line across his chest, deeper than the faint sliver from their first reacquaintance that had now all but vanished from his skin. With the sight of blood, her appetite was whetted. She lurched forward again, but this time he was ready. His closed fist landed square in her stomach, knocking the air from her lungs. He followed the blow with another to her arm, sending her dagger flying.

"You forget that I know your every move," Theseus goaded her, but she knew his was a false sense of security. Yes, she rehearsed the same drills with him repeatedly, not because she needed to, or lacked the inventiveness to fight otherwise, but because it was part of the choreography. A flurry of footwork and turns in which they both ended as victor. This was a very different situation.

Most women would have fallen to their knees under such force as Theseus's; even an Amazon woman might struggle. But she was Hippolyte. With no women to aid her, she reached up, grabbed his hair, and pulled hard, then struck behind his knees so that they buckled, toppling him forward. She twisted around, rolling with her weight on her hands, then landing to grab the dagger again, and spinning back to face him before he had seen where she had gone. She pushed the blade against the back of his ribs. Immediately, she felt his body slack beneath the metal. He raised his arms above his head and turned slowly toward her.

"How could I ever love another woman after you?" he asked, breathlessly.

That night, she told him it was to be their last. Rumors of the queen and her concubine could continue no longer. Besides, if her sisters were to return earlier than expected from the Gargareans, they would not allow him to leave alive, and the thought of his death stung her more keenly than she cared to admit.

"Will you have a drink with me?" he asked her, as they sat together, naked, in the dim light of the oil lamps. "If tonight is to be our last night together, will you indulge me in this tradition?"

Wine was something she had resisted in his presence. Wine and herbs, anything that lowered her inhibitions. Yet he gazed upon her with such pleading.

"Just a cup, and with water?" Theseus said again. "I believe I saw some barrels, over by your stables."

"Those were presented to us as a gift by the King of Phrygia. Years ago now. I do not even know if it can still be drunk."

"Old is better. Wine grows richer with age," he replied. "Let me go, to bring a barrel here. I promise, one cup only. A proper farewell to my queen. That is all I seek."

In the light of the oil lamp, his hair shone like fire. Besides her own, his was the only body she had come to know so well. She knew the lines along his jaw, and the tautness across his collarbone. She knew each of the scars on his body.

"Fine, one small cup, and with plenty of water. I will fetch the barrel."

"You stay here, my queen. I will fetch it. You will be expending more energy on my return," he said, kissing her heavily on the mouth before he left.

When he returned shortly after, wine in hand, he kissed her softly, before raising his cup in a toast.

"To us," he said.

———

Blackness filled her mind. A pit. An absence of thought, total and opaque, a deep-rooted numbness. An impenetrable swill of nothing. And then her eyes flickered. It was only a blink, yet that brief instant was enough for the light to blind her. A deep throbbing cut behind her eyes. The queen lifted a hand and pressed her fingers gently against her forehead, only to find the sensation change from searing agony to unfathomable dizziness. The feeling rolled through her skull, back and forth, as if she had taken a tumble from her horse and landed on hard ground. But it had been years since she had fallen from her horse, and even as a child, she knew how to land to protect herself. The ache spread downward. A thickness was building in her throat, her muscles slow and unresponsive. What had happened? What could have caused her to feel this way? Her mind was as sluggish as her body, as she tried to push herself up to a seated position, only to tumble backward and strike her head on the hard surface beneath. Was she sick? A fever? Never in her life had she or any of her sisters suffered from such an affliction, but some of her women had. Those whose cuts had become so infected and swollen with puss, it addled their minds. Was she in a such a state? She could feel no broken bones or open wounds. She could not recall an accident that might have caused such an injury. And the pain seemed to emanate from a place behind her eyes and the top of her spine.

Grinding her teeth, the queen pushed herself up, sat, and tried to channel her thoughts into a simple stream that she could follow.

Where had she been before this? She tried to recall. With her sisters, perhaps? No, they were absent. But not at war. No, they were with the Gargareans. That was right. They had gone, and she had stayed. The relief that flitted through her at this recollection was short-lived. She had been in bed. She had been with Theseus. The wine. She had drunk too much wine. But how? She remembered only two sips, and then—and then nothing more. She screwed her eyes tighter, as if the intensity of the action might bring to mind the situation, but found nothing. It was as if the time between here and there had evaporated, wiped clean from her mind.

It was only then, as Hippolyte rubbed the bridge of her nose, that she noted the difference in her surroundings. Her gray stone walls had been replaced by wooden planks. Her soft horsehair mattress nothing more than a wooden bunk. The smell of damp pervaded, heavy and briny. And the rocking motion, she noticed as she tried to move again, was not restricted to her, but afflicted the entire room.

She was on a boat.

She was on his boat.

He had taken her.

PART III

THIRTEEN

THE WOMEN WERE WELL INTO THE SECOND DAY OF THE journey back to their homeland, after a first day, which was always the most tiring and treacherous of the three. On that first day, they had ridden over steep ragged mountains where the horses were forced to travel in single file with barely a foot between them, and crumbling ledges that plummeted into ravines. Even with beasts as sure-footed as theirs, the rocks slipped under their hooves. Some faltered and refused, their riders forced to slap their heels into their sides to keep them moving. One young girl fell from her steed, and by the grace of the gods, caught her hands on the edge of the precipice and pulled herself to safety, her life saved by the strength in her arms. After that, the women did not talk again until they made it through the mountain pass.

Toward the end of the day, they reached the flatter lands, where they camped for the night, feasting on the meat the Gargareans had presented them—along with metals and leathers—as parting gifts. That night, the tiredness was overwhelming, and there was little to be heard in the way of songs or chatter.

Next morning, all of that changed.

They had packed up early, laughter already reverberating around them. The sky was immense, an endless expanse, adorned with great white clouds that hung like statues in the air above them, with barely a flicker of wind to abate the dry heat. They had departed for the Gargareans in spring, but summer was now encroaching, browning the grass and thinning the rivers to streams. Even in their homeland, the heat of the sun would soon be felt. But nothing, not even the most arid of lands or scorching of heats, could lessen the women's elation.

With the perilous terrain behind them, they were finally felt free to talk and laugh. And once the laughter had started, it was near impossible to stop.

There were too many tales to exchange. Too many tidbits of gossip to be sought out secondhand, or ideally from the women in question, most of whom were eager to shed light on the even the most salacious rumors circulating about them. Chatter and whoops of delight continued to reach Penthesilea's ears as she rode at the front, at a stately pace, for there was no need to rush. The happier the women were, the more fiercely they fought to protect their names. Her mother had taught her that years ago, and it was the line by which Hippolyte ruled.

Their trip had been fruitful, if for no other reason than to let off steam. When the women left Themiscyra, they had been tired, worn out from battle after battle, never able to fully relax in case duty called for them, unsought, in the night. The winter months had been tough on their bodies as they spent the days in training, perfecting their skills as if each sparring session was being observed by Ares himself. Such endless pressure caused tension to creep into their minds, warping their thoughts and wrapping its cold fingers about their spines, even if they themselves had not known how tight that tension had grown until it slackened. That could certainly be said for Penthesilea, who only now appreciated the weight she had placed on herself.

For the first two weeks of their trip, she had taken her leadership of the Amazons with a gravity that bordered on sobriety. She had not indulged in the herbs that the men had offered or in the burning of seeds they had brought themselves as gifts. She kept watch at night, more often than she needed to, and slept in a small tent alone, with her ax beside her. She had placed herself as Hippolyte would: absolute protector of her women. A regent queen who would be ready at all times should her women need her. But gradually, that veneer had worn away. Slowly at first, she joined in with the smaller fights, with those men that challenged her, for she needed to feel the heat of a striking blade in her grip. After a few days of sparring in such a manner, she took her first man to bed. He was one of the older ones, his body more scar than skin, the tight hair on his chest rolled into corkscrews of white and gray. After taking him, she had joined her women around the fires, watching the colors form in the flames as the scented smoke wove spirals in the air and through their minds. With the smoke came a freedom. The final loosening of the tethers and responsibilities that she felt back at home and to her sister, and that had bound her so tightly when she had taken up her temporary role as leader. From then, she was one with the other women.

She had spent the remainder of the days fighting with the men, then allowing the fights to lead wherever she fancied. The last night had been her favorite of the entire trip. Three Gargareans had decided to tackle her together. Finding her unarmed, they had approached her with swords raised and shields prepared to block her strikes. They had thought that their advantage in weapons and numbers would be sufficient to best the daughter of Ares. They had thought that to take her down—even outnumbering her three to one—would cement their reputations amongst the rest of the men, despite the fact that their elders had ridiculed them as they approached, and Penthesilea, too, had felt a twinge of sympathy for these young men. She had taken their shields and turned their blades on them before the first had ever managed to lunge at her. She had drawn blood. And that was where the fun had started.

She had taken them all together that night, and what they lacked in skill, they made up for in stamina and enthusiasm. Even now, the images of their three bodies entangled with hers and each other's brought a grin to her lips. Their bivouacs were not known for their warmth, and in the colder months the Amazons would rub their skin with a salve made from the oil of the halinda plant to draw their blood to the surface and create a heat so violent their body would sting. But it was not cold that night, and the heat that rose from their four bodies caused sweat to slide down her oiled hair and puddle in the canyons between their muscles.

"It is a daughter; I know it is. Every child Ouras has given me has been a girl." Melanippe's voice startled Penthesilea from her daydream. How long she had been lost in her reverie she could not remember, but her sister, who had until now been riding halfway along the convoy, was now parallel to her. "It will be a girl. I am certain."

With her mind now in the moment, Penthesilea found herself needing to temper her sister's expectations.

"You cannot know for certain. You may not even be carrying."

Her sister offered her a look of scorn. "I am carrying. It is from the first night. I know that I am, the same way I knew that last visit I was not. The gods have seen fit to repay my patience. I know my body. I know it as well as you know yours."

Her smile tightened as she surveyed Penthesilea's features for a telltale sign, yet Penthesilea remained stone-faced. Her absence at the beginning of the trip had reduced the likelihood, though it was certainly possible. Given Antiope's fertility, and her history of conceiving and birthing with every visit to the Gargareans, it would be reasonable to assume she was in the same state as Melanippe professed to be. It would not be inconceivable that this year, Hippolyte would be the only one of them not carrying. Inside, Penthesilea cursed the queen. Of course she would choose this year not to come. Once again, it seemed as if her childlessness was a slight from the gods, rather than due to the fact that she did not lie with so many men as rest of them. Not that she would be anything other than overjoyed for her sisters. The more of them that were carrying, the more there would be to carry on their parents' name.

"What do you think she has spent her time doing?" Melanippe asked, apparently aware from Penthesilea's expression alone that she was thinking about the queen. "I suspect she has been so bored she has lined up a dozen battles for us on our return."

"Or else she has been off and finished them already herself," Penthesilea replied. "Who knows how many wars she might have won single-handedly in the time we have been gone?"

"The poor women who remained there with her. She has probably had them scrub all the armor and sharpen the swords at least a dozen times in our absence. I do not envy them."

A faint smile rose on Penthesilea's lips. It was true, Hippolyte had an eye for the smaller details. An obsession, one might say. But she could not hold Hippolyte's foibles against her. They were some of the many things that made her a great queen. Greater than Penthesilea would have been had Ares chosen her instead? It was difficult to know.

That next night was to be their last camping, and when they rose in the morning, Penthesilea felt the shift in her women, and in herself. Pregnant or not, when they returned to Themiscyra, they would be returning to their true calling. For as playful as the last few weeks had been, a tedium arose after having gone so long only sparring. For all that Melanippe had spoken in jest when she suggested Hippolyte would have their next war waiting for them, Penthesilea suspected she might indeed be correct, for any tedium they might have endured would have been all the more significant for the queen. Training the youth, and spending time with the young children, had never been where her true strengths lay.

They approached Pontus from the southeast, their convoy significantly depleted from that which had left the Gargareans. Upon arrival in Anatolia, the nomadic women had separated from the group, with some who preferred warmer climes remaining further south. Others, in contrast, would travel north, as far as the boarders of Thrace, where the mountains and higher altitudes made for brisker weather. The rest of the women, those who resided in Pontus, rode at a steady pace with Penthesilea.

Half a day's journey before the plains of their forests came into view, their horses began to strain more forcefully against their reins. Most of the women, the princess included, dropped theirs altogether. They did not need reins for such a journey. The horses knew the trails and could easily be steered through rivers or across small passes with a tug of the mane.

"I am heading to the river to bathe and give thanks," Antiope said cutting her palomino gelding in a large circle so that she fell in front of Penthesilea and Melanippe just as the citadel came into view. "Many of the women are coming. Do you wish to join us?"

The cool running waters of the Terme bubbled with shallow

pools sufficient for bathing, or for the horses to drink from. Several women, Penthesilea included, preferred to clean themselves there rather than in the stagnant heated water of a bath, but she shook her head at the offer all the same.

"I should see our sister," she said. "No doubt she will have plenty to inform us about. I may make my way later."

Antiope nodded in understanding and turned to Melanippe to hear her answer, but before she could speak, the women's attention was distracted. Three horses were thundering toward them. Three women on horseback, but with no weapons she could see.

Something stirred in the princess. A deep concern, guttural, primal, and unlike anything she had felt before. Heat siphoned from her skin as she rode.

Galloping at top speed, she reached the women, breathless.

"What is it?" Her horse's hooves skidded in the grasses as she drew it to a stop. "What is wrong?"

The women were ashen, their gazes searching beyond the princess, scouring the women behind her. It was the eldest, Glaukia, that spoke.

"The queen?" she said. "Is she not with you?"

Penthesilea's face crumpled as she shook her head in confusion. "The queen stayed here, at Themiscyra. You know this. She decided against the trip this year."

Confusion was etched on all their faces. Confusion Penthesilea could not interpret. How was it not possible they did not know Hippolyte had been with them for a full two moons? It made no sense. But when she gazed upon the women, each one of them refused to meet her eye.

"She is gone."

FOURTEEN

S HE HAD GONE TO WAR. THAT WAS THE FIRST THOUGHT THAT ran through Penthesilea's mind. The queen had gone to war, just as she and Melanippe had joked earlier in the day. It would not be the first time she had left with only a limited army. Yes, a large army was intimidating, but so was the sight of a dozen women slaying a hundred men without receiving as much as a scratch in return. Penthesilea felt a twinge of envy. Those were some of her favorite fights. She had perfected the swing of her ax in such close quarters. She was ready to ask how long ago they had left—she already had some weapons on her, and it would be the work of but a moment to grab a fresh horse and retrieve her ax. But the words froze on her lips as she noted the atmosphere around her.

There was no humor in these women's voices. No hint of the pride that came when their queen was away, spreading their fame. Instead, their eyes were narrow, their foreheads creased with more than merely sun and age. A wind curled in from over the sea as they stood motionless, the manes of their horses blowing inland.

"What has happened?" She heard the question called out from one of her women, but no one replied clearly. Instead, whispers scuttled between the women. A cloud drifted in front of the sun, casting the sea in a dull gray light.

Penthesilea's eyes were trained on Glaukia. She was one of the oldest of the women and, when enticed by the fumes of the seeds, would gladly regale the rest of them with tales of Otrera and Ares in the early days of the founding of the Amazons. She was known for both her frivolity and her agility and had broken more than one bone attempting tricks on horses that she had not performed for thirty years. Yet the woman who stood before them now displayed neither humor nor light.

"There is something else," she spoke quietly, glancing behind Penthesilea and her sisters to the waiting women, who had now fallen silent, hoping to catch a whisper of what was being said.

"What is it?" Penthesilea spoke in equally hushed tones. "What else is there to know?"

The woman swallowed. Her hand trembled and a pallor blanched her skin as if she had taken a blade to the belly and was losing blood. So unusual was the response that it took a moment for Penthesilea to realize the emotion that the woman was displaying, for it was not one an Amazon would typically show, even when confronting death.

The woman was afraid.

"What has happened?" the princess asked, this time a fraction more firmly. "What has happened to my sister?"

The old warrior inhaled, casting her eye up to the sky as if offering a silent prayer to Ares himself before she spoke.

"The queen had a man. A man who stayed with her, in Themiscyra. And now they have both gone."

—

Hours had passed. The horses were brushed down, feeding on brittle hay and grass, the familiar scents of the earth and of moiled equine cloying around them. In the time it had taken the women to reach the city walls, the winds had brought rain that pelted down so heavily it rebounded around the women's ankles as if the earth itself were retaliating against the heavens. No women had gone to the river.

Penthesilea's feet were sore from constant pacing on the stone floor, her voice sore from her ceaselessly repeated words. She had plucked an arrow from somewhere, a table perhaps, and mindlessly rotated it over and over between her fingers. A thoughtless action, but a necessary one.

"I do not understand. You say she kept him with her. She"—it choked her to say the word—"*wanted* him here."

"I would say she enjoyed his company," Glaukia responded.

"In more than just a carnal sense?"

The old woman nodded, chilling the air in Penthesilea's lungs. "They were barely separated. Never at night. Ask any of the women; they will tell you. We all saw them together, fighting, riding. Laughing."

This last one Penthesilea had the most difficulty understanding.

"Do you think it is possible that she has left with him?" Melanippe asked. "That she has abandoned the Amazons?"

Unable to bear the despairing looks of the women, Penthesilea turned and walked to the edge of the room and gazed out on the vista before them. The moon was high, but the opacity of the clouds had transformed it into a shapeless smudge with a white halo that blurred into the darkness. There were seven of them in the room together: her, her sisters, and four others—the same three who had ridden with the news of the queen's departure, plus one more. Glaukia and Eumache were older, with their white hair worn in braids tight to their scalps. The other two were younger: Andromache, who had been injured in a battle in the weekend preceding the trip to the Gargareans, and Derione, whose skill as a wet nurse made her more valuable here than elsewhere. Even though her back was turned, Penthesilea could feel their eyes boring intently into her, awaiting her answer. But what answer could she give them? She would never have dreamed that her sister might abandon her people. Might abandon the honor bestowed upon her by Ares himself. But then, she could never have imagined that she would welcome a man with open arms into their home.

She turned back to Andromache. "You say he came with offers of marriage?"

The woman nodded. "Bold as brass. Not just once. That was the reason for his arrival, or so he said. I overheard him mention this several times. He had no shame declaring his purpose."

"And she did not rebuke this?"

"She did," Derione replied forcefully. "I heard her myself. Several times. She said she would never leave her home. That she would never choose to be the wife of a king when she was a queen in her own right."

Relief came from these words, words that Penthesilea could well imagine spilling from her sister's lips. It was as if the room had been allowed to breathe. Several sighs, including those from Melanippe and Antiope, filled the air around her.

But the relief was short-lived.

"Then he must have kidnapped her," Antiope said.

"How? She would have struggled. One man alone could not have taken her against his will," Melanippe countered.

"But there was the ship nearby," Derione offered by way of explanation. "And one of our boats has gone now, too."

Silence hovered. The arrow lay motionless across the bridge of Penthesilea's knuckles. This was not a piece of news they had shared with her earlier. Her immediate instinct was to rebuke them for withholding this, but she shook the feeling away. Anger would serve no purpose now.

"A boat is gone, you say?"

"Yes, a fishing vessel. Only a small one. And the oars within it."

At least they knew for certain how she had come to leave, which only served to reinforce the notion that it had not been by choice. Had she chosen freely, Hippolyte would only ever have left by horse.

"How many sets of footsteps led to it?" the princess asked. "If only one set led to the boat, we will know for certain that he has taken her. Many would indicate he had help."

Do not let it be two sets of footprints. The thought ran through her mind. *Do not let it be that she has left us by choice.* She could see the other women looking between each other, avoiding one another's eyes. It was clear their thoughts were all on the same theme.

"We did not realize she was missing until late in the day," said Derione. "By that time the tide had swept in and washed away any signs in the sand. Any footsteps that might have been there had gone."

Disappointment plunged through them, heavy as rocks in their bellies. So much breath held within the chamber, its absence adding further to the tension, like the moments before the winds swept in to tear up the land.

There was no queen. She was gone.

"Why did you not come and find us? Why did you not come to tell us this?"

A full moon. The queen had been gone for an entire moon. With a fleet of ships, who knew where Theseus might have taken her by now? The women hesitated. Finally, it was Glaukia that spoke.

"We thought…we thought that perhaps she had returned to join you. Ridden out at night when none of us had seen."

"Or that she had gone by choice," Andromache bowed her head, chagrined by her own words.

Unable to face the women, afraid that if she looked upon them, she might make an end of them there and then, Penthesilea turned to her sisters.

"I will take a small group at first light," she said.

"A small group?" Antiope responded. "We need our full force. Every woman. We will make this prince pay for the abduction of our queen."

"If she was abducted."

"You heard what Derione said. Hippolyte refused his marriage proposals. She did not wish to go with him."

"She refused them in public. We cannot ignore the fact that she allowed a man within the walls of Themiscyra. That in itself speaks volumes. If we attack first only to find she left us by choice, we will have waged war with no reason. Others will come to Athens's defense once they learn that we are in the wrong. We will be risking our home."

She knew it was not the response her sisters expected her to offer, and as she drew in a long, labored breath, they exchanged a look that spoke words she was not privy to. And yet she knew without doubt what they were thinking.

"This is not a matter in which I wish to gain glory." Penthesilea's tongue smacked against her teeth. "I am thinking only of Hippolyte. Of what is safest for our queen. My queen."

From their pursed expressions, she knew they remained unconvinced. They assumed her plan was to tear through Athens alone, to save her sister and seek all the glory that such a trial ordained for herself. And while it was true that such a thought had, indeed, visited her mind briefly, she had dismissed it just as fast.

"Then what?" Antiope said, still unconvinced. "If we find out that she has been taken, what do we do, then?"

"Then we will do what the Amazons do best," Penthesilea replied. "We will go to war. And Theseus will die."

FIFTEEN

THE JOURNEY WAS MORE ARDUOUS THAN SHE HAD ANTICI-
pated. From the moment they descended the steppes of
Pontus, the rain assailed them. Drops as big as pebbles blurred
the path before them and the landscape beyond, making it impossible
to establish which direction to ride in. The sky, swollen and gray,
pressed down on them with a weight that seemed to slow their minds
as much as their pace, while the water soaked through their boots and
their caps in such volume that rivulets formed in front of their eyes.

"Princess, we cannot keep moving like this. The horses, they
fall," called one of the women from behind her, though she did not
turn to see who, for the winds were too strong to turn against.

"We have fought in worse than this," Penthesilea shouted over
the storm, just as a bolt of lightning shot through the distant air,
momentarily illuminating the sky.

"Please, my queen. We cannot save her if we do not make it to
Athens."

It was the voice of Cletes that reached her, her tone crawling
with fear.

Penthesilea twisted on her horse and tried to determine their location. She knew from the sea and the sun that they had been traveling east when they had left at dawn, but now the clouds were so deep it was impossible to find even a smudge of brightness in the sky.

"We cannot camp here," she said, eventually. "Keep your eyes out for somewhere we can shelter. A rock face or a copse. And I am not your queen."

She heard the women's murmurs behind her, muted by the rain, and kicking deep into her horse's flanks, she pushed on.

The rain had still not abated when they reached a sandstone cave, cut into the rock face with a small overhang that afforded the horses a little protection. From the ashes that coated the cave floor, it was evident that the space had been used for shelter before now, by farmers, perhaps, or possibly by their own nomadic women. The thought did not fill her with comfort. She had hoped to be further on the journey by now, past the Sea of Marmara and into Thrace. As long as the rain hammered down above them, she knew she had no choice but to wait for it to pass. Perhaps in the morning, the clouds would have emptied themselves entirely, she hoped, but as night fell and the reign of Selene's silver moon came and went, the rain endured. Penthesilea and her women remained trapped within the confines of the cave, their clothes failing to dry in the saturated, musty air. Outside the whinnying of the horses grew more intense as they expressed their craving for warmth and for grass to graze upon.

And in their company, there was no humor, no lightness, none of the banter that would have flown had this been a normal expedition. This was anything but normal.

Five women had joined her: Klonie, Polemusa, Thermodosa, Derione, and Cletes. The first four she had picked not only for their skill in battle but for their appearances, too. All were entirely different, yet equally beautiful in a manner that would subtly appeal to the wandering gaze of any man fortunate enough to come across them. The muscles in their bodies, the curve of their hips, all impossibly alluring, and for Penthesilea's plan, that would be of benefit. And even if their beauty failed, their arms would not. They were each of them proven killers. Smart and ruthless. Efficient and deadly.

All except Cletes.

This had been Cletes's first trip to the Gargareans, after making her maiden kill in battle less than a year earlier. She would not have been Penthesilea's choice, neither for experience nor for looks, for there was nothing subtle within her beauty. Her dark eyes, mahogany hair, and eyelashes long enough to fan a wind would be certain to draw the eyes of any that fell on her. But she had begged Penthesilea to let her join them, having assigned herself the role of page to the princess. It was she who had brought food to Penthesilea on those first nights with the Gargareans, when the princess had stayed out in the cold, worried for her sister. It was she who had taken her horse to rub down when they had heard of the queen's departure and had ridden out to meet them on the steppes as they departed Themiscyra that early morning, dressed in her embroidered robes, the hope and optimism flowing from her very pores. Given all that she had done for her, Penthesilea did not have the heart to send the girl away. And so five women became six, riding together toward Athens.

She had decreed that Melanippe and Antiope would remain at home, a decision that was met with great animosity, particularly from Antiope. This time she did not shrink from her complaint, accusing Penthesilea of seeking glory outright, of wishing to make her name as renowned as that of Hippolyte. After all, should something happen to the queen, then she, Penthesilea, would be next in line. Antiope reminded her of this in words laden with venom, bristling and barbed, as if Penthesilea could ever have been unaware that she had been placed second by her father. Not quite worthy of his zoster. For that reason, Antiope insisted, Penthesilea should be the one to stay in Themiscyra, and Antiope be the one to lead the women to Athens. She was almost as clean a shot as Penthesilea, she argued, and certainly a greater warrior than anything the Athenians could muster. But Penthesilea threw her argument back at her. With Hippolyte gone, she was the one who ruled, and she would be the one to ride to Athens, not, as her sisters believed, for the glory. Not so that her name would be sung through cavernous halls and riotous taverns. Not for her name to be etched into history. She would go because she could not sit idly by and wait for news. Because the absence of her sister, and their ignorance as to what had befallen her, had turned Penthesilea's stomach to knots, full of thorny, jagged edges, which stabbed and tore at her insides and tightened with every passing hour. In all her life, Penthesilea had never succumbed to an illness like so many other women did. No sickness of the gut or malady that caused her temperature to rise. This was as close to sickness as she had ever come, and such ailment would only pass when Hippolyte was riding beside her once more. And if, *if* Theseus had abducted the queen, as she believed he had, then his death was imminent. Penthesilea would fight until Athens crumbled.

That was what she would do, once she heard the truth from Hippolyte's lips, but not before that. For however flighty and impetuous Antiope might think her, she would not declare a war in which she risked the lives of their women without her sister's acknowledgment. Not while she was still alive.

By the next morning, the sky had finally cleared, the sunlight shimmering as it shone unbroken on the sodden earth.

"We will stick close to the coast," Penthesilea told them as they fixed their saddlebags. "The earth will be drenched and precarious. Be gentle with your horses; we cannot risk lameness now."

The path itself she knew well enough. They had traveled from Anatolia into Greece countless times, sometimes for visits that lasted mere days, on other occasions for weeks on end, when king after king would call for their aid, one army and then another fearful of losing their lands, unable to summon the strength to crush their invaders with their own resources. They had turned green grass red here, had decimated armies who thought themselves invincible until they had seen the half-moon brass shields of the Amazons glint on the horizon. They had been called here to swing their swords and fire their arrows for so many wars that Penthesilea would need a full moon to recall them all.

But this was different. For every time they had ridden here before, to Macedonia or Thessaly or beyond, they had known who it was they were going to fight, or at the very least, who they were going to fight for. This time, all was uncertain.

They did not speak as they rode, pushing the horses into a gallop only when the terrain was flat and even and dry enough to permit it. Occasionally one of the women would point out a spring or stream where they could stop to drink, but other than this, even Cletes remained silent.

As they rode past the vast expanse of Mount Parnassus, the sky was a bright blue, the lush greens of cypress trees and cedars rising high above them. The air was thinner here, cooler, too, and dense orchards flourished on the mountainside, with the grapevines so prolific that they obscured the houses and bowed the trellises they had been tied to. The mountain was sacred to Dionysus, son of Zeus and God of Wine and Ecstasy. Given the abundance of fruit, it was easy to see why.

"There is a place a few hours south of Boeotia," Penthesilea spoke as the women slowed to traverse the rockier landscape. "We have a friend there. We will be able to rest for the night. Eat. Change our clothes."

"Our clothes?" Klonie asked.

"We cannot travel to Athens like this. It will arouse too much suspicion."

Trousers and tunics were the standard wear of the Amazons. Leather caps fitted close to the head were worn while riding and in battle, occasionally adjusted to fit a metal helmet, should the severity of the fight require it. She had assumed the need to change their wardrobes would have been obvious to her women, as obvious as leaving the horses and spears where no man would find them, rather than striding into Athens upon their steeds, declaring their warrior heritage for all to see. But their cheeks paled, and Klonie gripped her bow tightly.

"But our weapons?" she asked again.

Penthesilea inhaled sharply. "We can take whatever we can strap to our bodies, under our robes. Daggers. Knives. As many as you are comfortable wearing, provided they remain invisible. We cannot arouse suspicion. The rest will stay in Boeotia with Cletes."

The young girl opened her mouth, pink lips shining as an objection rose within her, then clamped her mouth tightly shut. The princess had spoken. Unlike her sisters, Cletes did not question her rule while the other women exchanged furtive glances of apprehension that Penthesilea did not dignify with a response. They did not need weapons. She had seen Klonie snap a man's neck between her knees on the battlefield, Polemusa break a man's jaw with the swing of her elbow. The damage that one of them could wreak with a single dagger was easily comparable to what any fully armed man might do within the walls of Athens. Weapons were a source of comfort; that was all.

Like Hippolyte's zoster when they rode into war. The comparison sent a shudder running down her spine. After all, Heracles's desire for that zoster was what had first brought Theseus to their shores.

They arrived at their rest point, southwest of Thebes, two days later than she had originally planned, the sky ablaze with stars. Great constellations draped across the firmament like mighty rivers, their thousands of tributaries glinting, bright white against the endless indigo expanse. Thousands of stories, held in perpetual stasis by the will of the gods. Sometimes Penthesilea could lose herself in their stories. Stories like that of Cassiopeia, the beautiful queen bound for all eternity to her chair in the sky.

While undeniably attractive, the boastful queen Cassiopeia had proclaimed herself even more beautiful than the nereids, the sea nymphs that accompanied Poseidon and aided sailors in their travels. The God of the Sea was protective of these nymphs and had taken great umbrage at Cassiopeia's remarks, sending the great sea monster Cetus to ravage her kingdom. In a desperate attempt to pacify the beast, Cassiopeia had tied her daughter, Andromeda, to a rock in the sea for Cetus to feast upon. The story told how Andromeda was saved. The hero Perseus, armed with the gorgon's head, had swept in upon the winged horse, Pegasus, and rescued her from certain death. But Penthesilea's thoughts remained with Cassiopeia. Unforgiven, she was tied to her chair and cast out to the stars, forced only to watch the world revolve beneath her.

"You will not be rash, will you?"

Penthesilea drew her eyes away from the sky. Cletes spoke from behind a burning fire, and hazy twists of smoke wove their way upward, darkening the air between them. The other women, upon the princess's order, were sleeping, yet Cletes had remained awake, beside Penthesilea, as if it were her calling to do so.

"I know I cannot ask anything of a princess, but please, if I could, I would ask you not to be rash. Not to try to kill him on your own."

"I would have left you in Pontus if I had have known you would start speaking like my sisters."

"Your sisters speak that way because they love you. I speak—"

Her sentence finished short, as if there were more words to be spoken. Words that would entwine them. Words that Penthesilea did not want to hear. Stillness engulfed them; impenetrable, it clasped them, threatening to swell to such proportions it would consume them both, when a crackle from the fire sent tiny amber sparks upward and melting into the air and drew the women's gazes away.

"You should sleep now," was all Penthesilea could reply.

When morning arrived, they dressed themselves in Athenian fashions, fussing with the fabric that fluttered between their legs.

"This cannot be right?" Polemusa insisted. "There is too much fabric here. How is one to run in a such a garment?"

"One does not run in such a garment," Penthesilea replied, attempting to conceal how she, too, struggled with the garment.

Given the length of the journey, they started on horseback. The women grumbled incessantly about their clothing, and gasps of frustration rang out every time a sharp wind whipped the cloth about them. Penthesilea herself remained silent on the matter, despite the discomfort she endured due to the thin leather sandals on her feet. Boots, she knew already from experience, were infinitely more practical for riding.

At midmorning, they found a small area shrouded by trees, where they stopped and dismounted. Immediately, the horses' heads dropped to the ground to eat.

"This is where we leave you," Penthesilea told Cletes.

"Be safe, my princess," Cletes replied, and Penthesilea saw a question glinting in her eyes. The need for a reassurance she could not provide. Turning her head, the princess tethered her horse to a nearby tree, before recommencing the journey without a word.

Now on foot, the remaining five women passed over rocky terrain and verdant farms filled with olive trees. Trunks twisted and snarled open into crowns of iridescent leaves. Goatherds kept their animals beneath makeshift tents, with wooden fences that, poorly built, seemed slanted and no match for a determined beast, or else left them to wander amid the shades of the groves. The women made no eye contact as they walked but kept veils over their heads and across their faces, leaving only their eyes exposed.

"People are staring at us," Polemusa whispered, as they passed a family feasting on the ground with flatbreads and oil. As the women drew closer, the family fell silent, and even after they had passed, the hush lingered, though Penthesilea paid it no heed.

"Possibly it is their land," she replied. "It does not matter either way."

The closer they came to Athens, the more fertile the farms and vineyards grew. Row after row of twisted vines cut across the landscape. Cultivated into straight lines, the endless vines were interspersed with wheat, the golden yellow a stark contrast to the bold green elsewhere.

At first, the air smelled of such forceful cultivation, of plowed earth and pollen, of freshly pressed oils and burning cedarwood. Gradually, though, those scents faded and were replaced by the fetid odors of life, both human and animal, an unmistakable rankness. And yet even amid the stench, when they reached the citadel walls, the women had no choice but to stop and stare, momentarily awestruck by the sight before them.

They had reached Athens.

SIXTEEN

THE FORTIFICATIONS OF THE CITADEL WERE UNLIKE ANYTHING she had seen before. A deep moat, dry and vast, had been cut into the earth in front of the first wall, which stood at the height of two men. This smaller structure was constructed parallel to the citadel walls themselves. The towers and battlements were roofed with terra-cotta tiles that glinted like burned earth, and the thinnest of windows were cut into the dense stone walls—thin enough for an arrow to be shot from but not shot into. Unless it were an Amazon behind the bow, Penthesilea thought. Her arrows could fly through those. If anything, it gave them a fixed target to aim for.

On either side of where they stood, the citadel wall wove up and down the mountainside, its yellow bricks encircling a city of which she could glimpse only the smallest fraction. A small fraction made visible though the enormous gates. There were several such gates positioned along the walls, she knew, but they had come from the north, the easiest approach to Athens, although they might need to reconsider this when they left.

"Come, we should move with these people. Arouse less

suspicion," Penthesilea said, gesturing toward a group of around fifteen. Most of them were men, but half a dozen women loitered behind them. Their pace was dragging as they exchanged conversation and gossip, and played deaf to the prattling of their men. With a nod of Penthesilea's head, the Amazons sidled up beside them and slipped seamlessly into step with the party and across the deep moat.

There was so much to gaze upon. Too much for her eyes and ears to contend with, although thankfully, her sense of smell had finally grown inured to the stench that only moments ago had made her retch. The vast number of buildings was the first thing to strike her, and the people themselves, even greater in number. Hoplites, Athenian warriors, were easily identifiable with their sculpted brass breastplates and polished helmets, the gleaming metal of which was imprinted with their crest. As Penthesilea passed them, she and the rest of her women attempted to slow a little, each taking note of the same things: the number of guards, the weapons they wore, the places in which the wall might be scaled if needed. The hoplites held spears and xiphos, the short swords that would prove useful weapons once the men had been relieved of them. But not yet, Penthesilea reminded herself. Not until it was necessary.

The topography allowed only glimpses of the citadel. Unlike the steppes in Pontus, where the ground rose and fell gently, as if shifted into their positions by the very breath of the earth, the hills and valleys here felt as if they had been forced into place with a hammer and an ax. There was no calmness to the curvature of the land. No ease or even logic that she could see. Just jagged peaks, great rocky ledges, and steep inclines, and all of them littered with yet more people and more buildings. Temples sat on the high points of the hills, the Acropolis, smothered in the smoke of incense and crowds outside, visible even from their low elevation.

The women shifted closer together, as if preparing for an onslaught of enemies.

"Are those temples?" Derione spoke with a hushed voice, noticing the buildings only now. "Why do they need to be so large?"

"Because they are Greek. They revel in the ostentatious. It is like shouting a prayer, rather than whispering it, and expecting it to be heard with greater force." She ladened her voice with cynicism, attempting to conceal the awe with which she viewed these edifices. These temples, these homes. Even the wall itself.

Although now a little disjointed, they continued to move with the group of men and women, toward, Penthesilea assumed, the agora. Athens was known for its trade, and the marketplace would be the heart of it all, a place in which people could barter for honeys and lamps and silver jewelry. She had seen plenty of agorae before, although usually in a state of depletion, before or after a battle. However, whatever expectations she might have had, they soon paled into insignificance at the sight before her.

"Where has this all come from?" Klonie asked.

This was Athens. The heart of it. A market so bustling, so astir that even the goats failed to lie still in their pens. Aromas of oils, not only olive, but deeper and richer, fragrances, rosewood and cinnamon, iris, cistus, myrtle, and hyacinth, wove invisible coils of perfumes in the atmosphere around them. Peppercorns, perfectly spherical, dark gray and flush pink, filled small wooden bowls. Salted fish were stacked high on tables, the colors graduating from deep pinks to a crystalline white. There were stalls selling leather, in pelts, or cut and shaped into sandals, fabric, wood, papyrus, the list was endless, with people flitting from one to another, some with urgency, others with a pace that was near stagnant. It was mesmerizing. So mesmerizing that Queen Hippolyte might have chosen to live her life here, perhaps? The question had barely formed in Penthesilea's mind before she shook it away again. Beneath the allure, the less appetizing aspects were all too apparent. Dung and rats were ankle-deep in places, and amongst the effluent, flies and mosquitoes buzzed around the lips and eyes of people and animals alike. Drunkards lay out in the heat of the sun, snoring, some in a pool of their own vomit, while children raced over their bodies as if they were corpses. No, Hippolyte would not choose this life. She was certain of it. Several pairs of eyes were now fixed on the women, and she realized they had now separated from the group with which they arrived. At least she had not bought Cletes with her, Penthesilea thought, for then they would truly be staring. Paying their observers no heed, she continued to survey the agora.

Under another canopy, a dozen men and women were nestled together, their arms and wrists bound behind their backs, dark- and light-skinned, and of varying ages. The princess's eyes were drawn to a woman with her back to her. Her dark hair was of the same tone and thickness as Hippolyte's, a little shorter, but weaved in a plait that her sister could easily have worn. Was it possible that this was what Theseus had planned? To kidnap the queen and see her humiliated as she was sold to the highest bidder? Penthesilea's pulse raced, and her feet slid on the ground as she approached, the dung and mud slipping over the sides of her sandals and onto the soles of her feet, but she did not even notice.

"Sister?"

The woman turned around. Her dark eyes were lined with kohl, and narrow and almond shaped. The square jaw, the long nose, the light brow; from this angle, there were no similarities.

"My apologies," she said and slowly backed away.

As they picked their way through the stalls, uncertainty churned within her. A sensation akin to souring milk was ripening in her gut, as if she were heading into a battle with no idea from which direction the attack might come. She knew that her women felt it, too. Even if it were somehow a straightforward thing to remove Hippolyte from the palace, they would not manage to escape a place as busy as this without casualties.

They had fallen, quite accidentally, into a formation in which they regularly fought, slowly moving, their eyes constantly scanning, their hands gripping the waistbands of their robes, at the place where the daggers were hidden. The noises were distracting. Men shouting, trying to sell their wares, children screaming and crying. Dogs barking, horses braying. They were so close to the earth, so close to nature, yet it was all but impossible to make out even the most zealous trills of birdsong above the cacophony.

"Garnets. Sapphires. Rubies."

A hawker was shouting at each person who approached, and seeing the group, aimed his voice at them.

"Garnets, the biggest you'll ever see."

"Where shall we go?" Derione whispered. A drumming had commenced beneath Penthesilea's rib cage. The push of adrenaline quickened through her veins. She was scouring the horizon, still unsure which way to turn, when a hand reached out and grabbed her by the wrist.

There was no moment to consider. No second to wait for her mind to order her muscles into action. Instinctively, the princess snatched the dagger from her waist, spun around, and pressed the blade against the hawker's throat. Immediately the remaining Amazons fell into position around them, blocking the view from passersby.

"You dared touch me?"

The hawker coughed, his throat jerking beneath the force of her blade. By instinct, she had chosen the angle carefully: high enough so as to not draw blood, yet with enough pressure to constrict the airflow through the windpipe and cause considerable discomfort.

"My mistake," he coughed. "I am sorry. Forgive me. Forgive me. Please, forgive me."

She loosened the pressure just a fraction and he fell back, gasping for air, the tears glistening in his eyes as they darted from side to side. Even though the knife remained in the princess's hands, he looked past her, as if the worst was yet to come.

A moment passed, and when nothing else happened, he slumped to his knees, relieved.

"You are on your own," he said, with a mixture of disbelief and horror.

The realization struck Penthesilea a full heartbeat before Derione spoke again.

"We have no man," she said, reading the man's expression. "That is why those people before were looking at us so intently. All the women here are with men."

Was it really the case? Penthesilea shifted her stance slightly, changing the position of her blade so that its tip was now pointed into the man's chest. She scanned the view around her. Now that her attention had been drawn to the fact, it was impossible to ignore. Of course, women had no rights in a place such as this, and as such it should have come as no surprise that a chaperone was required if a woman wished to roam in Athens. She knew this already, yet somehow it had slipped from her mind. Or perhaps it was simply that when she had been in such situations before, the rules had never applied to her, so she had paid them no heed. Now, however, the situation was different.

"Prince Theseus, where does he reside?" she asked, digging the dagger a little more firmly into his chest.

The man jerked his head toward the top of the Acropolis. Sitting at the same elevation as the Parthenon was a lower building, flat roofed with wide verandas. It was a sensible position for a palace, the princess considered. If an attack were to come, its occupants would be out of harm's way. Though even from here, she could see places through which they might scale the cyclopean stone walls if the time came for them to launch an attack. Something shifted within her. Her sisters' words. Cletes's hopeful promise. This was not to be a storming. Not a fight in which she was to prove her worth as a warrior. If she was to enter, it would have to be with the willing acquiescence of those within.

The thought struck, bold and sudden like a blunt arrow to the chest. With a smile on her face, she turned to the hawker.

"Pack up your gems," she told him. "You are coming with us."

SEVENTEEN

WHO ARE YOU?" STAMMERED THE HAWKER. HIS EYES WERE deep set and hooded. His bushy brows, once, presumably, bordering on black, were now graying, and met in the middle. That he was not a native of Athens Penthesilea had already established from both his skin and his accent, but that would be to their advantage.

"Do not speak," she said. "And wrap this shawl around your head. I do not need you to be recognized." There was no longer any need for weapons. If he objected, it would be a swift but bloodless end.

"Why? Why are you doing this? Who are you?"

"I am Penthesilea," she said. "Daughter of Ares. Sister of Queen Hippolyte."

"You are the Amazon princess?"

Any color that remained in his cheeks fled instantly, and the tremble in his hands migrated to his knees, forcing him to rest against his table in order to steady his balance. In such a moment, his age showed in the folds of his skin. He looked frail. Helpless even, although the princess allowed an internal flicker of satisfaction at his state. It was one thing to be feared with an ax in her hand, but another entirely to draw the same effect from her words alone.

"Must I ask you again, or do I need to be forceful?" she said.

Hurriedly he began to pack away his stall, all the while his eyes searching out an escape, any manner in which he might to draw attention to his plight, or else race away from his captors without it ending in his death.

"There is nothing you can do." Klonie spoke softly. Even simple sentences spoken by her had a lyrical lilt to them. "Either you do as she says, or you will not survive. Any one of us can end you in an instant."

He nodded, his shoulders slumping with the realization of the truth. Yet Penthesilea felt no guilt. A man who had accrued such a wealth of gemstones had not done so by making foolish, impulsive decisions. And to make an enemy of an Amazon would the last decision any man could make. With his bags filled, he stood up as straight as his aged, quaking frame would allow and looked at the princess.

"What do you want of me, now?" he asked.

The strength of his stare was admirable, particularly from one who, judging from the smoothness of his palms, had likely never seen battle in his life. An iota of respect flared within Penthesilea.

"Now you walk with us," she said. "You walk with us to the palace."

Incense bloomed thickly, sickly sweet with the saccharine scents of cherry blossom and citrus oils. Time and time again, Penthesilea found her eyes drawn to the stupendous buildings, captivated by the drone of the hymns reaching her ears like the rhythmic smashing of waves over rocks, or the drumming beat of a gallop on soft grass. *What did the gods think of such a display?* she wondered. It was no secret that both Poseidon and Athena had competed for patronage of the city, each presenting the old King Cecrops with gifts that would help his land flourish beyond his dreams. Slamming his trident on the stone ground, Poseidon had split the earth open, and from it sprouted his gift: a spring of water. Salty seawater, the likes of which could be found hammering against the cliff edges all around their peninsula.

By contrast, Athena, under the watchful gaze of Cecrops, had planted a seed, which grew before his eyes into a lustrous olive tree, bursting with fruit. Immediately, Cecrops saw all the possibilities. Fruit could be used for oils, to burn in their dark nights, or eaten, while they sat under the shade the leaves provided. It would provide wood that could be burned or carved into weapons. It was an easy decision for Cecrops to make, and the temples to Athena stood proud.

Her father, Ares, had never professed a desire for such edifices. He was content for his daughters to show their dedication though sacrifice and war. Yet from the rounded bellies of many Athenians, these offerings were still being well received. The citadel was wealthy. Prospering. But if that was the case, why would Theseus have taken Hippolyte when he might have his choice of women for his bride?

"Let your hands fall naturally," Penthesilea spoke to her women as they approached the steps to the palace entrance.

"Clasping our daggers is natural," Klonie replied.

There was no need for a reply. Penthesilea understood the women's concern. Discretion was not their forte. Hiding their intentions went against what any king would ask of them. They were Amazons. They rode into battle with spears raised, their heritage and legacy screaming from their very bodies. Every man they had ever faced knew exactly who they were. Until today.

Together, they reached the steps to the palace. The polished marble was slippery beneath their feet, slickened further by the mud and grime that covered their sandals from the long walk and the slurry of the agora floor. The veils that draped down over their hair and across their shoulders were little more than a thin gossamer, yet for Penthesilea it was claustrophobic enough, restrictive and, at times, suffocating. If they were to fight here, they would fight barefoot and in close contact, the princess decided. That way she could use the lack of friction and her opponent's weight to her advantage. They would need to place women around the citadel walls, too. They would have to decide which gate to enter through, and barricade the others so that no one could escape. A full-scale attack would be required if Athens were to fall.

The higher they climbed, the denser the crowds became. People hoping to gain an audience with the king. Hoping to kneel on the floor in the throne room, where a king might look down on them and, with apathetic disinterest, feign understanding of their plights. Perhaps Aegeus, the King of Athens, was different. Perhaps he truly listened to his subjects and citizens. She thought it unlikely. She had seen enough to believe such audiences were nothing more than the shroud worn by tyrants. She had seen firsthand what happened when a king was given a *suggestion* he didn't agree with. And just as the gem hawker had not grown rich without wiles, neither, she considered, did a king hold on to his kingdom.

Time seemed to slow as they inched forward through the press, yet patience was a skill her women possessed in abundance. Honed in the long summer months, stalking a lone roe deer over miles on foot, and perfected during those endless dark winter nights, where they would keep watch for the slightest glimpse of an intruder on their lands. Penthesilea could see the women studied their surroundings as she did, could see as they took a mental note of every person in their sight, if and how they were armed, and how they could be dealt with most efficiently.

Over two dozen hoplites guarded the entrance. The sight of the guards, with their plumed helmets and their formed cuirasses, pleased her. The presence of so many guards meant it more likely that royalty was within the palace rather than traveling. And if Theseus had taken Hippolyte, he would not leave her, knowing that she would escape at the first opportunity that arose.

Besides the hoplites, there was a man on his knees at the entrance, the bottom of his sandals worn through so that the calloused and bleeding flesh of his feet was visible. An aroma of husbandry emanated from him. The oily scent of lanolin and goats.

"It is the third time this has happened. Please, let me speak to the king I require a review with the polis."

"The king will tell you to make offerings at the temples."

"I have done that! I have done that. Please. Please. I am allowed another audience. The king will grant me that."

While the argument continued, Penthesilea scrutinized the hoplite with whom the man spoke, noting with interest how his weight was shifted to one side, causing his tunic to fall at a slight angle. He was taller than the other guards, almost Gargarean in size, but he had sustained an injury to his left side, and now it was slightly weakened. He was there for intimidation rather than force. Knowledge of this fact could be vital if it came to a fight. With the hawker still trembling, she slid a little to the side, garnering a better view from which she could study the other men that stood in the path between her and her sister.

The one closest to the palace door was smaller and slighter than the first guard. His eyes were moving constantly, not only to observe those men closest to the palace entrance, but also those further away. His ear was quick, too, his attention moving sharply at one sound and then another. When his eyes landed on her, they focused briefly, before she lowered her gaze and shuffled back closer to the hawker. Another difference between this and her usual form of battle—there, the men knew you had come to kill them. Reading their strengths and weaknesses was not something that had to be done discreetly.

"What are you here for?"

With the slanted accent and direct voice, it took Penthesilea a moment to realize that the guard was looking at her and her women. The man with the bleeding soles had moved on. Awaiting his next instruction, he stood by the edge of the palace walls. It was their turn now. This, it appeared, was the only hurdle being placed between her and her sister. Lowering her body into a deep bow, she glided forward.

"I have women here," she said. "I am to present them to Prince Theseus."

The hoplite sniffed, recoiling with an air of deepest repulsion.

"Why are you speaking to me?" He turned to the hawker, whose tremble was now so pronounced that it rocked his hands and rattled the gems in his bags. He opened his mouth, in a half gasp, before Penthesilea cut across him.

"My husband is a mute. He lost his tongue to bandits. It does not affect his ability to earn money, thankfully. No, as I have said, we have gifts. Women, for the prince." The hawker snapped his mouth closed as the hoplite eyed her with suspicion.

"I did not know of their arrival."

"They are a gift. From East Anatolia. A presentation to congratulate the prince." The guard remained stone-faced even as he looked past her to study the four pairs of eyes that shone at him through the slits in their masks. "They have been requested by Queen Hippolyte, as a gift to her future husband."

Was this not what the Grecian men did, bartering and offering women as if they were cattle? She had seen it often enough. Seen women passed from man to man, the spoils of war, as transferable as gold and jewels with the only real difference being that the value of a human descended far more rapidly. As antiquities, they became worthless with age rather than considered valuable for their wisdom.

"We are to see Queen Hippolyte first," Penthesilea spoke again. "She can confirm this for you. You can take us to her now. We have come from Anatolia."

She added a little force to her final words. If they were keeping Hippolyte there, then they would know who she was and should not be surprised by the presence of women on their own, women able to speak their minds, even in the presence of their husbands.

With barely a twitch of his finger, the hoplite gestured to one of the guards behind him. A moment later he was gone, and the guard, pointing with his hand, indicated that Penthesilea and her women were to wait by the palace entrance and the reeking goatherd.

"What now?" Polemusa asked when they were out of the hoplite's earshot.

"Now we wait."

"And if they do not allow us to see Hippolyte?"

Penthesilea drew back a breath. "We are asking as a courtesy, that is all. If my sister is in this building, I will not leave until I have spoken with her."

Beside them, the goatherd wheezed. He had dust on his chest, she suspected. Dust from the animals. No doubt he kept them in small pens and brought them into his home on the colder, wetter nights. There had been girls born in Themiscyra with such conditions.

Wheezing from the day of birth, or the moment they touched a horse. Such girls tended to prefer the nomadic life, away from large herds, and usually kept poultry, but they still had a place in Pontus and with the Amazons. Even it was not the life they had first thought that they wanted.

Penthesilea found herself wondering how long it would take them to find Hippolyte. The palace was grand but not so massive that a brisk walk would surely have covered it all in the time that the guard had been gone. Perhaps she had been wrong to assume Theseus had taken her sister here. Perhaps her refusal of his marriage proposal had seen him provide a more terrible punishment. She did not fear her sister's death, but then, she would not have feared her abduction, either. When the guard reappeared in the doorway, he beckoned for them to approach.

"You can present your gifts to the polis," the guard said. "They will decide if they are to be gifted as you requested."

"The polis is for men, but my husband cannot speak to present them."

"There is no need for words. It is easy enough to see what is offered here."

The guard lifted his hand toward Polemusa as if to grab her by force and shackle her the way they had seen the slaves in the agora. The women stiffened, each one fighting the urge to kill him there and then.

"No," Penthesilea replied, stepping between the pair before his hand could graze Polemusa's skin. "That is not what we requested."

A sneer twisted the hoplite's lips, his narrow eyes gazing past Penthesilea and lingering on Polemusa a moment longer before he addressed the princess once again with a look of deepest scorn, repulsion seeping almost visibly from his pores.

"You seem to forget your place, woman."

"And you seem to forget that the woman you are harboring here is the Amazon queen."

It was so fast, so instant, that only the Amazons knew it was coming. While the hawker looked on dumbfounded, the guard had no time to adjust his look of disdain before the women had surrounded him and shielded him from the sight of his comrades. Within the space of a moment, Penthesilea's hands had reached up, grabbed the side of his head, twisted his neck, and, in one swift, forceful movement, caused a snap to ring out and echo in the high ceilings above them. The knees of the hawker buckled, but Penthesilea caught him before he could hit the ground.

"Do not give us away, or you will meet the same end. Now, where would the women of house be?" A sound stuttered in his voice. Croaking and breathy and unintelligible. "If you cannot tell me anything, you are no longer of use to me."

His stuttering continued for a moment longer.

"The gynaeceum. The women's room. It will be near the center of the building, so they cannot see out into the street." She held his gaze for a heartbeat, trying to read any deception within it. Then, with a satisfied nod, Penthesilea patted him on the shoulder.

"There, I knew you had a use." She turned her attention to her women. "You stay with him. Stay hidden and find a place to put that body where it won't be discovered. If anyone finds you, deal with them without attracting attention."

The women nodded, and Penthesilea did not wait to see the satisfaction she knew would glint in their eyes at the hope of a killing.

Instead she headed inward, to find her sister.

EIGHTEEN

WEEKS HAD PASSED SINCE SHE HAD WOKEN THAT MORNING, the waves rattling against the sides of the ship, her mind dazed from the water beneath her and from the herbs that had mingled with her wine and caused her to fall into slumber. Herbs that had been fashioned by Theseus's hands, herbs that had driven her to a sleep so deep that it took two days to wake from. Two days with strong winds driving them from the shores of Pontus. The citadel of Themiscyra was far behind her now. They had passed though the Black Sea, and the narrow straight that led to the Sea of Marmara.

Even now she recalled how the chants from the deck had reached her above the crash of the waves and the *slap, slap, slap* of the oars against the water as her eyes blinked open, the saline dampness of the world taking a moment to reach her senses. Her mind was still dragging itself from the fog, when she brushed her hand down the length of her body, only to be startled by the fabric that she found there. No trousers or tunic completed her outfit. Instead she found smooth silk. Soft and near invisible, tracing the lines of her body. As she shifted to her feet, the drapes fell to the ground and over her bare feet. Where had this come from?

Slowly images formed in her mind. Disjointed. Fractured scenes in strange orders and accompanied by sounds that did not fit, as if her memory had been broken like an amphora dropped on a stone tiled floor and had been pieced back together so that the images no longer sat flush side by side. Her home. The horses. Making love to Theseus on the mattress in her chamber. Then, with a churning that caused the bile to rise in the back of her throat, she knew what he had done. She was naked when he had fetched her the drink. When he had drugged her. And this garment, this gown, fit so her perfectly, it could only have been tailored for her alone. Of course it had. This had been his plan all along. Theseus had come to steal her.

She had tried to stand but stumbled, the effects of the herbs still swam in her veins.

"Theseus! Theseus! Come and face me, you coward!"

Two more attempts to stand and she had been on her feet hammering her fists against the door to her cabin with such force that her hands bled and her throat scraped in agony. It was as if she were experiencing a detachment between her body and mind. The wood had been nailed together and, she suspected, reinforced on the other side. Either that or she was even weaker than she feared.

"Father! Father!" The words *help me* formed on her tongue before she swallowed them back down. Never before had she begged her father for help. She had offered him sacrifices, yes, but that was not the same thing. She would not ask him for help. Her throat had ached as if the tender flesh had been gritted with sand, and the raw, insatiable hunger that suddenly fell upon her offered a further indication of just how long she had been on this boat. Inching herself back to the bed, she noted the flask of water hanging on a nail behind her.

Opening the bottle, she poured its contents onto her tongue, mouthful after mouthful, gulping it down. Only when she paused for breath, and the earthy bitterness caught on her tongue, did she pause and consider her actions. Her head hit the wooden bed before she could even retch.

———

A plate of food had been placed on the floorboards the next time she had woken. Salted meats, dried fruit, and dry biscuits. The standard fare for those traveling. Theseus had told her that his men had enough food to last them, and now they had one extra mouth to feed. One they had no doubt planned for.

Sniffing the food, she surveyed the deep scratches on the heels of her hands and, more painful, the knot of ropes that were twisted around her wrists. She tugged, knowing she would find no slackness there. She had been bound. Tricked again. Shame coursed through her veins, sourer than any poison she could ingest. She had been enslaved by a man, and it had taken place in her own homeland. The ignominy mingled with the valerian tonic that had curdled inside her. A ship this size would have a crew of over fifty men, all of them loyal to Theseus. All ready to follow his command. Had she been on land, fifty sailors would have proven a moderate exercise, but that was all. Barely a challenge. But at sea? Even if she took command by killing Theseus, this was his domain. His father was Poseidon, God of the Sea. He would best her at every attempt she made. What she needed was to be on land. Then Theseus would get what he deserved.

She sniffed the food again, touching it only with the tip of her tongue, searching out that telltale sickliness that came with valerian. Yet even when she was certain the food had not been tainted, she did not take a bite. Something else had caught her attention.

The hard jerking motions of the ship had been replaced with a gentle sway. A rolling lull that rocked her back and forth, knocking rhythmically. And beneath that sound, another. Footsteps.

She stiffened as the footsteps grew louder. Closer. A heavy thud echoed by the pounding of her heart. When the footsteps stopped directly outside the door, she lifted her bound wrists, pointing her elbows as her only weapon.

The second the door opened, she flew.

With her elbows still raised, she slammed her full body weight into Theseus, yet he was prepared. With shield raised, he hammered it into her, smashing her toward the timber planks of the walls with such force that she felt them crack. Pain shot through her arms.

"Careful, my love. If you damage the ship, we may never make it back to Athens."

"What did you do to me? You have taken me!"

"I knew you would not come on your own. Your sense of loyalty ran too deep. It clouded your vision. But this is best, my love. You will see. You are free now. Free to rule with me."

"Free? You have captured me? Bound me!"

"A precaution, that is all. I knew you would need time. Time to see that this is best. That we should rule Athens together."

"That is not what I want."

"Is it not?"

He was bolder here. More self-assured now that was away from her homeland. It was understandable. In Pontus he was outnumbered hundreds to one. Here, she was the one who found herself in that position. It was also the first time she had seen him dressed in his armor. Naked upon his arrival, he had worn only what she offered him—trousers or, more often, a simple tunic. But here he was every bit the warrior. Knowing he would not go to all this trouble to see her harmed, she shifted back, allowing herself the indulgence of studying her enemy. Beaten brass molded the curves of his torso, and smaller pieces had been curved into rounded plates that sat upon his shoulders and his biceps. Some flesh was exposed. They were places she could attack, but she would need to get her hands free first. And subtly, so he would not see.

With a long sigh, Theseus took a seat on the edge of the wooden slats that she had been placed upon. How a man could make something less comfortable than rocks to sleep on was beyond her, yet these shipbuilders excelled at such a skill.

"Hippolyte, please listen. It is just the two of us here. You do not need to lie to yourself anymore. You do not need to be concerned that your women might overhear you, or with the effects of your disloyalty. I have taken the pressure, the weight from you."

"You have stolen me."

His forehead rose and crinkled, as if in disbelief, before he shook his head. "No, my love. I have made it so that we can be together. That is all I have done."

He put his hand against her cheek, pushing her toward him, but she would not move. She kept her face fixed away from him, her eyes down as her thumb and fingers worked slowly at loosening the knots. When he realized force would not make her move, he dropped his hand in defeat.

"Hippolyte, my love, I did not bring you here to fight. I did not. I did it because I saw the truth in your eyes, every time we kissed. I felt it in my body every time we were together, I saw that you wanted this, too. That you want us to be together."

"You kidnapped me!" But her words had no impact on him. It was as if he could not hear her voice, or understand the things she was saying to him. Without warning, he dropped to his knees.

"I need you. I need you as my queen. Please, Hippolyte, you love me, the way that I love you. I know you do. Surely you see this was the only way for us? We cannot be together in Themiscyra. I have a kingdom. The greatest kingdom in the world."

"You are not even the king! You are a boy with delusions of grandeur." Her wrist had gained enough movement to twist. Another minute more and she would have both hands free to throttle him with.

"No, I am the future King of Athens, and will be the greatest king on Earth. And you will rule beside me."

He rose and kissed the smooth patch of exposed skin on her chest. His own skin was smoother than that it had been during their time together. His scent more heavily masked with oils and soaps.

"No," she leaned her body into him. "You can't do this. You need to turn this ship around. You need to take me back to Pontus."

"I will not do that."

"I will make you."

"I would like to see that."

A smile rose on his lips, yet it had barely formed when she smashed her elbow across his jaw. The strike took him by surprise, and he fell backward and landed against the floor just as a surge from the ship caused her to topple forward. The queen was as ill-prepared for the tumultuousness of the waves as the prince had been for the ferocity of her fight.

"You will not get away with this," she said, raising her knee to strike him in the groin. But he caught her ankle before she could make contact and tipped her backward, slamming her down on the hard surface.

"There is no man alive who can tame you, save me. Do you not see that?"

Higher off the ground, now, she clasped her legs around his neck, then launched herself sideways, shoving him back down.

"I do not need a man." She readied to strike again, but he was there. Even as she kicked out with her feet, striking his chest and knocking him backward, he was upright and ready before she could land the fatal blow. She could not find a rhythm. It was, she knew, the fault of the sea. The way the floor moved and disappeared beneath her feet. The robe was nothing more than torn fabric now, twisted into a rope, which she swung out and caught around his throat. With all the strength in her arms, she pulled it tighter, and for a second his cheeks reddened and his eyes bulged until the boat knocked them again, freeing him from her grasp. The calm seas of earlier had been replaced by erratic lurches from side to side. Every time she struck him, he was ready with a counter. And while he was dressed in his breastplate and armor, her body was struggling from the drugs and lack of food.

"This is what you want," he said, the blood trickling from a cut above his eyebrow. "You want a man who can control you. Who can best you."

"There is not a man on this planet who can control me," she spat, tasting the ferrous tang of iron between her lips. The plate that the food had been on was smashed into fragments. Reaching down, she grabbed a piece as it rolled across the planks. Yet even as she bent, she felt the tip of a blade under her breast. The skin between her ribs yielding.

"I am your king," Theseus hissed into her ear. "And I will follow you to the end of the earth. You know that. Perhaps your love for me is not a fierce as mine is for you, but it will be. I promise you. It will be. And if you think it will not, then end me. End me now."

As he stepped back, the pressure alleviated from her ribs and a gasp of relief flowed from her lungs. He was standing away from her now, the knife offered out between them. The seas were silent. Not a ripple of motion. The sounds of the sailors a mere murmur beneath the panting of their breaths. Even their first fight in the shallows of the water, with the waves lapping at their feet, had not felt so intense as this. No fight she had ever engaged in had felt as intense as this.

"Take it," Theseus said, offering the knife again. "If you cannot love me, then end it. End it now. For I would rather succumb to you like this than live my life without you. So it is your decision, my queen. What are we to do?"

Her eyes locked on his. More than any other man, he deserved to feel the end of her knife in his heart, and she deserved to watch him die. So why was she not moving? Why did the thought of killing him cause her own body to become stricken in pain?

"You see," he said, stepping forward and taking her hands, the knife now forgotten. "You love me, too."

NINETEEN

THE SAME SMOOTH MARBLE STONES THAT HAD SO UNNERVED
Penthesilea on the steps outside the palace lined the floors
within it. Those who lived here clearly had not considered the
implications of such a surface when it came to fighting, either because
fighting at all was something that was rarely considered or because
the notion that a fight might reach the inside of the royal palace was
inconceivable. The distinct scent of resins and wax, no doubt used on
the ornate frescoes that lined the wall, caught in her throat. Freshly
painted, bold blues and ochers decorated the corridors as far as her
eyes could see. Her gaze was drawn in particular to a seascape, where
waves crashed on a cliff edge, a small bird flying above them. An owl,
she noted as she drew closer. Athena's bird for Athena's kingdom. She
offered it the slightest glance before continuing on her search.

The evening sun reflected off the floors, but the princess stuck
to the shadows, her fingers ever conscious of the weapons concealed
upon her. Following the hawker's advice, she moved inward, her
footsteps as silent as a single drop of rain on the sand. She stood
motionless outside doorways, pressing herself against the cold stone

walls as she listened for voices. Often, she heard them. Male voices, deep with raucous laughter, or at other times, hushed and laden with consternation. But no woman's voice. No Hippolyte.

More than once she was forced to dart into an alcove or take a blind dash behind a curtain as a server scurried past, burdened with silver platters and amphorae, but each time her concern was short-lived; the servants' eyes remained fixed on the ground. She had just evaded one such encounter when another set of voices cut through the cold of the corridor.

The laughter was unnaturally high-pitched, more like the titter of gossips than women in genuine merriment. Certainly Hippolyte would never giggle in such a manner. But it was a woman's voice, for certain, and the first that the princess had heard inside the palace. Shrinking against the wall, she waited and listened again. It was not beyond the realms of possibility that this was a private chamber. That a man was in there with the woman, or women, causing such a reaction. But after another moment, she heard a woman's voice again, speaking this time rather than laughing, and two more female voices followed quickly after.

Penthesilea looked around her, noting the cool stillness in the air and poised for whatever might happen next. Shadows cut across every inch of the floor. There was no light. No sound from the agora. This was the innermost area of the palace, just as the hawker had said it would be. A heavy tapestry, in blue and green fabric, hung in a large swath marking the doorway. She would have to step inside, or else wait for an eternity, in the hope of hearing her sister's voice. Tensing, as if preparing to swing her ax, Penthesilea pushed the fabric aside.

The sunlight came as a surprise, causing her to squint, for although the room was fully enclosed within the palace, an opening in the roof flooded the area with daylight. Tapestries of woven fabric adorned the walls but also lay incomplete with multitudes of threads lying in tendrils across looms. Plants and flowers, seemingly chosen for their brightly colored petals and aromatic scents rather than nutritional value, grew in large terra-cotta pots, which lined the stone fountain around which half the women were sitting, perched on the edge, their feet dangling in the water.

"Come in. Sit. Amalthea was telling us about her wedding night."

Penthesilea, stepping further inward, realized that she was the one being addressed. The attention of all of these women had turned to her, and they were looking and speaking as if her presence had been expected. Or at least, not unexpected. And yet, she could not move or offer a reply, for her eyes were fixed on the far end of the room and the woman seated on a couch there, her eyes trained downward. She wore an air of disinterest, of someone barely present at all, as if her body were there, in this room with these women and their gossip, but her mind was somewhere very different.

The sweet air had turned suddenly sickly in Penthesilea's lungs. Had she passed the woman in the agora, or even outside in the corridor, she would not have recognized her. The way her hair fell in gentle coils, glistening with oil and adorned with flowers. The soft draped fabric, falling so perfectly around her as if she had worn the outfit every day of her life. Yet Penthesilea knew that was not the case. Her heart quickened, beating so fast it felt like the buzzing of a hummingbird's wing as she stepped toward her sister.

"Hippolyte," she whispered.

The queen lifted her head, a small gasp floating from her lips.

"Leave us," she announced, standing.

The other women looked up from their gossip curiously.

"Our husbands—" one of them began, but she was not given a chance to finish.

"I said, leave us," Hippolyte repeated, in a tone even Penthesilea would not have disputed.

Hurriedly, the women rose to their feet.

"We are not to be disturbed," Hippolyte told them as they filed toward the door. "Take your leave until tomorrow. You are not to return until I ask for you."

The women fired backward glances and curious scowls at Penthesilea as they disappeared through the curtain and out of sight until, finally, the drape fell back into place and no more women remained.

The instant they were alone, Penthesilea raced to her sister, holding her in the longest, tightest embrace she had known.

She broke away, tears of relief in her eyes.

"They said you had fled. That you left with him. That you left of your own free will. Tell me it is not true?"

Her heart continued to race as she waited for the answer, beating so hard and so fast it felt as if a single word might sever it clean in two. All the battles she had fought, all the men she had slain—never had she felt such nervous tension as she felt now.

"No, it is not true. He slipped me a tonic. A sleeping draught derived from valerian root. I told him I would not leave with him."

"I knew the rumors were not true." Relief flooded through Penthesilea. It was as if, until this moment, her body had been unable to truly breathe, the tension wrapped so tightly around her lungs that every inhalation without her sister caused her more and more pain. She had not fled. She had been taken. That any of the women had doubted her for even a moment should, in Penthesilea's mind, result in a punishment unheard of amongst the Amazons. Yet she still had questions of her own.

"What about Themiscyra? Is it true you allowed him into our city?"

The dip of the queen's head was the only confirmation the princess needed, and her heart, which she had thought had been healed by her sister's previous words, now splintered and fractured a thousand times over.

"Why? Why would you do such a thing?"

"I cannot say." Deep creases formed in the queen's brow, as if she was unsure of what she was recalling, a dream whose once-sharp edges she was fighting to feel for against the cloak of unconsciousness that came with waking. "It felt natural. Heracles and his men had already been inside the citadel."

"When they threatened to kill you."

"I understand how you feel, but I cannot explain. Sister, please, I know you will not be able to forgive me for this. I cannot forgive myself. I never will. I was not acting rationally. Something about him makes me act that way."

A cold shiver prickled the hair on Penthesilea's neck. It was not the first time one of their women had claimed that a man made them act irrationally, although she could not recall it having happened to any of the women of Themiscyra. They were the nomads, who would roam the land, free to meet with their men whenever they chose. There was a suspicion that some perhaps lived with their men, too, at least in the colder months. It was possible they even raised their children together. It was something they never spoke of. But this was different. This needed to be spoken of. She needed to know the truth.

"You love him?"

This time, the queen showed hesitance in her answer.

"From what I know of love, I believe I may do."

What was left of Penthesilea's heart shattered still further. Love.

How could it be? Hippolyte, the strongest, the most fearless. Their queen. Their mother had loved Ares, and they knew of that, but that was something different. Ares was a god. She had always believed that she and her sisters were immune to such a folly. They loved each other. They loved their lands and their women. Wasn't that enough? What more could one man possibly bring?

"Does he love you?"

"I believe so. In his own way, yes, very much."

Why could she not read her sister? Before now, she had known her every thought, sometimes before Hippolyte had even processed it herself. She had known her plans of attack, had known the uses to which she would turn the spoils of war. She had known which men she would fight and lie with and which she would dismiss. But now, she could not for the life of her construe the workings of Hippolyte's mind.

Silence was sweeping around them, broken only by the rustling of the tree leaves. It was a mere infatuation, Penthesilea wished to say. Or worse. He had drugged her to take her away from them. Was it beyond possibility that he had been doing the same thing throughout his stay in Themiscyra? Her sister's body might be strong, but perhaps her mind could be addled with a concoction of Athenian herbs. Yes, Penthesilea thought to herself, struggling as the heat seemed to build around her. That had to be the answer. Her sister had been drugged. Yet before she could say as much, Hippolyte spoke again.

"There are no binds holding me here, sister," she said softly, causing Penthesilea's brief hopes to collapse around her. "I believe he could be a match for me."

Penthesilea struggled to fathom the absurdity of the words. "A match? What does that mean?"

"It means he challenges me. He does not coddle me."

"Why would you need to be coddled? You are Queen of the Amazons. You could have killed him a thousand times over by now."

"No. He is like us." Her voice dropped to a whisper, barely audible. Whatever she was about to say, she did not wish it to be heard outside of this room. "He has ichor in his veins. He is Poseidon's son."

This were the first words from her sister that caused Penthesilea to stop. The love she had spoken of was catastrophic and ridiculous, but this…this added weight to her theory. Weren't the gods known for their sleight and slyness when it came to the seduction of women? And Poseidon was the worst of them all. She had heard enough.

"You need to leave. You need to leave here now. You will be safe, I promise you." She reached out for her sister's hand, but Hippolyte did not take it. Rather, she took a step away from her.

"Hippolyte?" The princess's tone was low and threatening, yet Hippolyte merely pressed her lips together.

"There is more," she said.

The heat was near unbearable as Penthesilea waited for whatever torment her sister wished to inflict upon her next, but rather than speaking, Hippolyte simply moved her hands. It was such a simple gesture. So small, sliding her hands from beside her, where they lay with casual ease, to her stomach.

"I am with child."

The heat was replaced instantly with a chill so biting Penthesilea felt as though her very spine had frozen. Time, always so fluid, took on a new character, in which the same moment seemed to repeat over and over again. *I am with child.* This was what Hippolyte had wanted. What she deserved. But surely not like this. A thousand responses formed in her mind, only to fade before they made it to her lips.

"Are you certain it is his?"

"I am."

For the first time since she had arrived in the room, Penthesilea turned her back on her sister. The knife that she had kept hidden had somehow found its way between her fingers, as she paced around the central fountain. After two laps she was certain; her sister's mind might have been addled by some madness she considered love, but she would not allow the same for her niece.

"Your daughter is an Amazon. More than that. She is an Amazon princess. She should be raised as such."

"Assuming I have a daughter. If I have a son..." Hippolyte allowed her words to drift away into silence, but Penthesilea had no time to discuss such ridiculous notions.

"She will be a daughter. The gods would give you a daughter to carry on your name."

Hippolyte shook her head. "I do not know that. If this child is born a boy, then he will be a king. Heir to Athens."

"What are Athenians? Painters. Poets. Your child is a warrior. The descendant of the God of War himself."

"But if it is born a boy, we cannot raise him as one. That is not what we do."

"Then he will go to the Gargareans as all our boys do." She was exasperated. Why was this conversation even needed?

"They know their queen did not lie with them this year," Hippolyte continued. "They will know the child is not theirs."

"What difference does that make? They would be honored to have your child. And if, as you say, the father is half god, too, why would they not raise him?"

"It may not be simple."

The knife was moving in her hand now, turning over and under her knuckles.

"Then it is a bridge we will cross when we come to it." She had never had the patience of her sister—of any of her sisters—and felt justified in wanting to scream at the queen It was only the women waiting somewhere outside that stopped her inciting such a confrontation.

"Penthesilea, you must understand that if this child is a boy, then Theseus will kill anyone who stands in the way of his heir."

Once again, the princess paced.

"So what? You stay here? You abandon us? Your women?"

"The gods brought him to my shore. I have to believe that this is their plan. And I do believe that. You will make a better queen and leader than I ever did."

"That is not true."

"Yes, it is. It is a truth we knew before Ares offered me his zoster. It is a truth we have refused to confront or admit. You are fearless. Your bow cannot miss."

"And? What is a bow? If that was all it took to be a queen, Ares would have made me the leader long ago. He did not. He made you."

Hippolyte rose to her feet. The pregnancy was not yet visible on her sister's body, though a deep flush colored her cheeks.

"If it is a girl, I will return her to you. Theseus will understand. He will know that she must be raised as an Amazon."

"And if the child is born a boy, you will leave him here and return to us. Boy or girl, you will return?"

A new pain formed in her throat. Keen and scraping. Soundlessly, Hippolyte crossed the room to where Penthesilea now stood and pressed her hands against her sister's cheeks.

"This will not be the last time you see me, sister, I promise you that."

There were no more words to say. The ache that spread through her chest was if she had plunged her own ax there, torn her own heart clean from the cavity of her chest. Breaking from the embrace, Penthesilea turned silently and walked to the door, pulling aside the heavy fabric. She cared nothing for the heaviness of her footsteps as she walked back through the corridors to where her women and the hawker were hidden in the shadows. One more dead guard lay with the first, and a stain dripped down the hawker's chiton as if he had vomited there.

"We are leaving," Penthesilea spoke, striding past the women, without even second glance at them.

"What about the queen?" Polemusa asked.

"The queen has made her choice," Penthesilea replied, with no glee in her voice. "I am the queen now."

TWENTY

AS PENTHESILEA'S FOOTSTEPS RETREATED, THE QUEEN WEPT, and for all her strength, it was not the first time she had shed tears since she had been taken from her home. She had wept after that night on the boat, when she had not been able to take Theseus's life as she had intended. He had exposed the limitations of her abilities as a warrior, and this was how she knew her words to Penthesilea had been the truth. Her sister would make a far greater queen, for she would never hesitate to make the kill.

As she disembarked in Athens all those weeks ago, she had still been looking about her, searching for a way out. A weapon she could use. But his men had been told to keep their distance, their weapons hidden, and Theseus, for all the love he professed to bear her, had continued to drug her with valerian. She was awake. She could walk and talk to some degree, but it was as if a path had been severed between her thoughts and her actions. Every movement took longer, every word was a little less clearly enunciated.

For those first days, she had attempted to refuse the drink and food he gave her, had attempted to starve the poison out of her, and yet somehow, he managed to slip it back in, through the water, the fruit. Perhaps it was even in the air. Had she been able to kill Theseus then and there, she had thought, she would have done so. But she knew in her heart that it was a lie. And he knew it, too.

When Theseus had introduced her to his father, he might have brought a wild beast into his palace for the welcome he gave her.

"This is who you have chosen?" That was all Aegeus had said of her. "An *oirapata*?" *Slaughterer of man. How was it possible he could see her in that manner*, she wondered, *when she did not even have control of her limbs and speech?* She drooled and dribbled. Had slept more in a few short weeks than in any previous year of her life. Any moment, she thought, her sister would arrive and sever their heads in front of her. Any moment Penthesilea would come and complete the task she had been too weak to undertake, the task she yearned for and feared in equal measure. But at that time, she had not yet realized that she was with child.

The day after meeting Aegeus, Theseus came to see her with an apple in his hand. He took a single bite, before offering to her.

"There is no poison," he said, as he held it out. Hippolyte eyed the fruit. Its crisp red skin and white flesh dripped with juice, and though her every instinct warned her to refuse his offering, or else to take it and cast it at him, her stomach growled and gnawed at her from the days of resisting as much as she could. She grabbed it and moved back, devouring the fruit as if she were a beast consuming flesh for the first time in months, and when she was done, she eyed him from beneath a bowed head.

"You cannot keep me here," she said.

"I do not wish to keep you here. I would prefer that you would stay here willingly. I wish you to consider this your home. I want you to lead with me, as we spoke of in Themiscyra."

"And that is why you are keeping me prisoner? You wish for me to rule from here? To rule from behind high walls with my mind addled? Never to see the land I am to be queen of? Never to be part of a conversation?"

"No, I will show you what it is I want of you. And you will like it. I promise."

"When?"

"As soon as my father leaves. He has been invited to Salamis. I am encouraging him to extend his stay there and allow you some space to become accustomed to our ways."

She sniffed, now wishing she had savored the apple, for in the rush to satisfy her hunger, she had barely tasted its sweetness.

"And when will he depart?"

"They are preparing the ships now."

It took four more days, during which Theseus spent almost all his hours locked in the room with her, bringing her fresh fruit and wine. The fruit she ate, the wine she knocked over and spilled or, on more than one occasion, threw at him. They were only halfway through the second moon of the women's trip to the Gargareans. It would still be several weeks before Penthesilea came for her and ended Theseus. Yet the thought of it made her almost as sick as the thought of staying here. For now they fought each day, and each fight ended in the same manner, with their bodies entwined and their lips feeding off one another's frenzy.

That morning, his smile was wide as he took her hands and said, "Come. I have a gift for you. One I am certain you will love."

He had been right. She had struggled with the chiton back then, and with the way the fabric exposed so much of her skin. And yet she had felt so much ease in walking beside Theseus. Walking through the palace's colonnades and down to the temples of the Acropolis.

Perhaps it was the contrast with the lack of daylight she had experienced since her time on the boat, but the aromas of the air soaked into her skin with a freshness that imbued her whole being with a lightness and a sense of freedom she could not recall having felt before. She had no problems to solve here, save her own. No people who needed her. Looked to her. Depended on her.

They continued, descending until they had passed through the walls of the citadel and onto the farmland that surrounded it.

"Where are you taking me?" she asked.

"You will see."

They took a narrow path through a vineyard where the small grapes bubbled on the vines and the large green leaves were already ripe to be picked and blanched in brine to soften them enough to eat.

"Theseus?"

Rather than speaking he tugged her hand. And there, at the end of the path, they came to a clearing. A clearing that was filled with men whose faces were red with effort as they held ropes as tightly as they could.

"What is this?" she asked.

His boyish smile ripened on his lips.

"I knew you could not be content here without your horses, but I did not know what you would prefer to ride. I will be honest, though, your particular method of riding should be reserved for when my father is away. Still, I wished you to have a steed that you were proud of."

She was rendered mute by the sight before her. Horses. So many horses. But it was not simply the number that overwhelmed her but the sheer variation within them. Her eyes were drawn to a pale gray mare, small in stature, like those she had ridden a thousand times. Behind the mare stood a stallion. Every inch of his coat was jet black, and his mane and tail shone as if they had been dipped in oil. There were bays and piebalds, as well as palominos, whose pale coats glinted luminous as moonlight.

"Where? How?" she said.

"Some have been gifted to my father over the years. Not that he can even remember. I sent out a request, before I came to see you. I wanted there to be something here that you would be satisfied with. I sensed the first time we met that your horse would be important to you, if you are ever to see Athens as your home, the way I hope you will."

He had done all this before he had even taken her, Hippolyte thought, and the bitterness took root within her again. This was what he had planned, before she had he even taken him to her bed. Were the drugs still in her system? She could stand and speak with ease, but perhaps she had merely grown tolerant to their ways. But even as these thoughts flashed within her, she found it difficult to remain angry in front of such a sight. Stepping forward, she placed her palm onto one of the bays as it huffed a heavy breath of hot wet steam.

The area was too cramped for so many beasts, and several had already begun to paw at the ground. Of the men who held them, some were confident and relaxed, but others wore the familiar look of fear in their eyes at Hippolyte's presence.

"Do not worry yourself. My queen knows what she is doing," Theseus called loudly to the men. It was the first time he had called her such, at least in Athens. And it felt so natural. She was his queen, and this acknowledgment, surrounded by stallions and mares, filled her heart.

She moved between them, studying their heights and coats. Several of the horses backed away. Others came toward her, their feet and eyes skittish. But the mare remained exactly where she was, her stare locked on Hippolyte. Small and nimble, she would be the perfect creature on which to ride into a battle, assuming she could be ridden at all. But yes, Hippolyte could ride this mare. She was certain of it. In her eyes the queen saw a darkness, a desperation. She was not like these others, she was telling her. She was the same as Hippolyte was. The mare needed the freedom to gallop. She yearned to be ridden.

"It's just you and me," Hippolyte whispered as she stretched out her hand to the animal, her words so faint they were lost on the breeze as soon as they had formed. "You and I don't fit in here, do we? I think that's a good thing."

She took one more step toward the mare, and then another. Soon she was an arm's length away. The horse's ears went back, yet the sign of annoyance merely brought a little laughter to the queen's mouth.

"No, you don't mean that. I know you don't."

She stepped forward again until her palm was so close she could feel the mare's breath as she blew from her nostrils. The other sounds of the day, the whinnies and neighs from the other horses, the birds and the dogs, the people, all faded away. It was just her and this mare.

"I think we were meant to find each other here, don't you?"

At that moment the mare pressed her nose into Hippolyte, not against her hand, but lower, beneath her chest. And with such tenderness as if she were comforting a newborn foal. It stayed there, the rhythms of their breaths steadying to a single beat. And not two, but three heartbeats joined as one. Tears streamed down the queen's cheeks. It was all the confirmation she needed, for she had suspected it these last two days, and now she knew she was not alone in sensing it. As the mare lifted her head, Hippolyte pressed her own head into her coat, absorbing her scent, her affection, her everything.

That night, she told Theseus what the mare had confirmed for her. That she was with child.

He fell to the ground, tears in his eyes, and buried his head in her lap.

"This is the gods' gift to us. You know that. This is the gods' gift to us. My son. My beautiful wife and my beautiful son."

That was the moment she tried to hold in her memory as Penthesilea turned her back on her and walked out of Athens.

This will not be the last time you see me. That was what she had told her sister. And it would be true. If she bore a girl, then she would return to Themiscyra with the child. If it was a boy, she would leave it here and return by herself. She would leave both Theseus and her son.

The sun had set without splendor or ceremony, quietly withdrawing its light and plunging the world into a grayness in which the quiet of the gynaeceum overwhelmed her. Theseus would not visit her yet. Not with his father present. For while he had promised that she would live her life with the same freedom in Athens as she had enjoyed among her own people, Theseus was not yet king. His father was. And as prince, Theseus had been busy, visiting farmlands and acting as an emissary. She was not even sure if he had returned to the city yet that evening.

And so it was without a second's thought that she pushed aside the tapestry that sealed off the door and headed outside.

Perhaps she knew to which room she was heading. She would never admit that, either to herself or to Theseus, as she stepped into a chamber with a large fresco of a garden scene, complete with pillars and trees. And there, beside the window, his hands by his side as he gazed out on the whole of his kingdom, stood King Aegeus.

TWENTY-ONE

AEGEUS STOOD IN THE CORNER OF THE ROOM. AN ODOR OF fortified wine and honey mingled with the burning oils from the lamp. His eyes were lost on the dark vista outside, his gray hair and beard tightly curled and trimmed to equal length just below his jaw. He was very different from every other king she had met. Given the circumstances of Theseus's conception, she had expected a man who reveled in his wine. Who surrounded himself with courts and consorts that sang his praises and lavished him with compliments and affection. But this was a quiet man. Contemplative. The palace was his statement, rather than a venue for constant revelry. It was easy to see that Theseus had been honest when he spoke of his father's vision to turn Athens into a hub of art and the center of civilization.

She made no sound as she stepped into the room, and yet he turned to face her.

"Oirapata." It was only the second time he had addressed her, and still he used to the same term: *slaughterer of man*. Whether it was uttered in rage of disgust, she could not be certain. Possibly a mix of both. "Are you lost? The andron is a room reserved for the men of the household. Is your own gynaeceum and chamber not sufficient?"

She studied him, his bearing, and the timbre of his voice. He had not, as she had expected, demanded her instant dismissal or ordered the guards to remove her. Perhaps he knew that none of his guards would be a match for her.

"I am afraid I am unaccustomed to limits placed on a woman's location."

"It is something you are to get used to, if you are to stay here."

"I doubt that. You are not naive enough to believe that Theseus brought me here with the intention of changing me. I think that if he hopes to change anything, it is you and Athens itself, rather than me."

"Is that so?"

He scoffed, drawing the breath from his belly as he spoke, then wordlessly reached for an earthenware amphora placed by the side of his table and, despite the presence of a servant, poured himself a small cup of wine, which he then cut with water.

"I will take a cup, too," Hippolyte said, taking another step inward. "Although I will take mine with a little more water."

With the cup in his hand, he studied her face, as if searching for a trace of jest. Upon finding none, he stood and collected another cup from the ledge behind him.

Even at nighttime, the view across Athens was mesmerizing. The umbra of night intruded upon by the gentle glow of candles and lanterns, while the soft chanting of the priestesses made harmony with the cicadas' song to the rhythm of the slapping of waves on the cliffs. Aegeus kept his eyes fixed on Hippolyte as he returned to the jug and poured the wine, although against the queen's wish, he filled the cup with nearly as much wine as his, with barely room for a splash of water in the top.

He held the cup out but made no move to take it to her. A small smile played across her lips as she stepped toward him. She had had men try to throw their drinks at her before, always underestimating the speed at which her eyes saw the coming events and her hands moved to anticipate them. It always ended badly for them. With a man his age, even the slightest knock would pop his arm from his shoulder, but she would not attack unless he struck first. As it was, when she wrapped her fingers around the cup, she noticed that his hand was completely steady, without so much as a tremble to it.

"Queen Hippolyte," he said, raising his cup in her direction before taking another sip of his wine. "I have heard rumors of you."

"I suspect there are many rumors making their way across our lands. Is that not the nature of those vile things? That they so easily multiply? Tell me, what have you heard?"

"That you murder your children if they are born men. That you murder the men after they have served their purpose."

"They can serve their purpose more than once, you know," she replied coyly.

"Is that so?"

His eyes simmered. *How was it possible that she could see Theseus within them*, she wondered, *when she had seen the effects of Poseidon's blood in his veins?* Was it true, then? Could Theseus really be son to them both? The evidence certainly suggested it.

The king and queen continued to stand, facing one another. Hippolyte could stand quite comfortably for several hours without so much as an ache in her thigh, but here the position had its own connotations. People who stood were waiting for something—more often than not, a dismissal. And she was not going to be dismissed. So without waiting for a further invitation, she strode across the andron and took a seat on one of the burgundy-covered couches, and awaited Aegeus's response. It did not take long to come.

"And what about your breasts?" he said, taking a seat opposite her.

"My breasts?" The queen arched an eyebrow.

"I have heard that some of your women mutilate themselves. Remove their breasts so that they might hold a bow more easily. Shoot an arrow with better precision."

Hippolyte was not oblivious to the rumors that floated around them; the idea that they killed their newborn sons was something she had heard before, but this one was new to her. She couldn't help but laugh. Genuine laughter from a place of genuine amusement.

"I am sorry to disappoint you."

"So it is not true?"

"I suspect this is a rumor created by a man who wished for there to be some unsightly reason for our skills."

"And you do not kill those sons born to you?"

There was no malice and little judgment to his words. He was asking as if he were a scholar, attempting to absorb as much information about his latest acquisition as he could. It was an endearing quality, Hippolyte felt. One that, once again, reminded her of his son.

"No, we do not cut off our breasts, and we do not kill our sons. We return them to their fathers."

"So you wish only for daughters?"

"Women are our way of life. Women are the most fearless of warriors."

For the first time, a smile flickered on the old man's lips.

"Do not let my son hear you say that."

"My husband knows my feelings on the matter quite well."

"Yes, your husband…" His eyes drifted off as if this, Hippolyte's bond to Theseus, was not something he was yet ready to accept. There had been no ceremony between the pair of them, no visit to the temple to have the gods bless their union, but was the child in her womb not all the confirmation she needed of their approval? Was the very fact that he had swum to her shore, unaided and uninjured, not a sign that the gods wished them to be reunited?

Clearing his throat, Aegeus turned his eyes back to the queen.

"Theseus has told me that you are already with child. I assume you know that?"

"I do."

"So you must know Theseus would prefer a son. An heir to his kingdom. Would you resent that?"

It was a question she had already asked herself. She had asked it before her sister's arrival and almost every hour that had since passed. A daughter would mean returning to her women, the continuation of her name through the Amazons. A son would mean something very different. She could return to Themiscyra, but then what?

"I trust in what the gods will decide," she said and once again, Aegeus smiled.

"You answer wisely. I suspect you were a good queen to your people."

"I suspect I will be a good one to yours, too."

Them, without waiting for an invitation to drink further, or a dismissal, she rose from her seat and placed her cup down on the table beside her.

"Good night, King Aegeus. We will do this again, I believe."

———

When the moment finally arrived, it brought with it a pain she had longed for through many long years. The surging through her body.

The tearing of her muscles. She did not scream, as she knew some women did, but rather closed her eyes and breathed in the moment. She breathed in each swell and tightening of her abdomen with the scents of the oils that had been soaked into towels and pressed against her head, but she took none of the herbs offered to her for the pain. None of the remedies that the women of Athens relied upon to birth their children. This was it. This was the last moment in which she and her child would be truly at one. And she wanted to feel it. She wanted to feel it all.

In that last moment, when the child broke free from her womb and into the world, and their cry filled the air like a melody, it was as if her heart had been split into two and would never again be complete unless that child was beside her.

Tears pricked her as she reached down between her legs and lifted the baby to her chest.

"A son," she whispered, lifting her eyes to meet Theseus's. "We have a son."

PART IV

TWENTY-TWO

AFTER DEPARTING ATHENS, PENTHESILEA DID NOT RETURN immediately to Themiscyra. For two nights she and her women camped out in the northern hills of Attica, from where she obtained an excellent view of the citadel. There had been a mistake, she tried to convince herself. Hippolyte had been coerced into staying, and she would leave the moment she was free to do so. She had heard rumors of a witch in the Athenian palace before now, one that hailed from Corcyra and used not only potions and herbs but the power she willed from the moon and the darkness to wield the occult. Could Hippolyte be beholden to her?

The thought caused a rush of nausea to surge within her. She should not have left. She should not have left her sister. But what she could have done? Fight the queen? No, she should have found Theseus. He was the one she should have killed.

She did not speak to her women of what had been said, and they knew better than to ask her, so they waited those days, with the buzz of mosquitoes thwarting their sleep as she sought answers and found them. The witch, Medea, she quickly learned from a local, had been banished from Athens upon Theseus's arrival, and Aegeus, mortified by her trickery, would banish any others he believed to practice in her manner. There was no darkness in Athens, they told her. Theseus was a good man. A man who loved his new queen and lavished her with gifts. Gifts such as horses. These words made her sick to the pit of her stomach, and yet she knew the truth of them. She had seen the clarity in her sister's eyes. The resolution with which she had said she would stay until she had birthed the child. There were no spells holding her there, save the ridiculous notion of love.

Only when she told the others to return without her did Cletes question her.

"I will stay with you," she said immediately.

"I do not need company."

"But you should not be alone. You should have protection."

The princess frowned. Cletes was a good fighter, but she was not so long in battle as many of the others. If any of them were to require protection, it would be Penthesilea who came to their aid, and they all knew this.

"What do we tell the princesses?" Cletes asked upon realizing the folly of her previous comment. "Your sisters. What do we say to them?"

"Tell them that I will return before the tide reaches its highest point."

"And about Queen Hippolyte? What do we say of her?" Polemusa spoke this time, but her voice was tight. Wary. It was the question that had wavered in their minds constantly, and she knew they were entitled to an answer, yet each time Penthesilea had attempted to offer one, her throat closed dry, strangling whatever response she might have prepared.

This was the reason she could not return with her women; for what answer could she possibly give? Antiope and Melanippe would assume she had played some part in Hippolyte's decision, but even if they did not, how could she tell them that the queen had chosen the love of some man over love for her women? How could she say that their sister would return after birthing a child that might be raised by a foreign king in a foreign land?

"Tell them she is still in Athens," she said, turning her face away from them as she spoke. "I will let them know more on my return."

During the following week, Penthesilea remained on those hills in Attica alone, waiting for a sign that she knew in her heart would not come, and fighting the unending deluge of guilt that raged constantly within her. Guilt that she had not been able to convince her sister to return home. Guilt that she had not insisted she come to the Gargareans with them. Guilt that she had not killed Theseus and Heracles and every one of those men when they had first arrived on their shore. Guilt was all she felt.

Even as a warrior of her standing and lineage, Penthesilea was not immune to emotion. A good warrior always felt remorse. Guilt often stemmed from death: the young warrior cut down before they had barely even lived or the older ones that she might have protected better. But they had died in a manner that made themselves and the gods proud, and that was all the consolation that was necessary.

Such a death was always the chosen option for an Amazon. As she stared at the distant darkness behind, which she knew flickered with the perpetual lights of Athens and its temples, Penthesilea recalled vividly a young woman, Myrine, who had sickened from an illness that afflicted her lungs. Each breath, from the day of her birth, was a struggle, and the cough that hacked from her tiny frame sent her face puce every night. The mucus that collected on her lips and tongue was viscous and white. They had thought she would not survive her first winter, given the difficulty that she found in suckling and gaining weight, and yet she did. And the second. And the third winter. The strength her body lacked, her mind made up for ten times over. She learned to ride with a ferocity and determination that could have only come from the gods themselves, and the women crafted her a bow of a smaller size than even the youngest girls trained with so that her weakened arms could learn to carry and fire it. She was not agile, nor was she strong, but she was tenacious and headstrong and determined to prove herself worthy of the name Amazon. Year after year she continued in such fashion until she could leap fences on her horse and fire arrows from her modified bow to strike a target from some distance. The women genuinely believed that, now, she could take her place among them. That she would kill her first in battle and be crowned a true Amazon. That was the same year that the fever struck.

It came overnight, starting mildly enough, a light sickness that brought with it low groans and bubbles of sweat on her forehead. By morning, she was wailing, her body soaked in sweat, which drenched the thin mattress on which she lay. Those frail lungs that had battled unyieldingly since she was born emitted wails of such anguish that birds bolted from their roosts. Her skin was translucent, a green-blue web of veins beneath it shining like tributaries. That same morning, while the young girl twisted and writhed in her bed, they were called to battle in southern Anatolia. Penthesilea had not wished to visit the girl and say goodbye. She had been desperate to believe that Myrine would achieve yet another of the miraculous recoveries she had managed so often over the years. Yet the princess was not naive and knew the likelihood was that Myrine would be gone by the time the women returned. She could not wait until then.

As she entered the room, the girl opened her eyes.

"Take me," her voice croaked. Barbed and brittle, barely more than more a whisper. "Make me an Amazon."

Penthesilea had knelt down on the stone floor and combed her fingers through Myrine's hair, so sodden with sweat it was as if the girl had been bathing in a river.

"You are an Amazon."

"Not like this. Take me. Please. Do this for me."

Penthesilea did not ask for Hippolyte's permission. She rode out that day, Myrine perched on the horse in front of her, her body so weak she could barely keep her grip on its mane. More than once, Penthesilea considered the absurdity of the decision she had made and began to steer the gelding back to Pontus, but each time, Myrine cried out, pleading for her not to. She needed this. She needed to become an Amazon.

When they reached the battlefield, Penthesilea braced her body against Myrine's and wound her fingers around the girl's so that they gripped the bow together. When the princess pulled the arrow back, it was as if they were as one body, and the arrow that Penthesilea shot at the approaching man was shot by Myrine.

Even in the dust and squalor of the killing, Penthesilea saw the light shine from the young girl at that moment, her very essence lifted by the gods. Elevated into realms of which most women could only dream. She was Amazon. And she would have her victor's ending.

With little more than a nod between the pair, Penthesilea understood what had to happen next. She leaped from the horse, leaving Myrine alone with bow and horse, and swung her ax through the air, slicing it through spines and stomachs indiscriminately. The battle was swift, as so many were. The few men that saw sense and tried to flee on foot were run down and slaughtered, or else felled by arrows they did not see coming. When the dust had settled, only Amazons remained. But Penthesilea did not look to the living. She looked that day for the dead.

Myrine lay on the ground facing the sky, a gaping hole in her heart but a smile upon her lips, and Penthesilea knelt in the dust and wept tears of joy. They buried her the next day with that bow in her grave, for she had died a true Amazon.

Often Penthesilea thought of her, of that young girl, with a flash of pride at what she had given her. But now, alone upon the hills of Attica, she thought of her with guilt. What if she had not taken Myrine? What if the fever had passed as so many had done before? Then what more might she have achieved? And as for Hippolyte, what if she had insisted more vehemently that it was the wish of Ares, their father, the god himself, that she remained as queen? Where would they be if those things had happened?

The change came one morning, nearly a month after she had first set up camp in Attica. She had woken and sensed something new in the air, a crispness, carried on the wind, which danced around her like leaves in an autumn breeze. And when she sat up and opened her eyes, she saw before her a fawn-colored doe, standing beneath a cypress tree. Perhaps if the doe had been beside a hawthorn or a cedar tree, the princess might have dismissed the sight, but both the deer and the cypress tree were the symbols of the Goddess Artemis. She had prayed often to Artemis in her guise as the Goddess of the Hunt, but that was not her only role. For Artemis was also the Goddess of Childbirth, and as Penthesilea gazed upon that creature, standing brave and untrembling before her, she knew what it was telling her. Artemis would watch over Hippolyte. The queen was safe under the goddess's gaze.

Penthesilea tilted her head in deference to both the goddess and its creature, and by the time she had raised her head again, it was gone.

Immediately, she packed up her belongings and rode for Pontus. And beneath the pummeling of her horse's hooves, she heard a truth she had never expected to hear.

Penthesilea was the Queen of the Amazons.

TWENTY-THREE

MUSIC DRIFTED UP FROM ONE OF THE TEMPLES, PREPARA-
tions, no doubt, for a festival. At nighttime a thousand
candles would be lit, and the drums would beat out
rhythms that shook the citadel walls and echoed across the far
mountains while men danced in the dwindling light of the moon,
although she could not say for certain what the festival was. Had
she been with the Amazons, she would have known exactly which
feasts the women needed to prepare for and would be overseeing the
gathering of the sacrifices and the preparations for the celebrations.
Yet here she only oversaw events from a distance, sometimes offering
guidance, but more often than not leaving the tasks to the priestesses
who had offered their lives in service to the gods. This was their
calling. Not hers. As to what her calling was now…that had become
harder to identify.

On more than occasion, Hippolyte had tried to leave Athens
behind her. The first time had been several months after Hippolytus,
her son, was born. He was around the same age the boys were when
their Amazon mothers would take them to their fathers to grow up as

warriors with them, and before Hippolytus's birth, this was the date she chosen in her mind upon which she would return to her women.

She had fed him one last meal from her own breast, waiting until he fell into a deep slumber before she laid him down in his crib and kissed his forehead.

"Grow strong," she said, the last words she planned on speaking to him, and though her voice was only a whisper, he heard and opened his eyes wide and stared at her. She felt it then. The gnawing uncertainty. The insecurity and doubt creeping like vines around her, suffocating her intentions. Was this really the right thing to do, she wondered, as he stared at her, unblinking. He was still so young, and though Theseus was a doting father, it was always she, his mother, that Hippolytus sought in the dark of night. Biting down on her lips, she pushed past the pain, leaving him in his crib and stepping backward and away from him. Almost immediately his lower lip began to tremble. Still, she continued to back away, allowing a wet nurse to cross in front of her.

"I will tend to him, my queen," said the woman. Her voice was muffled, hollow and flat, and Hippolyte barely registered it as she took another step backward into the hallway and then turned and made her way toward the palace entrance, Hippolytus's cries echoing through the halls and corridors even as she moved further from him.

With a quickening pace she pressed on, bearing nothing save a small knife, and seeking naught else but a single steed. Yet her body felt heavier than she had ever known it. Her limbs dragged, as if she were wading through deep water and being dragged ever backward by an invisible current. Descending the steps toward the agora, laughter and chants and prayers from the Temple of Nike should have been sufficient to drown out her son's wailing, and yet above even this, above even the sound of the wind shaking the leaves on the trees, she could hear him. When she reached the city walls, the pain in her chest had grown so acute it was as if her heart were being torn out from beneath her ribs. No, she decided, glancing back toward the palace. This is not the right time to leave him. He was too small. He still needed her. But soon. She would return to the Amazons soon.

The night before her next attempt to leave, Theseus had come to bed later than normal, after ruminating on important matters with his father's closest advisers. When he rolled over beside Hippolyte, he groaned loudly, the pungent smell of stale wine wafting in his breath.

"You have drunk too much, again," Hippolyte said, choosing to kiss his forehead as opposed to his lips. Her husband moaned again.

"A man in my position would never do such a thing," he replied, moving as to kiss her on the lips, yet Hippolyte blocked the action with her hand, laughing at a pitch that made the prince wince in discomfort.

"Your current state seems to suggest otherwise."

Drinking wine in excess was not an uncommon trait amongst the Athenians, she had learned, although it was generally found in lesser men than her husband. It was a foible that did not please her, but she had grown used to it, nonetheless. Theseus was not drinking to forget or numb himself like those men she saw outside the tavern. He did not become raucous or aggressive. He simply had the habit of getting swept up in the moment, losing track both of time and of the quantity of wine he had imbibed.

"Perhaps I am coming down with a sickness?" he said the next morning when he woke. He pinched the bridge of his nose as he squeezed his eyes tightly shut. "I think it is best I stay here a while longer. You do not mind, do you, my love?" he asked and rolled over and away from her before she had even replied.

Not that Theseus's drinking was her reason for leaving.

She had not planned on saying goodbye to any of them, and parting with Theseus in such a manner in their bedroom seemed fitting, but she needed to see Hippolytus once more.

In her head she anticipated watching him from a distance and slipping away silently. This was a good age to leave, she had told herself. He was young enough that he would barely remember her. That was the way it was supposed to be, the way it was with all their male offspring. And yet, as she gazed upon him through the gap in the curtain, playing with a nursemaid who squeezed his chubby legs and tickled him until he laughed, she felt it again. That tangible tether. The physical bond that throbbed and burned at merely the thought of separation. How would she cope without him? How would she focus on her role amongst the Amazons if her mind, not to mention her heart, remained here in Athens? She would not, that was the truth of it.

It was not only Hippolytus that ruled her heart so fully. For all his flaws, her relationship with her husband had flourished in the years since Hippolytus's birth. The same intensity burned within them as when they had fought on the beaches in Pontus, but their relationship was more than merely physical now. The pair shared a deep friendship. A kindred understanding. Never had she spent so much time with any one person, other than her sisters. When he was away, she found herself missing his presence, his warmth, his touch and conversation, and when he returned, they were only parted when his duty as prince rendered it unavoidable.

Less than a month after Hippolytus's fifth birthday, the pair had spent the morning riding together. Theseus had recently been away for over a month, traveling as his father's emissary, spreading the vision of Athens and presenting works of Athenian art to the envy of the other kings.

On his return, he had lavished Hippolyte with gifts, including, once again, a new selection of horses to pick from. It was a tradition now, to mark the anniversary of her arrival in Athens.

"I have decided not to bother with the stallions anymore," he told her as they walked hand in hand down to the open fields where the horses had been gathered. "Are you aware that in the last five years you have never once picked a stallion?"

"Is that the case?"

"You know it is."

It had never been a conscious decision, but over the years she had become aware that the horses she chose always bore a striking resemblance to those she would ride out on the steppes. Small, nimble, quick to turn and redirect, often with a flame that flashed in their eyes.

"I do not know why you continue to bring me for them. I do not need any more horses. I barely have time to ride the ones here as it is."

"I bring them"—Theseus squeezed her hand tightly—"because every time you see them, your eyes look as though they have seen the greatest wonder the world has to offer. And that look in your eyes is a greater gift for my eyes to gaze upon than the true form of any god." He lifted his hand to her cheek and kissed her tenderly on the lips. After these years, they had still not grown tired of one another. She was not ignorant enough to assume he did not take other women when he was away from Athens, but when he was in the city, it was only ever her company he sought. When he broke away from the kiss, it was with a familiar glint in his eyes that told her that after this, they would retire together, and not emerge again for several hours. "And if you do not have time enough to do the things you love, then we must find you more time. Perhaps if you would let the nurses take a little more time with Hippolytus?"

The pursing of her lips was not intended as so clear a gesture, yet her husband responded with bright laughter.

"The fierce Amazon queen, undefeated warrior, feared throughout the world, bested by a five-year-old."

It was absurd, but it was the truth, and she found herself laughing alongside her husband. For Hippolytus had bested her in every way. From that first moment in which he lay, sticky and white against her bare chest, his eyes unblinking.

Now, though, he was at an age when she could converse with him, could revel in his company and the innocent eyes with which he viewed the world.

"You know, if you were any other mother, I would worry that your doting on him would make him soft," Theseus said as they continued to walk.

"You wish me to be harder on him?"

"You can teach him to fight and still be gentle with him, as you are well aware."

Hippolyte knew of what he spoke. Only that morning she had taken their son out to practice with wooden swords, the way she taught the Amazon girls. The slick palace floors were less than an ideal surface on which to train, but at least they were away from the prying eyes that followed him whenever he left the palace grounds. He held his weight solidly, blocking her gentle strikes, but it was not the same. Amazon children saw sparring and horse riding and arrows flying every day of their lives. They wanted to be pushed, harder and further, until their muscles ached so badly they would fall asleep on their feet. They tended horses twice their height, brushing their coats and picking the mud from hooves in clumps as soon as their chubby fingers would allow. They bruised and broke bones and knew that if they wished to be as strong and fast and fearless as they dreamed, they would have to shatter those invisible borders placed on their own minds by their own perceived limitations.

Yet here, the queen did not want Hippolytus to endure the pain of broken bones or even temporary failure. She wanted to keep him close. Protected.

"You would rather I adopted more Spartan methods of training, my love?" she asked, knowing the question would irk her husband. He gritted his teeth in feigned annoyance.

"Careful, or I shall return these horses whence they came."

TWENTY-FOUR

S EVERAL FOALS SKIPPED IN THE GRASS. LONG-LEGGED AND
spritely, they kicked out every few steps before stopping
abruptly and turning their necks from side to side, as if
observing their surroundings for the first time. Together, Theseus
and Hippolyte stood hand in hand, the queen watching the animals
move, judging their temperament and speed from the way they
interacted with each other. By contrast, Theseus looked only at her.

Unlike other the occasions on which Theseus had gifted her
horses, Hippolyte's eyes were drawn to a colt. Young and thickset, he
must have been less than a year old, although he nipped at the other
horses as if every one of them were part of his herd. His mane had a
shaggy wave to it, like drying hay in a summer field, and his eyes a
brightness that glinted in the sun.

"Him," she said, pointing to her husband. "It is him."

Theseus cocked his head quizzically, glancing at the horse then
back to his wife. "This is because of what I said about you only
choosing mares, is it not?"

"It is not. He reminds me of someone." The sorrel color of

his coat was almost the exact shade of her husband's hair, and the arrogance with which he strode reminded her of the young man who had swum up to her shores all those years ago. "I think it must be the way I saw him attempt to mount a mare who is well above his status," she said, coyly.

"Is that right? Honestly. You know I am to be king. Not a man to be ridiculed for my family's amusement."

"And you know that long before I met you, I was already a queen and could quite easily return to that life if I find myself dissatisfied with any aspect of this one. My husband included."

Once, Theseus would have heard these words as a threat. Especially when she was pregnant. If the child had been a daughter, then the only thing to hold her in Athens would have been him. Back then they had both doubted that his love alone would have been sufficient to keep her and her child from her sisters and the other Amazon women. But things were different now. They were a family. This was Hippolytus's home, shared with the people he loved most, and Themiscyra could never be that to him. So while her son remained here, so would she, with a husband that doted on her. There were certainly worse things to wish for in life.

"Then I shall have him brought to the stables," Theseus said with a nod to the horse.

"After I ride him, you mean?"

He was not yet fully broken. She could tell before she had even approached him. And those who had tried to tame him before had done so with a force and anger that had left him skittish at even the slightest sharp movement. So she coaxed him forward tenderly with her voice as much as her body. His muscles never relaxed, the tension rippling through him the entire time. Yet she stayed with him, never forcing, never rushing, her afternoon plans with her husband now forgotten.

Eventually Theseus left to return to the palace, leaving Hippolyte alone with the animal. With each stroke of her hand, she felt the tension loosen both in his body and in hers. Tension she was not aware had remained within her, here, in the city that had become her home, in a land in which she was finally content. But in this moment, and moments like it, it was as if she were young girl again, not much older even than Hippolytus. A young girl, out on the steppes and eager for her first kill and that first taste of battle that would claim her Amazon birthright on her behalf. A time before her father had named her as the future queen, before she had labored under the weight of all her women. A life when it felt as if she had all the time she desired to be at one with the earth. At one point she cast her gaze over the horse, expecting to see her sisters beyond it, breaking in their own new steeds. Instead she saw that a small crowd had gathered, shocked and in awe at the sight before them. The terrifying reminder of who their queen was. And with that, she mounted the animal.

Even now, Hippolyte relished those moments when the men and women of Athens saw her riding around their citadel, bareback on her horse, her chiton tucked beneath her, skin on display as her legs parted across her steed. Their jaws dropped. Some men stared, while others looked hurriedly away as if she were a gorgon and a simple glance in their direction would render them stone. Today her ride was short, the colt more receptive to her than she had anticipated, yet still jittery amongst all the people. After riding him to the stables, she dropped to the ground, with the promise she would return tomorrow.

At the palace Hippolytus ran into her arms. She lifted him up and hoisted him on to her hip.

"We saw you, Mother! Pappouli and I saw you! Can I come with you? Can I come riding with you next time?"

"You saw me?"

"Pappouli took me."

The queen looked past her son to see Aegeus behind her. His beige robe descended to his ankles, his leather sandals adorned with gold beadwork that matched the laurel wreath on his head. His skin was darker, more weather-beaten and liver-spotted than it had been when she had first arrived, yet his eyes remained as bright.

"He did, did he?" she said, with a smile at her father-in-law.

"There was quite a scene outside the citadel. My guards were concerned that something was amiss. Of course, I told them it was likely nothing but the *oirapata*, causing her usual trouble in my kingdom."

He smirked as he spoke his words. Over the years, the term had come to be one of affection between them. For even before Hippolytus had arrived, the two had found common ground. Leadership of their people and sacrifices to their gods. The differences between the Athenians and the Amazons were insurmountable, but the difference between good men and good women, Hippolyte had learned, were not nearly so great, no matter where in the world they were. And Aegeus was undoubtedly a great man.

"Look, Mother! Look at what Pappouli has given me!"

Hippolytus lifted his hand and showed Hippolyte the item clasped within it. The small terra-cotta doll was carved intricately with articulated legs and arms and a tall pointed helmet. Its hair was carved into a long plait that fell all the way down its back, and was painted the darkest of browns.

"It is the great Amazon queen, Penthesilea," Hippolytus said. "She is the greatest warrior alive. Look, her arrows cannot miss." He twisted the arms and legs around, making whooshing noises as if arrows were flying from its invisible bow.

"I saw it for sale in the agora. It seemed fitting, don't you think?" Aegeus said.

Hippolyte glowered. "Queen Penthesilea," she said, twisting her lips as she cast her most scathing look toward her father-in-law. "She is the greatest warrior alive?"

"That was what the seller said. In his defense, the gentleman was not from here," Aegeus added with haste and humor.

"Well, let us ensure he does not return," Hippolyte laughed, before turning her attention back to the doll. She was not certain what her sister would have thought of the likeness. The facial features were far harder, the brow deep set and the face frozen in a scowl. After another cursory glance, she spoke to her son.

"Shall I take you to your bath and tell you a story about Penthesilea, the greatest Amazon queen? And aunt to the future greatest king in Athens?"

"Really?"

"Really."

She caught Aegeus's eye once more before she left, the light twinkling so brightly it was as if he were lit from within. Love for family did that, she realized. It lit you from within.

That night, she joined her father-in-law in the andron, as had become their habit when there were no guests present. On days when the king entertained, the queen was forced to do her part, playing court in the gynaeceum, although surprisingly, she found she no longer resented this segregation. In some cases, she yearned for it. After all, the lone company of women was what she had grown up with.

She had left Theseus in a bath filled with oils, where he had found her and kissed every inch of her body before pulling her out, laying her on soft clean towels, and making love to her on the marble floor beneath the painted eyes of men and women that covered the walls of the bathroom. After that, he had taken her bath and had submerged himself in the water while she dressed herself before kissing her son good night.

"I had to pry that toy out of Hippolytus's hand," she told Aegeus when she arrived in the andron. "He fell asleep holding it."

The old man smiled. "Then I consider my gift a success."

"Although you are not yet forgiven for your *greatest warrior* comment."

"Ah, but it was not my comment." A half smile played across his face, and yet she could see behind it a heaviness in his eyes. Aegeus was a man who was not afraid to show his emotions, though they rarely varied greatly. He was a placid man with a gentle disposition, a very different creature from the boisterous, bullying temperament of the many Greek kings she had known. Far more temperate, even, than her husband. Another factor that strengthened the story of Theseus's linage.

Aegeus rose from his seat and did not wait to ask before pouring her a cup of wine. Unlike her first drink with him, he filled this cup only one third full of wine, before topping it up with water, knowing her preference. It was a preference she had learned here in this very room, along with her fondness for the sharper, more acidic wines as opposed to the sweet ones. She took the cup graciously, waiting until he had taken his seat before speaking again.

"Theseus will join us shortly. He says he has something to tell us."

"Is that so?" Aegeus nodded slowly but added nothing more. *Was there something Hippolyte should know?* she wondered. A war on the horizon, perhaps? If that were the case, she could help. Strategize with him. It would not be the first time they had done so. But before she could ask, Aegeus spoke again.

"You have never asked your sisters to visit here, or at least, I assume you have not. I would, after all, have been graced with an introduction had they called upon us."

The question was unexpected and caused Hippolyte's mind to flit back through time, to the moment when Penthesilea had stolen into the palace to bring her home. It was one of the most oft sought memories she bore, even the way her sister had turned and walked away from them. Several hours later, two guards had been found with their necks snapped and, sitting beside them, babbling while he wept, an old gem merchant. The guards tried to question him about the deaths, believing it impossible that a man so frail could have bested two hoplites with such ease, but it was as if the man's mind had been addled, for all that he could do was weep and mumble about having his tongue cut from his mouth.

No trials were ever held in relation to those deaths, not even for the gem merchant found with the bodies, leading Hippolyte to believe that Aegeus thought her responsible. But he had never referred to it. To place blame on Hippolyte would to be blame Theseus for bringing her here in first place, she assumed, and this was something his father would not countenance. Now, it was as if the incident had never happened.

"I have had no word from my sisters," Hippolyte said, her thoughts returning to the room.

"You are sad about this?"

"I miss them, but they must do what they must. As must I. And what grief their absence causes me is more than compensated by Hippolytus's love for me. And Theseus's. And yours," she added. The old man smiled, as if she had given the correct answer, although the smile was short-lived and drifted from his lips almost as quickly as it had formed.

"You cannot know how happy it makes me to hear you say this. You know, I always believed that had you birthed a son, you would return to your women. And yet here you remain. Year after year, still beside me. And now, as I grow older, I am worried."

"Worried? What for?"

He offered a sad chuckle that cut short in his throat.

"I worry that, should you leave, it would break this old heart of mine. Just a little, mind. I am made of tough things. But certainly, yes, I would be sad if you were to go."

Hippolyte thought back to only an hour ago, when Theseus had found her in the bath. Her body had been submerged beneath the swirls of oils and petals that fragranced her skin. He had not even removed his robe as he slid into the water and planted his lips on hers. And when he had slipped inside her, he had held her gaze so intently and her body with such passion, it was like the first time he had laid eyes on her. How could she ever leave that?

"You have sacrificed much to be here, with us," Aegeus continued, his voice returning her to the moment. "Sacrificed in a way that may be normal to women, but not to your kind. The gods sent you to us. I am certain of that. We are blessed."

As she held the old man's gaze, she could hear a pain trembling his voice. Was he sick, perhaps? Was that the cause of his anguish? She opened her mouth, ready to ask, before changing her mind and remaining silent on the matter.

After his declaration, the conversation turned to more mundane topics. Motions and proposals the polis had discussed that day, new experts that Aegeus was employing to help ensure a constant flow of water up to the citadel. How many new boats they planned to build, and which countries were currently at war with one another. But the weight of years seemed to sound through his voice as he spoke. A heaviness that she had not heard there before. This was new.

As was the fact that he had taken Hippolytus out of the palace to watch her ride. Hippolytus was a respite for him. A pleasure that he indulged whenever time would allow. But time did not always allow for it, certainly not on days when the polis had met. Something was playing on his mind. Something he was not yet ready to share with her.

By the time Theseus joined them, they were already on their third cup of wine.

Dressed in a full-length robe, he passed by Hippolyte, kissing her gently on the head. He smelled of the same lavender oil that had scented the bath they had taken with one another only hours earlier, and she lifted her face to share a smile with him. A secret smile that conveyed what they had done, and what they would do later that night. A smile he did not acknowledge.

Instead, he nodded to the servant at the edge of the room to prepare him a glass of wine.

"That is enough," he said, when barely a drop of water had entered the cup.

Hippolyte felt the twist of unease in her gut. Her husband would often take his wine stronger and longer than was good for him, usually in the days before he left Athens. Yet he had not told her he would be leaving again so soon.

"Will you not sit, my love?" Hippolyte said, as her husband continued to hover, lingering between them. Aegeus, too, was shifting in his seat. *Was it the same tension*, she wondered, *affecting them both?* And if that was the case, why did she not know the cause?

"I am grateful that you are both here," Theseus said, after draining his cup and holding it out to be filled again. "I have something I must tell you."

Hippolyte chucked lightly. "Theseus, we always meet here when we can. Why are you acting so peculiarly?"

She forced her smile to remain on her lips, but neither her husband nor her father-in-law reciprocated the action. Rather, Theseus stiffened his back further and cleared his throat.

"My darling Hippolyte," he said, "you are aware that we Athenians have many traditions of which we are proud. You have come into our world and graced it so flawlessly, my queen, that I could not ask for more. The men and women of Athens revere you. You have given them a prince, who will rule over the greatest kingdom ever to exist. But there are other things that come with living here. Things you have not yet been witness to."

The queen froze at the seriousness of his voice. The solemnity. She struggled to think what might elicit such a response. Death? War? She was not a woman to be thrown into despair by such things; surely her husband knew this of her. Yet when she looked and saw the gravity in his expression, the unease within her deepened. Unable to remained seated any longer, she rose from her chair, her eyes meeting her husband's head-on.

"Theseus, what is it? What do you need to tell me?"

Still the seconds ticked by. Aegeus's gaze was trained down on his clasped hands while Theseus's nostrils flattened against the side of his nose as he pulled in a deep breath.

"Tell me, my queen, what do you know of the Minotaur?"

TWENTY-FIVE

IS WORDS WERE MET BY A MOMENT OF CONFUSED CONTEMplation. Every man and woman in Greece, Anatolia, and beyond had heard of the Minotaur. Those same parents who frightened their children to sleep with tales of the warrior women with their axes and arrows would no doubt alternate such tales with nightmares of the monstrous creature, half bull, half human, that lived beneath the palace of King Minos. Tales had drifted to Pontus, relating its vile breath and insatiable appetite, all compassion and reason lost beneath the heavy horns and thick bedraggled fur of the creature that spent its days stalking a maze of endless twists and turns that lay deep below the palace.

More than once, Hippolyte had thought that, perhaps, King Minos would call for the Amazon women, to rid them of this terror, yet it had not happened. Being home to such a creature no doubt brought with it a reverence and respect that Minos was perhaps reluctant to relinquish.

If the stories were true—and Hippolyte had no reason to doubt them—then the beast had been born of a human mother, Pasiphae, daughter of Helios and husband to King Minos. No doubt it was her father's blood that had allowed her to give birth to such a creature and survive.

"Yes, I know of the Minotaur," Hippolyte said in response to her husband's question.

"Of course you do."

Although it had been he who had commenced the conversation, Theseus now focused a look of great intensity upon his father, as if seeking a sign as to how much he could say, or perhaps hoping Aegeus would continue speaking for him. Tension rippled between the pair as Hippolyte waited expectantly, unsure what Crete and King Minos's burden could have to do with them in Athens. After all, it was King Minos who had tried to trick Poseidon by sacrificing a stock bull, rather than the great white bull that had been sent to him. And Pasiphae who had birthed that great white bull's child after she had become besotted with the beast. These were acts that King Minos had brought upon himself and his kingdom, and Hippolyte could see no link between them and Athens. Until Aegeus revealed how they were so devastatingly entwined.

"Do you know why Athens is so great a city?" the old man asked her. His eyes pierced into hers, and for a moment she thought he truly wished her to answer, but then that instant was gone. And he continued before she had time to consider her answer.

"It is a great city, because I have built it from what I have learned," Aegeus said. "I am no longer afraid to erase my mistakes and do better. I no longer believe that my opinion is the only valid opinion and that I will always know best how to farm, or build a temple, or even pour a cup of wine." He lifted his cup to the servant standing silently in the corner of the room, and the man stepped forward to refill Aegeus's cup. The old man drank deeply, allowing the fluid to rest on his tongue before he swallowed it down. Hippolyte watched him, her eyes moving between the king and her husband. The tension that had been held so keenly in Theseus's body when he entered the room still remained there, and had now infiltrated her own. Only when Aegeus lowered his cup, did he continue to talk.

"No, I know that when it comes to many things, I am ignorant, although that is not the case with every matter. It is true that wisdom comes with age, but, at the same time, with age come mistakes, and I have made many of those, my young *oirapata*."

She remained silent, unsure how the old man might react. Occasionally, when guests had left, or he was awaiting the arrival of someone in particular, she had seen the king fall into melancholy. She had watched as he retreated inward and distanced himself a little from the world outside him. But she had not heard him speak like this. Never before like this.

"There have been dark times in my life, Oirapata. Many dark times, before Theseus found me, and I am certain he has told you of plenty of them. But not, perhaps, of this one. Not, perhaps, of the Minotaur."

Hippolyte shook her head, not wishing to speak and disturb the flow of words.

Aegeus nodded as he continued. "As is the case with many young men born into greatness, I was afflicted with arrogance. And arrogance always displays its most ugly self when it feels as if it has something to prove. You have seen Theseus with his dear friend Heracles. I am sure you can testify to that."

Hippolyte mulled the comment over. Had Theseus acted as if he had something to prove when she had first met him with Heracles? Not on the beach, perhaps, when Heracles was threatening their lives for her zoster, but later in the citadel, most certainly. After all, he had come home with the Amazon queen as his bride, had he not? She smiled slightly to show Aegeus that she understood and that he should continue with his tale.

"There was one young man around whom my competitive nature and arrogance would most often display its fiercest aspect, and that was King Minos's son Androgeus. He was younger than me by nearly fifteen years, so for the greater part of our lives, I had always been able to beat him at any challenge that arose. I know it is hard to believe it now, but I was quite the athlete in my youth. Then one year I returned to visit Crete, and he had grown. I had grown, too, obviously. I was older then than Theseus is now, and I am no longer ashamed to say that my body was not at the physical peak it had once boasted. I am not ashamed to admit such a thing now. But I was ashamed them. Androgeus, however, had grown into a pillar of strength and beauty. His hair was blond, so light in places you might have believed that he, too, was an offspring of Poseidon's bull, but he was good-natured with it. Humorous. Charming. A doting son and a beloved elder brother.

"That year I had arrived for the Panathenaic Games, as I always did, and this was the year that Androgeus suggested we might perhaps gain more from spectating than from participating. We could sit with his family, the king and his sisters and mother. We could drink wine and relax. That was what he said, and that was something my arrogance could not brook. I insisted we compete, convinced that he was simply fearful of me showing him up."

There was a pause in the tale as Aegeus, visibly repulsed by the memory of himself, snorted in disgust. "I thought he was casting about for an excuse. Even at my age, I believed I would outdo him. But it quickly became apparent that things had changed. Androgeus beat me at every challenge set. At running, he was the faster. At discus, he was the stronger. It did not matter what I chose; whatever event it might be, he bested me. He was crowned the winner, to my deepest humiliation. Which is why I offered him one last challenge. One last challenge, not in the eye of the public, but in private, that would determine for certain that he was the greater warrior. I told him we should kill the great white bull."

A cold chill swept in, fanning the heavy fabric curtains as Hippolyte pressed her lips together, trying to hide the dismay and disgust she felt at this revelation.

"Oh, I know what you are thinking," Aegeus said with a bitter chuckle. "You are thinking the gods would be angered. That they would seek revenge on us for killing their sacred creature. But revenge had already been visited upon Minos for *not* killing the bull. That was the very purpose for which the creature had been gifted to him. *Not* killing the bull was the reason that Pasiphae had had her way with it. But this is not about them now. This is about me.

"I suspect my thinking was twofold, each tine of the fork equal in its selfishness. I could gain favor with Poseidon for doing his original will and finally killing that bull, and, since I planned to sweep in and kill the creature before Androgeus could, I would prove that I was still the greatest and strongest of the two of us.

"Perhaps I thought I would offer the deathly blow while Androgeus battled the bull by its horns. Perhaps I thought I would get the blow in some other way. But there was no battle. It was over so quickly, as if the bull knew what we had come to do. It charged, its head down like a bolt of white lightning along the ground, and plowed its horn straight through Androgeus's stomach. He remained there for a minute, hanging like a broken puppet, arms splayed, legs drooping down. The moment for me to lunge forward and kill the beast had come; even with Androgeus in such a state, I knew that was what I should have done. But I could not. I was a coward. Androgeus had bested me in all the games, and if he had not survived the bull, then how would I? Like the recreant I was, I ran back to Minos, begging forgiveness for my deed. Forgiveness for the death of a beautiful young son."

As he spoke, his tear-glazed eyes lingered on Theseus, and it was plain to see where his thoughts had wandered. As the old man brushed away his tears, Hippolyte thought back over the incident. She remembered only vaguely some rumors regarding the death of King Minos's son, though she could not recall how far back that time was. However, the look on Aegeus's face told her that, for him, it was as if it had taken place yesterday.

"And so, now," Aegeus continued, "it is my people who must pay. Every nine years I am obliged to send fourteen Athenians—seven young men and seven young women—off to feed their monster, the Minotaur. You know, there is such a passage of time between the offerings that sometimes I almost allow myself to forget. No, that is not right, not to forget. To hope, rather. To hope that they will find another way. A way to subdue him. Or kill him. A way that does not require me to pick out Athens's finest and end their lives so brutally. But this is to be the third time the people of Athens have paid the price of my arrogance."

When he turned back to face Hippolyte, the flames from the oil lamps brightened, reflecting in the sheen of his eyes. "That is why I am sometimes this way, Oirapata. That is why you have seen me descend into the cavern of my own darkest thoughts on occasion. It is the least I deserve."

If she had been the type of person to do such a thing, Hippolyte thought that at that moment she might have embraced the old man like a daughter, and she wondered whether Theseus might do so instead. But Theseus did not move. Instead, he inhaled deeply, his shoulders moving down a fraction, as if his father's tension had somehow alleviated his own.

"And that is why I needed to speak to you both today," he said, causing Aegeus's eyes to jerk up from where they had been fixed upon a mosaic pattern on the ground. "Because I have decided that I am going to end this now. I am going on the boat to Crete with the next sacrifices as one of the seven men, and I intend to kill the Minotaur."

TWENTY-SIX

THE SILENCE HAD TURNED ICY AROUND THEM, THE AIR SO still and tangible that the curtains no longer fluttered, and the light of the lamps glowed without so much as a flicker. From outside came the distant bleating of goats and the sound of songs from the temples, but Hippolyte could not draw her eyes away from Aegeus. Words were ready to burst forth from her lips, in rage at her husband, but her mouth remained closed. She would not speak until she knew that she and the king were in agreement.

"No." The word escaped Aegeus with such force she could hear the smack of his tongue against the back of his teeth. "You cannot do it. I will not allow it. I forbid it."

The air loosened in Hippolyte, but barely enough to allow a comfortable breath. She knew her husband well enough to be aware that their approval was desired, not required. But at least the king was on her side.

"I need to do this, Father," said Theseus. "Surely you understand? You said it yourself; it is a cycle of pointless deaths."

"So you will add your death to the numbers? No, it cannot

happen. I will not let it happen." Aegeus was on his feet now and marching toward his son. "I did not go through all I went through to bring you into this world only to have you die because of one of my own mistakes."

"I have no intention of dying. I will kill the beast, and then I will return to you. I am capable of doing this. Hippolyte, tell him. Tell my father I am capable of doing this."

"Tell him this notion is ridiculous, Oirapata. Tell my son he has lost his mind."

Both men looked at her with pleading eyes, but it was to her husband's that she was most drawn.

Was he capable of killing the monster? The question rolled through her mind. He was the strongest warrior Athens had to offer, of that there was no doubt. But was he as strong as this beast? Was he even as strong as her? The only time he had bested her, her body had been hindered by the effects of the valerian root, and she had been struggling with the unfamiliar motion of a boat at sea. They had been on Theseus's territory. The Minotaur, in contrast, would be in its own home, surrounded by places and objects, sights, and smells that it alone knew and could use to its advantage. What was the probability that one man, even her husband, would win against such odds? But then—perhaps he would not need to. A spark lit within her.

"Let me come with you," she said.

"Excuse me?"

"Seven young men and seven young women," she said. "I am certain that I am not so old I would be denied a part. Think about it. What chance would the beast have against the pair of us? You, the Prince of Athens and its finest warrior, and I, an Amazon queen." She turned to Aegeus. "We could do this together. I am certain that we could achieve it. Then Athens would be free of this burden for good."

She watched the idea taking shape behind the old man's eyes, the pain and the truth swimming in his thoughts. This would work, she was convinced of it. But even before Aegeus could offer his reply, Theseus spoke again.

"No. You cannot. You cannot come." He objected with even more force than his father had only a moment earlier. "I must go alone."

"Why? That is absurd. The two of us together could end this once and for all."

"I said no!" Theseus's voice blasted with such force the flames on the lamps almost blew out. Tendrils of black smoke curled up as they steadied again.

"Theseus, listen to her, I beg of you. More rash words have been spoken." Aegeus spoke softly, but Theseus had no desire for softness.

"No. This is my calling. This is my father's legacy, and I must be the one to right it. She is mother to the heir of Athens, and her place is in the palace looking after him."

Hippolyte felt a pounding in her chest. A drumming beneath her ribs, rhythmic and hard, like the pulse to which she rode to battle. The heat rose to her cheeks.

"My place?"

She could almost feel her stature growing as she stood, her spine straightening out. How had it been that she had shrunk so much in her time here that she had not even noticed? Not even noticed the way her shoulders curved inward rather than pushing pack the way they would do when she held an arrow. Never had she been spoken across by a man, certainly not her husband.

"My place," she spat, "is that of an Amazon queen."

For the first time she could recall, Theseus paled at the sight of her, as if he had forgotten that the small creature he had brought into his home was not a kitten to be petted and tamed, but a wild animal, a tiger, with powerful jaws and claws, and that the only reason she had not yet ripped his head from his neck was because she had not yet chosen to. But at that moment, Hippolyte had been released.

"My place is where I wish it to be. I have beheaded men by the thousands, put arrows through the hearts of thousands more. I am here, in Athens, with you, my husband, because I choose to be. And if I were to choose to leave and kill the Minotaur, then that, equally, would be my choice. You seem to have forgotten whom you chose as a wife, *Prince* Theseus. Or rather, whom I allowed to choose me as a wife."

He stood like a small boy in front of her, seething with anger. Would he hit her? It would be interesting to see him try. There was a reason she always ensured her wine was watered down. Her husband should have learned such a skill.

"Please, my children, I can see you are both upset. Understandably so." Aegeus stepped between the pair, placing a hand on each of their shoulders as if he were attempting to abate a quarrel between two siblings. "Theseus, you must understand how ridiculous this is for us. You are risking your life. It is almost certain death. Hippolyte only wants to keep you safe."

"I do not need a woman to keep me safe." The petulance in his voice; he sounded like Hippolytus, she thought. Only the prince did not pout with such despondency. "This is not a discussion. I came here to tell you both tonight, not to seek permission. The boat leaves in the morning, and I will be on it." He turned his eyes to speak to Hippolyte. "I have issues that I wish to discuss with my father now. Perhaps you should retire to the gynaeceum. Or your chamber. I care not. Your presence is no longer required or welcome here."

The anger in her chest was transformed into disbelief. She

studied his face, searching for something, some hint of coquetry. An indication that his harsh tone was only in jest. But there was nothing other than cold unrelenting anger. She prepared her tongue again, ready to slice through him, when Aegeus squeezed her shoulder.

"Perhaps it would be best if I talk to Theseus now, my daughter." He locked his eyes on hers. Old eyes, weary, heavy, and tired, and Hippolyte thought of her own father. How he would never be affected by such a trivial ailment as age. Her heart filled with affection for her father-in-law. She nodded to him once, her eyes sweeping past Theseus, not daring to glance at him for fear that she would not be able to contain herself. Whatever the outcome with his father, tonight's comments would not be forgiven with ease, Hippolyte promised herself.

The night air was crisper in the hallways, yet she could not retire to bed, not with the anger flowing so violently through her. Instead, in spite of all its faults, she returned to the gynaeceum and the looms and the tapestries and everything she detested about being a female in this place. At least there was wine.

How dare he? How dare he tell her what she could and could not do?

She paced the room three times over. She should leave. She should leave now and return to Themiscyra. That would show him where her place was. And yet even the thought caused anguish to swell up inside of her. For her place now was not in Pontus but somewhere she had never expected it to be. Her place was with Hippolytus, her son. That was where she wanted to be. Always with Hippolytus. Slapping one of the tapestries as she went, she strode out of the gynaeceum, marching as if a shield were affixed to her arm.

Hippolytus was sleeping soundly in his bedroom, although he must have woken at some point, for he had removed the terra-cotta doll from the side of his bed and returned with it under the sheets, where he gripped it tightly to his chest. How could she ever leave him? Not until he was king, she thought. Not until he was married and had his own child, perhaps. Perhaps then he would know how deeply her love for him ran.

Breathing in his scent and the scent of the clean fabric, she leaned down and brushed his forehead before taking a seat by his feet. There she sat, listening to his slow, shallow breaths, attempting to conceive of a life without him in it. It was impossible. Those days before Theseus and Athens felt as if they were part of someone else's life. A splendid life, full of adventures. Full of wonderful stories that could be told over a fire to eager ears desperate to avert the call of sleep. But stories from which she was now almost entirely separate. Stories of someone else's battles, someone else's deeds.

Still watching the rise and fall of his chest, Hippolyte waited until her anger had begun to wash away. Soothed by this small figure, so blissfully unaware. And then, when her neck began to seize and her lungs could no longer contain the yawns, she kissed him gently on his soft pale skin and retired to her chamber.

Sleep did not come, not that she invited it, seated upright, waiting for Theseus to join her. Would he stay away from her all night? The question stirred around in her head. Surely not. He always came to her bed at some point, even on those nights when he and Aegeus entertained until the first splinters of dawn seeped over the horizon. And yet, as the night drew past its fullest, inkiest blackness, she remained alone, and only when those gray slivers of light slid beneath the curtains did his shadow cut across the doorway.

"I am leaving this morning."

He stood there, his shadow stretching toward her, though he himself made no attempt to move.

"You are leaving? Already?" Hippolyte sat upward. She did not know at what point she had fallen asleep, but her neck ached as she righted herself. "Do we not get to discuss this further?"

"There is nothing to discuss. The boat leaves this morning, and I must leave on it. I must make myself a sacrifice in order to rectify my father's actions." He paused. There was a bitterness in his voice as he spoke. A bitterness at his situation, surely, for why would he be bitter at her?

"Theseus, please. Will you not at least consider what I said?"

"There is nothing to consider. But I must ask something of you. If you do not find it beneath your station."

A sad chuckle formed in her chest. She had seen so many men like this. Weak men, who shrouded their fear by belittling those around them. Usually she killed them on the spot, but since this was her husband, the action did not seem fitting. So instead, she spoke as gently as she could.

"What is it I can do for you, my husband?"

Theseus sniffed.

"My father. He has not taken the news well. I would appreciate it if you could mind him in my absence."

She waited, to see if there was more he wished to say. Of course she would take watch of Aegeus. It was barely a chore for her. She thought back to the night before, when he had referred to her as *daughter*. It was a fondness he had not shown her so expressly before, yet one they had reciprocated for many years.

"You know I will."

"Thank you. And Hippolytus, too? You will tend to him in my absence?"

"Given that he is my son, and already I tend to him perfectly whether you are present or absent, I do not consider that too much of an inconvenience," she said, but her attempt at gentle humor evaporated even as she spoke.

The scowl on his face said it all. If he was not going to apologize for the words he had spoken last night, then surely a tender farewell would come soon. She waited, wondering whether she should rise and move to him, but decided instead to remain fixed on the bed.

"I will be seeing you soon, Queen Hippolyte," Theseus said, and then, without so much as a kiss, turned on his heel and left.

TWENTY-SEVEN

S HE WAITED IN HER ROOM, THE SOUND OF FOOTSTEPS APPROACH-
ing and receding echoing constantly in the hallways beyond
her. Every time the patter grew close, her heart would skip a
little, her breath quickening as she hoped beyond hope that perhaps
he had changed his mind, had thought better of his foolish obsession
with the Minotaur, or else returned for her so that they might fight
this battle side by side. But the footsteps always retreated. Would he
not at least return to wrap his arms around her and kiss her farewell,
the way he had always done before he left on his voyages? Surely even
an argument could not erase the love between the pair so completely?
But there was nothing, and soon a new silence fell upon the palace,
a silence that told her the black-sailed ship had departed Athens,
along with its cargo of fourteen Athenians who had been sent to their
deaths, her husband among them. His tenacity was a characteristic
she had always found endearing, but now, it seemed little more than
petulance.

"Where has father gone?" Hippolytus asked, as she brought a
breakfast of grapes and figs to his room. "He said goodbye to me

this morning. Where has he gone? He said he was going to kill a monster." After only a day, the terra-cotta doll had seemingly been forgotten, half-lost amidst the twists of fabric upon which he had slept. Hippolyte pulled it from the coils and placed it on the small table by his bed. "Father said he will return the greatest hero of all. Greater even than Heracles," Hippolytus continued.

"Is that so?"

Now ignoring both the doll and the food, Hippolytus jumped from his bed, where he picked up a small wooden sword and swung it through the air as if he were battling the very same monster his father was soon to face.

Hippolyte looked upon the object with a sense of disappointment. It was made of birch. A light wood in both color and weight, too flimsy to offer any real benefit when it came to training, being little more than a toy for farmers' children. More than once she had spoken with Theseus and his father about this. Toys were one thing, but there were so few people in the palace who might train with Hippolytus properly, who might engage him and teach him without being held back by the fear of hurting the future king, that the least they should do was furnish him with adequate tools. She sighed. She would remove it from his room while he slept and replace it with something more suitable.

"Here, place your feet further forward," she said, abandoning all hope of breakfast and adjusting his posture. "And lower your weight; yes, that's it. Like that. Now swing your sword at me again, but don't hit me. You need to control it. As you would your own arm and hands."

The young boy swung his sword at his mother only for it to strike her squarely on the shoulder. A look of shock flashed across his face, but Hippolyte merely smiled.

"What did I say about control? Go again, my love."

They played like this for some time, Hippolyte teaching him the different ways to swing and hold a sword, and how to use his legs to perfect his balance. She allowed him to strike her, and failed to block his strikes, pretending to buckle under his sallies, until his smile was vivid and wild, and the desire for food and breakfast finally too acute for the child to ignore.

"I wish to ride, Mother. Can we go and ride, now?" he asked, still chewing as he spoke.

"Of course we can, my love," she said. "But first I must go speak to your *pappouli*."

"I will come, too." Hippolytus stood, bread in hand. "I will show him what I have learned about slaying monsters with swords."

"Not this time," she said, pulling him into her chest and pressing her lips against the crown of his head. "But I will not be long."

As much as she wished to push the last image of her husband from her mind, the words Theseus had spoken about his father continued to ring within her. Aegeus would need her, and she would be there for him.

For Aegeus and the other men in his council, the business of the day took place in the megaron, a large open room with pillars of cyclopean proportions, tiled seats, and a flat central area where the king stood to make himself heard. It was not a place for women—unless feasts or such occasions were being held there—and though Hippolyte had tried to rectify this soon after her arrival in her Athens, the patriarchal dominance remained strongest in this part of the palace.

"The men find you too much of a distraction," both Theseus and Aegeus told her, after she attended one morning to listen to them engage in weak, desultory debate on how to strengthen their defenses and build their armies. Given her expertise on such matters, she had begun to voice her opinion when all chaos broke out. While some men shouted, raising their voices above her, desperate to drown her out, many cowered, convinced that this *oirapata* had come to do as her name suggested and end them all. Others were too stunned to speak or move.

"If your men are distracted by a single woman, fully clothed, then I suspect the issue is more with them than with me," she had replied to her husband and father-in-law that evening.

"It is not as simple as that. I have gathered these men from throughout Greece to guide my construction of Athens. Bithys's family hails from Pella. And he is not the only one."

There was no need for him to say more. Hippolyte knew well where the lack of simplicity lay. She had been called to Pella to end a war there, and she had done so swiftly, leaving no fighting man alive. No doubt these men were old enough to recall those attacks, which made the fear with which they observed her all the more understandable.

"The only way you are going to make them see that I do not want their heads is to let me sit with them," she said repeatedly, but Theseus and Aegeus were both in firm agreement. Now the only time she entered the room was to remove Hippolytus when he had run off in search of his grandfather. And even in those brief moments, she was able to enjoy the looks she received, the confusion in their faces. She knew they were wondering how it could be that she looked like any other woman in Athens—motherly, caring, doting even— but that beneath her exterior lurked a savage killer. An *oirapata*.

That morning she knew Hippolytus was not present with her grandfather, but still she walked into the vast room with her head held high. She had not intended to speak, just to meet Aegeus's eye and assess his state. But as she stepped from the corridor into the echoing chamber, it was not Aegeus's voice she heard.

An elderly man was standing in the center of the room, waving his hands as he declaimed on the subject of crops while the others looked on, entranced. Hippolyte stepped further in, scanning the view. Even amongst the sea of gray beads and white chitons, she knew she would recognize her father-in-law in an instant, and yet he was not there. As more and more men became aware of her presence, the nervous movements began. Shuffling in their seats, furtive glances until silence had fallen, and even the speaker had been reduced to a barely audible mumble. She had not intended to address the whole polis, but now that she had their attention, there seem to be little else she could do.

"I seek an audience with the king," she said.

The speaker, now shaking, cleared his throat several times.

"The king is unwell. He was unable to attend today. He asked me to...to..." His already pale skin turned a shade whiter. "Do you intend on staying?" he asked, a tremble to his voice.

Hippolyte smiled as serenely as she could, although she could not stem the twinkle in her eye.

"Not today," she replied. "It is the king I wish to speak to. Though perhaps soon I will sit with you all longer."

She turned her back slowly, hearing the collective sigh of relief from the men behind her.

In all her years in Athens, she had never known Aegeus excuse himself from matters of the city. Even last winter, when a cough had sunk deep into his chest and he was unable to manage more than two or three words without doubling over in pain, he had found a place to sit at the back of the hall, sipping on a syrup of thyme.

Retreating from the hall, Hippolyte headed to the andron, only to find the room empty other than a servant, who was attempting to sweep the dust into a pile, only to have it rise and fall again two feet from where he was standing.

"Where is the king?"

He gripped the broom tightly as she spoke.

"I have not seen him, my queen. It is the meeting of the polis, now, is it not? He should be there."

"He is not there."

The servant shrank inward, cowering as if Hippolyte were about to blame him for the king's absence. But she did not wait to ask him any more.

There were countless places throughout the palace and the Acropolis where Aegeus could go to seek solitude, and yet Hippolyte knew in her heart exactly where she would find him: on the southern veranda with a view out across the port and the seas beyond. It would be from there that Aegeus would have watched Theseus's ship sail away, and it was to there that she walked to find him.

A cool breeze billowed the fabric of his clothes, although the old man seemed not to notice as he stared out at the water. The clouds were white and fluffy, the sky blue, the wind gentle; there was nothing foreboding in the scene, nothing to imply that fourteen young people had sailed to their deaths.

"He has gone?" she asked quietly.

The king did not move at the sound of her voice but remained lost, gazing out at the waves. Several boats were smudged on the horizon. Was it possible that her husband was aboard one of them?

"How long will it take him to reach Crete?" she asked, trying again to draw the king's attention. Finally, slowly, as if trying to decipher the source of the sound, Aegeus turned around to face her.

In the few short hours since she had seen him, he had aged a decade. His eyes sunk inward, as if set in great gray hollows; his thin lips were dry and wan. Etched into his wrinkled face were deep frown lines that cleared only briefly before he began to speak.

"I think the reason I enjoy my grandson's company so much is that I never knew Theseus at this age. You are aware, I suppose, of how he came to be here? How I left him with his mother until he was old enough and strong enough to fulfill his destiny?" He had not answered either of her questions, though she knew she did not need to ask again. Instead, Hippolyte nodded, allowing the old man a silent pause with his thoughts. "I wonder now if that was a mistake. He is a good boy, my Theseus, as you know, but this desire to prove himself… Sometimes I worry how far he will push himself. I wonder if this yearning to demonstrate his strength comes from not having had me there to guide him as a child. Not teaching him of my mistakes. I wonder if perhaps I am to blame."

The guilt in the old man's words echoed within Hippolyte as she moved into place beside him. She knew of similar pain, from her times at war, when women had lost daughters, sisters, friends, and she knew that once blame has settled, it sends out roots so strong that no mere words can break them. So instead, she chose silence. For a while, the two of them stayed there, motionless, two minds set on a third and what would await him when he finally disembarked. Perhaps he could find someone to aid him in his task. Perhaps the inevitable could somehow be avoided, if he only learned how to escape the labyrinth in which the Minotaur was contained.

"You have been such a gift of life to me, Hippolyte." Aegeus broke the silence quite suddenly. "I want you to know that. If anything were to happen to me, or to my son, this will always be your home. You will always be welcome here."

"He is strong," Hippolyte said, only to realize how trite and patronizing she sounded. Still, the old man smiled.

"I cannot bear to be in this world without my son, Oirapata. I cannot. I know he has faults, but who among us does not? We have made an arrangement. So that I do not have to live in Athens without him." A flurry of anxiety fluttered within Hippolyte at these words.

"Your Highness, please, you should not be thinking in such a manner."

"We have made an arrangement," Aegeus repeated. "I know, it may seem morbid, especially to one such as you, my daughter, but I have had my time. If the gods choose to take him from me, then it will be my time to go as well."

Hippolyte did not give herself time to consider what that outcome might mean for her. Her son was next in line to the throne. If both Theseus and Aegeus were gone, the wolves would come knocking. Would Athens be able to defend them? And would her women fight for her son when she had left them for so long? Before she could explore these thoughts, Aegeus spoke again.

"I asked him to ensure the sails were changed," he said. "You should know this, too, so that you are prepared. If his ship returns with white sails, it will mean he has succeeded, that he has been victorious and my son, the hero, will have returned to us alive. And if the sails are black…"

He let his words drift into the air and evaporate into nothing. A weighted void sank within her like a boulder through a glassy lake. Hippolyte took her father-in-law's hand.

"If they are black, then I will be right beside you, and we will get through this together."

TWENTY-EIGHT

E STIMATING TIME AND PREDICTING EVENTS WERE SKILLS
Hippolyte felt she had truly mastered as an Amazon. She could
look at a clear sky and know beyond doubt whether it would
remain that way long enough for them to complete their chores
outside or the rains would come sweeping in off the mountains.
When dark clouds appeared, she knew whether they would break
above them or would wait until they reached the sea before lightning
struck and thunder burst the clouds open. She would know how
long it would take her women to win a battle from her first sight of
the first enemy warrior, and more often than not, she would know
how long it would be until that same weak king called upon the
Amazons for help again. And yet here, it was as though time itself
had become knotted.

Some days moved so slowly it was if the threads that dragged
them toward nightfall had become tangled, matted, unable to shift or
move forward. Together she and Aegeus would lose hours, watching
wavelets form and grow on the sea or the sun move inch after inch
across the sky. Other times, the days were so swift they disappeared

in a blink, pulled in one mighty movement into the past, and she would feel as though dawn had barely broken before they were lighting the lamps and once more ushering Hippolytus back to bed. And yet throughout all the uncertainty, one consistent thought remained.

Theseus.

At first her mind stirred endlessly over the question of whether he had reached Crete. If the winds were strong, and they encountered no obstacles, the journey could be completed in under two weeks, but she had no evidence of such. Perhaps it would take another day. Another four days. And even then, she did not know what would happen. Were all the sacrifices offered up to the Minotaur the moment they arrived on the shore, or was there time yet? A period of grace to allow the young people their final revelries? A chance to dance and drink and eat and feel the heat of the sun on their faces and the sand between their toes before they were fed to the beast? Were they offered up all at once or one by one as the dreaded sense of the inevitable swelled within the remaining tributes?

At one point Aegeus had mentioned that games were held in honor of Androgeus, but the comment was made in passing and not directly to her. They were just words he whispered to the wind, as he had taken to doing more and more with each day that passed, and however deep her own anguish might be, Hippolyte did not want to add to her father-in-law's by pressing matters further.

Aegeus had taken to waiting on the cliff edges every morning, from the moment the sun glinted on horizon, his eyes scouring the view for the hint of sails. Other boats came and went, some days by their dozens, some days many more. But not the one they were waiting for. Not Theseus. No white sails, no black. Nothing but waiting.

"He saved me," Aegeus said. "Did he ever tell you that? Did he tell you of my wife, Medea? She tried to have him killed. No doubt she would have done the same to me, too. But Theseus saw through her. He saw her for the witch she was. Without him, I might never have met my grandson. Or seen my city thrive."

"And you will both continue to see it thrive for many years, still," Hippolyte replied. "And you will live to see Hippolytus grow into a strong brave man, just like his father and grandfather."

After a week, she took to joining him at the cliff edge during those hours, where they waited together, sometimes holding hands, sometimes seated at a distance, but in either case, rarely speaking. As the sun came into full view and there was no sign of the ship, Hippolyte would feel the first flutter of relief echo within her, yet she knew the day was long from over. For hours they would sit there, and only when the sun reached its zenith and the turn of the tide ensured that no more boats could make it to Athens before nightfall that day, would she watch the anguish that gripped every inch of the old man drain away from his body. *Not today.* Those were the words she heard spoken in her mind each day the sun blazed down from above them. After Aegeus would stand up, offer her a short nod, and say he had business to attend to. *Not today.*

With no husband to occupy her time, Hippolyte spent the rest of her time almost entirely with Hippolytus, busying him from the moment he woke so that he did not dwell on his father's absence or catch wind of the insidious gossip regarding her husband's inevitable demise. It was time she treasured, moments in which she saw him grow as she never had before. Time she came as close to training him in the Amazon ways as was possible in such a removed location. But all the hours they spent together practicing with bow and sword left him tired—sometimes so exhausted he fell asleep against her as he picked at his dinner, and she had to carry him to his bed, leaving her alone with her thoughts. Thoughts of her family, both here and beyond.

Over the years, she had garnered what information she could of the Amazons, from the markets and the women in the gynaeceum, not to mention tidbits she picked up outside the polis, when the men looked at her and muttered their distrust. *Penthesilea had led a battle in Dascylium and won. Penthesilea had aided the king in Sardis and decimated her opponents. Queen Penthesilea. Queen Penthesilea. Queen Penthesilea.* Sometimes it felt as if that was the way it had always been. Or at least, that was the way it was meant to be. And she felt no animosity, for she had found a different form of peace in Athens.

Three weeks after Theseus had left, Hippolyte learned through her servants that a sickness had struck in the agora, one that came with a heavy fever. The wives of four farmers had been left widows that week. One potter's wife had died, leaving him with seven children, including a newborn that was not expected to survive. Hearing of such long, lingering illnesses and deaths only made her more grateful for the Amazons' way. No sickness had ever taken her before, nor did she expect it to. But whatever protection might be granted her by the blood of her father was not extended to her son.

She noticed it first as he trained with her in the courtyard, on the fifth week of Theseus's absence. How Hippolytus struggled to lift the sword. It was true, she had replaced the light birch for a smaller brass piece, which was admittedly weightier, but he had lifted it and managed to swing it cleanly several times the week before. Yet that morning, he could barely raise it from the tiles. By the afternoon, his forehead and neck were gleaming with sweat, and the next morning, the sheets upon his bed were soaked to the point of translucency. All day he refused to eat, sipping with trepidation at water, remaining in his bed, listless and lethargic, and by the time night fell, the fever had taken a full hold.

"This is too warm." Hippolyte snapped at the servant who brought bowls of scented water to place on his brow, in an attempt to abate the fever. "He needs ice. Where is the ice?"

For hours she had tried to ease the swelter that made him burn her at the touch. His skin was flushed, clammy, bright red in places and stark white in others, emitting an aroma of soured milk.

"We have no ice." The servant bent so low to the ground she was almost kneeling as she spoke and backed away.

"Find some!" Hippolyte ordered. Never before had she felt such hopelessness. Over a hundred had succumbed to the illness in the last fortnight, men and women of all ages, children included. Children whose health had been no different to that of Hippolytus. But her child was not any child. He was a future king. He had to live.

She felt her pulse hammer against her ribs as she contemplated a future without her son. She would not lose him. She refused to. It was not unheard of for Amazon women to come down with fevers, yet they were almost always caused by an infected wound, never swept in on the air as this one had been.

When morning came, there was no improvement. Now, the affliction had spread past his skin and body to his mind and words, too.

"Father! Father!" Hippolytus writhed on the bed, his eyes rolling back and forth. His dark skin was pallid and clammy, and the sour scent had strengthened. Hippolyte snatched away the warmed compress and replaced it with a cooler one.

"I am here, my love. I am here," she repeated, combing her hands through his soaked hair. "I am here."

She did not eat, or even drink water, as she stayed there that day, watching her son's complexion alter from red flushes of heat to white boneset chills.

At one point, his cries became whimpers, sad and pitiful. At other times he spoke words, although very little made sense. He called for his favorite steed. He called for his father and grandfather. But most of all, he called for her.

"I am here, Hippolytus. I am by your side," Hippolyte said time and time again, her mind fighting an exhaustion the likes of which she had never before experienced. It was not as if her body had not been tired before. Nor her mind. She had endured more physical tests than any other warrior could imagine, had suffered the loss of friends, had been taken unwilling from her home, but seeing her son like this, so close to a precipice from which he would not return, was draining the very life from her. Night brought a darkness so complete that even the stars could not fight their way through the black cloak that enveloped the citadel, and Hippolytus's stirrings had slowed. No more writhing of twisted limbs. Just soft, exhausted groans.

Unable to leave his side, Hippolyte fell asleep. She did not know when or if she dreamed, but her rousing was abrupt and unexpected.

"Mother. Mother, I am hungry."

Hippolyte twisted slightly where she lay. A fog of sleep shrouded her eyes and mind, and her right arm was weak from sleeping at a peculiar angle. This was unusual for her. Even after all these years, she tended to sleep lightly, always ready in an instant to rise to her feet and reach for a weapon, but at that moment her muscles and bones creaked as she sat up, stretching her neck and clicking out the knots that had formed in her muscles.

"Mother, did you hear me? I said I'm hungry."

Now upright, Hippolyte blinked at her son.

His skin was pale, and the dampness, left over from the fever, still clung to his skin. But there was a light in his eyes. A brightness that she had not seen for two long days. She pressed her hand against his back and found the temperature a near perfect match for her own. The relief flooded through her as she pulled her son into her chest and kissed him repeatedly.

"Does that mean I can have some food?" he said, wriggling out of her grip.

"Yes, my darling. I will fetch you some now."

She moved to rouse the attention of the servant in the room only to find the place empty. A spark of anger alit within her. What if something had happened? What if she had needed someone in the night? But the feeling did not last long. Somewhere in her mind a memory glimmered. Had she not asked all the servants to leave her and her son alone? Obviously, they had followed her instructions.

"I will fetch something for you, now," she said, kissing him again before rising to her feet.

Outside, dawn was on the cusp. The stars had already melted from the sky, although the first of the sun's rays were not yet evident.

Only a few steps out of the room, and she caught a girl by the elbow.

"Hippolytus requires food. Please, bring it to his room."

"Yes, my queen."

"Make sure there is plenty. And that it is fresh. Today's harvest."

Hungry from the days spent without food, Hippolyte was about to turn back the way she had come when the sight of the first rays of sunlight stretching across the marble floor reminded her of Aegeus. He had been to see her last night, had stood in the doorway and inquired about Hippolytus's health. He had done the same the day before that, too. A pang of guilt struck within her. Had she been aware that her son's fever had broken in the night, she would have risen to join the king and watch for Theseus that morning. Daylight crept in fast at this time of year, but he tended to linger on the cliffs a while, even after he had seen that Theseus's boat was not present. With a little luck, he would still be there, and she could tell him of his grandson's recovery.

Out on the cliffs, the dry earth crunched beneath her feet. The rugged landscape was stark and austere in comparison to that of Pontus, and yet there was a beauty in it, in the way the rocks glimmered with the sunlight and the plants grew even through the aridity. She continued to climb, aware of the grime that covered her clothes from the days spent tending Hippolytus. She knew Aegeus would not judge her for such a thing.

Disappointment struck when she stepped out from the citadel and found no silhouette waiting for her on the cliff edge. She had been too late, she assumed. Aegeus must already have returned to the palace for food, just as she would do now. As the thought crossed her mind, it was countered by another. If that was the case, and he had returned, then surely she would have passed him on the path here? There was only one route, the same well-trodden track she was standing on. Unease churned within her as she continued toward the edge of the cliff, only now, for the first time, she fixed her attention on the horizon.

The sun was a semicircle, perfectly bisected by the horizon, its rays turning the clouds a deep magenta, their stately progress mirrored in still sea.

And there, in the center of it all, a ship, with black sails.

TWENTY-NINE

T HE AIR RUSHED FROM HER LUNGS, A SEARING PAIN CLAMPING
around her ribs, every breath causing her to gasp.

Black sails. Theseus was dead. Her husband was dead. Her son had no father. And Aegeus? A new pain struck, in the same place as the first, like a knife making quick work of the task an arrow had already begun.

"Aegeus! Aegeus!"

She twisted around on the spot, as if she might have simply not seen him, as if he might appear from the scant shrubbery, and yet she knew that would not happen. After a moment's hesitation, she raced to the edge of the cliff, and the air fled from her chest for a second time.

His blue robes were splayed outward, arms spread, the waves crashing repeatedly over his body, which lay crumpled on the gray rocks. He had landed in a small crevice, a gap that brought him that much closer to land.

"Aegeus!" she called again. The foam turned red as it rolled over his body while, above them, seabirds squalled and circled. "Aegeus!" she repeated.

His body rocked to the side with a lurch. A lurch that brought hope to Hippolyte's chest. Such a movement had to be caused by more just the momentum of the waves? Yes, there was blood, but the water had diffused the red inkiness, making it seem worse that it truly was. He was still alive. He had to be alive. She would not lose them both.

The quickest way to reach him was directly down, Hippolyte knew, as she hitched her chiton inward and clambered down the first face of the cliff. The wind whipped her fabric as if it were sail, forcing her in directions she did not want to go, while the spray from below showered her, soaking into the stones and making it almost impossible to find any purchase against the rocks. With a glance down, she saw that his body had shifted slightly toward the cliff. Had he tried to crawl there, perhaps? He was still face down, but she could not but hope.

Breathless and teary-eyed, she hoisted herself back up to the cliff edge and looked down again at the body, hoping to spot another route down to it. If there was still the slightest sign of life in him, she had to try, but how? Not in this way. Not risking her own life traversing these cliffs.

Pulling the fabric back over her body, she raced away from the cliff. In her head she heard her women crying. The clanging of metal and the thundering of hooves. This was not a fight for the Amazons, or a war for the king. This was a fight for all that remained of her son's family.

In all her years in Athens, she had never run like this. Feet pounding. The hard stone stinging her feet, which had softened from all the years of indulgence and time spent indoors with Hippolytus. The sound of blood rushing in her ears as loud as the waves she would soon be chasing.

There was no need to go to the palace; she did not need guards. She just needed a boat. A small boat.

"Your majesty?" she heard more than one confused voice call to her, yet she did not stop. Perhaps she would get there in time. Perhaps the gods had seen fit to save him. That was all she could hope for.

She dreaded to think how many minutes had passed before she reached the port. She stopped, her breath steady, eyes skimming the boats in front of her. This was the way she had always acted in war. Looking. Scrutinizing. Deliberating.

There were dozens of boats docked and bobbing up and down. Dominating the docks were the larger vessels, loaded with nets—and behind them she spied the black sails that told of her husband's death drawing ever closer, but she paid them no mind. She could not think about Theseus now. She would mourn him later. She needed to cling to the hope that Aegeus could be saved.

Her mind went to the small crevice beneath the cliff where he had landed. Against the rising tide and surging swell, a large boat could easily get broken up on such rocks. Instead, her gaze fixed on the small rowing boats of the type children would take out as they practiced their fishing skills or the sort owned by the poorer fishermen who struggled to catch enough to eat each day. A small man, older and grayer than her father-in-law, was hunched over one of these, tidying the nets within it. Hippolyte lunged toward him.

"I need your boat," she said, fists clenched and body braced to take it from him.

The old man righted himself slowly and had opened his mouth to speak, when his eyes widened.

"Queen Hippolyte."

"Your boat. I need it. And your oars. You have oars?"

"Yes. Yes," he kept his head bowed, shuffling back away from her, but she could not rescue Aegeus on her own.

"You must row us," she said, as she climbed in. "Over to the south side. The cliffs directly below the palace, you know them?"

The old man hesitated, the crumpled, leathering skin on his neck bobbing as he swallowed, but before she found herself obliged to issue a threat, he had climbed aboard and fixed the oars in his grip.

The old man's arms were sinewy and darkly tanned, but he still struggled against the force of the wind. His motion was disjointed, his sockets grinding and creaking with every movement he made. *How is it possible that he could move so slowly?* Hippolyte screamed inside her head, but instead, she simply barked an order.

"Give them to me."

The man did not hesitate to hand the two oars to the queen.

Using all the strength her shoulders possessed, she pushed back against the waves and the tides, the blades cutting through the sea before rising out, ready for her to plunge downward and slice back through the water again.

"Please, please…" she muttered to any god that might hear her. "Let him live. Let him live."

From behind her came the whip and slap of the black sails approaching them. She could not look upon them, could not bear to think about them. Not now. She had to get Aegeus. With the pace her strength provided, they moved swiftly around to the edge of the cliff.

"Here, take over. You need to keep the boat steady." As she handed the oars to the old man, she pushed herself to a standing position. The boat rocked beneath her feet, but the waves were rhythmic. A repetitive pulse. It was no different than standing on a horse in full gallop, she told herself, no different to that constant motion she was so at ease with, for she could stand on a horse while Zeus himself raged above her.

The waters broke into white foam as they flooded down the

rock face, but beneath the surface, they were opaque, as dense as copper and dark as a starless night. Straining her eyes, she tried to see through the undulating mass. Where was he? Her pulse was soaring again, but her feet were holding steady with the beat of the sea.

Briefly, from between the white and black, she caught a glimpse of something bright. A lighter color. His robe, perhaps?

"There!" she shouted. "Row me there!"

But it was no use. The old man had no more strength now than he had at the harbor and was struggling to keep the boat in place against the tide. She looked down into the water. Shadows merged and blended, bleeding gray into one crashing wave and then another. There was so much movement, the constant surging making it impossible to tell where the water ended and the rocks began. Try as she might, she could not catch another glimpse of him from above the surface. But from beneath, there might be a better vantage point.

The thought came to her in an instant. Yet even as she placed her foot on the edge of the boat, a weathered hand grabbed her by the ankle.

Frozen in shock and confusion, Hippolyte twisted and faced the man with a snarl.

"How dare you?"

"My queen, you cannot. Please, this spot, it is known. My own son lost his life here. The water will drag you under before you can even draw your first breath."

Never before could she recall being quite so taken aback. "Release me, while you still have the ability to do so," she said quietly. The waves were rising around them, the higher tide bringing a greater force with it. Yet she had found her balance. Her stillness in the tempest. It was the fisherman who struggled to remain seated. Despite this, he kept his grip on the queen.

"You cannot. You cannot save them. I promise you. Not here. Whoever it is you seek, they would have known that. Every man and women of Athens knows that. If this person you seek is of Athenian blood, then they chose this point deliberately."

Hippolyte cast her eyes back out over the water. The tide had risen so far and so quickly that she could no longer tell if this was even the place that Aegeus had fallen. Perhaps that was the problem. Perhaps she had chosen the wrong place to look.

She stepped back into the boat, and the man's hand released her.

"Give me those," she said, and snatched the oars back.

She spent that morning rowing around the cliff edge and back again, screaming Aegeus's name loud enough to drown out the gulls above her. Loud enough to drown out the thunderous crash of water against the rocks. Yet not loud enough to drown out the pain she felt. She could not go back to Athens. She could not return to the palace. How would she look at Hippolytus and tell him that he had lost the two most important men in his life? How could she tell him that Athens, his home, had no ruler? That his tender years would attract older, fitter, stronger men to take a crown that was rightly his and would show him no mercy. She continued to row until the sun was high above them. Only then did the old man's voice ring through the air to her.

"I am sorry, my queen."

The cold sank into her bones, weighing them heavier and heavier with every breath. He was sorry. How little that meant.

When she reached land, she cast her eye to the black sails of the ship now docked. Her lungs burned anew. Although she could not admit it to herself, she knew that the time she had spent searching for Aegeus had kept the truth from rearing in her mind. She had not even allowed herself to think the words since that first moment.

Theseus was dead.

Theseus was dead.

The man whose child she had birthed, who had loved her and prized her from the first moment he had seen her, was dead. And she would have to tell their child.

Her pace was trudging, her soaked body shivering, although whether from cold or the torment of her thoughts she could not tell. With each step she felt as if she were leaving part of herself behind, as if her dark sodden footprints were fragments of her soul and would soon be lost forever.

When she reached the palace, she found worried eyes darting fleetingly about. Hushed whispers, too quiet to be intelligible, reached her ears.

"A towel," she said as she reached one of her servants, her own gaze remaining forward, the shivering now deep within her bones.

Only when she had passed him did she realize the servant had not moved.

"Did you hear what I said? I need a towel."

"Yes, my—Queen Hippolyte. Yes," he said, and scuttled off.

Her first inclination was to head to Hippolytus and tell him the truth, but she could not. Not yet. Today he had risen with color in his cheeks, seeking food, feeling well. And now his world would be ripped out from underneath him. If she could delay that a little longer, she would; if anything, it was her duty to do so. So instead, she headed though the palace, numb to it all.

When she reached the megaron, she stopped. What was the point of going inside? She would find neither of them there. The polis had not gathered, and no voices echoed from within, yet something made her push the curtain aside and step inside the room.

He was standing with his back to her, forming a silhouette whose edges were so bold and strong against the sun that he seemed more than a mere demigod. Hippolyte felt her knees buckle beneath her.

It was her mind, she thought, as she forced her legs to hold. It was all in her mind. He could not be here. And yet, she knew that form. Those shoulders, those hips.

"Theseus." She could barely hear his name as it drifted from her lips. Her eyes blurred with tears. "Theseus, is that you? It cannot be."

Slowly the figure turned. He was dressed in stately fashion, in purple robes, a laurel wreath crowning his head. He had been marked as a hero. In that moment all the pain that had sprung up within her was washed away by a deluge of gratitude surging from every fiber within her.

"How? Your ship, your father… Theseus. Oh Theseus."

She ran toward him, a quake in her legs unlike anything she had every encountered on the battlefield. Her heart thumped with the power of the greatest stallion. The gods had gifted her. They had gifted her husband, and she would never let him go again. She opened her arms, ready to feel his embrace, when a new sight caused her to draw sharply to a halt. Behind him stood a young woman. Blond hair and large eyes ringed with kohl. There were many such women in the palace. Many who came to gynaeceum and drank her wine and gossiped insidiously.

But this woman was holding on to his arm, holding on to Theseus and pressing herself close against him.

"Theseus, who is this?"

He lifted his chin, a slow, considered inhalation before he tilted his head ever so slightly toward the woman.

"This is Phaedra, Princess of Crete," he said. "She is to be my wife."

THIRTY

SHE WANTED TO KILL HIM. THERE WERE VASES TO BOTH THE left and right of her, gargantuan objects that served no purpose other than to display the scale of Athens's wealth. Even at the neck, the red clay was thicker than her thumb, but they would be easy enough to break with a strong kick of her heel. She could use a shard to slice his throat, or his belly, or plunge a thinner piece through his eye and let him bleed out in agony. She could take the fabric curtain from where it draped casually behind him and wrap it around his throat while he gasped for air and his eyes bulged in his head. There was no rocking from the sea to protect him from such a fate here. Or she could simply use her bare hands. Snap his neck. Beat him until his ribs cracked and pierced his lungs. There were endless options at her disposal. And yet she did not even move.

"Theseus, what is this?"

He shuffled slightly, adjusting his posture so that he blocked Hippolyte's path to this woman. This girl. This Phaedra. She asked again. "Theseus?"

"I do not have time for this." He rubbed his temple with the heel of his palm, as if exorcising an ache that had formed there. "I need to see my father. Wedding arrangements have already been made. He needs to be aware."

Hippolyte studied his eyes. Eyes that narrowed as they caught her gaze. So many emotions rippled behind those dark pupils. Fear— fear of her most likely—and distrust, too, but along with them, a new sense of pride and arrogance. Pride that he had returned when no one thought it possible. Arrogance at whatever game this was he was playing with her. Yet amongst all those emotions moving behind his eyes, one was missing. Grief. Only now did his request to see his father register with her. He did not know.

"Aegeus is dead." She spoke with as much compassion as she could muster.

Creases formed in his brow. A crumpled confusion. And when he spoke, he sounded exactly like Hippolytus, on those occasions when he had been requested to do a task that he had never before performed and was perplexed and unable to piece together what was required of him.

"I do not understand," he said.

"Your sails, Theseus. They were black. They were black, and your father saw. He threw himself off the cliff's edge. I am sorry. I tried to save him. I tried to save him."

His legs buckled visibly in front of her. Silent tears streamed down his cheeks.

"I...I..." he stuttered, and the girl at his side grasped him a little harder. Hippolyte averted her eyes away from them.

"I searched the water. I took a boat out..." she began, but it sounded frivolous now. She had not even dived beneath the waves to find the body. Theseus would have done that, but then Theseus would have had his other father to guide him through the water.

"Why? Why did you not change the sails?" she asked. "That was your agreement, was it not? He told me. White sails if you lived, black if you died. How could you forget that?"

He opened his mouth to speak, only to close his mouth again. And then she noted it. The manner in which his hand rested against his head. That cradling motion. She had seen him do it a hundred times before, and always with the same cause. A self-inflicted one. The anger that had only moments ago subsided into at the sight of his grief now reformed, blazing hotter than ever.

"You were drunk," she spat. "You forgot to change your sails because you were drunk? Did you even recall the arrangement you had made with him? Did you even think of him once, you selfish, arrogant—"

"You will not speak to the king like that."

"You are no king!"

From behind him came a small whimper, like a puppy locked in a cupboard. Phaedra was standing to the side, now, Theseus having shaken her free, her arms crossed over her chest. Theseus's eyes went from her to one of the servants.

"Take her to her room. Overlooking the temple."

"Theseus," she whimpered.

"Do not worry, my love," he said, taking Phaedra's hand and kissing it. "I will be with you shortly. There is a conversation I must have first." And when his eyes met Hippolyte's, she could see the guilt flowing even faster than his tears.

The megaron was not the place to hold such an intimate conversation. The large space allowed their voices to resonate around them. But Theseus made no attempt to suggest a more private venue, and Hippolyte was not going to ask. The pair waited as Phaedra's footsteps receded, the silence growing heavy like the pressure before a storm, the air closing in around them.

Her teeth ground together. She, it appeared, would have to be the first to speak.

"What is this, Theseus? Who is that girl?"

"As I said, her name is Phaedra. Daughter to King Minos. She is to be my wife."

She shook her head in disbelief.

"You have a wife. I am your wife."

Her response elicited a laugh so bitter it should have burned his tongue.

"Is that what you are?" he replied. "For there has never been a ceremony to say so. No agreement has been made, no dowry passed from your family to mine. You have been a guest. That is all. A guest who has outstayed her welcome."

Her jaw dropped. Never before had he spoken to her in such a manner, not even in jest, and she could think of no deed of hers to merit such a response. Whatever had happened had wounded his pride so deeply, it was irreparable. There was only one thing she could think of that might possibly have elicited this reaction.

"This is because of what I said. Am I right? Because I wanted to come to Crete with you? Because I wished to aid you on your quest?"

"But I did not need your help, did I?" Theseus snapped at her. "I did it. I killed the Minotaur alone. I did not need a woman's help to complete a hero's task."

"And so this is your vengeance on me? Please, make me understand what has caused this."

He sighed, heavy and full of petulance.

"There is nothing for you to understand. The betrothal of Phaedra and me has become even more important, now, with my father gone. Athens needs stability. It needs a queen who will not repeatedly consider leaving. You think I am unaware of all those occasions on which you have contemplated leaving me? I have had eyes on you since you first arrived here."

"You do not trust me?"

His words punctured her heart almost as much as anything he had said before.

"How could I ever trust you, Queen of the Oirapata?"

For so many years it had been used as a term of endearment, and yet here the words were thrown up at her, acerbic and full of venom, intended solely to inflict harm.

"You love me," she whispered. "You love me."

"I love Phaedra."

"How? You don't even know the girl. And she is a girl."

"A girl who will grow to be a magnificent woman and queen. What I do and who I love has nothing to do with you."

She felt her knees crumbling beneath her, her hands reaching out for him in her dizziness.

"It has everything to do with me. I cannot believe this is true. I cannot believe you have fallen out of love with me. Please, Theseus."

"Your begging is repugnant. For someone who considers themselves a warrior, I am surprised you are not disgusted yourself."

Those were the words she needed to hear, for it was true. She did. She was disgusted by herself. She was disgusted that she had believed his lies and trickery and words of love. She was disgusted by this sniveling woman she had become. She was disgusted by this slothful life she had become so content with, away from her women, and her steppes and her sisters. As she rose to her feet, Theseus stepped backward, sensing the shift.

"I will arrange for a ship for you immediately." He spoke as if he were sending some emissary on their way back to Kephallenia. "I will ensure you have passage back to your home."

Home. Yes, because Athens would never be that again. "A ship? I am an Amazon queen. And I will travel as such."

"As you wish."

She stiffened her back. Pushed back her shoulders.

"Hippolytus and I will travel immediately. I will gather our things now. I would appreciate it if you could ready the horses."

This time it was Theseus who stiffened. The moment of satisfaction that had glinted in his eyes at her submission was erased.

"Hippolytus is not leaving with you."

"Of course he is. He is my son."

"This is not negotiable, Hippolyte."

His words riled her to an extent she had never before experienced.

"On that at least we can agree. You have a brought a new *queen* into my home. She is young enough to provide you with a dozen more sons. You cannot have it both ways, Theseus. Hippolytus is coming with me."

The fury that flashed through her was red and raw and tore at the bloodless wound he had already inflicted. Bile burned the back of her throat, stinging as she forced the words out between her teeth. Yet Theseus replied with just as much venom.

"Hippolytus is my son, and he will stay with me. You are an Amazon. You are not capable of raising a son. You women burn babies born men. It is a miracle he has been safe in your presence as long as he has."

He spat the lie at her, and she knew his sole intention was to inflict the deepest wounds he could. She had told him exactly what happened to all the males that they birthed. She had told him on those first days before he stole her from her family, and countless times since. Countless times she had expressed her gratitude at keeping Hippolytus by her side as he grew, rather than sending him to the Gargareans as would have been his fate with the Amazons. Countless times she had thanked Theseus and the gods for allowing her this privilege. He knew this of her, and yet he uttered these words, words he knew would damage her the most. This, a man who had professed his love for her. His endless love. His undying love.

Her voice cracked, words choking through the tears.

"You bastard. Every child born to us is raised with love. Raised to be a warrior."

"And it shall be no different here. I shall ensure he is taught to fight and kill as well as any of you womenfolk could."

She scoffed at his arrogance.

"As if you are even capable. I have seen you with a bow, remember? You might be able to swim like a fish, but you fire an arrow like one, too."

His face hardened. Teeth bared, he stepped toward her, his breath so close she could smell the stale wine from the previous night curdling in his stomach.

"Tell then, great queen, if we can still consider you that, where will Hippolytus go? You truly believe he will be welcomed by the Gargareans? He is not one of theirs. He is nothing to them. If anything, his very presence is a symbol to them that the Queen of the Amazons was dissatisfied by their seed."

"He is my son. He will have a home with me."

"In Themiscyra? The only man, raised amongst women? Truly? How do you think he would feel about that? Moreover, how do you think the women would feel about that? Each of them forced to hand over their sons and yet you intend to strut in, years absent, with Hippolytus riding high on a horse? You think they will be grateful for his presence? You think they will trust him? He has my blood in his veins, remember? The blood of the man who stole you from them.

Perhaps they will think he is there as a spy. Perhaps they will wish to rid the world of him."

There was no containing the tears now, as they spilled down her cheeks, pooling on the cold marble floor beneath her. This pain. This tearing within her, how was it possible that one could inflict such agony without the use of a weapon?

"You cannot keep him from me." She spoke the words, but her voice rasped, for she knew the truth as well as he did.

Theseus straightened his back and lifted his chin as he spoke.

"I am King of Athens. You have no idea what I am capable of. Now gather your things, unless you wish to learn what will happen when one queen, a shadow of her former self, attempts to contend with an army?"

THIRTY-ONE

NEVER BEFORE HAD SHE EXPERIENCED SUCH PAIN. HER chest throbbed, and her eyes and throat burned, yet somehow, she kept her gaze forward, past the servants, who had waited upon her for years. Past their smoldering looks, some of pity, some glee, some relief that they would no longer share a roof with the *oirapata*.

Gather your things, Theseus had told her. But what things? If this home did not belong to her, then what of the items within it? If even her son, whom she had grown in her belly and raised on her milk could not be considered hers, then what else even mattered? When Theseus had taken her on the boat, all her weapons had remained in Themiscyra, but he had gifted her many over the years. A bow, carved from bone engraved with images of women upon horseback. Knives of varying length, xiphos with garnets encrusted in their smooth metal handles. She had dozens to choose from, but in the end chose only the bow, three knives, a zoster of dark-stained leather, and a quiver with four arrows. These were not chosen out of sentiment, but because they were the weapons she would need for the journey.

Whatever memories might previously have been attached to them were now little more than ashes in the embers of the relationship.

One of the blades, however, had been given to her by Aegeus, the old man who had become like a father to her. *How would he have reacted to his son's admitting this Phaedra to the palace?* she wondered. Would his love be as fickle as his son's? She doubted it, but then, before this had happened, she had doubted it was possible for a person to endure so deep a wound and yet shed no blood. Taking this blade, she attached it at the front of her zoster; it would be the first one she drew, should the need arrive, and part of her hoped it would. Part of her hoped that plunging a knife into a man's heart would lessen the pain of her own, yet at the same time, she knew that even a thousand deaths would not remove this agony from within her.

With her small leather satchel densely packed, and her weapons secured around her hips, she had all she needed to depart, but there was still somewhere she had to go. She had to say goodbye to her son.

Early afternoon sun illuminated the walls and floor of his chamber, and an aroma of warm earth rose through the palace. Mere hours had passed since Hippolytus's fever had broken and he had woken her with the desire for food, and yet it felt as if she had been swept through days, if not weeks, in that time. Aegeus's body on the rocks, the small boat, Theseus and Phaedra. As improbable as it was, she stood there a very different woman from the one who had left her son that same morning.

She watched him from the doorway. His back was to her and his hands busy in something close to his lap. He had always been such a busy child, always needing a way to keep his mind and body occupied. As soon as he was able to crawl, he had wanted to walk and run, and anytime he was required to sit quietly, he would squirm and fidget as if his body were rebelling against the constraint. And he here he was, quietly muttering to himself with whichever toy was in his hand. She could watch him for hours like this, Hippolyte thought, and the breath was torn from her as she realized that she never again would. Not for hours, nor minutes, nor even for seconds.

Before she allowed herself to shed another tear, she stepped inside the room. She waited for a moment, then coughed, alerting Hippolytus to her presence. Immediately his face beamed with light.

"Mother. Mother, come and see!" His eyes gleamed at her. "I have made an arrow, see? I chipped the wood the way you showed me."

Lifting the object that he had been so intently studying, she saw that it was true. In his hand he held a small knife and small branch of cedarwood, which he had whittled at the end to produce a point. It was rough, the piece of wood far too knotted and misshapen to form an actual arrow, but it was the first time she had seen him do such a thing without being prompted. Tears that she had hoped to avoid choked her throat.

"Goodness," she sniffed, swallowing the pressure down and forcing a smile onto her lips. "With a point that sharp, you would be able to pierce the hide of boar. Maybe even the skin of the Nemean lion."

Her son beamed at the praise, his eyes alight.

"You mean that?"

"Your mother is a warrior. There is no one in the entire world who knows arrows better. And that"—she lifted the arrow from his lap—"is a perfect arrow."

How could it have been that only a day ago she had feared for his life? Been terrified that the fever would take hold and not let go? It was absurd, now she considered it, her reaction to a single fever in a child who had been so strong for all his life. But then, she had been strong. The strongest, and nothing had prepared her for this.

"Hippolytus," she said, patting her lap. "Come sit with me. I have something to tell you."

Obliging, but still holding the arrow, he moved and sat by his mother. He smelled so sweetly of the cedarwood. Of his own youthful musk. Did all young men smell like this? No, it was not possible. It was him and him only. A scent that would remain with her like the aroma of rains on the steps of Pontus. She closed her eyes, inhaling all she could, and praying silently that she would find the strength she needed. "You mother has to leave you for a while," she said.

He frowned. His bottom lip protruded slightly.

"For how long?" he asked.

Of course he would ask questions. He always asked questions. Questions as to why chickens roosted but owls flew at night. Questions as to why the lightning struck before the thunder roared. All the time, he wished to know more. To know why, or how, or when. Why would this be any different?

Only this time it was different, Hippolyte knew, for this time she had no answer.

"I cannot say," Hippolyte stroked his hair, breathing again that cedar scent. "But your father is here. And you father will take you care of you."

"And Pappouli, too? Pappouli is here, too."

Tears clogged her throat. The burning behind her eyes deepened. Never had she had to do such a thing before. Amazons lost mothers, sometimes at this age, but the group was formed in such a way and with bonds so strong that some young girls did not even learn who their birth mother was until they were eight or nine years old, far less their grandparents. They were all family.

"I am sorry, my darling. Pappouli has had to go somewhere, too."

"With you?"

"No, somewhere else."

"So why can I not go? Why can I not go with you?"

Why? Why? Why? Guilt roiled through her, penetrating the very marrow of her bones. Was this her doing? Had she stayed silent before Theseus had departed for Crete and the Minotaur, had she possessed the faith that he would complete the quest on his own, then perhaps he would have not taken it upon himself to find a more *permanent* bride. But no, she would not allow herself to take on the burden of another man's actions. This was Theseus's choice. He made the decision to abandon his family. And she could control his actions no more than she could control the winds of the sea, the strength of Helios's blaze, or the tears that wove down her cheeks.

"You will be happy here, my love," Hippolyte offered her son the only truth she could find. "You have your father here. And he has all his adventures to tell you about. You know he defeated the Minotaur?"

Once again, the child's eyes widened, the whites glistening.

"He did?"

"He did. Your father is a hero."

She hated it. She hated the words spilling from her lips, but what choice did she have?

"He is here? He has returned?" Hippolytus asked.

"He has returned."

Within an instant the boy was on his feet and darting toward the door, the arrow abandoned on the floor.

"Hippolytus," Hippolyte called after him, catching him by the hand. The boy stopped, confused. "Can you hug your mother goodbye, please? Remember what I said? I must leave you for a while?"

The young boy stood there, torn between his mother's request and his desire to see his father and hear all the new tales of his heroism. Begrudgingly, he walked to her and wrapped his arms around her neck.

She could no longer attempt to contain the tears, but let them roll freely down her cheeks, tumbling onto the marble tiles beneath her feet. Perhaps she could simply stay there and not let go. Hold onto him, feeling his heart beat against hers. Feeling his warmth against her skin and hearing his breath in her ear. Why was this so hard? Why was the thought of walking out of the palace and not seeing him so much harder to bear than anything she had ever faced before?

"Mother, you are squeezing me too tight." Hippolytus squirmed in her grip, wriggling to free himself. She did not want to release him, could not bear to release him, yet as his struggles intensified, she knew she had to. She dropped her arms, and he spun around, already racing to the door and to his father.

"Hippolytus?" She called his name again. Once again, the boy turned, his expression now full of annoyance at these constant delays. "Be strong. Be fearless. And remember your mother loves you."

She had barely finished speaking when he raced away from her, his footsteps fading into the depths of the palace. Lying on the floor was that thin stick of cedar, coarsely whittled to a blunt point at one end. No, it would never make an arrow, not even with her hand to help. Yet she picked it up and slipped inside her quiver all the same.

PART V

THIRTY-TWO

THE BAGS WERE SO HEAVY THEY WERE FORCED TO SPLIT THEM between two dozen horses. Some of the payment had been agreed in advance: the metals—brass and copper—and the sacks of salt, too. But the king had been so impressed with the swiftness with which they dealt with the situation that he had lavished them with everything he could spare: gems, necklaces, silver platters. And there was more besides: large quantities of earthenware, vases painted in orange and black, many of which they had refused to take due to the sheer size and impracticalities of carrying such objects. Several of the women had been handed items personally. Two of the youngest had been gifted gold necklaces, which draped their necks and fell awkwardly onto their chests—a disadvantage that did nothing to stop their recipients wearing them with such pride.

Penthesilea had suspected the battle would be straightforward enough. An army of only three hundred men would not take long to dispatch, and so she had picked this particular night to bring along the young girls, some of whom had never been to war before and whose virginity in battle remained intact. The older, more seasoned warriors had been given their instructions, to intervene only if necessary, but where possible to let the young girls do their part. And they had.

Arrows had flown through the air, crisscrossing, sweeping up and down like a murmuration, piercing one heart and then another. They whistled and struck and stabbed and severed. One man and then another fell before they had even realized they were under attack. By the time they knew who it was they were facing, it was too late for them to flee. They were surrounded. The men did not know the age of the girls or that they were as yet unbroken, but it did not matter. They were Amazons. Every girl that came with them that day had killed, and every one of them lived.

"We must pay a great sacrifice to our father today," Antiope said over her shoulder as she rode. "We must thank him for your prosperity. He will be proud of what you have accomplished in his name, too." She slowed until she was parallel with Penthesilea and spoke more softly. "And he will be proud of you, for all you have accomplished as queen."

Penthesilea kept her eyes forward as she rode, her ax held by her waist, the heavy mass counterbalanced by her bow quiver and knives.

"I have done only what has been required of me," she replied.

"Maybe that is true. Yet what you did today, and the number of women that have been anointed, have given us the largest Amazon army we have ever known. You have proven yourself to be a great queen. Greater, perhaps, than Hippolyte herself."

The fact was undeniable. Every year since Hippolyte's departure their numbers had grown, not merely through the fortune of birth but due to her and her sisters pushing the young girls to train faster and harder. She took them to battle not when they believed they were ready but when she knew they would have to prove themselves or die. And each time, her gamble proved astute. In all those years, they had lost few and had gained the strongest set of warriors she had even known.

Despite this, it remained a natural instinct in Penthesilea to rebuff all compliments and defend her sister's name as true Queen of the Amazons. Rumors of Hippolyte had ebbed and flowed in the years since she had left. When it was discovered that she had birthed a boy, many of the women had assumed she would return to them, Penthesilea included. She had laughed and felt a joy that she would not have expected at the anticipation of handing over her crown, a crown she had never felt she truly deserved. But when Hippolyte had not returned, a bitter seed had sprouted within several of the women.

"She has abandoned them," Antiope said.

"You do not know what he has done to her," Penthesilea tried to reason with her sisters in private. "He stole her, remember. He drugged her and dragged her away. There is nothing that is beneath this man."

"She stayed of her own accord. She is the Queen of the Amazons. If she cannot overpower a single mortal prince, then she is not worthy of our father's name."

For that Penthesilea had no response. She had told them only selected parts of her conversation with the queen that day in the gynaeceum. She had related how he had drugged her and stolen her away, how she had refused his marriage request just as the women had said. She had told them that Hippolyte was with child and would not risk the war that Theseus would bring to their shores should she try to leave with his child. She had said nothing of love, though.

Instead she had said Hippolyte would return when she could. She would take up her place as queen again. Yet as the years went by, it was harder and harder to defend these claims. She heard no rumors of further children or pregnancies to hold her in Athens. Could it be that Theseus had threatened war if she left, even with his child in his safety? That was the only explanation she could think of. Apart from the other factor. The factor that she feared to dwell on for too long for fear of the anger it provoked within her. The fact that her sister Hippolyte had left them for love.

And so, this time, as they rode over the rippling hillsides and short verdant grasses that led back to their homeland, she was not quite so quick to rebuke Antiope as she might have been.

"Our father blessed us today," she answered diplomatically. "I only hope that he will continue to do so."

They were traveling from the north. The battle had taken place close to the Gargareans' lands, where the valleys and dips were steeper than those of their homeland, and the seas dense with salt. The yellow rocks crumbled beneath strong hooves, and the trees angled so sharply from the winds it was a wonder that they still stood. But the weather had been temperate, and the cloudless sky was illuminated with a moon so candescent it allowed them to ride on well past sunset. There was the temptation to keep going further; riding through the night would allow them to reach Pontus by dawn, but the young girls had earned their rest, and thus they camped out beneath the shimmering constellations, creating several small fire pits, which they dug deep enough in the earth to prevent any sudden winds from extinguishing the flames.

From somewhere in the distance came the clipping of hooves on rock. There would be farmers here, families with herds of goats, but they would pay them no mind. Lighting a fire sent a clear signal to all around. These women did not fear intruders. And so Penthesilea laid back and closed her eyes, letting the warm air wash over her.

It was difficult not to feel a sense of calm and happiness listening to the young girls talk about their kills. About the arrows that had cloven both wind and enemy alike. About those who had feared the worst only to find a strength they did not know they possessed. They were not young girls anymore. They were Amazons, and the next year they would join them on the trips to the Gargareans.

A silent smile rose within the queen. She recalled so clearly the sense of power and elation that came with that first battle. The pride that swelled with the realization you were truly part of something greater. If need be, they could leave a little later in the morning. Allow the women time to sleep. After all, there was nothing to hurry back for. They would need to hunt, to prepare their sacrifices, but there would be time enough for that.

Still lying on her back, a set of footsteps approached, and the smile deepened within her. She did not need to open her eyes to know who was beside her.

"Do you wish for any food, my queen?"

At the sound of the voice, Penthesilea opened her eyes. Cletes had grown into a warrior whose skill surpassed all of Penthesilea's expectations. Talented with both sword and bow, she could shoot two arrows in a split second and hit two targets six feet apart with perfect accuracy. Her arms were rippled with muscles carved as if by the hand of a god. Her long hair, worn in a single braid down her back, and so dark it was almost black, was a vivid contrast to the azure of her eyes and the pink curvature of her lips. She knelt down in the earth at the side of the queen, causing Penthesilea to raise herself up onto her elbows.

"Thank you for the offer, but I have eaten."

"Then a drink? I can fill your flask at the spring if you have not already done so."

"No, you have already filled it for me, remember? When we first set camp."

"Of course. How could I have forgotten?" The woman's eyes locked onto hers, a small smile toying on her lips. She took her finger and traced it along the outside of Penthesilea's thigh "Then is there, perhaps, another way I can be of service to you?"

Sparks spread up through Penthesilea's body as she looked around at her women and tried to distract herself from the heat that was building inside her. It would not be the first time she had taken Cletes to bed with her. In fact, she had lost count of the times that the two had fallen into one another, their bodies entwined, immersed in heat and pleasure.

Their union had first occurred with the Gargareans, where they had shared a tent, and then the same men, and then each other. An insatiable lust arose within them both upon touching one another's bodies. Upon returning to Pontus, and without the men, they found satisfying each other alone equally gratifying, if not more so. And nothing could build up Penthesilea's desire more than a good battle. Cletes had lowered herself down, shifting closer to the queen, and her warm breath only deepened the yearning within Penthesilea. She was not the only woman to have lovers within the Amazons. It was far from unheard of, and yet something about this moment did not feel appropriate.

"I believe I will be greatly in need of your aid when we return to Themiscyra," she said, aware of the breathiness of her voice.

Cletes smiled, her eyes gleaming in the moonlight. "You are certain there is nothing I can do for you now?"

The thirst for her touch was agonizing, as Penthesilea drew in another breath, as Cletes slid her hand toward the queen's inner thigh. Before she could reach any higher, the queen grabbed her wrist and twisted it away from her. A yelp of surprise flew from Cletes's lips, which turned quickly into a grin.

"As you wish," she said rising to her feet. "Tomorrow night in Themiscyra it will be."

Then she stood and walked back to the women, ambling with deliberate slowness, so that Penthesilea could watch her move in the firelight and observe all that awaited her. It would be a difficult and lonely night's sleep.

When Penthesilea awoke next morning, Antiope was already moving about, packing up the gear and filling the canteens.

"The young ones are still asleep," she told the queen, offering her a piece of dried meat. "Do you wish me to wake them?"

Her instinct was to say no, to let them sleep, but clouds had drifted in during the night. Deep purple, they threatened both rain and lightning. This side of the mountain pass was notorious for tremendous downfalls, and it would be best to reach the other side before they came.

"Yes, wake them. We need to start riding."

A sense of festive celebration remained within the young women, but it had transformed, now, into more thoughtful reflection. What they needed to work on, where their areas of weakness were. Who they needed to ask to help them with sword fighting or horsemanship. How they were to gain the confidence to strike without hesitation. Penthesilea smiled to herself. This desire to better oneself, this constant need to improve as warrior, as a fighter, as an Amazon, was at the heart of who they were, just as much as the battles were. There was a reason that they were unbeatable, and she was listening to it behind her as she rode.

The sea came into view first. A silver sheet with barely a ripple on the surface. Quickly, the green grasses of the steppes followed and then, set back and on the crown of the hill, their citadel of Themiscyra. Against its clear desire, Penthesilea drew her horse to a standstill, turning in an arc to face her women.

"From now on, the rest of the day is yours," she called to them. "You are free to spend your time as you wish. You can sleep; you can train. You can hunt. We will hold a sacrifice for Ares tonight. You will offer up your gift then, but whether you hunt for it now or later, it is your decision."

She smiled to herself as she spoke these words, for she knew that none of her women would choose sleep over hunting, particularly not when a sacrifice was required, and this despite the fact that many of them needed it.

She would ride straight back to Themiscyra. Melanippe had waited there, and she would want a full account of all that had taken place.

"I think I shall hunt as well," said Antiope, as the women resumed their canters. "I will ensure they do not become overzealous with their kills. It will not serve us well to anger the Goddess Artemis after such a fortuitous battle."

With a nod of approval from Penthesilea, the princess steered herself further south and toward the thicker areas of the forest, the majority of the women breaking off to follow her.

As she rode, Penthesilea rolled her neck from one side to the other, feeling the satisfaction of pulling the stress out from her muscles. Tonight she would take a long bath, would soak away the aches and prepare herself for Cletes to join her. Or perhaps Cletes could join her in the bath. They had experienced great pleasure in that manner in the past, and no doubt Cletes's muscles required as much relaxation as her own. Her mind was still wandering over such things when she caught sight of a figure astride a horse a little way in front of the citadel.

It was the steed that caught her attention first. It was broader than those they rode. Taller, too. She had seen such animals before on their travels. Often, they were used to pull chariots in the garish games the men fought to try to assert dominance over one another. They had owned one or two such creatures in her time, too. Payment for services rendered to this king or that. But none of such particular coloring. None with so pale a coat.

It was at this point that her eyes rose from horse to rider. She was not dressed in Amazon wear, or the garb of any of the nomads from Anatolia. There was no cap tight to her skull, no leather boots or trousers on her legs. And yet she sat astride the horse the way an Amazon would, straddling it in her Grecian attire. And even at a distance, there was something about the way she held herself. The strength and security with which she sat. With a sudden thump from her heart, Penthesilea heard a gasp fly from her lips.

Hippolyte had returned.

THIRTY-THREE

THE THREE SISTERS GATHERED TOGETHER, ALONE AND OUTSIDE the citadel. Melanippe's voice was a hushed whisper, like the sigh of the breeze that fluttered through the trees around them. The sun had sunk low onto the horizon, its last rays illuminating the frayed edges of the clouds above it with a dusky pink while the sea glimmered serenely, barely a white crest upon it. Yet Penthesilea had learned long ago that silence could be deceptive.

"Has she still not spoken a word to you?" Melanippe asked her. "You are the queen, now. Surely she has told you why she has chosen to return?"

Penthesilea shook her head, uncertain whether she could still refer to herself as such, even in her thoughts. The true queen had returned. Ares's choice as queen. And yet the Hippolyte who was now within the walls of Themiscyra was not the queen who had left them.

"She spent all day training," Antiope said "All day. She was up before sunrise, and her fingers bled from the arrows, but she refused to stop."

"We need to give her time," Penthesilea replied, knowing the response her words would elicit before they had even left her mouth.

Antiope's scorn punctured the hush they were attempting to maintain.

"How much time? Three days have already passed. Three days, and she has told us nothing. What if she is laying a trap? What if she is keeping us idle here so that the Athenians may attack us? You know the nomads have been gathering to see her. It would be the perfect opportunity to strike, with all our women gathered in one place. She may just be biding her time until her lover arrives."

Her eyes locked on her sister, Penthesilea pulled her dagger from its sheath and twisted it between her fingers, knowing that Antiope would heed the warning. It was not a threat, more a reminder to consider carefully which words came next. The sisters had never fought one another in earnest. They were always by each other's side, whether on the field of battle or in the daily running of the kingdom. But things could always change.

"Hippolyte was queen." She spoke slowly, judging her tone with every consonant. "She is the rightful queen, anointed by Ares. She would never put our women at risk."

"You do not know that. You do not know what she would do anymore. It has been nearly than six years. We need to know why she has returned. If she will not speak to us, then we have no option but to assume the worst. To prepare for the worst."

"You are wrong!" Penthesilea's wrath spewed from her, demanding agreement. "We have every choice. Every choice to trust her. *I* trust her."

"Yes, and you are queen now," Melanippe said, her quiet tones a gentle antithesis to Antiope. "But you are one of only thousands of women here, Penthesilea. Already inside the walls, women are talking. Fearful of her presence. If you do not have answers soon, you may face a revolt."

"There has never been a revolt among the Amazon women," Penthesilea replied, outraged that they could even suggest such a thing.

"No, and there has never been an Amazon queen who married an Athenian prince. Please sister, we do not say this to be cruel. We love Hippolyte with all our hearts; you know we do. But you must find out why she has retuned, and what she wishes to do. And you need to find out soon."

Twisting her face away from them, Penthesilea clenched her hand around the dagger. She was defeated. Outnumbered. She had been backed into a corner, and they all knew it. So that was it, then. Hippolyte must talk.

———

A small lamp had been placed in the corner of the room, its shallow flame leaving powdery ash marks against the walls and the ceiling above it. It provided barely enough light by which to see, much less perform any tasks of meaning, and yet it was the light by which Hippolyte sat upon her bed, drawing a whetstone against the side of her blade, the grinding noise echoing on the bare stone walls around her. This was not a room she had been accustomed to sleeping in. This was a room that the pages used. For a time, Cletes had slept here, before she had found a more permanent place in Penthesilea's bed. Was that how Hippolyte viewed herself, now? As nothing more than a page?

"Antiope took your horse to the pastures, with the other ones." Penthesilea had carefully considered how to open the conversation before she had entered the room. This seemed as inoffensive a remark as she could begin with. "I hope that was the right thing to do?"

Hippolyte nodded, her chin still down. The grind of stone against metal was rhythmic. Hypnotic. Grind and clink. Grind and clink.

As an Amazon woman, Penthesilea had learned that you could not force someone to speak without a solid threat. Though her job did not call for the tasks of interrogation, death and confession often went hand in hand. Men would say anything if they thought it might spare their lives. Of course, Hippolyte's life was not at risk, or if it was, she did not seem to care.

Knowing the difficulty that awaited her, Penthesilea took a small stool from the edge of the room and moved it closer to her sister. She had hoped that mentioning the horse might bring about a simple, straightforward conversation, but that hope was gone now. She had no choice but to say why she was there and pray that the truth would bring a swift and peaceful resolution.

"Our sisters think you come to betray us," she said. "That you are waiting here as a trap."

Hippolyte's hand sprung up from her blade, her whetstone hovering motionless in the air.

"You do not believe that, do you?" she asked.

No, Penthesilea wanted to reply. *No, with all my heart, I do not.* But she knew that if this was the reply she gave, Hippolyte would fall silent again, and they would be no closer to learning the truth of her return. Instead she said, "I struggle to know what I believe."

A heartbeat's silence separated one moment from the next, and then Hippolyte's hands were back, working on her blade, although her motion lacked its previous steadiness. Her hands were shaking, the rhythm stuttering and syncopated.

"You said you would return after your child was born. Boy or girl, you said you would return to us."

Hippolyte kept her eyes down. "I believed I would."

"So why did you not?"

The metal rang out, reverberating, as she hit the blade a little too hard with the stone. Yet still the old queen refused to speak.

Out of desperation, Penthesilea reached across, grabbed her sister's shoulders, and shook her once, forcefully.

"Please, Hippolyte! I need you to talk to me. I need you to tell me. The women are worried. Whatever it is, whatever happened, we will help you. We will forgive you. But please, please talk to me."

Her pulsed hammered. Her sister was weak. Not in body, but in spirit. She did not fight back or even respond to Penthesilea's outburst. Beyond the room, footsteps pattered lightly. She should have known that Antiope and Melanippe would be listening, anxious to ascertain that the account Penthesilea gave them of the conversation was accurate. There would be no lying, no claim that Hippolyte had provided an explanation or confession. Not unless it was the truth.

Penthesilea squeezed her hands a little tighter on her sister's shoulders. No shaking now. Just flesh against flesh.

"Please, Hippolyte. Whatever you can tell me. We need to know. The women need to know. Otherwise...otherwise..." She allowed the consequence of silence to drift wordlessly between them. There was quiet now. No whetstone grinding. No footsteps outside. One moment passed, and then another. *Do not make me say it*, Penthesilea prayed, as slowly Hippolyte's eyes rose to meet her sisters. Even in the dim light, the sheen of tears was clear.

"Otherwise, I must leave Themiscyra?" she asked. "Otherwise, you will make me leave?"

Silence was the only answer Penthesilea could offer, and yet they both knew its meaning as certainly as if she had shouted the words from the top of the highest steppe. Sitting up in the bed, Hippolyte drew in a long, deep breath, then placed the sword on her lap.

"I heard rumors in the palace. Rumors when I first arrived of the things he had done. The people he had killed. Not warriors. Not monsters. Just people. Some of the servants, they would shrink away from him. Lower their eyes as he passed. But they were servants. Slaves to him. That is how they act, is it not? They fear their masters."

Penthesilea remained silent on the matter. As long as Hippolyte was talking, she did not wish to stem her words.

"There were other rumors, too. Rumors that he had kidnapped a young girl, Helen, when she was but a child. When he was a child, too, for that matter. I asked him about it. I asked him about all the rumors, but that was all they were, he said. Slander. The play of two young children that jealous people had attempted to tarnish. And I believed him. With my whole heart I believed him. Even after what he did to me. Even after he had taken me."

Her voice drifted off, as did her gaze, disappearing to a place that Penthesilea could not see but could only imagine. Her fists clenched at her sides.

"He showed me so much love, Penthesilea. He did love me. I am certain. Why come back for a person after so many years if it were not for love? Why welcome them into your home? But his love… Even when his father jumped. Even when he knew it was his fault…" Hippolyte shuddered as if a cold breeze had rolled in through the window, and yet Penthesilea could feel nothing but heat in the room.

"I tried to save him. I tried to save Aegeus, for him. And Hippolytus. My Hippolytus. I do not know what I will do. How could he do this? How could he do this to me?"

The lamp continued to flicker and burn as Penthesilea sat and listened. There was silence from the hallways, her sisters motionless as they listened. Her sister's words came in fits and bursts, no simple narrative, but rather fragments of events, often told without connection, at least no connection that Penthesilea could spy. Yet slowly, she drew lines between the pieces and brought them together to form an image. An image of a man, and a child, and his wife. An image of pain and betrayal and loss. Penthesilea asked no questions, not about Theseus, or Hippolytus, or this woman he had taken as his wife. Only when Hippolyte drew the heels of her hands to her forehead and said one simple thing, did Penthesilea finally feel it was her time to speak again.

"What did I do wrong?" Hippolyte asked. "Why was I not enough?"

The fury that rose in Penthesilea at the question was as hot and dangerous as smelted metal on a man's skin, and she made no attempt to cool it.

"You? It was not *you* that was never enough. You were too much for him, sister. Always too much. Too strong. Too powerful. Too smart. Too compassionate. Too brave. Too loving. He tried to bring those things down in you, but he could not succeed. He did not replace you because he wished for something better, my darling sister, believe me. He replaced you because he knew you were more than he could ever live up to."

Her sister's jaw wobbled slightly. She must see the truth, Penthesilea thought. Hippolyte was the true Queen of the Amazons. Invincible in human terms. Fearless. How was it possible that a man could break her in such a manner? A wave of appreciation for Cletes's devotion flowed through her. Never had she doubted her loyalty, and never, she hoped, had Cletes doubted hers.

"Sister. He has wronged you. Wronged you in so many ways."

Hippolyte laughed, a sad, bitter chuckle.

"Even if that is the case, what is there I can do? He is King of Athens, now, and he has my son."

Her lips pressed tightly into a line as Penthesilea turned her head to the doorway. She had no doubt that her sisters continued to listen outside, and hoped that for once, they were in agreement with what she was to say next.

"What do you want to do?" Penthesilea asked.

Hippolyte's eyes went down to her lap and to the blade that she had placed there before telling her tale. With one finger she stroked the length of the metal before lifting the knife and turning it over in her hand.

"I want him dead," she said quietly. "I want my son back and my husband dead."

For the first time since her sister's arrival, Penthesilea felt a genuine smile come to her lips, and the familiar sensation of heat flow within her. She raised her voice by just a fraction, to ensure her sisters outside could hear her.

"In that case, I suggest we do what we do best. We go to war."

THIRTY-FOUR

THE SMILE THAT ROSE ON HIPPOLYTE'S LIPS WAS ONE OF humor, and it blended into the lightest of laughs as she reached forward and kissed her sister on her cheeks.

"Go to war with Athens? That is a war I fear even we cannot win."

Penthesilea frowned. "We have won every battle we have ever fought. Why would this one be any different?"

"For a hundred reasons. The size of their army. The arrangements and structures that surround and support them. The weave of the city streets, that every soldier has to commit to memory. The defenses that must be surmounted even to enter the citadel are greater than everything we have faced before."

"In that case, we shall relish the challenge."

Penthesilea held her sister's gaze. It was clear now that Hippolyte had considered her suggestion to be little more than jest. That words of war were nothing more than a light and sympathetic comment intended to raise her sister's spirits. But even as they watched one another, Penthesilea could see realization dawn in her sister's eyes, the understanding that she had spoken in earnest.

"You are serious?" Hippolyte's voice lowered. "You believe we can do this?"

"I know we can. You want Theseus dead. I want him destroyed for what he has done to you and to this family. I want him to suffer in ways he cannot conceive. I want his walls to fall and his city to burn, and if you search in your heart, I know you want that, too." The words came in a deluge. This was what she had desired more than anything since the moment Theseus had stolen her sister away. "We can do this," she pressed again. "I swear on all the gods, and on all our lives. We can take Athens."

Her breath quivered in anticipation as Hippolyte's eyes, still locked on hers, glinted with something she remembered from all those years ago. Slowly, her sister dipped her chin. *Was that a nod?* Penthesilea wanted to ask her. Had she agreed? Hippolyte's movements were so tentative and delicate, as opposed to the vigor she had once shown. Then, with a shallow inhalation, Hippolyte spoke.

"If you truly believe we can win, then we should start preparing," she said.

———

From the moment of Hippolyte's abduction, Penthesilea had dreamed of the moment she would attack Athens, take Theseus, and retrieve her sister. But this was better even than the dreams she allowed to run wild in her head, for this time she would watch as Hippolyte sent an arrow though Theseus's heart.

The call went out to summon the nomads back to Themiscyra, and messengers were sent far and wide to their allies to secure the warriors, horses, and food required to besiege the city. In the normal course of events, they would send scouts to Athens to assess access to the citadel, locating its weakest point for entry, along with those areas where they would likely to meet the most resistance. This information would ensure the battle was swift and efficient, but there was no need for such expeditions now. They had Hippolyte.

"Each of the gates will have to be barricaded, but we will need to enter from here to commence the battle." She pointed to her sketch of the citadel. It was far from comprehensive, missing the places she had not visited, but from what Penthesilea had seen, she knew that the palace offered a broad and sweeping view of the lands below. "There are high points through the citadel that we can use to our advantage. This one here"—she pointed to an area to the west of the Acropolis—"should be the first place we take and establish a stronghold."

"We can sacrifice to our father there," Antiope said. "It is only right that we do so."

The other sisters nodded in agreement. "The Areopagus, then. In his honor. This hill is the one we take first. Then we move further east from there."

As Hippolyte continued to speak, Penthesilea scrutinized her sister with a calculating gaze. Her tone had altered since her return. She approached each task with detachment, as if the places she named were unknown to her rather than ones that she previously had considered home. Her reticence also extended to their discussions about the women and the other tribes, deferring to Penthesilea when any major decisions had to be made.

They recalled all the nomads and the Amazon women who had settled in Ephesus in the west of Anatolia. They reached out to those lived in auls, camps gathered on the steppes with large tents in the center of which fires were lit to ward off the winter frosts. They called on the Thracian tribes with whom they had formed allegiances over the years. Then, when all had promised their aid, they loaded the horses with enough supplies to last them until they had starved out the citadel. With all this in hand, one final task remained.

On the day they had chosen, the sea was high with gray swirls of sky reflected in its raged waves. Half a moon had passed since Hippolyte had returned, and finally they were as prepared as they knew they could be. They had ridden through their lands and passed the Sea of Marmara, where they offered up their most significant sacrifice on a dark and craggy outcrop. Every woman rode with them there. The old, who suspected this battle would be their last, and young girls not yet blessed with the blood of a kill. There, to Ares, they offered up horses from their homeland. Beautiful male beasts, loyal and strong. Gifts that were worthy of their father. Even with all the blood she had seen, Penthesilea forced herself to watch the light flicker from every stallion. There was no waste here. Ares would see their sacrifice and reward their dutiful observance.

The scent of blood was thick and cloying as the last animal was led to the rock, a dark bay, which Hippolyte guided by a single rope, slung over its neck. Kneeling on the ground by its feet, she whispered words that only she and the gods could hear before she plunged the knife upward into his heart.

Afterward, they danced.

From sunrise through to sunset, they danced with spears in their hands. The chants and cries and the stamping of their feet against the ground sent their prayers far and wide. Penthesilea had prayed in such a manner countless times before. She had danced at festivals, at celebrations, and feasts to honor the gods for the bounty bestowed upon them time and time again, but she had never danced with such urgency in her step. Never with such force had she stabbed her spear down into the ground, again and again. She was lost in it all, in the sounds of the women's voices rolling around her, deep and resonant and mesmerizing. When the fires were embers, and the sun had slumped beneath the horizon, they took to their beds, for tomorrow they would ride to Athens.

Shallow moonlight glowed around them as Penthesilea knelt in the shallows of the water. It was colder here than on the shores of Pontus. Yet the icy sting on their fingers was refreshing after the smoldering heat of the dance. Antiope was sending women off, uttering orders to meets with kings and the leaders of tribes between here and Athens to ease their passage. Melanippe had disappeared to tend to some issues with supplies, but Penthesilea had chosen to stay close to Hippolyte.

Somehow, despite all these years away from the women, she had lost none of her accuracy with a bow, nor skill with her spear and sword. She must have trained in Athens, Penthesilea assumed, perhaps with Theseus. Or perhaps the gods had simply honored her with this gift. She did not wish to ask. But while her body remained firm and fierce, her mind did not. Penthesilea often glanced at her sister and found her eyes drifting away, a gaze lost somewhere beyond the horizon. She would lose track of her words, stopping and restarting sentences with an uncertainty Penthesilea had not seen in her before. And the distrust that the women continued to show in her, despite this planned attack, meant that Penthesilea kept her near at all times, even going as far as to sleep in the same bed as her at night, which necessitated Cletes's absence. An absence she wished to rectify swiftly.

As they washed their hands in the water, Hippolyte turned her head to look at her sister.

"I need to ask you something of you. Something more," she said.

Penthesilea lifted her hands from the water and dried them on the seat of her trousers.

"Anything. You know that. You know you can ask anything of me."

"I do know that, yes."

"And you do not need to fear. I know you are concerned about the size of their army, but this siege will succeed. We will take the citadel and we will reunite you with your son."

Hippolyte nodded, yet she did not respond. Rather, she took her hands and pressed them together tightly before releasing them to fall back into the water.

"I am sorry," Penthesilea spoke again. "You wished to ask something of me. Please. I will listen to you."

Hippolyte lower her gaze a fraction, and Penthesilea felt something pull at her heart. How was it possible that eyes could convey such sadness? Were they not the same eyes that had shone with laughter and joy and compassion and love? But then, a heart was the same heart in war or in lovemaking, and still it had the ability to change and shift. To allow darkness to rise and fall within it.

And at that moment darkness dwelled so deeply in Hippolyte, there was no light reflected at all.

"I want him to die. I want Theseus dead for what he has done to me and for all the atrocities I am certain he has committed before and will commit again if he is not stopped. I want him dead."

"I know, I understand." Penthesilea clamped her mouth quickly closed, remembering her promise to listen.

"You are certain that we can defeat him?" Hippolyte asked again. "His army is great in numbers and his hoplites well trained."

"We have destroyed great armies before. Armies double, triple, ten times our own numbers."

"This will be greater even than that."

"And the rewards that the women reap will ensure that this war is never forgotten. That the Amazons are remembered forever, as the greatest warriors ever to have lived."

A pause stretched between them as the waves continued to lap over their knees.

"I am worried that if the moment comes, I may not be able to do it myself," Hippolyte said, finally. "I am worried that I will not be able to kill him."

Penthesilea stopped scrubbing at the blood ingrained in her knuckles and held her sister by the shoulders. Water ran down her back as she pushed Hippolyte upright, and the queen's gaze had no choice but to lock onto her.

"You are the Queen of the Amazons," Penthesilea said. "You cannot miss him. Sword or spear or arrow, he will die by your hand."

A half smile passed across Hippolyte's lips, but it could not form there. Instead, she shook her head. "With him, it is different. It is not a failure of my strength that I fear. It is my mind. When he speaks to me, he uses words which seep too deeply into my thoughts. I love him. I know it is wrong, and I want him dead, but nevertheless, I love him. He will make me doubt myself, I am sure of it."

"Perhaps he might have done such a thing to you before, but we will be beside you now. We will not let that happen."

Despite Penthesilea's confidence, Hippolyte shook her head again.

"I need you to promise me that, if the moment comes and you think I may not be able to take it, you will do it for me. You will kill him."

To her surprise, Penthesilea hesitated. She had dreamed of plunging a knife through Theseus's heart, but what Hippolyte was asking was far more than just the death of the treacherous man she had considered her husband. The Amazon women took pride in their accomplishments. Gloried in them. For Hippolyte to consider herself unable to kill such a man concerned her. Perhaps her sisters were right. When all this was over, would Hippolyte be fit to rule again as queen? Penthesilea shook the moment away.

"When you are there, when you are in the battle, you will see things differently. You will find your strength."

"Perhaps. But perhaps he will find my weakness. Please, sister. I cannot face Athens if I do not know that you will promise me that. Promise me that, if I ask you, if I signal to you that I am unable, you will take that shot. Do this for me."

Knowing there was only one answer she could offer, Penthesilea spoke, although the weight of the words fell heavy in her heart.

"If you cannot do it, then I will. I will kill him. But first, we must take Athens."

THIRTY-FIVE

T HEY RODE WITH HORSES LADEN AS NEVER BEFORE, THE SWEAT turning their coats dark and slick beneath their blankets as their hooves pummeled the ground. North first, then west again through Thrace. Even Hippolyte, with all her years on the battlefield, knew that what a formidable sight awaited the Athenians as the Amazons galloped onwards, their patterned tunics glinting, quivers loaded, and bows at the ready. Men and women bolted into houses, children crying, and adults cowering at the sight as they rose past settlements and houses. The wind whipped over their tightly capped heads, whistling in the air, no voices between them besides the occasional word of instruction from one of the princesses or tribe leaders.

It was no wonder that Hippolytus had spoken of Penthesilea as the greatest Amazon queen. Riding like this, Hippolyte was under no illusion as to just how proficient a queen her sister had been. The women hung on her every word, rapt and awestruck, each speech she delivered more inspiring and rousing than the last. They rode together, not as individual women, but as one mass. One weapon. And somewhere, in her very depths, she allowed a glimmer of hope to spark into life, the hope that Theseus would understand just what he had done in taking her son from her.

The numbers of warriors had grown, too. She was not blind to that. So many of those children, those young girls who had struggled to nock an arrow or stand atop a galloping horse when she had left were now riding out, caps close to their skin, tunics and trousers already stained with the blood of the battles gone by.

Before departing the Thracian lands, they changed their horses for fresh ones, gifted by King Tyragetae, whose settlements they had ridden through. As much as Hippolyte wished they could move faster, time had to be spent with each of the tribal chiefs and kings, talking tactics, repayments, and prizes that would be presented to them when the citadel was brought to its knees. Such a delay was necessary to ensure that their supply needs were met, should the siege extend longer than they anticipated.

"So it is true?" Tyragetae asked, the same question each of the leaders before him had put to her. "Theseus truly kidnapped the Amazon queen?"

Each time, Hippolyte felt herself squirm, as if her skin had shrunk and become too small for the body it held. They did not ask if she had fallen in love with him or whether the son she had borne was a prize worthy of any war, and so she simply answered them honestly: Theseus had kidnapped her and taken her, just as Heracles had bested her without a fight simply by wearing the skin of the Nemean lion. They had defeated her. Perhaps it was not a coincidence that under Penthesilea's reign, the army had grown stronger than ever before. Perhaps she was simply the better queen. All evidence indicated as much.

With the horses changed, they continued the journey. The closer they came to Athens, the deeper Hippolyte's nerves resonated, and yet the calmer she felt. Soon she would be fighting, swinging her blade at the enemy and spilling blood on the sandy stones of Athens. And nothing made her more at peace than killing.

"We will leave as soon as the moon is it at its highest," Penthesilea told them as they camped in Attica, to the north of Athens. On Hippolyte's advice, they would enter through the Pirean Gate on the east side of the citadel. There were places there, hills, without buildings and structures, where they could form their strongholds. She only hoped her memory had not let them down; had she known it would come to this, she would have insisted that she see more of the citadel during her time there. She would have roamed daily, learning all the weaknesses of the city, all its shortcomings and vulnerabilities. But then, they were a lot of things she would have done differently, had she known that this moment would arise.

If Theseus was expecting an attack—and, she considered, he would be foolish not to—then he would expect an attack from the north. This would be the more obvious route, with several gates by which they could enter. He would think only of numbers of men and would expect a short bloody battle rather than considering the topography of the land and the likelihood of a siege. More men would be placed on those northern gates. She understood him, could anticipate the way he would think. So there had been advantages to their relationship after all.

Penthesilea had asked her to make the speech. To rouse her troops to fight for her the way she had done all those years before. For a brief moment, she had considered it, but this was not her army anymore. It was Penthesilea's. Not just because she had trained these women and lived with them, but because they trusted her.

"Perhaps," she had said softly. "When he is dead, they will trust me again."

She felt none of the pain she had expected when uttering these words, for it was the truth, yet even as she spoke, she thought it unlikely. How could they trust her when she did not yet trust herself? What would she do when Hippolytus was returned to her? Where would her true loyalties lie when she was forced to decide the fate of her son? The same question had been poised on the tips of her sisters' tongues for as long as the battle had been planned, and she had watched them swallow it down again and again, for they, she reasoned, did not want to hear an answer, any more than she was able to provide them with one. And so it was Penthesilea who stood before three thousand women. Amazon women, Thracians, Scythians, and Samaritan allies. And she, Hippolyte, stood behind with Antiope and Melanippe, daughters of Ares. An Amazon princess, if nothing more.

All watched in awed silence as Penthesilea lifted her eyes to the moon, as if able to glimpse Olympus and the gods residing there, listening to her every word. She paused for a moment, before lowering her gaze back to the women.

"I do not need to tell you that not all of you here today will return to your homelands." A slow rumbling rippled through the women. Several older hands squeezed younger ones. There was no need for reassuring smiles. It was a rite. A privilege. The young ones were thirsty for it; the older ones knew that, whatever happened, they had done their part. Still, Penthesilea continued. "This will not be a short battle. We will not gain our victory in an hour, or a day. Perhaps not even a month. And we will not gain it without loss. But we will gain victory. Athens and its rule will fall. Those of you who do not survive will be warriors. You will die heroes. We are all the daughters of Ares. We will show Athens that. We will show them that we are all the daughters of Ares!"

She raised her spear to the sky.

In the instant that followed, three thousand spears rose into the air, their tips shining in the moonlight. They were formidable. They were unbeatable. They were the Amazons.

————

When the time came, they left the bivouacs along the roadside with their supplies and a hundred or so warriors to protect them. If the battle lasted several weeks, as they all expected it to, they could use this place as a camp; somewhere to send the injured while the others fought to strengthen their advantage. Besides, no Athenian would ransack them. They would be too busy trying to stay alive.

Clouds obscured the stars and moon above them and the lights around, only the faintest flickering from the distant citadel guiding them to their destination.

"They will put many guards around the palace. You know that, don't you?" Penthesilea said to her as they rode. Barely a hair's breadth separated the women. There were no fast gallops here. No cantering with free reins and eyes. For the longest while, no words had been spoken, but as the lights on the hills grew brighter, it was Penthesilea who broke the silence, speaking only to Hippolyte. "The moment they see us coming, he will be protected. It will only be a small group of us who are able to advance on Theseus. We will need our best women to break through his guards."

"And take Hippolytus," Hippolyte reminded her sister, with more sharpness than she had intended.

"And take Hippolytus. We will get your son, Hippolyte. I know why we are here."

After that, she found there was nothing more to say.

As the sky lightened and the stars melted one by one, the city walls came into view. At first, they were nothing more than a silhouette, a long snake of black, slicing through the hillside and over the horizon. But as they drew closer, the image cleared: the cyclopean brick structures, the heavy gates, and, at the apex of the hill, upon the temple, the last of the night's candles stuttering out. The guards that spotted them were silenced before they could utter a word, much less raise an alarm. The tension quivered back through all the women.

As they reached the Pirean Gate, Penthesilea drew the women to a stop and turned once more to her sister.

"You should start this," she said. "You should send the first one out."

For a moment, Hippolyte considered refusing the request, as she had refused to address the women the night before. But just as it had not been her place to speak then, it was her place to start this.

And so she did. Her breath held, Hippolyte drew back a flaming arrow, raised her bow, and released it over the walls and into Athens.

War had begun.

THIRTY-SIX

T HEY RACED THROUGH THE GATES, PUSHING FORWARD AS
torrents of arrows flew overhead, hiding the sky above and
silencing every hoplite within range. Once through, the land
opened up a fraction. Hippolyte stayed low her on her steed, her
back level with the horse's flank, offering her opponents only the
smallest slice of visible flesh to strike at while allowing her the reach
to pull used arrows from dead hoplites and fire them again. Behind
her came a scream from one of her women. A scream of pain, of
agony. One of their number had fallen, but she could not look back.
They never looked back.

A hundred or so women were inside the city walls by the time
the alarm was raised. Torches were lit, one after another, until the
entire citadel was aglow, the lights on the walls encircling them, dawn
coming to Athens before Helios had ordained. At that moment,
every man, woman, and child within the city walls knew they were
under attack. Theseus would know, too, and he would know exactly
who had come for him.

"We must get to the higher ground," Hippolyte shouted,

pointing the areas out to the women nearest her, including the rocky landscape that Antiope had wished to name in honor of her father. "We must get our women to these points, and then we will have the advantage."

It was she and Penthesilea who had entered the city. Outside the walls, Antiope would be doing her part, placing women on every gate, arrows and blades ready for any Athenian who tried to escape. Melanippe had taken the west side, and two of her strongest women, Dorymache and Antandre, were at the south. They had them surrounded. Now it was simply a case of waiting and killing.

By the time the Athenian soldiers had sallied forth in such numbers as might have inflicted some harm upon them, the women were already well within their walls with room to fire their arrows and swing their swords as effortlessly as drawing breath. The hoplites moved in a tight formation, shields raised or else thrust forward, creating a metal shell around their bodies, glistening spears poking out as they marched on. Each collective footstep was thunderous, reverberating through the ground and shaking the leaves from the trees. But their movements were slow. Small steps, tentative steps. The Amazons were more decisive than the former queen had ever seen them before.

The women had split off into groups, some riding toward the Areopagus, others diverting both north and south to two of the smaller hills. There was no respite. No lull. As one arrow met its target, another was loosed, and then another. Men fell, their shields clattering in the dust as those behind them scrambled over, attempting to protect themselves from the onslaught.

"Here! They are coming from here!"

The queen turned to the west side of the mound. The slope there was steepest, and thus they had considered it their least vulnerable flank, but several men had scrambled upward and were swinging their swords viciously through the air. One strike and then another lay down their women. The queen blanched at the sight of a dozen of her women, lying wounded or worse on the ground.

"Keep control here," she shouted to Penthesilea as she rode through to the men at the edge of the rock, bringing her horse to a halt and dismounting in one fluid motion. Her arrows were gone, now, every one of them embedded in the bones of an Athenian soldier, but her aim with her sword was just as good. Her feet skipped a dance over the ground as she leaped and lunged, striking metal and muscle, suit and stomach. Time and again she withdrew her sword only to plunge it once more into flesh. She had been a wife, she had been a mother, but she would always be an Amazon.

On and on they fought, until the sun claimed the sky, gently at first and then faster and faster until it blazed golden above them. Dust and blood surrounded them. Bodies—men and women scattered across the earth. In the rising heat of the day, the blood had already dried, soaking rust-like into the earth, its stench filling their nostrils.

"They are retreating," Penthesilea said, wiping a brown-red smear of sweat, blood, and dirt from her forehead. "They are retreating. They know we can beat them."

Hippolyte held her bottom lip between her teeth as she surveyed the scene. She, too, could see the Athenians moving backward. Shields raised but no longer with their spears held aloft. They were not fighting back. Her sister was right. They were retreating.

Around her she could hear the jubilation rolling through her women. It would be gracious to allow them this moment of joy, but this was not what they had come for.

"This is but the first battle, sister," Hippolyte said, wiping her arrow on the seat of her trousers. "We are here to win the war."

As the weeks wore on, she saw just how true those words had been. The days grew repetitive in nature—the fighting commencing before daylight, bloodshed and screams replacing the sounds of the agora and the chants of the temples she had become used to during her time there. The mud and grime that covered the ground was now a deep red, reforming every time rain washed it away. The use of so many women to barricade the gates had reduced their numbers inside the citadel, such that they were outnumbered by the hoplites, who Hippolyte knew to be at least nine thousand strong, assuming Theseus had told the truth on the matter. Still, position was everything. The Amazons had three strongholds. Three hills from which they could view the scene, send poison-tipped arrows into homes, and watch as the Athenians scattered in terror.

That was not to say that victory was certain. The Athenians had made their advances slowly, but they had advanced. Their attacks had come from the Lyceum and the Palladium and the Hill of Muses, areas the queen knew would have to be conquered if they were ever to take Athens in full.

Fighting drew to a close at sunset, at which point the arrows would rain down with less frequency until night fell in earnest, and the Athenians gathered their dead before retreating into their homes or temples, preparing for morning, when the battle would recommence.

"We should advance," Penthesilea said almost every night. "We should advance, now, while they are sleeping. We can take their homes, reduce their numbers, weaken them that way."

"They are not sleeping," Hippolyte countered her, "just as we are not sleeping. They are plotting, readying their weapons. They are tending to their wounded. They are burying their dead and preparing their next attacks as they attempt to devise a way to defeat us. They will have guards at every post, ready to wake every soldier at slightest sign of movement. They are not resting, as we are not resting. And let us not forget we have our own injured to deal with. And our own dead."

It was true. More wounded than expected, and more dead, too. Her women were strong and fearless, but that did not mean they did not succumb to pain or even to death when facing numbers over three times their own. This was not an open field. There were places to hide, ambushes that the Athenians had long planned, forearmed with their knowledge of the citadel. It should have come as no surprise that the hoplites were well trained. Theseus had wanted a wife whose name would ring through the ages, and a city that would never be forgotten. Of course he would want an army to match.

"We are starving them out," Hippolyte reminded her sister. "They will not be able keep fighting us when their food runs out. We will starve them, and then we will take them. That is the way we will win this. That is the only way we will win this."

And each time Penthesilea agreed, yet Hippolyte felt the frustration growing within her. Each death she felt so keenly. Some days so many fell that they were not able to remove them all in one night and had to wait until the following evening, when the bodies had begun to grow disfigured beneath their bruising. She understood why her sister wanted to act with force, now, but she also knew why they could not.

The quiet after a battle was a quiet like no other. It had always been the same. No cicadas, no owls or caterwauling. No drunkards singing and swaying as they stumbled down the streets. The light lapping of the sea against the cliff was the only counterpoint to the howls of pain that beat a constant ostinato through the night. It was only those who could be saved that cried aloud. The others, those injured too badly to survive, met swift ends, their pain and suffering over as quickly and as kindly as could be managed.

When the others caught sleep in the hours between battles, Hippolyte would find her eyes wandering up toward the highest point. She could not see the palace from her position here, and yet in her mind's eye, it was as clear as day. Did Hippolytus understand what was going on? In their time together, he had hardly left the palace unless he was with his grandfather, but he could not be oblivious to the constant screams that filled the air. What had his father told him? Had he told him that it was his mother who brought death to his kingdom? Had he told him the great Amazon queen, Penthesilea, who he so admired, was his beloved aunt, firing arrow after arrow at the soldiers defending him? Was he afraid? She had brought him up to be strong, not to fear noises or shadows, but would that be enough?

One evening, four weeks into the siege, Melanippe paid them a visit in the night.

"I do not think it will be much longer," she said, her youthful optimism infectious. "They have stopped attacking the two eastern gates. I think they have seen that they cannot defeat us there. They are worried. Saving themselves and their energy. Soon they will be weak enough that we can overthrow them."

"Perhaps," Hippolyte answered.

"You do not think so?"

"I think we should maintain our guard. How are the injured?"

At this point, Melanippe's optimism faded.

"We have never experienced such a number. They are healing, slowly, but we have lost many. As have you here?"

"Too many to consider."

It was true. After all the increase Penthesilea had presided over during her reign, their numbers had been decimated. But they were still Amazons. Every one of them was surely worth ten of Theseus's men. They would still be victorious. Hippolyte did not say this aloud, though.

Sieges were not the preferred tactic of the Amazons. They were not made for the waiting that came between battles. A restlessness grew among them, which only expanded as the time between the fights increased.

At one point, over two months into the siege, a full seven days passed without a battle. The stench of sweat and sewage had grown ripe and rotten. The natural color of their skin was gone, burned by the days in the sun, buried under the weeks of blood and grime. Their legs were indistinguishable from the crud boots that caked them.

"We need to end things soon," Penthesilea said to her sister as the pair sat on the edge of the Areopagus. They could see candles and lanterns lit at the Acropolis, more than at any other time since their arrival. "The women will get sick in such a place as this."

"He is offering up a sacrifice," Hippolyte replied, staring at the lights, her sister's words barely registering. "He is asking the gods for help."

Who would he be asking for help? The question brought a quiet unease rippling through her. He would not be arrogant enough to seek out the help of Ares. Athena, perhaps; the city had been named for her, yet if she had wished to protect it, would she not already be there, defending her heroes? Phobos, perhaps. The thought sent a chill down her spine. Phobos, the God of Fear, Terror, and Military Rout. If that was the case, it only served to underline their desperation. As long as Phobos did not answer Theseus's call.

The next morning, the winds changed.

THIRTY-SEVEN

T HE ROAR CAME FROM EVERY DIRECTION AT ONCE. AS IF SHE were underwater, the noise resonated around her skull. Around all of their skulls.

"Hold this point!" Hippolyte yelled.

"They are coming from the south now, too! Do we attack?"

"Hold your ground. Arrows only. Do not be drawn in. Do not be drawn away! Keep the gates blocked."

They had come like a tsunami. Those seven days of quiet had lulled the Amazons into a false sense of security. Why would the Athenians wait so long to attack again, if it weren't for decimated numbers and to delay the inevitable final defeat? Any moment, they had assumed that an emissary would come to negotiate for a truce. Yet when the Athenians returned, it was not with a truce, but with a great surge.

Numbers they could not have imagined poured out from buildings on every side of them. The drumming of their feet and clanging of their shields formed a metronomic pulse that shook the ground and rose trembling through the earth and the soles of the Amazons' boots.

"Do not let them reach us," Hippolyte shouted again, but distance did not matter, for the Athenians were no longer constrained by the use of swords. The weapons that flew toward them were heavier than arrows. Cast in thick metal, yet shaped to a tip, they severed the air with such force that they did not stop moving, even when plunged through the heart of an Amazon. Phobos had answered their prayers with such a weapon.

"Sister! We will not hold," Penthesilea shouted over her shoulder at she spun her ax horizontally across her body and brought down first one hoplite and then another. "Where do you wish to concentrate the attack?"

Confusion flooded Hippolyte. Never before had she seen her women so outnumbered. It was not a case of being outfought by greater skill. Her women fought more effectively than any of their men. But there were simply so many of them. Theseus had called on all his forces to fire these new weapons. He had liberated his slaves to fight and die for him. All of this to keep her from her son. Her thoughts flitted across the citadel, to the gates where her sisters and the other women had given their blood to fortify them. She did not wish to acknowledge it, but there was no doubt: the Amazons were, for the first time, losing.

"I need to get to Theseus," she said. "There is only one way we can end this. If their king is dead, they will have to submit."

Penthesilea nodded. "Show me the path you need clearing," she said.

Still fighting off soldiers like ants on a spill of honey, Hippolyte glanced behind her. They had to get down the hill and around to the other side of the Acropolis to climb the steps to the palace. It was a challenge that would be made far easier with the aid of more women, but there were none to spare. Those still standing were barely holding the Areopagus, and the departures of both Penthesilea and Hippolyte would weaken their defenses still further. It was best the pair went by themselves.

"We should go through the agora. The marketplace," she said, pointing her arrow to a spot that was swarming with soldiers. They would be outnumbered a hundred to one, yet she knew her sister would not refuse.

"Then let us go. You move forward. We shall fight on, clearing the path."

They had fought in such a manner before, the two of them breaking away, killing endlessly to force a pathway through enemy soldiers. At such close quarters, Hippolyte relied on her kopis, the small swords that swished through the air ceaselessly and too fast for her enemies to see. Every moment of her blades, each twist and turn yet another death for the Athenians, and another step toward Theseus and Hippolytus. From behind her came the sound of Penthesilea's ax cleaving Athenian flesh with the same relentless fluidity.

One by one the hoplites fell, and to her surprise, Hippolyte found herself filled with admiration for these men. Admiration and sympathy. They fought fiercely, knowing death was imminent, all to serve a king with fewer scruples than a bandit. *He was my husband,* she wanted to shout at them. *He promised me a lifetime of love, and this is how he treated me. He does not care about Athens, about his people. He cares only for himself.* But there was no time for words. No time for sounds other than the grunts and huffs and guttural screams that rattled from the hoplites as death greeted them at the end of her sword.

"There!" Hippolyte called, momentarily pointing her blade in the direction of the steps to the palace. A hoplite thrust his spear toward her, but before the tip could reach her armor, she kicked outward, sending him tumbling back and making swift work of both him and the soldiers behind him.

No other women had made it this far into the citadel, and the soldiers here were more densely packed and more heavily armed than anywhere else. A human blockade. A wall of beating hearts. A churn of dread rolled through the former Queen of Athens, for she knew exactly what their presence meant.

"He knows," she said. "He knows I will be coming for him."

"Then he knows you are going to kill him, too," Penthesilea replied. "You will do this. You will end this today."

Her arms were ablaze, a throbbing heat quivering within them as her muscles pulsed like snakes. The seven-day standoff had given her time to recover. Time for the Amazons to regain their strength, but it had done the same for these soldiers.

Through midday they fought. Each step upward was bought with a dozen deaths or more. Streams of sweat poured off their skin. The heat was scorching, as if Helios were unwilling to descend from his peak. The golden rays reflected off the buildings, blinding them as they turned, pivoted, and pitched, as they flung themselves against sword and shield and each time rose up to do the same again.

"We are nearly there," Hippolyte cried, reaching the final line of reinforcements. Down below them lay a channel of Athenian bodies. However certain Theseus might have been that Hippolyte would come for her, the dwindling numbers of guards told her that he had been equally certain she would not make it this far, for as she passed the threshold into the palace only a handful of hoplites remained.

A handful of men she had seen every day for nearly six years.

"You know how this ends," she said, with as much kindness as she could muster.

"Oira—" She cut the man's throat before a further syllable could escape.

Inside, the palace was cool. Quiet. The clanging of the battle down below them was muted here, deadened by distance and the sound of her own heartbeat. The heat of the midday sun had bled away through the cold white marble, the dark shadows turning the sweat and blood icy on her skin.

"Where will he be?" Penthesilea asked. "Where do we go?"

Hippolyte pressed her lips together as her eyes scanned the corridors that had been so familiar to her for so long. The same tapestries still hung over the same doorways, muffling the sounds of their footsteps. The same painted frescoes graced the walls. And yet this place seemed more alien to her now than it had even in those first days, when Aegeus had met her with distrust, and her drinks had been dosed with valerian. She did not doubt that Theseus would have been watching her, cheering loudly as he witnessed the massacre of her family.

And there was one room that offered the best view from the citadel.

"The andron," she said with certainty, quickening her step. In her mind the room remained Aegeus's domain, his sanctuary, and without warning, a maelstrom of grief and anger rushed through her. Theseus had murdered his own father. Not with blade or poison, but with his selfish, self-absorbed arrogance. And when she killed him, it would be justice for Aegeus as it was for herself. Her throat dried, narrowing as she readied herself for what was to come. With the edge of her sword, she whipped the curtain aside and lunged inward, to find the room starkly empty.

The scent of wine hit her immediately, momentarily flooding her with memories. The old man, picking up Hippolytus, placing him on his lap and bouncing him there. Their late-night conversations, the stories they shared of the battles they had fought. The longing within both of them for a child that had finally been satisfied with the arrival of Hippolytus in their lives. She had laughed in this room. She had laughed and breathed and felt at perfect ease and comfort. And now she was preparing to shed blood in it.

"Hippolyte, they are not here. Where else? Where else would they be?"

Her sister's voice buzzed distantly behind her as she gazed at the soft furnishings of the room. Nothing had changed in her absence. The same vases stood on the same tall tables. The same lamps waited to be lit.

"Hippolyte!"

The sudden snap of her name snatched her from the daydream. If they were not here, then where? It was possible they had retreated to the throne room, she supposed. Given the urgency of matters outside the building wall, it would be a space large enough for all the advisers to gather and discuss strategies. Yes, that would make sense. Without sheathing her blade, she returned to the corridors, only to draw swiftly to a stop once again.

At first, she assumed the sounds she heard came from outside. A distortion of cries and wails bellowing from the battle. But these noises were not cries or wails. They lingered, growing in intensity then fading again, only to swell even greater than before. She sheathed her sword, exchanging it for her bow and arrow as, stepping forward, she strained to hear.

"Is that laughter?" Penthesilea asked. "It sounds like laughter. Like a feast."

No sooner had her sister spoken than Hippolyte's legs were

moving again, racing. Leaving rust-red footprints on the white floor, shedding dirt with her every step.

A feast. A banquet. She could hear it. Smell it, too, now. The warmth of roasted meat, the tart tang of salted cheeses. The waft of wine. The closer she came to the hall, the more intense the laughter and the cheering. Were they toasting victory so soon? No, surely even Theseus could not be as arrogant as to celebrate, now, while his men continued to die for him.

And yet as her feet slowed, it was not just laughter she heard. Nausea swelled in her stomach as the sound of a lyre trailed through from the room. Music. Music in a time of death. Never had her blood boiled so furiously, her pulse pounding in burning rage. These men were not afraid of them. There were not hiding. Not cowering like every other man did when the arrival of the Amazons was imminent. Why not? Suppressing an unexpected tremor in her fingers, she nocked her arrow, but, before she could move toward the doorway, a hand reached for her shoulder.

"Wait, sister. We must first find Hippolytus. If we act now, he may be lost to us."

The drumming in her ears had set something loose inside her head, had sent rivers of mud to confuse her thoughts. But on this, she was clear. He was celebrating. He was celebrating his own wife's death.

"I will take Hippolytus," she spat, eyes trained on the doorway in front of her. "I will take Hippolytus, and then I will slit Theseus's throat."

Her hand was no long shaking as her fingers squeezed around the arrow. Yet as she stepped out of the corridor and the light of the banquet hall hit her, she froze at the sight.

THIRTY-EIGHT

WHEN SHE HAD FIRST ARRIVED IN ATHENS, THE SCALE OF the feasts had taken some time for the queen to become accustomed to. The excess to which they ate and drank with so little regard for their bodies and even less for the bounty of the earth with which the gods had blessed them simply disgusted her. Fish and meat, flaking from the bone, dried fruits, sweet sticky honey scattered and drizzled over crumbling white cheese. No expense was spared, no taste left unsatisfied. And yet this was how they celebrated. And the Athenians celebrated often.

On one occasion, around the time of Hippolytus's second birthday, she had attempted to eat as they did, filling her plate with everything that the platters had to offer, gorging beyond the point of enjoyment. Her body bloated. Her arms grew sluggish, so much so that she wondered, perhaps foolishly, if Theseus had drugged her wine again. Yet watching the others, she saw it was not only her that was so affected. This was the way of the Athenians during their festivities. Eat to excess. Drink to slightly before excess—or, in Theseus's case, once again to excess. Listen to music and laugh, despite the fact that your distended body could no longer lift itself to dance properly. And the effects did not end when the feast did. Even the next day she found herself groaning, her belly swollen almost as if she were growing a second child. After that event, she had always shown restraint, regardless of the temptations that faced her.

And yet what she saw before her was greater than any feast she had attended in all her years here. For it was not a celebration of victory, she realized.

It was a wedding.

He sat at the top of the room, at a table raised higher than the others. His hair was thickly oiled, curling down his shoulders in greasy tendrils as if he were a gorgon, and the purple tunic he wore was elaborately embroidered along its edges. Upon his head sat a crown of gold-stitched flowers twisted with threads of purple and red, and a wreath of gold twisted leaves, set with garnets the size of bird's eggs. Beside him sat the young girl he had brought into her home. The young girl he had said he was going to make his wife.

The room had fallen silent, every pair of eyes on them. Several women were holding their hands to their mouths, pushing their men forward toward the intruders. But the men did nothing other than grow paler and paler by the second. She recognized them as men of the polis. Men who had looked upon her with disdain and distrust from the moment she had been dragged to this place. They looked upon her as a monster. But she knew the truth of it. It was Theseus who was the monster here, and as Theseus himself had so recently proven on Crete, monsters could be killed. A new clarity took shape within her mind as she tipped her head to one side and spoke.

"It would appear that my invitation has gone astray," she said.

From the table closest to her came a series of whimpers, the cries of a woman whose hand was shaking so badly that the wine spilled over the top of her cup. The man beside her—from his age it was impossible to tell if he were her husband or father—straightened his back.

"You are not welcome here. You are defeated. You should leave now."

"The queen is speaking." Penthesilea's voice was low and refined. As direct as the point of her arrow, which, at that moment, she pulled back and aimed at the man who recoiled, his reserves of bravery depleted. Still, it was a better display than that mounted by the rest of the guests, who sat cowering in their seats.

Hippolyte waited a moment for the assembled company to reflect upon her sister's words, and then she spoke again.

"I fail to see how I have been defeated," she said, increasing the tension of the bow, the arrow pointed directly at Theseus. "To me, it looks like there is an arrow trained upon your king. No one else in this room needs to die. All I want is my son. My son and my husband's head."

With a nod, Penthesilea took a step toward Theseus, taking Hippolyte's place and fixing her aim directly on his temple while Hippolyte turned around to examine the room. At her best estimate, there were two hundred people in there, old men, young men, and women alike, all Athenians, many of whom had tears of fear trickling down their cheeks. Of course, visitors from outside the city would not have been able to attend. The Amazons' siege had seen to that. And amongst the Athenians were children. Several children, dressed in their finery. But not her child.

She marched toward Theseus at his table. "Where is he?" Spittle mingled with blood as it flew from her lips. "What have you done with him?"

It was Theseus's turn to tip his head, as if in mockery of her. "Am I supposed to know of whom you speak?"

The grinding of her teeth sent reverberations down her spine.

"Where is Hippolytus?" She enunciated each syllable of his name, and yet still Theseus played the same game, crinkling his face in mock confusion before widening his eyes.

"My son? He is not here, as you can see."

His tone was unhurried. He was enjoying the moment. Enjoying the opportunity to ridicule her. From behind her came the fluttering of fabric, so light and quiet it might have been nothing more than the fluttering of a bird's wing to the untrained ear. But hers was not an untrained ear. Swiveling on the balls of her feet, she fired off an arrow before the other guests had even realized what was happening. The arrow struck straight into the heart of an old man. The dagger in his hand dropped a second before he did, his body landing ten feet from the queen. Soldiers a hair's breadth from the queen had failed to blow against her; the fact that the old man had thought he might hit her with a dagger from that distance aroused a brief flutter of sympathy for him. Stepping forward, she kicked his body, rolling it over to pull out the arrow and fix it back in her bow before addressing the rest of the party.

"Do not test me," she said, locking her eyes on as many of them as kept their hands from before their faces. "I will kill every one of you to get to my son."

The arrogance in Theseus's face had shifted slightly. Beside him his young bride was white with fear, and she clutched at her new husband's arm.

"This does not end well for you, Hippolyte. Leave now. Let my wedding be. Take your remaining women, and I will send word of Hippolytus to you."

"I do not believe you. Every word you speak is a lie."

"You cannot escape here alive. Your women are dying out there. You know that. Today, tomorrow. They will fall."

"No one will fall until I have my son."

"You would do that? You would offer up the life of every woman in your service for a child you did not even want?"

"I always wanted him!" she cried. "I am not playing games, Theseus. Tell me where he is now, or I will kill you. I will kill every one of your guests, and I will start with this child you call your bride. It will be a mercy killing for her. Better to free her now than condemn her to a life of misery with you, do you not think?"

Her question hovered, as menacingly real as the motes of dust that glinted in the air around them. She had seen him for what he was. A liar, a manipulator, a narcissist. But he had seen who she was, too, and he knew that every word she spoke was true.

As Theseus's lips twisted and pursed, he turned to his new, younger wife, with a jerk of surprise, as if he had forgotten she was there. As he looked to her, Hippolyte noted the downward glance of the woman. The way her hands shifted from the table to her belly. Could it be, already? Was that possible? Before they were even married? Surely a princess of Athens was not so liberal. As she thought of the child that might already be blooming in the girl's belly, her mind raced from present to future. What would become of Hippolytus should this woman have another son? What schemes might hatch behind the blue eyes of this young queen? Certainly, none that would be favorable for Hippolytus.

"I am done with this," she said, and aimed the tip of her arrow at her husband.

Finally shaking off Phaedra's grip, Theseus rose to his feet and stepped out from his chair. His voice, when he next spoke, was barely a whisper. None of the arrogance of before. His eyes met hers, a deep pleading within them.

"Please, Hippolyte, not here. Not like this. This is between us. Let us talk? Let us talk like the rulers we are."

"Talk? Like you wished to talk to me when you came back from Crete? Like you wished to talk when you brought a child to my bed, when you dishonored all your father stood for? Will you speak to me like we spoke then?"

A pallor had crept across his skin. "I was wrong. Please, Hippolyte. You have caused enough destruction. You have said it yourself, your women are strong. They may still return from the fight outside. Please, don't do this here. You can take me; you can fire an arrow through my heart if that is what you think is just. But not here."

Again, those pleading eyes. The eyes she had seen for the first time on the beach at Pontus. So much depth stirred behind those irises, and when he next moved his lips, no sound came from them, yet she saw the shadow of the word in the air. *Please*, he mouthed.

"Hippolyte." Penthesilea's voice was jarring behind her. Sharp and quick, and intended to remind her of their promise.

"I want to know where Hippolytus is," she said, her resolve hardened again.

"And I shall tell you. But outside. Not here. Please, let these people drink their wine. Do not be the woman they think you are, Oirapata."

It was the second time today she had been called such a thing in this palace, yet this was not uttered with malice, the way the guard had spoken. Not spat at her the way he had addressed her on her last day in Athens. This was said with a twinkle in his eye. A twinkle intended to cast her back to those times in the andron, to remind her of Aegeus. Of Aegeus's love for them both. "I heard what you did," he said, softly. "How you tried to save him. They told me later how you rowed out into the waters and searched for his body. I never thanked you for that. I am sorry."

The memory stirred within her, yet she did not reply. She would not. She would not let her voice betray her.

"He loved you. He loved you very much," Theseus continued. "Please, let us talk. I will tell you where Hippolytus is."

Her chin nodded of its own accord, as if it were her body that were asking to be with him, rather than her mind. Behind her came a sharp intake of breath from Penthesilea. With a shift of her posture, she addressed her sister.

"Wait by the door and shoot anyone who moves," she said. "When I know where my son is, I will end this."

She stepped back, allowing Theseus to walk in front of her. It would be so simple to kill him now, she thought, with his back directly to her, but then what? Ransack the palace and the entire citadel for Hippolytus, in the hope that she would find him before someone killed him out of spite? Young children had certainly been killed for less. Besides, she wished to see Theseus beg. Then and only then would she kill him, and she would make it as slow and painful as possible.

THIRTY-NINE

INDISTINCT VOICES REACHED HER EARS, DISTANT CRIES. Penthesilea blocked them all out. She had to focus on the moment. On the promise she had made to her sister. She had voiced her concern and had her disapproval rejected, and now she must be ready for whatever was to come.

She remained both armed and alert as she glided across the floor, positioning herself so as to have a view of the guests—most of whom were weeping pathetically, and some of whom had fainted—and still observe her sister and listen intently to the conversation she was engaged in with Theseus. More soldiers would be on their way to the palace, now, troops diverted from other duties to protect their king, yet Hippolyte seemed oblivious to the danger. Oblivious to all except Theseus.

Callous men were not new to Penthesilea, and neither were arrogant kings, but the revulsion that swelled within her was stronger and harder to bear even than her encounter with Heracles had been.

She wished she could give her sister as long as it would take to extract an answer about her son, for without doubt the queen needed resolution, but Penthesilea needed to think of her women. It had been four days since she had seen Cletes. The likelihood that she was still alive was growing slimmer with every passing minute. An ache ignited within her. Regret for the moments they had not spent together. Immediately she rejected it before it could distract her any further.

While her eyes remained trained on the wedding guests, she noted that Hippolyte had stopped walking. Any moment, now, she would end this.

"This is far enough," she heard Hippolyte say. "Now tell me, where is Hippolytus?"

Theseus's inhalation was audible and slow. Aggravatingly slow. It was all part of his plan, thought Penthesilea, for the longer he took to breathe, the more chance that aid would reach him in time. The tactic was crude and juvenile, and the fact that Hippolyte might have considered herself in love with such a man appalled her. Her fingers twitched with the urge to send an arrow through his heart, but she resisted. Her sister would not forgive her for such an action, not if it lost her her son. Only stuttering, staggered breaths came from the hall. They were, for the moment, safe from the rest of the army.

"He is not here," Theseus said. "I have sent him to Troezen."

"To Troezen?"

"To be raised by my mother."

A sigh of relief rose in the princess. That was it, they had all the information they needed. They could reach their women now. Reach Cletes. Penthesilea threw a glance over her shoulder, ready to beckon her sister to leave, when three guests simultaneously rose. Young men, with broad shoulders and barrel-like muscles, each armed with a knife. An attack planned in silence. The first leaped onto a table, but for all his speed he had not a fraction of hers, or her skill. The arrow she fired sent him toppling back onto the men behind him, as one of his comrades hurled his knife straight at her skull. His aim was good, and it might have struck someone lesser, but for Penthesilea, a slight step was all that was necessary for the knife to fly harmlessly past and bury itself in hit the wall behind her. Within an instant, she had fired off two more arrows, straight through the accomplices' eyes. Screams rolled into the air around them, but she did not listen. Instead, the sound that reached her ears was the wheezing pain of her sister.

"How could you? How could you do that?" Hippolyte's voice was breathless. Emotional. This time Theseus answered promptly.

"Do you not understand? I had no choice," he said.

"I was right. You wish to replace him as your heir. Let me guess, her belly already swells with another of your bastard children? I should have known."

At the edge of her vision, Penthesilea saw the shallow shake of the king's head, a head that was long overdue the time when it should have been severed from his body. But to go against the queen would undermine their very structure. Any hope she had of the women trusting and following Hippolyte again would evaporate if she killed Theseus without her sister's command. And yet their women were in danger, more of them dying even as this drama played out in the corridors of the palace.

"No, you misunderstand me, Hippolyte," Theseus spoke again. "You have gotten this wrong."

A shudder of satisfaction rolled through Penthesilea. No one told the queen she was wrong. Certainly not in such an outright manner, and not if they hoped to live. She had seen it enough times with men, with rulers who had sought their help, only to refuse payment, or to claim that their involvement had not been paramount to the victory. No one told the queen she was wrong, and yet here was Theseus, stating it as fact, and still standing. She waited for the blow, the scream of his pain, yet it did not come. Instead, it was she who spoke.

"Hippolyte," Penthesilea voice was low. "This needs to happen. Now. We know where he is. We can fetch him. We need to go. Finish this. Or tell me to."

While her sister did not appear to hear her words, Theseus dropped to his knees, clasping his hands.

"Please, try to understand how difficult it was for me, having him here. Seeing his face that reminded me so deeply of you. Of what I had said to you. Of the terrible mistake I had made in sending you away. I love you, Hippolyte. You know that. I loved you from the first moment I saw you. I waited years for you. Years, with no other love in my mind. You know this is the truth. I was rash, that was all. Just angry. Forgive me, please. I will call off the wedding now. Come back to me."

And in that moment Penthesilea understood why Hippolyte had asked for her help, for the sincerity in his voice would have softened even the hardest of hearts, even those who knew his words to be false. In the hall, the new queen was sobbing, but nobody moved to comfort her, all of them afraid of what a simple shift in their position might mean for them.

"Hippolyte…" Penthesilea spoke again.

"I will send her away," Theseus continued. "I will send for Hippolytus. We can be back together, as a family. The way that Aegeus always saw us. We can do this."

"Enough. This has gone on long enough." Penthesilea pivoted and trained her arrow at Theseus. "Say your farewell, sister."

She locked her gaze on Hippolyte, and the tears that filled her eyes. What was this man that he could do this to her? That he could cripple the Amazon queen? For the first time since seeing Theseus,

Hippolyte looked at her sister. She swallowed visibly, her chin dipping by barely a hair's width.

Later, Penthesilea would recall this moment over and over, and that simple tilt of her sister's chin. There had been a time before this war, before Theseus, when she could read every one of her sister's movements without misinterpretation or doubt. When she had known what a single flick of her hand or brief purse of her lips would portend. Perhaps it was because she was waiting for the signal, anticipating it with such fervor that she saw something that wasn't there. Or perhaps it was there, perhaps it was indeed what Hippolyte had wanted at that precise moment. But the second Penthesilea released the arrow from her bow, her sister's expression changed. The blood drained from her lips and cheeks, the whites of her eyes shining more brightly than polished marble. And Penthesilea watched as her arrow, with perfect precision, flew toward Theseus. It would not miss. It never did. At this range it would puncture his ribs in an instant and render him dead in minutes. That was what she knew would happen, what she saw in her mind's eye. That was what she was certain the gods wanted to happen.

Until it did not.

FORTY

A S A CHILD, HIPPOLYTE HAD DREAMED OF THE WARRIOR'S
death. Hers would strike her in the greatest battle of all,
but not until she had single-handedly led her women to an
unrivaled freedom and power. Thousands would watch on, awed by
her skill and strength, although what precisely dealt the final blow,
she had never been quite certain. It was, after all, a child's dream, a
moment she had thought of only in terms of courage and power. The
honorable end of the queen's reign. Of death, she had been certain.
Love, on the other hand, she had found it harder to believe in.

Whether it be romantic love, passionate love, love for which
wars would be waged and armies brought low—it was a ridiculous
notion, she thought. Countless times she had ridiculed the concept,
particularly on those occasions the Amazons had been summoned to
aid some king whose entire people had gone to war for *love*. Fighting
for family, for honor, for wealth and land—those things made sense.
But the love of a single person, when thousands of others walked
this earth? Why anyone would choose to do that had always been a
mystery to her.

That was not to say she had dismissed love entirely. The love she felt for Hippolytus burned before she had even met him, and the first time she gazed upon his deep blue eyes, she had felt a surge in her heart so immense it was as if the very organs within her had been reshaped to make room for this tiny child. But Hippolytus was not her first love.

As queen, the emotion she felt toward her women was undeniably love, even though it was a different feeling from the love she felt for her sisters. The bonds the Amazon women forged between one another evolved over years, resting on deep foundations of blood and trust built in battle and beyond, and fortified by experiencing each other at their strongest and their most vulnerable. It was rational that she would love these women. Rational that she would love her sisters, whose blood she shared, whose minds and beliefs she valued as dearly as her own. But her love for Theseus was not rational. It had no roots in logical thought. It was raw, and it was raging, and it was uncontrollable. This was the love for which men went to war without the briefest consideration of what it would cost them, the love that angered them into losing their minds. And it was every bit as real as the blood that flowed in her veins.

"I will send her away." She could hear what Theseus said, but it was as if she were in a dream, the words drifting in and out of focus and barely intelligible above the roar of her own thought. "I will send for Hippolytus. We can be back together, as a family. The way that Aegeus always saw us. We can do this."

She attempted to focus on her task, on her responsibility to the women outside the palace walls, women who were dying in their hundreds for her. And yet, simply being in his presence changed her. It shifted her perspective, the view now suddenly wider and vastly different. His love somehow elevated her into something more than what destiny and the gods had demanded of her. He had given her a new path.

"Enough. This has gone on long enough." She could hear her sister's voice, but her mind was elsewhere again. Theseus had loved her once, of that she was certain. All he had endured in bringing her here to Athens, in choosing such a woman as his queen, it had not been for nothing. She had hurt his pride, and he in turn had responded as any injured beast would, by baring its teeth and snapping its jaws at whoever came close enough to feed it.

"Say your farewell, sister."

This time she caught the note of impatience within her sister's voice. And not merely impatience; unlike Hippolyte, Penthesilea still had hope. It was a mistake, had always been a mistake, and whether Penthesilea would admit the truth to herself or not, they were overrun. They should have retreated during those seven days of quiet while their numbers were still strong enough to survive, and Hippolyte should have come here alone. But she had needed her sister's strength and unimpeachable resolve. As she stood there, waiting to give her command, two thoughts contended in her mind.

The first was that a world without Theseus in was, to her, a world full of darkness. He had shown her a new life. She had been a queen and a wife, but now, she could return to neither. She had no place by his side, however deeply she loved him and however convincingly he lied. But if he died, whether by her hand or by her sister's, there would be even deeper repercussions. Ripples that would spread out in time. The immutable traditions in which her son had been raised demanded that a father's death be avenged. If she killed Theseus now, or if she let Penthesilea do as she had asked of her, Hippolytus would have no choice but to come for her. And yet if Theseus did not die, his men would continue to kill her women until the Amazons were merely a thing of myths and legends.

As she looked to her sister, a stray tear tumbled and caught her cheek, and the sensation caused her to turn her head a fraction, nodding to shake the droplet away. She realized a moment too late what the movement had looked like.

The arrow flew from the bow, its glistening point heading to straight to Theseus.

The paradox of loss. Could she call it that? Either all her women died now or her son would be the one to cause her own demise. And Theseus. Theseus…

She moved before she could contemplate her own thoughts, diving in front of her husband. She knew where the arrow would strike, exactly as Penthesilea had aimed it.

His heart.

So it was there that she thrust herself, her arms wide, pushing him backward and moving her own body forward and toward its end. In that final second, she closed her eyes and thought of her son and the days they had spent together, playing with wooden swords and ceramic figures of Amazon queens.

FORTY-ONE

NEVER HAD SHE FROZEN IN BATTLE. NEVER HAD THE stench of gore, or the screams of the injured, or even the torrents of blood spewing from the maimed and dying been too much for her to endure. Never had she found herself not knowing where her next arrow would fly or where the blades of her ax would next swing. She had seen plenty of men freeze. Warriors, beasts of men with muscles glistening, men who came at them, teeth in a snarl, skin oiled and spears raised, only to find themselves rooted to the ground as one by one their friends and allies fell beside them. Some did not even get that far. Often the mere sight of the Amazons hurtling toward them, the ground shaking under their horses' hooves, would be enough to render them paralyzed with fear. It was always a matter of when, not if, these men would die, but for those who could no longer even lift a shield to cover their faces, the end was always swiftest.

There were occasions, though, when it had not been their opponents, but an Amazon who had frozen. And not just those younger and less accustomed to the sights and scents of the battlefield. Sometimes the affliction took an older woman, rendering her helpless and immobile by the sight of a loved one—a daughter, a sister—succumbing to death beside her. They knew, of course, that with battle came death, but they were mortal humans after all, and Penthesilea could recall a dozen times when she had been forced to call out to a woman across a plain, or, if the distance between them was too great, to fire an arrow with such accuracy as to whistle past her ear, fanning her hair and livening her senses so that she was once again alive to the battle.

But not her. Not Penthesilea. She was a princess, a daughter of Ares, and she had never frozen in battle.

Not until now.

The blood had pooled on the marble floor so quickly, a carpet of crimson spreading toward her, encroaching on her feet, already stained with the blood of a thousand others. But not Hippolyte's blood. Never was it meant to be Hippolyte's.

She had watched on helplessly, had seen the moment before it happened, powerless to change things. She had watched as the point of the arrowhead forced itself through the metal of her sister's breast-plate. She thought she had heard the tiny details of every sound that followed. The puncturing of the skin, the cracking of the bones, the cleaving of the heart.

And yet even as she saw the moment unfold, even as the red pool crept toward her, her sister's actions remained incomprehensible.

"She is gone."

It was not her voice, but Theseus's. His was the voice that stirred her. Hippolyte had fallen back onto his bent knees, and now his arms cradled her torso. How? How? And why was he gazing at her in such a manner, Penthesilea asked herself. But she could form no sounds. Not until the moment Theseus gently brushed the hair that had fallen across Hippolyte's eyes.

"Get away from her," Penthesilea snarled. His head snapped up, and yet he remained where he was, crouched on the ground, his arms holding her in a gentle embrace. "I said, 'Get away from her.'"

Still, he did not move. There were no tears in his eyes, yet his skin had grayed, deep crevices forming between his brows, his cheeks sinking inward. He cast the briefest of glances at Penthesilea before returning his gaze to her sister.

With a swiftness that spoke of her lineage, Penthesilea slung her bow over her shoulder, removed her ax from her belt, and hoisted it into the air. Her heart thundered within her, blurring her thoughts with its ferocity.

"There is no one to save you, now," she said, breathless. Her hands quivered, the ax's handle magnifying the tiny tremble to a quake. Never before had her blade not been steady and sure, but now it wobbled as if it were in the hand of a tavern drunk.

Still, it did not matter. Her strength would be enough. It was the least that Theseus deserved. Her resolve once more in place, she stepped toward him.

Immediately, his hands flew to the air.

"Think of Hippolytus!" The urgency in his voice was the same she had heard from many a man who knew he was about to die. "Think of Hippolytus. If you kill me, he is as good as dead. People will kill him and claim Athens for their own."

"I care nothing for Athens, nor for the boy. He is nothing to me."

The king paled further. Words streamed from his lips.

"I understand. But you cared for you sister, and he was her world. You must know that. That is why she could not return to you. That is why she sacrificed herself. Not to save me, but to save Hippolytus. You must see that. You must understand that."

"Your words of manipulation do not work so easily on me, *King* Theseus."

The tang of iron sparked on her tongue as she twisted the ax in her hand. One blow. So why had she still not completed the act? As she glanced around her, searching for some answer to her confusion, her gaze fixed upon her sister. Glassy and unfocused, Hippolyte's eyes remained open and locked onto Penthesilea, regardless of how she shifted her position. No depth or light shone behind those pupils, and yet, by their very presence, they were judging her. She felt the air thinning around her, growing thornier and more grating with every breath. Those eyes. She had to close Hippolyte's eyes or at least stop her gaze from penetrating her. Yet she could not move without giving Theseus an opportunity to strike her.

As if reading her mind, Theseus shuffled back, slowly at first, with the weight of Hippolyte's body on his knees slowing his movement, then, with a sprightliness she had not anticipated, jumping up and onto his feet. Hippolyte's head landed with a crack on the marble.

"Queen Penthesilea, you have lost." He did not shout, but rather sneered though a small crack in his parted lips. "Your women will have been defeated by now. You know that. And if my life ends, then so will yours, one way or another." A snarl curled on his lips. "And wouldn't your sister be upset if you had risked it all for nothing? Poor Hippolyte, she did miss you terribly."

"Do not speak of her! Do not say her name!" Tears burned the back of her throat, raw and acrid. Still, the ax wobbled in her grip. So what of Hippolytus? She had never met the child. She had never met any of the Amazons' sons beyond their first months. Why should she feel loss for this one? And yet she knew exactly why. This was not any Amazon child; this was Hippolyte's son. Could she really live with his blood on her hands, too?

The decision was made within a split second. She was, as Theseus had already said, the queen now, and as queen it was her duty to get her remaining women to safety. Those of her women that remained living, and Hippolyte, too.

Leaning down, she pulled the arrow from her sister's torso. More blood than she had expected gushed from the wound as she picked up the fallen Queen and flung her over her shoulder, knocking her own bow from her shoulder in the process. Without a second glance, Penthesilea abandoned the weapon; she would not be able to fire it and maintain the balance of Hippolyte's body. She had her ax. That would have to be enough.

"Goodbye, Queen Penthesilea," Theseus said, stepping forward and offering a mock bow. "Give my regards to your *great* warrior women."

Outside, the massacre had reached truly monstrous proportions. The Athenian numbers were so great, it was near impossible to make out where her women were amongst them. Bodies encrusted the ground, male and female, piled one on top of another as if a new layer had formed to cover the earth. Had any of her women survived? Everywhere she looked, she saw embroidered tunics, caked in blood and dust and grime, unmoving on the earth. The Amazons would not have retreated without an order to do so, and neither she nor Hippolyte had been there to give that order. Perhaps, she thought, with a faint spark of hope, Antiope would have had the sense to withdraw, if only to save a few.

Down below, several hoplites had noticed her descending the palace steps, though none proceeded toward her. They did not need to, for they knew that the only way out was past them. She jumped downward, balancing on the upturned shields of one soldier and the helmet of another, pinning Hippolyte's body as close to her as she could, to stop the sway of her legs toppling her balance.

With hoplites having swarmed the Areopagus and the surrounding hills, she had to find another route out of the citadel. The east gate. That was the position Melanippe had been barricading. If she could reach it and find a horse, then she would be able to give her sister the burial she deserved.

They came at her from every direction, jabbing spears and firing their immense metal arrows. The extra weight on her shoulder altered her balance, and a single arrow cut at the fabric of her tunic. A flush of surprise and anger heated her skin. In all her years, it was as close a strike as any man had managed. Leaping downward, she raised her ax above her body, and in a single swing parted four men's heads from their shoulders.

"I will kill you all, if that is what I have to do to leave this place," she snarled. Still, more came toward her. The noise was deafening, the endless clang of metal and the dull thud of flesh striking stone as men plummeted face-first to the ground.

Three hoplites approached, a pair from her left and right and one dead in front, meaning to trap her and offer no escape. The reddish-brown hue to their skin, right up to the elbows, told her this tactic had worked on at least some of her women. Usually such a sight would have posed no threat to her, but now she turned cold as she remembered how she had frozen in front of Theseus. Would the same happen again? No, it could not. And still they approached.

"Perhaps we will keep you alive," one said. "We were ordered to kill you, but I think we can have a little fun now, don't you?"

Penthesilea adjusted her weight, countering the mass on her shoulder. She would kill this one first. The others would lunge without thinking when he went down. She readied herself to strike, knowing now that she would not freeze, and yet they were still several feet from her when their eyes widened, one then another, and their jaws dropped as in deep surprise. A second later they fell, one by one, to the ground, an arrow in each of their backs.

"This way. The gate is open. We can retreat this way."

She stood in a doorway, her face smeared, her eyes bloodshot and yellow, and yet never in all her life had Penthesilea seen a more beautiful human. A gasp like pure air filled her lungs.

"Cletes," she whispered.

FORTY-TWO

THE MOMENT EXPANDED AROUND HER. SHE WAS NOT FROZEN. Nothing could hurt her, not now. A part of her heart, a part she had not believed would ever be whole again, had instantly reformed, as if the tear between the two sides had been stitched together with the thinnest of threads. Cletes was still alive. Standing strong, her half-moon shield dented and battered but fixed firmly on her forearm. Her bow still quivered from the arrows it had released just moments ago.

"Come. Quickly." As she called to Penthesilea, Cletes's eyes flickered momentarily to the body draped across her shoulder, and yet she said nothing, but rather beckoned her queen forward while simultaneously firing an arrow at the hoplites that still surrounded them.

Together, they fought their way back, although it was unlike any of the battles they had fought inside the citadel walls so far. The hoplites' numbers had thinned, the men less willing to risk their lives in their king's name now that they knew the battle had been won. Some fired at the women from a distance, their actions now merely defensive, and many scurried hastily away, happy to allow the women space to retreat if it meant their hearts continued to beat for another day.

For her part, Penthesilea killed only the men she had to. After all, if she could not kill Theseus, what did these men matter? She had failed. That was the truth of it. Their lives were meaningless to her. There was no glory in their death.

Together she and Cletes staggered and stumbled through alleys and across broken stalls and burning buildings, her eyes scouring shadows and dark nooks. Time and time again she flinched at the eyes of dead Amazon women staring up at her from the ground. Most had fallen with their weapons still in their hands, and all bore deep lacerations and purpled bruises where they had fought for their lives. There must be more, Penthesilea told herself with each woman she passed, unable to pick up or cast a prayer for them. Cletes had survived. They could not be the only ones.

When the pace of combat slowed enough that she might have asked about the others, Penthesilea remained silent, and only when the east gate came into view did Cletes speak again.

"We need horses. We can make our way to the camp at Attica." She spoke as the last of the hoplites blocking their path fell beneath their blades. "That is where the princesses told us to gather."

"My sisters are alive?" Penthesilea's knees trembled at the news, but there was no time to rejoice. Any moment, Theseus could give orders for the hoplites to leave the citadel, to chase the women down and slaughter them where they stood. They had to move fast, but the soles of her feet were red, raw, blistered, and blackened from the weeks fighting on the hot Athenian earth with no way to bathe and no manner in which to dry themselves.

"Here! There are horses here!"

Cletes had raced ahead to an olive tree where four Amazon colts struggled against the coarse ropes holding them there. "Take this one," she said, loosening the knot and flinging the rope over the horse's neck.

Without consideration of her dignity, Penthesilea threw Hippolyte over the neck of the horse, before leaping on behind her. Taking a moment, she readjusted the fallen queen, hoisting her upward from her shoulders, then lifting her waist so that her legs straddled the animal and her weight rested on Penthesilea, almost as if she were sleeping.

They had traveled this way so many times before. Penthesilea's earliest memories had been shaped sitting like this, with Hippolyte's right arm pinning her tightly, as she taught her sister to read the movement of the animal between them. They had ridden through storms and over riverbeds. They had ridden in leisure and in war, picking one another up midbattle so they might fire in both directions at once or race to higher ground and continue to fight from a more advantageous point. But Hippolyte's body had always been warm, had been pumping with blood and laughter and life. The figure that she clung to now could not have been further from the woman she had been, the queen who had commanded her Amazons with grace and valor.

The dead queen's head lolled forward, her chin banging repeatedly against her chest, her weight dragging her from one side to the other as the horses took the steep turns that zigzagged up the hillside and away from Athens.

Behind them, the citadel walls shrank into the distance, and the sounds of the hoplites' cheers grew fainter. There would be feasts in Athens tonight, she knew. Not only for Theseus and his new bride, but for all those who had survived. The thought sickened her to the core.

Continually, she found herself casting her eyes backward, waiting, although for what, she knew not. Soldiers on foot would be no match for them now. Even the fastest could not match their pace. No, she was looking for women. Amazons who, for the first time since Ares had blessed them, would be fleeing from battle, as she was fleeing from battle.

The ground was dry and brittle and crumbled beneath the horses' hooves while above them dense clouds blanketed the sky, a massive sheet of gray penetrated by only the dullest shafts of light. Attica had felt so close when they had stormed Athens all those weeks ago. A short ride, quickened with adrenaline and the thirst for Theseus's blood, to a fight in which her sister Hippolyte would ride beside her as she had ridden so many times before. But now, every stride of her horse seemed to catch, each second dragging as if it had been stretched to the point of fracture. And even though Athens was barely visible behind them, she felt no closer to their destination.

Cletes rode a short distance in front. Normally the pair would ride side by side or share a horse, the way that Penthesilea and the queen's corpse now rode. A thousand times, words formed on the tip of Penthesilea's tongue. The thanks she wanted to give to the gods for Cletes's life. The indebtedness she felt to her lover for returning so that she might escape with her sister in her arms. Yet giving thanks at such a moment felt insolent. Greedy. For why should she have even a glimmer of joy when so many had lost everything?

As they closed in on Attica, they slowed to a canter, then further still to a trot and, finally, when the tents of their camp came into view, the slowest of trudges.

It was a scene she had witnessed before so many times. Hundreds and hundreds of injured, screaming, weeping, knowing their ends were moments away. Her eyes watered at the stench of soiled clothes, catching in the back of her throat like rotting offal. Those who could still help rushed around, unable to tend to all those who needed aid and knowing that so much of what they did would be in vain. They had ridden away from such sights so many times, leaving the defeated armies, the dead and the dying, satisfied in the knowledge that they had caused this devastation. But never had she seen one of these camps filled with her own women.

"No! No!" The voice came from one of the tents, the shadows of its doorways folded inward, yet Penthesilea did not need to see the person to know the voice. A second later, Melanippe ran forward, her hands clasped over her mouth. "No. It is not possible. It is not possible. How? How?"

As she reached the horse, Penthesilea allowed the queen's body to drop into her sister's arms.

"How did this happen?" The question repeated over and over, yet Penthesilea could make no sound. A thick lump had lodged in her throat, tightening against the words she could not form. Hippolyte was the daughter of Ares, a woman who had lived her life with such energy and vivacity that no man could ever have extinguished that spark. And no man had extinguished it. It had been her.

The same sense that had overcome her as she faced Theseus inflicted her again. The inability to form a cohesive thought, or barely a thought at all. She felt hands on her, supporting her, guiding her to the ground and to the place where Melanippe wept over her sister's body.

Melanippe buried her head in Hippolyte's chest, her tunic stained so deeply with blood that none of the patterns within it could be made out. Time ebbed and flowed around them, and all Penthesilea could do was watch on. Cletes's fingers were wound around hers, the tight squeeze offering only the faintest comfort. Any moment,

Melanippe would find the hole in Hippolyte's body and would know which arrow had caused it. She would blame Penthesilea, and rightly so, just as she deserved to be blamed. And then…and then only the gods knew what would happen.

"Where is Antiope?" Penthesilea asked, finding her voice shallow and hoarse, knowing that she could utter these words only once. "She should be here. She needs to be here, too. Where is she?"

It was at the sound of her other sister's name that Melanippe lifted her head from Hippolyte's body, her eyes so bloodshot that the whites were no longer visible. It was those eyes that fixed on Hippolyte, tear-glazed and shining, before she lowered her head and shook it once.

The pain that ripped through Penthesilea was so intense, so excruciating, that she dropped to her knees.

"No! You cannot mean that! How? She cannot. It is not possible. It is not possible."

Together the two women knelt, their cries echoing on the hillsides around them, the smallest circle of those still able to stand watching on from a distance.

"There were so many men," Melanippe answered in stutters. "We could see them swarming. We knew that we would lose the gates if we did not go in and help. She did what she could. She took so many of them. So many of them. But they surrounded her from every angle."

Images swirled in Penthesilea's mind. Antiope had taken on hundreds of men before. How was it possible that these would succeed where all others had failed? Why would the gods have done this to them? She wanted to voice the question aloud, for the first time in her life, but fear, raw and unfathomable fear, had gripped her.

"What do we do?" she asked instead. "What do we do now?"

FORTY-THREE

WHILE CLETES AND MELANIPPE FOCUSED ON THE INJURED, Penthesilea kept watch, waiting for other women to return. And at first, they came, although only in trickles. Pairs of women, holding one another up as they rode or walked to the camp. Like her, they struggled to speak after the horrors that they had endured. Some arrived bruised from head to toe, having been captured and used by the hoplites for their enjoyment before they managed to escape. For some, early wounds had cracked open and were seeping foul, pungent pus. None arrived unscathed, and most were too badly injured to risk moving them to Pontus for some time.

"We have allies in Macedonia. We could take them there. It would only be a two- or three-days' riding," Melanippe said.

"Which is two or three days more than they would survive. Besides, who would help us there? We asked our allies to ride to their death with us. No king will help us now."

"We cannot stay."

"We have to. Besides, we must wait for the others. There will be more to return to us."

She said the words with such confidence, ignoring the glance that she knew Cletes and Melanippe had exchanged while she was not looking.

There had to be more women. There simply had to. When they had left Pontus and ridden through Anatolia, they had been nearly three thousand strong. And yet between those injured and those still standing, there were barely a hundred. How could it possibly be that their numbers had been so badly depleted? There had to be more women somewhere. Camping out in the houses of Athenians. Waiting for the moment when they had recovered their strength and could slip out of the gates and hurry back to them.

For four days and nights, she waited. Nights, Penthesilea decided, would be the best time for the women to escape, and as such she stayed alert, listening for the slightest rustle in the trees or snap of a branch.

On the fifth night, Cletes came and sat beside her, close enough that her shoulder pressed against Penthesilea, her scent of pomegranates long since lost in the aroma of the siege.

"Talk to me, my queen."

Penthesilea flinched. "Do not call me that."

"I called you my queen when you led us before, as did every Amazon woman. You are our queen, now, more than ever."

Penthesilea stared into the flames. The fire was small, built only from twigs of kindling, which crackled as they sent tiny sparks up into the air. If only they had known the truth about what would happen when Theseus had arrived on their shores with Heracles all those years ago. *Xenia* be damned, Penthesilea would have slit his throat without a second's thought. For how could the wrath of the gods be any worse than this?

"I do not know what we are supposed to do," she said, quietly.

Cletes pressed her hand against hers.

"We will rebuild. We will return to Themiscyra, and we will rebuild."

"What if we cannot?"

"We can."

"I do not think that I am able to do that. I do not think…I do not…"

What? What was she trying to say?

They had buried the bodies there. It was not as it should have been. All Amazon women deserved to be buried in their homelands, on the soft gentle steppes, beneath the wings of the eagles, under the endless sky. But that was not to be their fate. Not even for their queen. The Athenians had dumped bodies outside the gates, and they had collected them during the night, just Penthesilea and a dozen other women riding back and forth, gathering the corpses, many of which had swollen and were tinged with green. Others were unidentifiable from their wounds. They had been buried here. In this land.

"At least the queen is with her sister," someone said, as they laid Hippolyte and Antiope in the ground. They garnished their bodies with all they could: their bows, their shields, their breastplates, all went into the ground with them. Penthesilea thought back to the zoster, the belt that Heracles had taken from Hippolyte. The zoster should have been buried with her, her gift from her father, for her to take with her into the underworld. And yet it was not.

"Tell me," Cletes said softly. "Tell me what happened."

Penthesilea continued to stare into to the flames. The fire was growing stronger, now, the heat of it burning her skin, and yet she did not care. She could not reply. Melanippe had seen the arrow wound when they had bathed and dressed Hippolyte's body, and though she did not ask, she had avoided Penthesilea's gaze. She did not want to know the details. The manner of Hippolyte's death did not change the outcome. But the truth of what she had done burned within her.

"You know what happened. You already know," she whispered to Cletes.

Her lover nodded slowly. "It was your arrow," she said. "Your arrow killed her."

"Not my arrow. Me. I am the one who killed her." She attempted to wrest her hand free from Cletes's grip, but Cletes held on firmly, twisting Penthesilea around to face her. In the firelight, her skin glowed as if she were luminous, a gift from Helios himself. Was it really she that was half god and Cletes fully mortal? For it did not feel as if it could be that way.

"Tell me what happened. You must speak of this; you must release your burden. Please, my queen. I am afraid for you."

"Afraid for me?" The laugh that broke from her lungs was unnatural and high. "Why in the gods' names would you be afraid for me? I am the only one in this place who stands without an injury. Not so much as a broken wrist."

"Penthesilea, tell me what happened."

"All these women here. All those you are trying to save. You know some of them will never walk again. Never ride. We are waiting here for them to die. That is all we are doing. If I were a better queen, I would kill them now. Kill them in their sleep."

Her voice was raised, and she could hear the whispers drift from the camp behind her, and yet Cletes remained calm and composed, her eyes only on Penthesilea.

"Tell me what happened," she repeated again. "Tell me how we can put this right for you."

The laugh came again, this time throaty and bitter. "You cannot put this right. I killed her. My arrow. She chose it. She chose to save him. To save him. And I am the one that killed her. It was the arrow sent for him. It was the arrow I sent for Theseus." It was the first time she had spoken the words aloud, and the ache in her chest did not loosen but rather tightened and bound her so fiercely that it would not permit other thoughts to enter her mind. "I did it. I killed her. It was meant to be Theseus. It was meant to be Theseus."

The air entered her lungs in great gulping gasps. "It was meant to be Theseus." Tears tumbled from her eyes, cascading down her cheeks. With each breath came another wave, an insatiable, unstoppable surge.

"You are not to blame," Cletes said, pulling her into her chest and rocking her as gently as if she were a small child who had done no more than break an amphora and spill water on a tiled floor. "You are not to blame."

"Yes. Yes, I am. I should have known. I should have done it earlier. I should never have taken her with me. I should have not led this damn war. I allowed it. I encouraged it. I encouraged her to seek vengeance when she did not want to. I am to blame. I am to blame for everything."

And there it was, the truth that she had not allowed herself to speak. It was not merely that she had allowed Hippolyte to sacrifice herself. It was that she had suggested this war. Encouraged this war. How many times had Hippolyte tried to talk her out of it? How many times had she tried to dissuade her? How many times had she mentioned the size of the Athenian army and all that supported it, not to mention Theseus's ruthlessness? But Penthesilea had been too stubborn to believe it was true, too headstrong, too enthralled by their reputation to concede that the Amazons could be ever defeated.

"We can rebuild. Grow. You did it for us once; you will do it again," Cletes told her. But Penthesilea shook her head.

"It was different then. Look at who remains. Even assuming each of the women here lives to return to Pontus, which they will not, how many of those do you think would survive the ride to meet the Gargareans, much less carry a daughter to be born fit and strong? We are done for. I have ruined everything. I have destroyed my father's legacy. My mother's legacy. My sister's. And Theseus, he still lives." The words caused a tremble to spill down her spine. Theseus was still alive. Her finger flexed, itching for a weapon. When she found none, her fingers clawed. "I should have stormed his palace alone by now. I should have killed him already. That is what I must do." Her body quivered with rage as she imagined his blood pooling on the marble floors. She would show no restraint. Offer him no honor. She would destroy him.

"You will not do that," Cletes said quietly, resting her hand on Penthesilea's shoulder.

"I will. I must."

"You cannot. You know you cannot."

Penthesilea fought her lungs to reply. She opened her mouth, attempting to rebuke Cletes's claim, but in the end, it was Cletes who spoke the words that neither Penthesilea nor Melanippe had the strength to say.

"Hippolyte allowed that arrow to strike her," she said softly. "She allowed herself to be killed, because she knew that if Theseus died, then Hippolytus would be forced to come for his murderer. She knew he would come after you. Not immediately, but eventually. That is why she died. To protect you, her sister, and her son. So, if you want to protect her legacy, that is what you should remember."

Silence fell around them, impregnable and unyielding, absorbing everything but the feeling of failure she had brought upon herself. Cletes spoke only the truth, but it did not ease the shiver that now consumed Penthesilea. Hippolytus was only a boy; what did he matter to her? Nothing. That was the answer she wanted to tell herself. He meant nothing to her at all. But he had been Hippolyte's world, and that had to be enough. So that was it. Theseus would escape unscathed. Not a scratch on his skin while Hippolyte's body lay cold beneath this earth.

"It is not fair," she whispered, a guttural sob stuttering her words. "It is not fair."

"I know, my love. I know."

Time slipped past, the flames of the fire dimming into a soft amber glow, yet neither of the women moved to replenish the wood. Wrapped in Cletes's arms, Penthesilea continued to cry until she could cry no more.

"You must sleep," Cletes said softly. "I have not seen you move from this place since the battle ended. Please, rest. I will keep watch. If any other women arrive, I will find you and tell you."

And then she pulled Penthesilea to her lips and planted a kiss on the top of her head, as if she were a child being bidden to sleep by a gentle parent. And like that child, Penthesilea rose to her feet and retired to her tent.

No women came that night, nor the day that followed. And while they lost several women during that time, there were others in the camp who had recovered to a point that they could stand and even ride.

"We should head back to Themiscyra now. It is the best thing to do," Melanippe said.

"Themiscyra is too large to defend," Penthesilea replied. "With our numbers so depleted, we cannot keep guard on both gates and place lookouts across the land."

The absence of Hippolyte and Antiope had been felt every moment. Two women, Penthesilea had discovered, were not enough to conduct productive discussions. There was no one to take a side and shift a majority when they formed opposing views. No one to explain or reinforce ideas or add a third counterargument on which they might all agree. As such, they had formed a court of sorts, bringing into their discussions the strongest of the survivors. Klonie, Polemusa, and Dorymache were among them. Still, Melanippe labored her point.

"There is security in those walls. We know the city paths. If we were attacked, we could keep the intruders at bay, confuse them as we slipped around the city."

"Or they could simply block the gates and starve us out."

Just as Penthesilea might have predicted, Melanippe shook her head in disagreement.

"That will not happen. Theseus has let us go. He has returned our dead. He shows no indication of wishing to retaliate. We have relationships we need to repair. It is vital that we remain in Themiscyra, where we can be found and called upon when we are ready to fight. Please, come, sister. You know as well as I do that we have fought plenty of battles you could have won single-handedly. The Amazons will return again if you let them."

Her words were almost a reflection of what Cletes had said, but this time she heard something different in them. A clear line of thought that stuck in her mind and told her exactly what she had to do.

FORTY-FOUR

G UILT ROLLED THROUGH HER AS HER HORSE PADDED GENTLY
away from the camp. The air was biting, and the breeze
from the sea strengthened and ebbed without any clear
pattern. In the heat of her clothes, her body smelled thickly of newly
turned earth, dark soil rich in humus and rotted life. She could still
feel it all, the leaf litter, the mollusks, and all the other creatures
that had crawled out from the graves they had dug in the previous days. So many graves. Her hands were blackened beneath the
nails, embedded so deeply with dark clay that no white remained. A
darkness in her nails that spoke of another darkness within.

She had taken over the watch from Enchesimargos. Before
Athens, Enchesimargos had been almost as renowned for her skill
with a spear as Penthesilea had been for her ax. She had led armies
of her own, a nomad of the greatest renown. But she had taken a
spear to the shoulder. Her throwing shoulder. Not content with
damage he had already caused, the hoplite that had struck her had
pulled the weapon out, tearing the muscles from her bones, dislo-
cating the joints so they fell at irregular angles. To most it would be

considered a miracle that she had survived at all, a miracle that when she had fallen to the ground, one of her women had been there to catch her, to stem the blood flow, to help her retreat to safety. For days Enchesimargos had slipped in and out of consciousness until, finally, she rose lucid. But was she glad? Penthesilea thought not. She could see from the darkness that now clouded Enchesimargos's eyes and the monosyllabic tone in which she spoke that she wished her rescuer had left her there to die. For what was she now? Broken. Incapable of living the life that was as necessary to her as breath in her lungs. Penthesilea might have pondered over the future that awaited Enchesimargos and those like her, but she did not yet know her own path, much less that of anyone else.

She waited until Enchesimargos had gone to her tent, then waited a little longer still, estimating how long it would take her to strip off her weapons, lie down on the hard earth, and fall asleep. Once such a time had passed, Penthesilea slipped back to her own tent and retrieved her satchel from where she had placed it, just inside doorway.

She had promised that she alone would keep watch in those final hours between night and day when Selene's moon grew weak and frail against the brightening of Helios's sun. She had told Cletes that she would remain there, looking out, until the sun had tipped over the horizon, that she would raise the alarm if Theseus's men approached, or if any of their women returned. But she realized the truth now. Her promises were worthless. Had she not promised Hippolyte that they would kill Theseus? Had she not sworn that their siege on Athens would lead to victory? The truth was that there were no more women to come. These few survivors were all that remained, the last fragments of the most formidable army the world had ever known. The Athenians no longer saw them as a threat. They had weightier matters to occupy them. The Amazons were nothing to them now, no more than another tale to regale their companions with over wine.

And so Penthesilea left by the road beside which they had buried their dead. So many plots had been required that not a scrap of unturned grass remained along the roadside.

She rode first through Boeotia, and past Mount Parnassus, toward Thessaly. When hunger struck, she plucked overripe fruit from trees and used her bow to hunt rabbits, which she skinned and roasted on a low fire, sharpening her ax with stones while she sat by the flames waiting for her meat to cook.

Melanippe would have known the truth the moment she woke to find Penthesilea missing. She would have known that the women were hers to rule alone, now, and would have ordered them to pack up their belongings, fold down their tents, and ride homewards. They would ride through Thrace and across the Black Sea to the lush steppes of Pontus. And while part of Penthesilea's heart yearned for that soft billowing grassland and those rushing rivers, she continued north.

Five days passed before she fought again. Her plan had been to ride as far away from Athens and Themiscyra as her horse would allow her to and to lose her mind, and hopefully her life, in the heat of the battle. She did not care whose side she fought on, or what she fought for. Just that she fought. But the fight that found her did not come on the battlefield, but rather in a small farm, a few miles east of the coast, in Epirus.

The grass was a verdant green here, the crests and peaks of small hills rolling over one another, as if set into motion by the ripples of waves. The trees, narrow in the trunk, were loaded with fruit, and the fields filled not with just olive and grapevines, as had been the case with the land farmed around Athens, but with citrus fruits, oranges, lemons, and limes, the scents of which saturated her sense. She had stopped to harvest of handful of oranges, to fill her satchel and keep them for the journey, when the screaming began.

Screams were nothing new. She had been weaned on the screams of the battlefield and on women sparring to better their skills. She had spent her last three months immersed within such sounds, but this was different. This was a singular sound of desperation. Dropping the oranges to the ground, she mounted her horse in one leap and kicked her heels into its side with such force that it reared upward before racing toward the noise.

The whitewashed buildings of the farm were set behind a small wall, hip height. Vines created a covered canopy so dense that no sunlight could penetrate it, and a fountain had been placed in the center of the small courtyard where water ran from a natural spring. To the right of the farmhouse was a small paddock where goats were bleating loudly while a barnlike structure stood behind them. It should have been a peaceful place, the type of place an eremite might find his longed-for seclusion. Yet this was where the screams had come from.

Dropping from her horse, she checked the position of her bow on her back, then placed her ax between her hands and trod quietly toward the house. There was no rhythm to her pulse. No pounding in her heart. Just slow, considered steps. Whatever was happening behind the walls, she would end it.

The screaming now sounded different to that first call she had heard. Younger, perhaps, or more desperate. As much as she prayed she was wrong, she knew what she was going to see when she stepped inside the building. A young girl was pinned up against one of the whitewashed walls, held in place by two men while a third was in the center. The girl writhed and screamed, kicking out as she tried to escape the men's grasps. But there was nowhere for her to go. She must have known that, Penthesilea thought to herself, her mind momentarily distracted. And yet, still, she fought.

Without further hesitation, Penthesilea pulled an arrow from her quiver and slung the bow in front of her as easily as one might shrug their shoulder. The weapon fell into place, the arrow nocked before she had even taken a breath. Then, without moving her feet, she shot straight. The man in the center, the one inflicting his body upon the girl, fell first. He slumped forward and onto the girl, whose screams had reached a new crescendo. As the second man turned to face the Amazon, he, too, received an arrow straight though his chest. The third managed to open his mouth as if to form a question before he, too, fell.

Two more men came running from the back the house, knives in their hands, shock and anger written across their faces as they jabbed at the air with their feeble weapons, still clinging to bags jangling with what they had ransacked from this place. Silver and gems spilled onto the ground when she took her ax and sliced through their bellies. These were not soldiers. They wore no breastplates, no protection, and the softness of their flesh parted as though it were milk. With all five down, Penthesilea moved to retrieve her arrows from the first three.

The young girl was still pinned against the wall by the body of her assailant, a man who looked to be five times her age and covered in more hair than a bear. The girl grunted as she pushed with all might, attempting to free herself.

"My sister," she wheezed, still gasping for air. "Inside the barn. A man, he took my sister into the barn."

FORTY-FIVE

As the girl dropped onto her knees, retching and weeping, Penthesilea twisted on her heel and sprinted out of the house. Her footsteps were long, and she sprang over the wall that had penned the goats as easily as if it were a crack between flagstones.

The doors to the barn were open, and the young girl inside had already been forced to the ground, the man on top of her grunting as he thrust. Even from a distance Penthesilea could smell the wine, thick on his breath, so strong it could have been seeping from his skin.

This time she did not use her bow but brought her ax clean down on his neck, one swift motion penetrating down the length of his spine. Blood sprayed outward as he toppled onto the young woman beneath him, his entire weight falling on her chest. There was no grunting now. No thrusting. Nothing but the spilling of blood. With one hard kick Penthesilea pushed him off the child beneath.

Her lips were split and bleeding, straw and dirt in her hair, and her right eye was swollen so badly it was nearly closed. Already the bruising had begun to purple.

"Calista!" The elder sister ran in. She dropped to the stone floors, pulling the younger child, Calista, inward and enfolding her within her arms. Together, the pair sobbed.

Sisters. Penthesilea had known that, of course. That was what eldest had said. That her sister was here. And yet seeing the pair in such an embrace brought an image to her mind. It was so similar. The pair on the ground. The tight embrace. The bloodied bodies. And yet these two were both alive, and her sister was not.

The humidity increased. The air thickened, and the wheezing that had moment ago afflicted the eldest daughter had somehow relocated itself to Penthesilea. She needed air. Cold air. She had to be on her horse again and galloping away from here. But as she turned to leave, a voice called her back.

"Please, wait." The elder girl was back on her feet. "Thank you. They would have...they would have killed us. Please, our brother... Our mother... We... They...they are gone." The girl's breath juddered, catching and hitching as if the air were being stolen from her each time she went to use it. After a moment, she found her voice again.

"Stay with us," she said. "Please. There may be more. They may come back."

"They will not come back."

"We do not know that. There have been others before. But my father, he has always seen them off. Please, they may come back."

"Where is your father, now?" Penthesilea asked. "Is there a man in the house to protect you?" Hearing these words in her own voice, as if a man would be the only source of protection, made her want to vomit, but she could see from the paleness of the girls' skin, and the lack of callouses on their palms, that they were not the type to have wielded hoes or trowels, much less swords or spears. A farm in this condition, with silver accumulated in such high quantities, would likely mean their father would be planning on securing a good dowry for them, if he had not done so already. No, they would not know how to fight.

"My father and our other brother have taken a trip to Dodona. They will not return for another week at least. Please, please stay with us. We have money. Silver we can give you. And food. Please. Please. Anything you ask. You can take anything you wish."

The girl's hands were pressed together, her fingers pinching her top lip, unable to stem the tremors while the younger sibling clung to her robes, incapable of uttering any intelligible sound.

"You should be able to protect yourself," Penthesilea said, and turned away. She had made it only two steps when the girl grabbed her by the back of her tunic, jerking her toward her.

It was an impulse reaction. Penthesilea spun around, cutting the ax through the air, her muscles flexing tight, acting purely on reflex. For months there had been no training, no drills in which they had to stop before they went too far. It had been a blow to kill, or not at all. The ax split the air as it whistled toward the young girl. The blade edge touched the skin on her neck, and Penthesilea saw the child in front of her, her eyes wide and shining. Unblinking at the death that hung millimeters away from her.

"Please," her hoarse voice croaked. "Please, teach us."

Blood pounded through Penthesilea's veins. The heat, burning up through her chest and arms and all the way to her fingertips. How was it a girl could be like this? So weak? So unable to defend herself? And yet—she had not blinked at Penthesilea's ax.

"I am not a teacher," Penthesilea said. Turning again. But the girl was scrambling forward, blocking her exit from the barn. Her nails, already broken and pleading, clung to the Amazon's tunic. "Please, just teach us something. Anything. If they come back, we will not survive."

"Survival is not always the gift you believe it to be." Penthesilea yanked her tunic so that the girl dropped to the ground, finally defeated.

Without her willing them to, Penthesilea's eyes returned to the younger child, who stared solely and intently back at the Amazon, as unblinking as her sister had been. Their eyes met, a matched darkness swirling within them.

"I am sorry. As I have already told you, I am no teacher." Shifting her gaze down, Penthesilea strode past them and out into the open, plucking a lime from a tree before mounting her horse and riding on.

She traveled for half a day, barely noting the position of the sun, allowing her horse to make as many of the decisions as to which path they took as she did. For the first time since leaving Attica, her thoughts were not fixated on Hippolyte, and the images in her mind were not solely those of the arrow piercing her beloved sister. For now, she had another distraction. Calista. The younger of the two sisters. The name of the eldest, she did not know. The girl who had fought those men with teeth and claw, as if she were a caged animal. The girl who had thought only of her sister upon her freedom. No matter how much Penthesilea tried to distract herself, her mind refused to be steered away from them. Her brother and mother were already dead. Those young girls would have to deal with their bodies. And the bodies of the men who had come for them.

If more returned, they would not survive. It would be worse; they would be made to pay for what they had done. For what she had done. The gurgling of a river caught her attention, and, in one of her first conscious acts since leaving the farm, Penthesilea steered the horse toward it, suddenly grateful that this gift had come when her flask was near empty and the sun about to claim its highest point in the sky.

The river she had found was smaller than she had expected, more of a brook, with a rocky bed that caused the water to foam white. As narrow as it was, it was deep and fast moving, and icy cold as she scooped up a handful and held it to her mouth. Beside her, her horse pursed its lips, siphoning in all it needed to quench its thirst. Then momentarily, it closed its eyes. For a while they stayed there, the babbling of the water and the birdsong above them almost sufficient to drown out Penthesilea's thoughts.

There was nothing special about these girls, she reminded herself. They were not royalty, gentry. They were likely to be married off in the next year or so and produce more girls, exactly like them. Weak. Feeble. More young women who did not know how to hold a knife or defend themselves. And Penthesilea could hardly save them all. Hardly teach them all. Besides, most of them did not want to know.

But these girls did. These girls did want her help, and these two she could save.

She waited a short while longer, until her horse taken its second drink, then filled up her canteen and rode with a destination in mind for the first time in days.

———

At the farm, it was as if time had stopped the moment she left, although the bodies of the men she had killed now buzzed with flies, their hands splayed out at the same angles they had been in when she had ended their lives. The scent of death was ripening. Still just a shallow hum, but soon it would be a fetid backdrop to the smell of the farmland around them.

This time, Penthesilea saw the mother and brother that had been spoken of. Tucked in a corner of the room, they were younger than she had expected, and the mother had marks on her hands and across her arms. Downward slices where she had tried to block the men's blows and protect her child. It had been an admirable death, Penthesilea thought.

Among all the bodies, though, she could see nothing of Calista and her sister. They had certainly made no attempt to clear up the mess and prepare the bodies for burial, although perhaps they did not know how. Deciding to check the barn, Penthesilea had turned to leave when a small sound, no louder than the squeaking of a mouse, made her stop and turn. There against the wall she saw it. A wooden door, the joinery so fine it was near invisible. A pantry, most likely.

Slowly she stepped toward it.

She could feel it, the fear that radiating from behind that little door, the atmosphere so tense, it was as if it were straining to keep the whole world still. She stepped forward again, hearing the creak of her footsteps on the ground beneath her.

When she pulled on the door, her heart sank. The two were pushed as close to the wall as possible. The youngest, Calista, was sitting behind her sister, whimpering with her arms wrapped around her knees as she rocked back and forth. The elder girl was on her feet, a small blunt blade in her hands. In the dark light, her pupils were so wide they offered no color at all. Her hands trembled and the knife wavered so wildly it was a miracle she managed to hold it at all. When she saw Penthesilea, she dropped to her knees and buried her head in her hands.

"I will stay for one night, that is all." Penthesilea said. "And if you do not listen to what I have to say, I will leave you before then."

FORTY-SIX

TIME AT THE FARMHOUSE SLIPPED AWAY FASTER THAN SHE would have imagined, and the act of being busy, the simple fact of having a purpose, kept her mind moving in ways she had not known she needed.

On the first day, there was no training after all. The younger girl, Calista, had to be coaxed from the cupboard. She might have been small, but she dug her heels into the stone floors as if they were thick clay, and she gripped at the wooden shelves until the splinters ripped at her skin. She stank of urine and had soiled herself. She reminded Penthesilea of a dog. A puppy. A runt of the litter, who until this point had done nothing but lie listlessly by its mother's teat and refuse to eat. The moment the owner decided that a dip in a river inside a hessian bag would be the kindest course of action, the runt found its strength and refused to go without a fight.

Had a girl behaved in such a manner back in Themiscyra, Penthesilea would have dragged her from the cupboard and thrown her to the ground. She would have forced her to clean up her mess, to apologize to those she had inconvenienced, and then she would have been set about training her harder than ever. But here there was none of that. And probably deservingly so. The training for the Amazon women was tough, but it was tough so that they never had to experience what Calista had already endured.

Her elder sister, Aikaterini, crouched on the ground in front of her, murmuring sweet comforting words, but still she refused to move. She stared out at the light of the main building, shivering, the scratch marks on the tiles a cruel reminder of what the men had tried to do to her.

So while Aikaterini continued to coax her sister from the pantry, Penthesilea used her time removing the bodies from the house. The men, she burned. No coins in their mouths. No treasures to take with them to the underworld or to pay Charon to row them across the Styx. They deserved none of that. Rather, she left their bodies to smolder, burn, and sizzle, filling the air with the scent of charred meat.

The mother and the younger brother they buried in an orchard of peaches and fig trees just before sunset, after Aikaterini had finally coaxed Calista from the cupboard. The canopy of leaves scattered the amber light into tiny shards, building a mosaic on the ground. The pair had collected some of their favorite of items to go with them: a small handheld mirror with a twisted silver handle for the mother, and a bone comb carved with a delicate pattern of hares. For the young boy, a toy horse, carved rustically from wood.

Burials had once been a rarity for Penthesilea. Now they were more commonplace than sunsets.

As the evening sun disappeared behind the rolling hills, she saw that the young girls were in no fit state to learn anything. Pale and limp with exhaustion, Aikaterini had, upon Penthesilea's advice, filled a bowl with warm water and salt, to bathe Calista's hands and draw the splinters. She had found clean linen to press on the skin. Several small fragments of wood remained, buried deep in the soft pads of her hand, but she had removed the worst of it. As well as any of her young girls would, Penthesilea considered.

With the hands cleaned and wrapped, Aikaterini gave each of them a small meal of goat's cheese and bread, which she prepared under the light of single lamp placed low to the ground. It was a sensible decision, to make the glare of their presence less obvious, and Penthesilea wondered whether she had been taught such a thing, or if it had been intuition.

She had not cried, Penthesilea realized, as Aikaterini fell asleep upright, her arms still around her sister as she fought the tiredness and strained to stay awake. She had not panicked, or retched, or refused to touch the dead men. She had not complained as she mopped blood from the ground or changed her sister's soiled clothes. In another time or place, she would have made a fierce Amazon, Penthesilea thought, but even thinking of the Amazons brought the pain sharply back, and she stood, snuffing out the rage as best she could. Outside, the night was as quiet as she had known. No winds rustled the trees, and the tinkling of the fountain was the only accompaniment to her footsteps across the courtyard. She had tied her horse to a tree close to the barn where it could feast on the same hay that had been left for the goats, but now she reflected that it would be best to keep it closer to the house. After all, she had spotted few horses on her journey. To lose him would cost her immeasurably.

"Don't eat too much while you are here," she whispered to it as she worked the knots in the rope and led it back toward the house. "I do not want you to become accustomed to this life."

The horse whinnied and nuzzled her, as if it knew what she was saying, and Penthesilea felt a sad smile falter on her lips.

"This is better," she said, and tied him to a post directly in front of the door. With a final stroke across its broad cheeks, she took the steps back up to the house only to find herself face-to-face with Aikaterini, brandishing a knife.

"You said you would not go anywhere. You said I was safe."

"You are safe. I was checking on my horse," Penthesilea said. Still the weapon remained raised. Gently, Penthesilea wrapped her hand around the girl's forearm, close to the wrist, feeling the tremble resonating through the fragile bones. "I will not go anywhere," Penthesilea whispered again. "You can sleep now. You are safe."

For all that she had kept the tears at bay until then, sleep brought terror back to Aikaterini's mind. Listening to the girl's whimpers and mews, Penthesilea found herself wishing she had paid more attention to the sleeping draughts her women had concocted in Themiscyra. As things were, there was nothing she could do other than keep her promise. To stay.

When morning arrived, the silence of the night was replaced with a cacophony. While the sea was too distant to be heard behind so many hills and trees, the goats bleated loudly, demanding their morning feed, and chickens she had not seen the previous day had entered the house, where their feet scraped loudly on the stone floors.

"You will teach us, now?"

Aikaterini was awake when Penthesilea stretched out in the chair. She had slept well, considering. Perhaps it was the four stone walls that offered a security she had not experienced for so long. Perhaps it was the fact that she knew she would be able to handle whatever came through the doors. Aikaterini, by contrast, looked even more tired than she had before they had slept. Her skin was blotchy, and her lips were cracked and bleeding, yet it was the furrow between her eyes that aged her by a decade.

"You are in no fit state for me to train you," Penthesilea said. "You will injure yourself."

"You promised!" Aikaterini was on her feet. How was it possible that a girl could be so thin? So frail? No muscle on her legs or chest. No strength in her arms. Her ribs all too visible. It seemed inconceivable that anyone could survive past infancy in such a state, and yet there she was, standing up to the Amazon queen as none had dared before and hoped to live. Not that she had any idea to whom she was speaking. Perhaps, Penthesilea thought, she should tell her. Perhaps that would change matters.

"I am stronger than I look," Aikaterini replied, noting Penthesilea's look. "I help my brother and father on the farm. I milk the goats. I carry water. Please. You promised."

On the mattress, Calista was turning and twisting, half gripped by shallow tides of sleep. Her hands were still red.

"I know who you are," Aikaterini whispered quietly.

Penthesilea shifted. "What do you mean?"

"You wear trousers. You ride a horse with a cloth on his back. And you shoot arrows from your bow better than any man and any army. It is not hard to see who you are. You are an Amazon."

Penthesilea twisted her lips together, an impulse to deny everything rolling through her, which filled her once more with self-loathing. Never had she wished to deny who she was. Never had she considered denying her heritage, her parentage, the calling that made her stand above all others. And yet there she was, hesitating to respond to this girl. It was for their safety, she tried to convince herself. It was for Aikaterini and Calista. It was safer that they did not know who she was, given all the enemies she had made.

"I am a warrior of sorts," she said. "But you are not. And I will not be able to teach you. You are too old to learn."

"How do you know you will not be able to teach me if you do not try?" the girl responded.

FORTY-SEVEN

THEY MOVED OUTSIDE. DESPITE AIKATERINI'S BEST EFFORTS, the floor inside was still tacky with blood. Besides, outside offered more room and fewer memories.

If she had had more time, Penthesilea thought, she would have taught them to make their own weapons, the way the young Amazon girls did. After all, a poorly constructed knife that broke under pressure could cause more harm than good when trying to defend oneself. But instead, she asked them to seek out what they had. Knives for skinning rabbits or peeling vegetables. Those that her father used when sacrificing goats to the gods.

"You are aiming to kill," Penthesilea said. "You must think of nothing else. You must always be trying to cause your opponent as much harm as possible. Because that is what they wish to do to you. Now, you are short and light and should be swift on your feet. You need to use that to your advantage. You aim here"—she pointed to the soft pouch of flesh under her jaw, nicely within their reach— "and here." She drew a line across the belly. "Soft areas only. You do not have enough strength to break ribs, and your weapons are not made for it. The neck is a good spot, too. But you want to attack from the front if you can. The back will be harder for you to cause sufficient damage."

Calista sat on a nearby rock. The chickens that had invaded the house that morning had gathered around her, and she threw them seeds that she pulled from nearby sunflowers and watched vacantly as they pecked at the ground by her feet. Her bottom lip slanted as she bit down on one side, exaggerating the lopsidedness of her face that the swelling had caused. Periodically, she would cock her head or tilt an ear toward the house as if she had heard a noise from inside. She would stay like that for a moment before returning to the animals, seemingly oblivious to Penthesilea and her sister.

In contrast, Aikaterini hung on every word Penthesilea said. Barely blinking, she absorbed every sentence as if it were a blessing from the gods. Despite her size, she mimicked the actions of the Amazon, a miniature mirror to the mighty warrior queen. Her legs were black and bruised, the insides of her thighs scratched and red, yet she did not flinch. Did not complain.

"I can do better," she said, as she stabbed into the air, only for Penthesilea to knock her arm to the side as easily as if it were a crisp brown leaf ready to be separated from its branch. "Try me again. Try again."

The Amazon stepped backward, noting that Calista had moved and was now staring absentmindedly up at an orange tree.

"You have done enough," Penthesilea told her. "Your body is not used to this. Your muscles will be sore tomorrow."

"It is only midday. I want to learn more. There is more I need to know."

"That may be so. But if you wake tomorrow and your hands have been worked so hard they cannot even grip a broom, how will you protect yourself? Part of being a warrior is learning when you need to fight and when you need to rest. And now, you need to rest."

More words teetered on the tip of the girl's tongue before she pressed her lips tightly together and nodded rapidly.

That evening she ate. Eggs, boiled in water. Milk and cheese from the goats. Penthesilea watched on with a slight sense of pride. Pride that evaporated the moment she shifted her gaze from Aikaterini to Calista, who had huddled herself in the mattress, which once again reeked of fresh urine.

"Do you think she will speak again?" Aikaterini asked softly. "It has only been one day. She will speak again, won't she?"

Penthesilea switched her gaze from one child to another. False hope was something she had rarely been forced to bestow, so she tried to imagine instead the words that Cletes would offer in such a situation.

"Like you say, it has only been a day. She will need time. And the young are resilient. More resilient than many older people are."

Aikaterini nodded hastily, approving of this answer.

"Perhaps tomorrow she will train with us, too. I will ask her. She is strong, you know. Stronger than me. She will be good. You will see."

Seized by a new spirit of optimism, Aikaterini rolled her egg, cracking the shell before peeling away the broken fragments. Yet it was an optimism Penthesilea knew she must extinguish.

"I will stay with you a second night, but I will have to leave in the morning."

Aikaterini stopped peeling.

"But we need more help."

"I have given you help. More than anyone outside my family has ever received from me."

The egg rested in the palm of the girl's hand, the center still soft, oozing slowly onto the plate beneath her.

"What if they come back?"

"They cannot return. I have killed them, remember?"

"But there may be others." Her voice was panicked and high, the composure that she had shown while training draining away. "There may be others."

"And you know how to defend yourselves now. Trust me. You showed skill. And you have a thirst to ensure that no man takes advantage of you again. Besides, your father will return in just a few days."

"Please..." Her voice warbled. Those tears that had been kept in check now welled in her eyes. "Please."

"You have my answer. You will fight for yourself and live, or you will not." The harshness in Penthesilea's tone took even her by surprise. Aikaterini recoiled, her lower lip trembling. Leaving the egg on the plate, she fixed her gaze on the queen as she shrank back from the table and joined her sister on the damp, urine-soaked bed.

That night, her own words echoed in Penthesilea's head together with the look on Aikaterini's face and the disappointment that radiated from her. She could not face that again, and so once the pair had fallen back into fitful sleep Penthesilea slipped outside, mounted her horse, and pushed her heels into his flanks. Outside a cascade of stars spanned the sky, illuminating it with the vibrancy of ten thousand lamps. It was time she moved on. She had already stayed too long.

———

She sought out first one battle, then another. Any size and clan or tribe or king, it did not matter. The larger the war, the better. She arrived fresh from one fight, the sweat still slick on her horse's coat, and joined the next, always choosing the smaller army to fight with. That was her only condition, that she be outnumbered, and the greater the disadvantage, the better. She was never outnumbered for long. It was just as it had always been, her arrows unstoppable, her ax unforgiving. More than once, she changed alliances partway through a battle in the hope that, if both sides combined to defeat her, they might succeed. But they never did. She left every battle standing.

She had to die on the battlefield. She knew that. The death that had come to both her sisters was the death that she sought. And yet it evaded her at every turn.

She knew it would need to be a true fight, one where she was honestly bested in the art of war, but her mind puzzled as to where a daughter of Ares might find such a thing. Even in Athens, it had not been Theseus or any of his men who had managed to best Hippolyte. It had been her. And who was left that rivaled her? Melanippe? Not even her, that was the truth of it. Melanippe had her strengths, but Penthesilea's superiority with ax and bow meant she would defeat her sister in any true trial. Besides, Melanippe would not fight her. She knew that. And so Penthesilea continued riding.

With the changing of the seasons and the rise and fall of the tides, months and then years passed. Her horses had been changed, her tunic and boots restitched, and she rode further north than she had ever ventured before. She traveled to lands where the snow buried her horse to its knees, and the air was so cold it formed a cloud with every breath. She traveled to towns and cities beside lakes, with walls that looked impenetrable. To citadels defended by moats, deep and cavernous. And in each of these places she fought. Again and again, she fought, never receiving so much as a scratch to the arm.

At some point, she realized she no longer cared which direction she was heading. She returned to her old habit of following the clear skies, turning south or west, or whichever course allowed her to evade the rain. She traversed mountain ridges, waded through deep

ravines, and tasted fruits both sweeter and tarter than she had ever
before encountered.

To those that asked, she answered that she was from Thrace. A
nomad all her life. Yes, she told them, she knew of the Amazons,
they were legends, but no, she was not one of them. Once a nomad
had called out her name, "Queen Penthesilea," suspecting her true
identity, but Penthesilea had laughed and changed the subject, before
thanking her for her hospitality and continuing on her way. Year
after year she continued in such a manner, but it did not matter
where she went; death would not meet her.

The day she saw it, the air was rich with freshly burst pollen and
the irresistible tang of spring. The grasses had been growing steadily
more verdant. Thick and luminous with dew, they rippled like waves
across the water. In contrast, the sea was a perfectly unwrinkled
plane, and seabirds sat upon their own shadows, bobbing gently to
the lull of the waves.

Deep down she had always known it was coming. She had been
traveling east for several weeks, watching as the sky expanded and the
hills softened to a gentle roll. The horse she was riding was a dapple
gray, given to her as payment for a battle well fought and won on the
borders of Macedonia. The king there had stood with his queen at
his side, although Penthesilea had averted her gaze and looked only
upon the man. The looseness of the woman's robes, and the flowers
that garnished her hair, reminded her too much of that first time she
had seen Hippolyte in Athens. The king had offered various rewards
for her efforts, including gold and gems and even men or women for
her use if she wanted. But the metals and stone weighed down her
saddlebags, and she had no desire for any of the men or women that
had been offered, so she took only the horse.

He was larger than those she usually rode, his legs thick and cumbersome, but what he lacked in agility, he made up for in strength and fearlessness. Not once in the battles that she had fought upon him, did he rear or shy away, or even flinch at an oncoming spear. His pace, whether a canter or gallop, was steady and rhythmic, allowing her the flexibility to twist and shoot her arrows, knowing he would remain sure of foot. They had built a relationship that should have taken years to form but had somehow been there from the beginning, and he rode into battle just as she did: as if it were his very purpose.

But she did not name him. She could not bring herself to do so. Not when she knew that one day he, too, would leave her.

As the wind teased the stray hairs from her cap, she stood upon the steppes and gazed out at the citadel beneath her. It was smaller than so many she had encountered on her travels, and even from this distance, she could see the simplicity of the place. But it was hers. It was home.

It was Themiscyra.

The quietness struck her out on the steppes. Where were the clangs of metal? The angry shouts of the women training? Where were the whistles of arrows as they flew to meet a target, the shrieks of children, and the whinnies of the horses, so vast in their numbers that their aroma should have hung thick in the air? Where were the Amazons?

Had they been attacked? she wondered as she stared up at the walls before turning her attention out to sea. There were no ships. No invading armies, now, at least. And none of the kingdoms through which she had ridden had spoken of war in Pontus. The sea remained perfectly still, as if it were holding its breath, waiting for her, and it knew, just as she knew, that the slightest ripple might cause her to dig into her horse's flank and gallop away.

But she did not. She dismounted, rubbing her hand against her horse's neck as, footstep by footstep, she led him on a single rope up the twisted stone path to Themiscyra.

FORTY-EIGHT

THEY SAT OPPOSITE EACH OTHER. THREE SMALL LAMPS CAST shadows, which gathered in the corners of the room. Once, a room this size would have been lit by a dozen lamps. Now there were only three.

Melanippe was seated in a chair, her hair loose around her shoulders. Creases folded themselves into her skin, sweeping upward and across her brow. She was the youngest of them. The one who had shown what seemed like endless energy, eternal youth. If this was what Melanippe looked like, Penthesilea dreaded to think of her own reflection. She had not seen it in so long. Perhaps it would be best if she continued to avoid mirrors.

"You look tired," Melanippe said. "But strong. You have been fighting."

There was no question. The words hung between them in the musty humidity. Had Themiscyra always been so humid, Penthesilea asked herself, feeling her back beginning to grow clammy. Perhaps it was the time spent north that had made her more susceptible to such heat.

"I have fought a little," she responded.

Melanippe only nodded. Where was the young girl that spoke constantly, Penthesilea wanted to ask. The one who could fill any silence with her words. That girl was gone, now, Penthesilea realized. In her place a woman. A queen. And an aging one. The pauses between each question expanded.

"And what now?" Melanippe asked. "Are you planning on staying here? Planning on ruling?"

Penthesilea swallowed forcefully. The humidity that had drawn the moisture from her skin now dried her thoughts, and her tongue with them. She had known the question would come, and still felt unprepared. After all, she had no answer to give. So instead, she did as she had grown accustomed to doing, and diverted the attention elsewhere.

"Have you visited the Gargareans recently?" she asked. "I could not hear any children when I approached."

A hard light shone in Melanippe's eyes; she knew exactly what game Penthesilea was playing. And yet she answered her question all the same.

"I decided we should stay in Pontus for now. There are too many risks. Should we be attacked, our numbers are not great enough to defend ourselves. Besides, the Gargareans..." She allowed her sentence to fade, and for a moment, Penthesilea wondered how it might have ended. With a sickening shame, she realized. They did not want to meet with the Amazons. Not now. Not after they had lost so many of their women. Not after they had lost their queen and one of their princesses. Not after they had proven themselves weak.

"They think we have lost favor with Father." Melanippe said, suddenly. "Do you think it is true? Do you think we have lost his favor? Because I have tried. I promise I have tried."

HANNAH LYNN

In that moment the mask fell. The old woman in front of her was still that same younger sibling, in need of Penthesilea's assurance. And Penthesilea had no comfort she could give her. No way to ease the burden she shouldered.

"We are still alive," Penthesilea said, although her bitterness laced the words more harshly than she intended. "Have you been sacrificing to him?"

"Of course. Have you not?"

Penthesilea turned her eyes toward the lamp. The flame had grown. Bolstered by a breeze, it spread, its amber tongues licking upward.

"No," she said. "I have not. Not for some time."

She expected the confession to ignite a gasp of incomprehension from her younger sister. But instead, all she received was a simple nod of the head.

"Cletes is still here. She has taken a room on the north tower. Facing the sea. I am certain she would like to see you before you leave again."

It was the first hint of animosity she had experienced since her arrival, although now it had been loosed, its presence could no longer be contained. "We know what you have been doing, sister. We know that you have been fighting battles on your own. And we know why. You believe you have a better chance of victory without us by your side."

Penthesilea's jaw dropped.

"That is not why I fight on my own."

"It is not? Why, then? You have good women here. Strong women here, who fought by your side in Athens, and left with their lives."

"I know that."

"Then why did you not call upon us. Upon me?" There was a hardness to her sister's voice. A hardness where most people would show tears. But she did not cry. She had nothing left to cry for.

370

"I...I needed to be alone,"

"For seven years?" Melanippe rose, the gust of wind from her movement setting the shadows whirling on the walls behind her.

"I did not realize it had been so long," Penthesilea lied, with a feebleness she knew her sister could see straight through. Of course she knew how long it had been. She had watched the seasons change, watched the caps of the mountains turn white and watched as that whiteness sunk lower and lower until it covered the ground she stood upon, before retreating again, replaced with the kaleidoscope of spring. Yes, she knew that she had suffered from more than one scorching summer sun, and more than one frozen winter. But still, was it really that long since Hippolyte had died in her arms? How was it possible that so much time had passed, when she could still see the light leaving her sister's eyes?

She straightened her back, preparing to stand. "It is best that I go. I can see I have no place here."

Before she could rise to her feet, Melanippe had crossed the room. Towering over her, her teeth tightly gritted as she spoke.

"You have no place here because you chose to have no place here. Because you chose to leave your women when they needed you the most. You chose to leave me when my other sisters had no choice. You are the one who decided to do this, Penthesilea. No one else. Now, if you are leaving, please do so. I have crops to think about and grain to store and more than just your ego to attend to."

Penthesilea left the citadel and headed north, to gaze upon that beach where Theseus had first arrived with Heracles. She found herself turning over the same thought she had turned over a thousand times. How much suffering and death might have been saved if she had ended his life on this very beach, all that time ago?

The moon was a thin crescent, reflected perfectly on the surface of the sea. She could wade out into the water, she considered. Offer herself to Poseidon. But why? He would not want her any more than her father or any of the other gods did. And so, she simply stood.

The sea had begun to move a little, flurries of white foam distorting the image of the moon, when a voice cut through the darkness behind her.

"You have been out here for quite some time. Some may think you are waiting for something."

Penthesilea closed her eyes and squeezed them tight, as if doing so might keep the voice beside her. She had heard that voice in her sleep. Heard it call across the battlefields, only for the vision to evaporate the second she drew near. She had seen her, too, in those same fields, a glimpse of black hair between raised spears.

"Cletes," she said, softly.

"So, do you care to tell me what it is you are waiting for? For if it is a boat, you may find yourself out of luck. I believe they only stop here once every ten years or so."

She could not turn. Could not face seeing her, yet she could still picture the small smile curving her lips as she waited for Penthesilea to reply to her joke. And in spite of herself, Penthesilea felt a single gruff laugh force its way from her throat.

"No. No boats for me," she said.

"Good, I am glad that as least some things have not changed."

In years past, the pair had shared so many silences. Silences together, as they lay under their bivouacs, staring up at the night sky, watching the stars and the moon sweep across the horizon. They had shared silences in death. In the burials of their women after battles. Cletes was someone Penthesilea could speak to, away from her sisters. Someone she knew would never judge her. And yet at that moment, she felt judged.

She wished she could think of words to say, words to fill the void that had been cast between them, but there was nothing, bar the soft lapping of the waves as they rolled up onto the shore, then back down to lose themselves in the waters.

"I know what you have been doing," Cletes said, stepping forward and taking her by her hand from behind. "I know what you have been hoping to achieve. We have heard of the battles you have taken upon yourself. Alone, against hundreds and hundreds."

"I have been fighting. That is what we do. That is what I was born to do."

"No, you have been trying to get yourself killed. You know, I heard one rumor that you went into battle without even a breastplate upon you. Is that true?"

Penthesilea kept her eyes fixed on the moon. She had thought little of all the rumors that had reached Themiscyra when she had lived here. It was how they gained work and learned of the kings who were likely to be in need of their assistance. But, now, the rumors shared in whispers behind the citadel walls were about her. Whispers that changed things.

"The breastplate was damaged. I did not have time to fix it," she said. Offering an answer as close to the truth as she could. Cletes would not believe her, though. She knew that.

"There is not a woman in our army that you would allow to ride into battle in such a state. You have been reckless."

Penthesilea wished that she could refute this claim. Defend herself. Find her sharpened tongue and insist that Cletes did not know of what she was speaking. But she could not. Not to Cletes. She could find no other words, nothing except the truth.

"I deserve to die, Cletes. You know this. I deserve to die for what I have done. I cannot endure living like this, and yet death will not greet me. What do I do? What do I do?"

The strength in her knees vanished, and she dropped to the ground, but Cletes was already there, pressing her hand to Penthesilea's shoulder. All this time, and her scent had not changed at all. That sweetness of pomegranate, that deep muskiness of the earth. She would recognize that scent anyway, Penthesilea thought, as she drew in the deepest breath her lungs could hold. Perhaps this would be it. Perhaps the gods were granting her one last night with Cletes before they took her.

Wordlessly, Cletes lifted her hand to Penthesilea's chin and raised it, so that their eyes met. There was so much softness in her eyes. Melanippe's gaze might have hardened during the years of her absence, but the light in Cletes's burned as bright as it always had.

"I think there is somewhere we can go," she said. "Someone that we can see who could help you."

FORTY-NINE

S O MANY YEARS HAD PASSED SINCE HERACLES'S ARRIVAL AT THEIR
shores, the details had faded in Penthesilea's mind. She
remembered the most important facts, however. He had come
into their home, he had taken Hippolyte's zoster, and he brought
with him Theseus, the man who had destroyed them all. That was
enough. But Cletes remembered the smaller, finer details of those
days. Not only what Heracles had done, but what he had said. The
reason for his arrival on their shores. It was to seek purification and
redemption for killing his wife and child. And it had been a king
who had granted him this.

"It is a gift the gods bestow on the kings, to grant absolution for
such acts. This could be your way. Ask a king for purification. He
will set you tasks, and once they are completed, you will be cleansed."

"But if it was Apollo that sent him to King Eurystheus, I need
a god to come forward and allow my cleansing. None have been
forthcoming. I have been to temples. I have asked for forgiveness."

"But you have not spoken to a king regarding the matter.
Perhaps you must seek someone whose knowledge is greater than

ours. We tend not to require purification for our killings." Once again, there was that same toying smile, a smile that only hours ago would have drawn Penthesilea in, and have seen her placing her lips against Cletes with the hope of never again removing them. But, now, her thoughts were stirring. Was it truly possible that she could be absolved in such a manner?

They sat only a short while longer on the beach, watching the dark silhouette of an eagle cross the moon, before Penthesilea's impatience got the better of her.

"I should go; I should speak this through with Melanippe. If what you say is possible, then I should leave as soon as I can."

Still seated on the ground, Cletes rose slowly. She was barefoot, Penthesilea now noticed, and a new tattoo coiled up over the arch of her foot and toward her ankle.

"I understand you wish for answers," Cletes said softly, "but even if you do not need sleep, Melanippe does. Come, spend the night beside me. You can go to her at first light."

Seven years, and no one had laid so much as a hand against her body. Any softness Penthesilea had once possessed had hardened. Her skin was looser, sullied by the elements. But Cletes looked upon her as she always had. As if she were a gift.

"You have been missed, my queen."

"Don't—" Penthesilea began, but Cletes pushed a finger against her lips.

"You will leave again soon. We do not have time to waste with words."

———

She woke with the first light. She had forgotten, on her travels, the strength with which the sun cut across the horizon in Pontus, and the manner in which the sky would transform from deep blue to burning umber in the span of a heartbeat. She had forgotten how intense the song of the birds could be as they fluttered in the rafters and made nests between the tiles in the rooftop. She had forgotten, because she had forced herself to forget. Because remembering was unbearable. And now she would have to forget it all again.

It was not only in her looks that Melanippe had changed. Now, she was up well before dawn, and, after a brief time scouring the building, Penthesilea found her down with the horses. One of the animals was resting its knee in her hand, its leg crooked at an angle as she chipped clods of mud out from its hoof with a small hook.

"Sister," Penthesilea bowed her head a little as she spoke. "May I talk with you?"

Melanippe's head remained down. The horse waited patiently, using its tail as a whip to flick the flies from its back.

"I have to finish this first." Melanippe replied. "Two horses have become lame in the last week alone."

"I understand." Penthesilea tightened at the coldness she knew she deserved and stepped back, feeling herself shrink by a fraction. Still bent over, Melanippe continued to chip out the mud before pausing and looking up at her sister.

"I suspect this will take some time," she said. "Perhaps, though, when I am done, we could eat breakfast together. If you are hungry, that is?"

"Yes," Penthesilea replied hastily. "I am."

———

Melanippe approached every task now with thoughtful consideration, from the cleaning of the horses' hooves to the preparation of breakfast. The same consideration showed again as she rested her chin against the knuckle of her forefinger and contemplated Penthesilea's question. The old Melanippe would have let her thoughts be known immediately, for good or evil, whereas, now, Penthesilea struggled to read her expression at all. The thought made a sadness swell within her. It had been the same with Hippolyte. That change. That inability to read her sister's expression that had cost her her life.

Squeezing her eyes shut, Penthesilea pushed away thoughts of one of her dead sisters and focused instead on the one that still lived.

"So, do you think it is possible? Do you think there is a king that would do such a thing?"

Removing her finger from her chin, Melanippe clasped her hands together. "King Priam," she said.

"King Priam? Of Troy?"

"The very same. He is Thracian, and Father has always favored him. Besides, his wife, Hecuba, hails from Phrygia. It is close to us. If any king is to come to your aid, it would be he. But you need to consider the consequences of what he may ask you to do. Heracles was sent to perform harrowing tasks, remember? The skin of the Nemean lion, Hippolyte's zoster, not to mention his passing into the underworld. Could you perform such deeds?"

"I can face anything other than this guilt," she said honestly. "He can keep me in his house as a concubine if it absolves me of this."

For the first time since Penthesilea's arrival in Themiscyra, a small smile flitted on her sister's face, and for that instant the youthful light returned to her eyes.

"I think Queen Hecuba may have something to say about that," she said. "But you should go, sister. This is what you should do. Perhaps what you should always have done."

Before last night it had been so long since Penthesilea had embraced another person. So long since she had wrapped her arms around them and felt the heat of another body. Melanippe pulled her in close, perhaps closer than they had ever embraced, with her hands pressing against the back of her ribs so firmly it was as if they were one. And when they broke away, Penthesilea felt the absence as keenly as if they were seas apart.

"When will you go?" Melanippe asked.

"Tomorrow morning. Troy is reachable in two days. The sooner I arrive, the better."

"And will you take Cletes with you? We are short of women here. Most of them have taken to life as nomads. They feel safer on the steppes than confined within the citadel. I understand that. But I will need to make some arrangements if she is to go with you."

Penthesilea shook her head. "No, I need to do this alone."

"I understand."

Penthesilea could not count the number of times she had ridden away from Themiscyra. She could not recall the number of times she had looked over her shoulder and seen the walls of the citadel retreating behind her, watching the buildings fade into the haze of heat or blur into rain and clouds. Yet never had she looked at it the way she did on the morning she departed for Troy. Never had she looked at it as if this were the last time she might ever gaze upon those yellowed bricks and the stone laid by her ancestors.

Penthesilea could not imagine what trials King Priam would assign, or if she was even capable of purification, but she knew she would not return to Themiscyra until she found out.

FIFTY

TROY WAS POSITIONED IN NORTHWEST ANATOLIA. DESPITE ITS proximity to Pontus, it was not a place that Penthesilea had ever visited. There had been no need for her to. The Amazons came to kings in need, kings who required protection and faced battles they feared they would lose without the women's help. King Priam was not such a king.

Throughout her travels, she had heard rumors of the citadel, whose fortifications made those of Athens seem paltry by comparison. She heard of vast walls and towering turrets surrounding hectares and hectares of land in which the citizens farmed and worked and lived a life so full there was no need for them ever to leave.

She had heard rumors of the king too, of his humor and virility, and although she could not recall the names of his daughters, she knew that Hecuba had birthed at least one son. One boy, who she assumed would be trained to grow into a formidable warrior. Hector, if she recalled correctly.

At first, she rode slowly, attempting to predict the acts he might assign her. Wondering how long her future would be pledged to this man of whom she knew so little.

A damp drizzle filled the air, growing heavier as she rode further east and toward the coast, and by the time the city had come into view, the sky was leaden with clouds. But dark skies and stormy weather could no nothing to diminish this view.

Athens had taken her breath away and made her reconsider the wonders that man could achieve, but this…this was a marvel worthy of the gods. It was no wonder her father had favored such a place.

The entire city was enclosed within walls of sandstone yellow, thirty feet high, topped with turrets and towers that pierced the clouds, and bristling with armed guards at every point. Her journey should have seen her arrive from the eastern landlocked side, yet she knew that the strongest defenses would be on the west, by the shore, for if anyone were foolish enough to attack Troy, they would come not from Anatolia but across the sea. And so she circled around, to ensure that she was seen. She wanted King Priam to know that she had arrived.

She had taken clothes from Themiscyra. New boots, calf-high and thick-soled. Leather trousers and a tunic with a bright geometric pattern freshly sewn into the fabric, and a new hat that tapered to point; all undeniably Amazonian. She might have hidden her true self from the world for the last seven years, but now she wanted all to know who she was.

As she approached the gates, a great clang of metal rang out, grinding and grating as the massive gate pushed outward, opening not for her to enter, but so that the Trojan men might swarm her. From the moment the gap was large enough, guards raced out, one after another encircling her and her horse, their spears raised and their shields up. When enough men had been released, the gates clanked closed enough. Penthesilea noted the defenses with interest. If this was how they handled one woman, who knew what they would do in a war?

"Who are you?" The soldier who spoke held his spear angled toward her, but the tip quivered, the length of the weapon amplifying the tremor in his hand.

"This display would suggest that you are already aware of who I am," she replied.

The man jabbed his spear toward her. It was a pointless action. Foolish, even, for no man would prod a snake if he did not wish to get bitten, but she was here to withhold her venom. For now, at least.

"Tell King Priam that Queen Penthesilea is here to speak with him."

The man's lips twisted, his Adam's apple rising and falling as the trembling of his spear increased. With a twist of his head, he nodded to two men behind him, who backed away from the circle, leaving a gap that filled again instantly as the circle tightened around her. A moment later the gates reopened, just wide enough for the soldiers to slip inside. *How long would it take the news to reach Priam?* Penthesilea wondered. It might take a man on foot an hour to cross the whole of this citadel, and the palace was sure to be central, high up. She knew she had no choice but to wait.

She shifted slightly on the saddle, her only intent to adjust the weight on her pelvis, but the instant she moved, every spear rose toward her. Even in such a situation, she found the scene comical.

Her horse, for its part, looked somewhat indifferent to the whole display.

"Would it help if I offered you my ax?" she asked.

She posed her question to the soldier who had spoken to her, who now hesitated as if she were setting a trap for him to fall into. He pursed his lips. The detail on his armor implied he had the authority to make such a decision, but he also appeared to have a modicum of common sense. Was accepting an Amazon's offer to take her weapons more or less dangerous than letting her keep them?

"And your bow and arrow, too," he said, eventually.

She dropped the ax to the ground, where it landed with a thud and sent a soft plume of sand rising upward.

"I will need that back when I leave," she said. *If* was the word that had wavered through her mind before she spoke. *If I leave.* And yet her tongue had tripped and chosen *when* instead. Another soldier scampered inward to pick up the ax, but his shoulders slumped forward, surprised by the weight. When he looked back up at Penthesilea, the fear in his eyes had been replaced by a new sense of alarm.

"The bow next."

With a small nod, Penthesilea reached over her shoulder, her fingertips pressing against the warm wood they found there. Cletes had offered her this bow when she left Themiscyra two mornings past. It was newly made, strengthened with bone, and engraved with a pattern of deer and eagles. Cletes had made it for her, she told her, for the day she finally decided to return.

"We will hunt together with it on the steppes," she had said, and Penthesilea had smiled, knowing that they might never do such a thing.

"I will give you my arrows." Penthesilea said to the soldier. "After all, the bow is useless without them."

Her answer was received without grace, the distrust glowed in the men's eyes, but they accepted her offer, and Penthesilea slipped the quiver from her belt and allowed it to fall to the ground.

From there, there was nothing to do but wait.

The length of the beach was immense, and though rocky outcrops rose boldly at either end, the majority of the expanse was deep golden sand, soft and silty, with rounded pebbles scattered closest to the water. A beach this long would be enough to land a thousand ships, should any army ever choose to invade. And for the invader, there would much to gain, for without doubt Troy was in an advantageous position. Trade routes throughout all of Anatolia passed through here to Greece, and as such it was unsurprising that such a fort was required. But, while a thousand ships might land on this shore, the invader would need as many to take their war to Troy, and no king in all of Greece or beyond had such numbers.

The gulls squalled as she waited, and her mind slipped back into its usual train of thought when she found herself surrounded by men with weapons. Where would she strike first? There was, after all, a chance that things could go badly and that Priam would refuse to see her. He might have formed allegiances with Athens she was unaware of, and no matter how much she wished to die, she knew she would not be able to sit there and allow an arrow to strike her heart without a fight. She would need to find a way out. Only then would she be able to die as a warrior, if that was to be the gods' wish.

She would require weapons first, but they need not be her own. The men were foot soldiers, looking to the general for orders, so she would take the leaders out first. By that point, she would be able to reach either her arrows or her ax. After that, she would forge a path leading close to the wall. It would be a foolish tactic for the inexperienced, for those who did not know how to escape when penned in, but for her, it made sense. It was the best way to control a stream of opponents so that they could approach her only from one direction. She would pick them off, one by one, and when the time was right, she would make good her escape on her horse. Priam would not send more soldiers for her. Not knowing how they would end. These would be the sacrificial lambs.

Her mind was still moving through this scenario when the gates parted again, just a sliver, and once more a soldier stepped through.

His face was flushed, an indication of the haste he had employed, although he slowed before he spoke.

"Let her in," he said. "The king will see her now."

FIFTY-ONE

WITHIN THE WALLS, TROY BUZZED WITH LIFE. NOT JUST with buildings and people, but with agriculture. Farmlands. Acres and acres hidden from view, full of crops and animals, not a scrap of land going to waste. Golden wheat reflected the ocher of the stones while goats grazed in the thin, scarred grass that grew under the limited sunlight beneath grapevines that had been twisted high into canopies. Passionflowers burst with color as butterflies flitted between the vibrant petals.

This was an oasis, worthy even of Themiscyra, and her senses were overwhelmed. Walking both behind and in front of her, the soldiers' feet provided a steady thud on the ground. The sun beat down with ferocity, reflecting off every wall and door and elevating ordinarily dull materials, like stone and wood, to the heights of precious metals.

She watched as animals drank from a long trough and looked longingly at their fleshy tongues lapping impatiently at the water. That would be her, if Priam did not offer her a drink upon arrival; she had finished the last of her water that morning.

The deeper into the city she moved, the more condensed the buildings and people became. Men and women bustled through the day, arms jangling with copper bracelets as they traded wares, while children ran about their legs, laughing and taunting stray kittens with dangling pieces of string. Hawkers shouted with booming voices. Animals skipped and scampered in every direction, just as they had in Athens, with chickens tripping underfoot and mice and rats scurrying under doorways and out of sight only to reappear a moment later. The air was rich with aromas of roasted nuts and honeyed fruits. So much life. So much vibrancy.

And all of it faded as Penthesilea approached.

A hush descended. Taut and steely, it spread around her. Men who had been sleeping sat up, rigid, as if woken to find their nightmares a reality. Mothers pulled their children behind their legs, rocking babies, and clutching them close. Even the animals, who had been bleating with such animation, now fell silent. If this was a portent of the greeting Priam would offer her, then she shuddered to imagine what labors he would see fit to impose upon her.

When they reached the steps to the palace, the soldiers at the front stopped and parted, indicating for her to keep walking up alone, step by step.

Never had she approached a palace the size of this one on her own. The kingdoms that she had fought for during her solitude had been similar in size to Themiscyra, and her stays there as brief as was required to take her fill of food and collect any bounty she wished. And these might well be the last steps she ever climbed.

When she reached the top, King Priam was waiting for her. It was easy to see, from the stature and poise with which he held himself, that he had been a warrior, and possibly still was, although likely past his prime. His short curly hair had begun to gray, and his tightly twisted beard was cut close to his skin. He was dressed in a simple chiton with red embroidery. The air held still around him, and from a fleeting glance below at the Trojan men and women who stood watching, Penthesilea could see that his people revered him. He was loved. Respected. He was a leader.

As she climbed the final two steps, his eyes were locked solely on her. Not on the bow she had refused to surrender. Not on his soldiers, indicating that they should prepare to strike. But on her. Something churned within her, sending her chest fluttering, uneven and fast, slicking the palms of her hands with sweat. The sensation was so unfamiliar to her that it took a moment to understand what she was experiencing. Nerves, she realized. This was what it felt like to be nervous.

She took the final step, halting there, for there was nowhere left to go. *Was she expected to bow at this point?* she wondered. She never bowed. She was Penthesilea. Daughter of Ares and once Queen of the Amazons. Who could possibly be worthy of her bow? And yet, she reminded herself, she had journeyed here for Priam's help, and if showing deference was what it took, then she would have to do so.

She readied her shoulders and stomach, stepping one foot back as she prepared her muscles to perform a movement as strange to her as the nerves that continued to rumble through her belly when Priam spoke.

"Queen Penthesilea." He dipped his head. "I am so sorry for your loss."

He beckoned her into his home, welcoming her as if she were a known guest, an acquaintance of many years, or a friend who had been missed for some time. Knowing it was all she could do, she followed him though the twists and turns, up a staircase, and back down through narrow corridors. Red and white mosaic tiles formed geometric patterns on the floor beneath their feet while similar motifs decorated the large arches that they strode through. Stark and simple, the redness of the stones gave the impression of aridity, which disappeared entirely when Priam led her into the courtyard.

Every shade of green shone as vines grew around trellises, and trees twice her height sprouted up from immense pots. Tables had been laid plates of food and jugs of wine. A large fountain gurgled joyously, as dragonflies danced around it, occasionally resting on the stone sides or flitting over to the buddleia and honeysuckle that grew there.

"Please, you must be thirsty after your ride," he said to her. Immediately a young girl in a blue chiton stepped forward and offered a cup of water on a silver platter. Penthesilea drank it gratefully, before replacing the cup on the platter, whereupon it was refilled immediately.

Prior to their arrival in this courtyard, he had spoken continually, offering apologies that he had not been at the gate to greet her and for the hostility she had faced, for had he known of her arrival, he would most certainly have prepared a proper welcome.

Smiling as graciously as she could, Penthesilea had remained silent, her eyes moving across the walls at the frescoes painted there. Although they were somewhat lacking in detail, compared to those she had viewed in Athens, they more than made up for this in their warmth. The scenes of men and women lounging together, eyes creased with smiles, food at their fingertips. Priam had asked her no questions, seemingly content with the sound of his own voice, but now they had reached the courtyard, which appeared to be their final destination, and Penthesilea knew she could not rely on his loquaciousness to hide the fact that she had questions of her own to ask, as well as others that she would be required to answer.

"I heard tell of the events in Athens," Priam said taking a seat on a long plush couch and gesturing for her to do the same. "I can only offer my most sincere condolences. Your sister, she was taken by Theseus, was she not?"

Penthesilea nodded, her gaze involuntarily sliding toward the ground. She did not know what to say. How much she should give away. *Did purification warrant pure truth?* she wondered. It seemed likely, but there were some truths that were hers, and others that were Hippolyte's, and she did not want to sully her sister's name by pretending she knew them both.

From his seat, Priam let out a long and heavy sigh, and Penthesilea noted how his lips pressed together tightly, as if, for the first time since her arrival, he was contemplating what he should say. Then he nodded, gently, and spoke again.

"You know, your father has always blessed us graciously here."

"My father always spoke fondly of Troy," Penthesilea replied immediately, echoing the words that Melanippe had spoken, even though she herself could not recall him saying any such thing. Swallowing another sip of water, she filled her lungs with air, and prepared herself to speak.

"King Priam, you should know that I have come to you for a reason. I have come to you for redemption and purification for my sister's death. For her murder. Committed by my hand."

The words had spilled from her in an unexpected torrent, as if they could no longer be contained, and upon their expulsion, she took her cup and moved to fill it again, only to find her hand trembling with such ferocity she feared her grip might not be strong enough even to hold a feather in its grasp.

"I heard of Queen Hippolyte's death," Priam said. "Of your arrow. Of—"

Whatever else it was he might have heard was cut short, as a shout from the corridor drew their attention.

"Father, Father!" A young boy raced into the courtyard, his cheeks flushed and face shining with sweat as he came to a halt inside the doorway.

"Father," he said once more, now with relief that he had found the man he sought. A relief that was short-lived as his eyes shifted to Penthesilea. Immediately his expression changed.

"So it is true. She is here. Queen of the Amazons. Queen Penthesilea." Mouth agape, he dropped to his knees, so sharply and completely that his head near knocked the stones beneath him. Laughing, King Priam stood and crossed the courtyard to where he pulled his son up by his shoulder and slapped him lightly on the back, a hearty chuckle escaping from his throat.

"Queen Penthesilea, may I introduce to you my eldest son, Hector. As you may have already gathered, he has quite a fondness for you."

The boy, who looked to be around ten years of age, was a miniature version of his father in many ways. They shared the narrow-bridged nose and the same hazel eyes, but Hector was stockier than Priam, and despite barely a fuzz of hair to his cheeks, already stood less than inch shorter than the king. Beneath his thin robe, she could see the width of his thighs, and knew that the breadth of his shoulders would only grow. In the coming years, he would be a man to rival the Gargareans.

She rose from her seat, dipping her head slightly.

"Prince Hector," she said. "My pleasure."

Grinning as if in disbelief, Hector appeared unable to tear her eyes from her, and it was only when Priam slapped him lightly again on the back that he shook and once more noticed his father's presence, at which a new level of excitement struck him.

"Have you asked her, Father?" he said, practically bouncing on his toes. "Have you asked her yet?"

"Where is your patience, Hector? The queen has only just arrived. We have barely sat down."

"But you will ask her, won't you? You promised you would."

This was clearly an extension of a conversation from earlier in the day, and she could feel the energy radiating from the boy. The enthusiasm. He had a contagious optimism about him that reminded her of Cletes.

"Is there something I should be made aware of?" Penthesilea asked, realizing that, the sooner she attended to Hector's request, the sooner she would be able to seek clarification of her own. "Do you wish to ask me something, Prince Hector?"

His cheeks flooded a new shade of crimson, as deep as the embroidery on his father's robes, and the confidence he had shown only moments ago now ebbed away.

"You wanted to ask her; now here is your chance," Priam said. His eyes met Penthesilea's, twinkling in appreciation. She knew that all kings favored their sons. They were an extension of themselves and preserved the legacy of their names in history. Yet this seemed to be something more. There was a connectedness between the pair of them. Deep adoration. This was love.

"Come, Hector. Now is not the moment to go quiet. A true hero needs to show bravery at all times. Even when faced with such a beautiful young woman as our Queen Penthesilea."

Penthesilea was not sure which words caught her more by surprise, *beautiful* or *young*. She had not felt either in years. But, she supposed, she was younger than Priam.

"You wish to be a fighter? A hero?" Penthesilea asked, standing to speak.

The boy nodded eagerly, his hair bobbing up and down.

"That is a very brave thing indeed."

She watched as he swallowed, once, then twice, and wondered what type of king or warrior such a boy would be. This positivity and energy. Penthesilea had always believed you needed harshness to grow up strong. You needed to be tested. To face trials, like those her mother and father had set for them when they trained as youths. She struggled to see what hardships, if any, Hector had faced.

"I have an ax," the boy said suddenly. "And arrows and a sword. I have lots of swords, and you can choose whichever one you want. I promise I will listen. You can tell her, Father, can't you? You can tell her how good I am at listening. At learning. Have you told her how good a fighter I already am? I promise you won't be disappointed." The train of words muddled in her head, yet still he continued. "Is now a good time? I can come back later if that is better? When you have finished talking with Father?"

He gazed upon her expectantly, eyebrows raised. He had asked her something, but whatever it might be, she could not find it amidst the slurry of words he had offered her.

"I am sorry," she looked to King Priam. "Is there something your son wished for?"

While she looked at the king, she saw again that light in his eyes that reminded her of Cletes. He was one who saw all, heard all, remembered all. But it was not Priam that replied to her. It was, once again Hector, now bouncing on his heels as if his legs had been replaced by those of a frog or a rabbit. Unable to stand still for even a second.

"I wish for you to train me," he said.

FIFTY-TWO

SILENCE FOLLOWED. A SILENCE IN WHICH PENTHESILEA WAS unsure how she was supposed to react, although the moment did not last long. In a home with a child such as Hector, she suspected silence never endured.

"You have not trained men before, have you?" he asked. "I'd be the first. I would be the greatest. Tell her, Father, tell her how strong I am. Tell her how good a fighter I am."

"You wish for me to train you?" she repeated.

His body was springing higher than ever. Any more energy and she feared he might hit the doorframe. She stared at him, confused, perplexed by such a request asked for with such ease, by a boy.

"I do not train people," she said, quashing the memory of Aikaterini before it could rise. She had taught her and her sister enough to stay alive. Whether they had needed to use those skills was not her concern.

"But in your citadel of Themiscyra. You must have trained with the women there? You must have practiced? Or else how did you get so good?"

"Being a good fighter does not mean I am a good teacher. Trust me. It is my sisters you need, not me." *Sister*. That was what she should have said. Only Melanippe remained. The thought churned heavily within here.

"But you are Queen Penthesilea." Hector spoke the words as if they were an explanation for everything. Disappointment descended onto his young shoulders. The flush of excitement was replaced with sallow regret. Tension was building within the courtyard. The water's gurgle longer sounded inviting. The birdsong above them had turned shrill.

"King Priam, if you and I could finish our conversation?" Penthesilea said, unable to bear Hector's gaze any longer.

The boy was looking up at his father now. She could see in his eyes the soft sheen, the tears he refused to let form.

"Hector, let me talk to Queen Penthesilea. You have said your part, but now there are things we need to discuss."

The boy's eyes once more returned to Penthesilea, although she lowered her gaze quickly. He glanced back at his father before disappearing in haste from the room.

With a rise of his brow, Priam let out a short sigh that turned into a wide smile.

"Believe it or not, he is a fantastic warrior," he said. "He will be quite formidable when he is grown. Half the men in my army already run in fright from his sword."

If it was the truth, she did indeed find it difficult to believe. All the same, she smiled politely, tight-lipped, waiting to say what she needed to.

"King Priam, the reason I am here."

"For purification. I understand. Word spreads quickly, particularly word of an Amazon queen. As I said before, I am sorry for what happened to your sister and for the part that you played."

Condolences were kind, but they were not what she required. Again, she asked him, this time with no room for ambiguity.

"Will you do it? Will you grant me purification? I know I will be beholden to you. I understand that. Whatever tasks you ask of me, I will be at your disposal. Any gifts you wish me to relinquish for you. Any enemies you wish me to dispose of. Whatever you require, I will do it for you. However long that may take."

And then, without force or awkwardness, she dropped to her knees, just as Hector had done before her only minutes earlier. Yet rather than raising her up, the king roared a full-throated laugh.

"My dear queen, Have you seen Troy? I am in need of nothing here. I do not require your aid."

It was as if the arrow had struck again, this time piercing her own sternum. King Eurystheus had required fame, notoriety, power. That was why he had sent Heracles to endure such labors, for they gave him glory that alone he would never have possessed. If King Priam wanted for nothing, then she was not needed. And if she was not needed, then why would he purify her?

The marble floor seeped its chill through her knees as the king moved toward her and offered her a hand adorned with gold rings studded with stones, counterparts to the thick gold bangles clasped around his forearms and biceps.

Still Penthesilea hung her head, the weight of her disappointment pinning her to the ground as if metal shackles bound her there.

"I was wrong to come here." She rose to her feet without the aid of Priam's outstretched hand. "I am sorry. I should leave now." The temperature in the room had dropped, the air soured. A sudden dizziness blurred her vision, and she hastened to the doorway. Yet she had barely managed two steps when Priam spoke again.

"You misunderstand me, my queen. I said I did not need

anything from you. Not at this moment. But that does not mean I will not perform the purification for you."

Penthesilea stopped and tilted her head toward him, confused.

"I do not understand. You want nothing from me? You will purify me of this deed for...for nothing?"

Even as she said the words, their absurdity swirled thick in her mind. No king performed acts from the goodness of his heart. After all, a man did not become a king through philanthropy. There was always a plot. A clause. A twisted web of nuance, which, once the bargain had been struck, entrapped the petitioner forever with no more hope of escape than the maidens and youths who had once been trapped in the labyrinth beneath Minos's palace. She waited, hearing the rush of her own blood as it pounded with in her ears, for King Priam to set out his conditions.

"There is nothing I need from you now. Nothing I require. Perhaps, though, if the moment arrives when Troy is in need of help, and if ever it seems as though our walls are to be breached, perhaps then, you might come to our aid. And if possible, bring your women to fight against our foes and bring the battle to a quick close."

Penthesilea remained silent. If he knew of Athens, then he likely knew how few of her women remained. Still, she waited, and the pause stretched out between them until she could endure the silence no more.

"That is all? That is all you ask of me?" she asked.

"That is all," he said, although he stopped abruptly in a manner that caused her stomach to tighten. Here it was. Here came the inevitable sacrificial blow she had been waiting for. What? What could he say that required such prolonged anticipation? A smile curled at the corner of his mouth.

"Perhaps, though, you might take an hour out of your time and make a young boy very happy?"

———

It took time to prepare for the purification, Priam told her. She could rest if she would rather, and see Hector the following day, if that was what she preferred. But she shook her head. This purification had come at so little a cost. To ride to battle and fight for Troy. That was all she had to do. As long as there was breath in her lungs and strength in her legs, she would continue to fight. To do so for a king who was favored by her father was more an honor than a burden.

As so Priam led her through the winding corridors of the palace, where the sounds of laughter drifted between the songs of the bird. It was impossible not to feel small in such a place as this, not to see the meagerness of her significance amongst the glories of the gods.

"This way, my queen," Priam said. "The young prince will be practicing."

He led her down a set of steps and out into a wide space, open roofed, the clean sunlight pouring in, less a courtyard, more a small arena. The ground was tiled, like elsewhere, but made of sand and stone, and the scent of hot dust filled her nostrils. Around the edge of the space, a variety of weapons from knives to spears and bows were displayed.

"A father's indulgence, I'm afraid." Priam smiled. "Hector wants to learn to be a hero. And who am I to stand in the way of such a noble calling?"

"You came?" Hector called, bounding up toward them. He had changed from the robe he was wearing before and was dressed in a short tunic, exposing his long tanned legs. "Does this mean you will show me how to fight? You will teach me?"

He reminded her of a young Melanippe, who had no doubt said those exact words to her at this exact age. "I want to be the greatest warrior in all of Troy," he continued. "I will protect Troy. Command the army. Keep my wife and children and family safe."

"A wife, already," Penthesilea half smiled, as she exchanged a look with the king. "I have a little time," she continued, moving past Hector and examining the weapons on the wall. They were of great quality, the metals burnished and polished, the handles sanded smooth then inlaid with bone. What detail the frescoes lacked was more than made up for here. She skated her fingers over the edge of a sword, feeling the heat seep from her skin.

"You can take anything you want," Hector said, appearing beside her once again. "Father bought them for me. I would not mind. If you want, you can take anything. You can keep it. It would be my honor. My gift to you."

Again, Penthesilea's eyes found Priam's. "He has a good heart, your son."

"Very much so. He must have gained it from his mother."

This was, she realized, the longest conversation she had exchanged with a boy of this age. The only such conversation, even, and the thought saddened her a little, as images of the nephew she had never met rose through her.

"Let me see how you attack first," she said, lifting a shield from the wall. "Once I know where your skills lie, then we will look on what I am able to teach you."

Unbridled joy poured from the young boy's face as he chose his own sword, then shuffled backward into the center of the space, keeping his eyes on Penthesilea the entire time.

"Now, your aim is to try to hit me."

The sound of clanging metal, sonorous and clear, rang out, echoing off the walls, and sending vibrations of varying pitches through the weapons that hung patiently awaiting their turn. Hector moved his feet constantly, landing strike after strike on Penthesilea's shield. There was no escaping the fact that the child was gifted. His feet danced with intuition, the sword's movements as fluid if it were an extension of his arm. Time and time again, his blade came down, striking with a force that reverberated through her body. Each time the weapon ricocheted, he had control, already readying for the next strike. By the time they had stopped, an audience of a dozen people had sprung up. In the center, beside Priam, was a young woman with flowing hair that rippled like blackened waves, a young child on her hip while another two stood by her side, one clinging to her robe.

With a brief nod to Hector, Penthesilea motioned for him to lower his sword and left the boy to approach the woman.

"Queen Hecuba," she said, again bowing. Somehow it was easier to abase herself in this way before a woman.

"Queen Penthesilea. It is an honor to meet you. As you may be aware, we have a great deal of admiration for you within these walls."

Now they had stopped sparring, Penthesilea saw just how hard she had worked the young prince. His arms gleamed with sweat, and his breath, which had been so focused and controlled when they were fighting, was now quickened and labored.

"He is exceptional" she said in all honesty. "There are few I have ever seen who could fight like that at such an age."

The same sense of pride she had seen in Priam washed over Hecuba, as the Queen of Troy reached out her arm. Obligingly, Hector came and took it.

"He is our pride. They are all our pride."

A brief moment passed before Penthesilea spoke again.

"King Priam," she said, with an intensity that conveyed all she needed to say. "Is it possible? Have arrangements been made?"

The king nodded. "The temple has been prepared, if you are ready now. There is no rush. We can wait if you require any more time."

But Penthesilea had already waited long enough. "I am ready," she said.

FIFTY-THREE

S HE HAD CHANGED HER CLOTHES. DRESSED IN A SIMPLE ROBE OF pale blue that Hecuba had procured for her and, thankfully, assisted her to dress in. It was only the second time Penthesilea had worn such attire. She would not allow herself to think of the first.

Standing in a chamber with a small bed, she had stood awkwardly as Hecuba clasped the material at the shoulder, folding the pleats so that they gathered around her waist and fell gently to her ankles.

"Your hair is beautiful like this," Hecuba said, having unplaited the braids, so that Penthesilea's hair now possessed the same soft waves as her own. "You should leave it like this."

She offered Penthesilea a smile that the queen did not have the strength to reciprocate. The woman possessed the same endearing quality she had seen in both Priam and Hector. *What would it be like to live in a city with these people as your king and queen?* she wondered. She could not imagine Hector growing into a man who would take and drop wives as easily as cups of wine, as Theseus had done. But then, if she had learned anything of people, it was that you rarely knew what they were capable of until it was too late.

"You should go to the temple now." Hecuba stepped back, scanning Penthesilea up and down, as if assessing her handiwork. "I will take you there. The king is waiting."

Outside night had fallen, and in the corridor, shadows crisscrossed in lines, turning the floor into a grid that shifted as the winds enlivened the flames of the lamps. Whether it was cold or not, Penthesilea could not tell.

"He is inside, waiting for you," Hecuba said when they reached the temple. She grasped the queen's hands, clasping them tight as if they were the dearest of friends. The action caused Penthesilea to jerk in surprise and flinch as if in pain. Yet Hecuba seemed not to notice.

"He will purify you of this deed," she said. "You have nothing to fear here." A moment later, she dropped her hands and turned away.

It was a small temple, in comparison to the scale of the walls that surrounded the citadel, not a place where the citizens of Troy came to worship or lament. This was a private sanctuary for the king to pay his respects to the gods, an intimate and personal place, and he had allowed her to be a witness to it.

Lamps had been replaced by tallow candles, the fat of which burned with thick clouds of smoke weaving lazily up, filling the space with a strong and bitter aroma.

The temple was sparse. A large bowl had been placed on top of the stone altar and a single cushion on the ground in front of it. *Had it been emptied for her?* Penthesilea wondered. Had all the silver and gold and extravagant offerings been removed? It was not beyond the realm of possibility.

King Priam slipped out of the shadows. He, too, had changed his gown, and now wore a solid block of blue fabric and a heavy gold necklace made of joined plates, which hung so low on his chest it might have been armor. He offered none of his characteristic smiles or twinkling eyes, just an air of great solemnity as he crossed toward the altar and knelt over a small box that had hitherto escaped Penthesilea's notice in the darkness of the room.

The piglet he withdrew was dark pink in color and, judging by the viscous blood and thick white cream that coated its skin, could not long have left its mother's womb. Its mouth moved hopelessly, opening and closing in search of a teat from which it might suckle warm milk, but no such thing would be forthcoming in Priam's grip. Gesturing with his head, the king indicated for Penthesilea to take her place.

As Penthesilea lowered herself onto the cushion, the piglet let out a squeal of fear. No longer quiet and vainly suckling, it squirmed in Priam's hands, writhing and fighting hopelessly against his grip. Such small lungs, yet its wail cut through the air, again and again, piercing her ears.

Priam, however, seemed not to notice. He held the animal with complete calm, unconcerned that it might wriggle from his grip. Perhaps he knew it could not. Perhaps that was why he was so at ease.

"Your hands," he said, blocking her line of sight to the altar.

She stretched her hands outward, turning them over so that the palms faced upward, not wanting to look at the frail, impotent creature whose lungs and legs continued to battle to the bitter end.

"Great Apollo, we beseech you. I call on the gods to witness this cleansing. For these hands that have bloodied..." Priam's words were suddenly muted, muffled in the sweltering heat that had caused the fabric of her robe to cling to her skin. *I have killed my sister. I have killed her*, Penthesilea reminded herself, over and over again. *Please allow the gods to draw that blood from my hands. Let them take the images from my mind that haunt me at night. Allow me to die a warrior's death, deserving; allow me to honor Hippolyte's name. Allow*

*me to bring honor to my father and mother and to the Amazon women
who deserve a true ruler.*

She had done so much wrong in this life. She knew that now.
She could see it. But this was her chance.

Words echoed around her mind as she watched the melted
fat from the tallow candles pool, then run down the candlesticks,
hardening on the cold surface of the altar. The words from Priam, his
request to the gods, and the piglet squealing for its life, all of it was
peripheral to her. Until the silence came.

Silence, complete and absolute, followed the splatter of warm
water that woke her from her thoughts. The writhing had ceased,
too, and a knife glistened in Priam's grip. Blood, not water, cascaded
down onto Penthesilea's hands, forming a well that deepened and
deepened until her palms were overflowing, the pattering sounds now
the only noise to break the silence. The hot red liquid spilled over
her fingers down her wrists, under her nails. It dripped between her
fingers, landing to form circles on the ground and on the pale-blue
gown, seeping further, onto her knees and legs. Her heart pounded
with fury. A pain so keen seared through her, it felt as if the blood
were coming not from the piglet, but rather being drawn directly
from within her. As if it were being taken from her chest and her
ribs, the hollows of her bones. Why was there so much pain? Why
did she feel this now, here, where no blade had touched her skin? She
would have asked if she had been able to. But her tongue was of no
use to her. Fat and cumbersome in the thick throat that refused to
let her speak.

Her eyes went up to the piglet. No signs of life remained in the
creature. Its body was limp, its eyes glazed and absent, as if covered
by a sheen of thinnest gossamer. Priam's head was lifted toward the
sky, toward the gods, as he continued to mutter words of reverence,

words she still could not hear. How was it possible that so much blood could come from such a small creature? How was it possible that one small act, a single slice to the throat, could end an entire life? The blood no longer gushed, but had stemmed to singular drips, slowing in frequency and shrinking in size until, without a word, Priam crossed the room with the creature still hanging limply in his hands and placed it on the altar.

"Queen Penthesilea." He gestured for her to stand.

As she did so, the pooled blood rushed from her hands, pouring onto the tiles beneath her and over her feet. Dizzy with the heady, cloying scent, she followed Priam to the edge of the altar, where the dead piglet now lay with eyes closed on the cold stone. Beside it, the bowl was filled with water and oil, the steam still rising.

Colored petals floated on its surface, drifting on richly scented oils of lavender and rose. Priam stepped back, allowing Penthesilea the space to wash her hands in the bowl. And yet she hesitated. The blood had stained every inch of her hands, darkening the skin around the knuckles and every crevice in her palms. How could such a small bowl remove so much blood? It could not. It was not possible.

"It is time you were cleansed, my queen." Priam said softly.

Her heart pounding with apprehension, her every movement staggered, Penthesilea plunged her hands into the water. The feeling was instant, the warm water coiling around her submerged skin, the scents of the oils lightening her chest.

"It is done." Priam said. Penthesilea frowned. The water had indeed turned red, but she had fought in more battles than any man, and she knew that blood like this would need to be scrubbed. Palms and thumbs and knuckles would have to be kneaded together, else it would dry in those tiny cracks and leave an endless web of red on her skin.

"It is done," Priam repeated with just a fraction more force. "See for yourself."

With the pounding still constant in her ears, Penthesilea withdrew her hands from the water and gasped at what she saw.

Not a drop of blood remained on her skin. Not beneath the nails, not on her knuckles or on her wrists, which had barely touched the water. All the blood that had coated her skin, so thick, so viscous, all of it was gone. She had rubbed blood from her hands a thousand time before, but never had it dropped from her skin like this. What Priam had said was true.

She was purified.

FIFTY-FOUR

A SERVANT BROUGHT HER A TOWEL ON WHICH SHE COULD DRY her hands, hands that she could not stop staring at, still unable to believe how clean they were. After some of their most bountiful sacrifices, during which the blood of her horses had caked her skin to her elbows, she had known the stains to remain embedded in her nails for days. And yet, now, when she should have experienced at least a dark tanning on her palms, there was nothing. It was, without doubt, a gift from the gods. Unfortunately, the same could not be said for Hecuba's robe, the fabric of which was sodden.

Guilt flowed through her at this, only to turn to elation. This was a ruined dress. Something easily replaceable. A problem that had a solution, a burden that could be eased almost as quickly as it had arisen. The other guilt, the ironclad specter that had shadowed her day and night, molding itself to her form, howling of its presence, had gone. She had been cleansed.

"A bath has been run for you, my queen," the servant girl said. "And the queen has placed fresh robes in your room for dinner."

"I will not be joining them for dinner," Penthesilea said in reflex.

It was the response she almost always offered when asked to stay. But now she realized, with sudden embarrassment, that this was not the same situation. The girl stood, confused and unsure how to respond. "My apologies," she said, shaking her head as the girl frowned deeply. "What I meant to say is that I will require some time in the bath before I can join them. That is all. But please tell the king and queen I am grateful for their invitation. I will join them shortly."

More satisfied by this answer, but still wearing an expression of wariness, the young girl nodded before retreating down the corridor.

A different array of flowers and herbs had been placed in the bathwater. Curls of orange peels, pitted and porous, skimmed the surface as Penthesilea submerged herself within the warmth of the bath. It had been years since she had last bathed in such a manner. More than seven years, for certain. A sense of stillness drifted around her as she closed her eyes and inhaled. She could feel it. She could feel the difference in her. She was cleansed.

"Thank you, sister," she said to the air. For she knew that even with the gods' graces, Hippolyte would have had to play a part in this ritual. And she would make her sister proud again. She would make all the Amazons proud again.

She dressed for dinner in a manner that she had never before experienced. Two new servants appeared after her bath to oil her hair and adorn it with petals and flowers, and to offer her a choice of gold necklaces, embedded with jade and garnets and amber.

"Gifts from Queen Hecuba and Prince Hector," they said. Her immediate inclination was to refuse; after all, she had not come for gifts, and if anything, she should have been the one bestowing every endowment she could upon them. But she knew that acceptance of such items was often the greatest form of gratitude, and so she picked the garnets, somehow convinced that this was Hector's choice.

While she had no doubt that the servants had fashioned her clothes and hair in the most acceptable of manners, a wave of self-consciousness rolled through her as she approached the dining hall, deepening as every pair of eyes, from the king and queen and their numerous daughters to every male in every seat, turned to look at her. She could feel a flush of heat and knew her cheeks had turned a deep pink. Had she not held the gaze of over a hundred men outside walls of this very city only that morning? And yet this felt different. Then, she had been upon her horse, armed and dressed for war. Here, she was exposed.

In the quiet of the room, a chair scraped against the stones of the floor as young Hector left his place beside his father and rushed to her.

"You are beautiful," Hector said, seemingly astonished. "And you wore my necklace."

"It is true," Queen Hecuba had moved far more gracefully from her seat and took Penthesilea's hands. "You do indeed put the rest of us to shame. Now, come sit; tell me what you wish to eat. Or drink. You do not favor wine in Pontus. That is correct, is it not?"

She was placed in a seat between the queen and Prince Hector, whose loquacity had not faded even a fraction. "You ride with your quiver facing backward?" he questioned. "So that you can reach your arrows more easily?"

"I do."

"And you can stand on your horses when they gallop?"

"I can."

"What of firing with your feet? I have heard that some of your women can stand upon their hands and loose an arrow using only the strength of their toes."

"I cannot do that," she said, and the boy's face momentarily fell, before the queen continued. "But my sister Antiope was most skilled at that particular trick."

The spark within him reignited and the questions continued. At several points through the night, Hecuba was forced to go to the aid of one or more of her daughters, and Priam took over rocking the baby, dipping his finger in the wine and holding it against the infant's lips as he gurgled. Despite the grandeur and the opulence, they were, Penthesilea saw, a family.

"Tomorrow, will you teach me to use a shield? I want to try to defend myself from you, like you did yesterday. Can we do that?"

Priam placed a hand on his son's shoulder.

"The queen cannot stay here, Hector. She has her own kingdom to run, remember?"

Disappointment fell like shadow across the boy's face, although he held the emotion within him far better this time.

"I am sure I can spend a little time before I have to leave." Penthesilea glanced at Hector. "Provided you do not mind rising at dawn?"

"I can wake earlier," Hector answered.

"Dawn will suffice," she smiled.

When Penthesilea retired a little later, Hecuba walked her back to her room.

"There will be servants here if you need anything," the queen said. "Or if you feel more comfortable leaving now, please do not feel you must stay. I can tell Hector that you were called away to battle. He will understand that."

"I am looking forward to training with him again," Penthesilea replied, finding more truth in the words than she had expected. "And I am grateful to you and your husband for your hospitality. For everything you have done for me."

"We Anatolians must be strong together, must we not?" Once

again Hecuba clasped her hands, and this time Penthesilea did not flinch, but rather allowed her skin to absorb their warmth. "I know that nothing can ever replace what you have lost, but please, if you ever need to, then think of me as a sister, or at the very least a friend. I hope you will do that?"

A lump formed in Penthesilea's throat.

"Thank you," she said. "I will."

She slept soundly that night. More soundly than she could recall for years. Her mind was filled with dreams. Dreams of battles. Dreams of her sisters, in which they rode victorious, over the steppes and the rough sand of the Black Sea where she bathed in the water, letting the waves lap at her ankles, at peace. And when she woke, the same stillness remained with her.

She stretched out, clicking the muscles in her back as the chorus of birds confirmed that it was well past dawn. Noting that another of Hecuba's robes had been draped across a chair, she ignored these and instead collected her own clothes, her tunic and trousers. After dressing in her full armor, she made her way through the maze of corridors that led to Hector's training hall.

The prince was alone, practicing drills with his shield, just as he had seen her do the day before, ducking down onto his knees, then rolling over and back up with speed to avoid a strike.

"You should move your left foot back a fraction when you do that," Penthesilea said. The boy stopped midmotion, a wide grin breaking on his face.

"I had thought you had left. Mother said you might need to leave in the night. You know, for a battle."

"I will have to go very soon," she said. "But first let me see how you are defending yourself with that left arm again. It looked a little weak to me in comparison to your right."

Part of her wished to stay longer. The boy was a sponge to her words, absorbing every piece of advice she offered him, never needing to hear an instruction more than once. His speed was phenomenal, as was the accuracy of his striking. But as much as she wished to stay, she also wished to leave before the sun reached its pinnacle. The quickest way back to Pontus was to cross the desert, but even skirting around it, as she intended to, meant traversing dry and arid lands where water would be sparse. The earlier she left, the less time she would spend in these desiccated plains.

Together she walked with Hector and King Priam to the great gates of the citadel, and when they stopped, the guard who had greeted her the day before was waiting with her full quiver and her ax. While she fixed her ax onto her belt, she held the quiver out in her other hand.

"Here," she said, extending the item to Prince Hector. "Take it."

"You mean this?"

"I do."

With an air of disbelief, he ran his hand over the leather before pinching the feathered arrows with his fingertips.

"Do you see this, Father? Do you see this? These are arrows from the Amazon queen herself. With these, I will be invincible."

"I think it requires a strong archer and not just a strong arrow to be invincible," King Priam replied, diplomatically.

"Then I shall practice all day. All day and all night."

"I know you will, my son."

With Hector now absorbed entirely by the weapons, Penthesilea turned her attention to the king.

"I have so much to thank you for," she said.

"You have my blessings. As I said, if ever I am in need, I am certain you will come."

"I will. You have my word."

"Which is all a king could ever ask for."

She rode slowly back to Pontus, noting things that had been absent to her on the journey here. The sound of the wind through the trees. The birds, circling and stalking their prey from a height at which they would not be seen. She saw a new color to the grass and the trees, a verdant brightness that had been missing, not only during her last journey but from all her journeys since her sister's death. Perhaps even before then. Perhaps since her sister's departure.

And when she reached Pontus and the citadel appeared on the horizon, Penthesilea allowed the wind to whip at her tunic and sting her bare skin. She drew in a breath that filled her lungs, and held it there until she felt herself quiver.

This was her home. This was Themiscyra. And she would make it great again.

PART VI

FIFTY-FIVE

F OR YEARS THEY WORKED, TRAINING YOUNG WOMEN WHO HAD
only been girls when they fought in Athens, passing on their
skills and ways so that they might never be lost to the capri-
ciousness of time. They traded what they had for new horses, which
they bred and rode as soon as their spines were strong enough,
or else milked them to make cheese, which they ate salted and
covered with scattered nuts. In their forges they made weapons of
the highest quality. They trained, they farmed, they told each other
stories, spending the nights around the fires with their youngest
girls, recounting all the tales they could recall of Ares and Otrera,
of Queen Hippolyte and Princess Antiope. They told them of their
battles, of their hunts, of the laughter they had shared together. The
same stories were repeated yearly, monthly, sometimes even nightly,
and often by her own tongue, for Penthesilea was determined that
each girl should be able to recite the lives of their ancestors, word for
word. Over the years, this had become her dream. A way to honor
her sisters, which she hoped would continue for generation after
generation, etching the Amazons' place in history. Yet new births

were infrequent, and those mothers who had been lucky enough to bring forth a daughter often chose the nomadic way of life, rather than returning to Themiscyra.

"They are still training them in our ways," Melanippe assured her. "They are still turning young girls into warriors. But this place hold memories for them. There are too many shadows lurking in these walls. Perhaps, when there are enough children, they will return," she said.

"Perhaps," Penthesilea replied, understanding all too well the echoes that taunted her among their hallways and suffocated her with stillness where once they had resonated with laughter.

She herself had borne no children since returning. It was true, she was far older now than when she had first gone to the Gargareans and laid with men, but there were women far older than her who were still carrying children. Two years following Penthesilea's return from Troy, Cletes fell pregnant. Celebration whispered in the walls, tentative, but hopeful. And yet the baby was lost before it was even born. It would have been a girl.

Still, they made their way in life with more than fifty strong women who could be called upon to take to the battlefield, more than enough to ensure that their coffers were filled, and they were able to trade on the rare occasions that they found themselves in need.

The land continued to supply their requirements, just as it had always done, but with their depleted numbers, it proved impossible to harvest all the produce each season, and much rotted on the vine, a feast for hordes of ants.

The once grand buildings of Themiscyra were beginning to crumble, areas left to the elements, for the women no longer had any need for the gargantuan dining halls or the vast arenas where they had once watched one another spar and train. Vines had taken hold of some of the smaller turrets, smothering the windows, blanketing their lookouts with an opaque wall of green. They stayed in the smaller buildings, the one- and two-room homes that were easier to maintain and repair, although Penthesilea promised herself they would one day rebuild the rest of the citadel. When numbers returned, she told herself, time and time again. Bigger than ever, if need be.

Despite all the room now available to them, she and Cletes would often sleep on the steppes under nothing but a thin canopy of fabric, or even less. On occasion, they might have been hunting for the day, traveling too far south to return within daylight hours. Sometimes, in Themiscyra, Penthesilea woke in the night to find a flush of sweat drenching her skin and her breath quickening as the closeness of the walls overwhelmed her, and Cletes would rise with her and suggest a walk along the beach to watch the moon reflect in ripples on the water.

They met with the nomads to watch them train their daughters with hawks. They filled their time and their minds so that the years slipped by almost imperceptibly.

Only when the first strands of gray broke from the queen's scalp did she realize how much time had passed since her youth.

"Pluck it!" she had insisted of Cletes, whose hair had retained the same unbroken ebony tone through the years, the effects of age seemingly pertaining no more to her than to a goddess.

"I like it. I think it is regal."

"I was a queen long before my hair turned silver," Penthesilea countered, distraught. This was a physical sign. Soon others would follow, stiffness in her limbs, lethargy in her mind. How long after the first silver hair did one become incapable of ruling? Two decades? Three? She knew these thoughts were folly, yet they plagued her, nonetheless. Laughing, Cletes reached up and plucked the offending strand from the root, causing a sting that vanished almost as quickly as it had arisen.

Penthesilea often found herself thinking of Hippolyte, of the terrible times, but also the joyous ones. Their younger years, when they had seen the miracle of life in everything from the rising sun to the birth of a new foal. Their invincible youth, when they would ride in the Black Sea, the waves crashing around their steeds, the briny taste of spray filling their noses, offering them a taste of pure, unadulterated happiness. There were other memories, of course. Those she tried to suppress, for fear they would allow the darkness to seep out from the corner of her mind and consume her once more. But when such images did recur, she forced her thoughts instead to the legacy that her sister had left behind. Not just of the Amazons, but of Hippolytus, too.

Often, at night, against the soft measure of Cletes's warm breath, Penthesilea would think of Hippolytus. Where he must be. What aspirations he had. Whether she would recognize him if she saw him in a busy agora or in the heat of a battlefield. He would be a young man by now, and no doubt Theseus would be considering his need for a wife, or rather, Athens's need to build more alliances. Then again, perhaps Hippolytus was not so great a concern. It was rumored that Theseus's young wife, Phaedra, had borne him sons, too, although they were sickly and insipid and wrought with maladies, if the tales on the breeze were to be believed.

As well as her nephew, images of Antiope took root in Penthesilea's mind almost every time she mounted a horse. Whether within the citadel walls or out in the long grasses as they swept back and forth in the breeze, she could see her sister, her hair billowing as the wind augmented her gallop. In the beating of the waves, she could hear her euphonious laughter, and the harsher, more potent tones that she employed on the battlefield. She thought of her sisters constantly. And, occasionally, she thought of Priam.

During those first few months back in Pontus, she often considered the Trojan king and the gift he had granted her so nobly. Each moment of joy she experienced, she knew was a result of his hand and his grace. Each night with Cletes, a reminder of his generosity. She thought of the boy Hector, a man, as the years went by, whose name now echoed in the same breath as those of Penthesilea and her sisters. And although her ruminations on the men of Troy faded over the years, they returned with a vengeance when news of the war arrived.

Troy and King Priam found themselves under siege from King Agamemnon of Mycenae as he rallied the combined might of Greece on behalf of his brother, King Menelaus. Despite his wealth and standing, Menelaus had been powerless to stop his wife, Helen, when she left Sparta with Hector's younger brother, Paris. Some claimed that it had been her choice, that she had been overcome with passion and lust at the sight of young Paris, a hero all the more magnificent when set against the bloated, rotund brute that her husband, Menelaus, had become. Some insisted that was not the case, that it was Paris who had become so enamored with Helen that he had snatched her away in the night. It was a story that bore echoes too uncomfortably familiar for Penthesilea. Either way, the outcome was the same.

A thousand ships. That was what she had heard. A thousand ships had set sail for those Trojan sands, to declare war on the gracious King Priam.

"The Greeks cannot get into the city." All the women she spoke to offered the same opinion on the matter, regardless of whether they had seen Troy with their own eyes or not. "The wall is impenetrable. The Trojans will win. There is no way they can be defeated."

She took their words, hoping to find comfort within them, yet all the while assailed by apprehension, a feeling in the air, ebbing and flowing like a distant storm that, for now, was kept from the shore by a favorable wind but would eventually come crashing onto their lands.

From everywhere came rumors of Achilles, the young warrior, both undefeated and, so they said, undefeatable. Upon hearing this Penthesilea would scoff, for she had learned from bitter experience that no man or woman was undefeatable. Besides, for every tale of Achilles's prowess, there was another of Hector's. He was now the leader of the Trojan army, a prince known for his justice as much as his fighting ability, but one who was as skillful with a sword as any man ever seen in Anatolia. And at these words, Penthesilea would smile to herself, recalling how he had learned from her, and wondering whether he ever thought of her when he sent an arrow through the air or jabbed his spear into the breast of another man.

"We should go and help," she said one evening to Melanippe. They had dined out by the sea at a small campfire, feasting on fish that one of the youngest girls had caught with her spear. "It was my arrangement with Priam, as you may recall. That I should offer aid if ever he needed it."

"I thought the arrangement was that if they were ever in so dire a state that they worried for Troy, then you should go? No one is concerned for Troy. No one doubts Priam's position. They have held the citadel for more than five years, now, while the Greeks camp out in the squalor of the sand, away from their homes, miles from kingdoms that are being usurped even as they fight another man's war. Priam can hold Troy for another fifty years, sister, believe me."

Penthesilea pressed her lips together as she pulled the white meat from the bones of the fish, watching it flake, before bringing it to her mouth and hesitating.

"I have heard tell of a prophecy, sister. One given by the great seer Calchas, who says that the war will last for ten years. Do you think that is possible? That it could continue for so long?"

"If they remain in a siege in this manner, then why would it not be possible? The Trojans have food in Troy; the Greeks can receive it by ship. Do you not agree?"

She did. She thought exactly the same thing.

Five more years, but then who would win?

"We should wait," Melanippe said, resting her hand on Penthesilea's knee. "If they truly need us, then we will talk of this again. For now, you have your own women here to think of." And Penthesilea agreed.

The years passed with the continual rising and setting of the sun and the waxing and waning of the moon. Several more children were born to the Amazons, including a daughter to Cletes, and several sons who were returned to their fathers. The horses grew so great in number that they were left to roam, only a fraction being broken to ride. The rest of the time, they would stand in the rivers in their herds, as the faint morning mist rose around them.

Patience was what was required of her. Penthesilea saw that now. If the Amazons were ever to return to their former strength, it would not be yet. It would not be now. Perhaps not even in her lifetime. But perhaps in the lifetime of Cletes's child, Antianeira, who was a love to her that she could not have imagined. Each day spent with the child helped her understand more readily Hippolyte's reluctance to leave Hippolytus. If only she had been blessed with this wisdom all those years ago.

All the while, rumors of the Trojan war reached them like scattered leaves on a light wind. There was dissent in the Greek camps, not only between the soldiers but between the leaders, Achilles and Agamemnon in particular, a feud galvanized by the plague Apollo had sent upon them.

"Perhaps the Greeks will give up," Cletes said after this news had reached their shores. "They have lost many men."

Penthesilea did not share her optimism. "No. If they were going to leave, they would have done so already. Agamemnon is tenacious, he will not retreat now. He will not leave without a win, one way or another." Cletes nodded, though she said no more on the matter.

It was on the ninth year of the battle at Troy that Penthesilea spoke on the matter again with her sister. Dusk was settling on the steppes, bringing with it a hazy warmth that cloaked the lands. The two sisters were seated on the crumbling steps of what had once been their vast arenas, the distant lapping of the shores coming faint through the air as they stitched patterns into the tunics of their trousers. But while Melanippe's mind was lost in the task and in the rhythmic motion of her needle, Penthesilea's could not rest. Placing the leather down on her lap, she lifted her head and addressed her sister.

"I wish us to go to Troy," she said. "We have stood on the side long enough. The war will end soon, and this Achilles is still strong. I believe we are the key, sister. We are the key to ending this war, and ending it in favor of the Trojans. We should leave. Soon. Our separation is what has caused this war to drag on in such a manner. I will tell the women to ready the horses tomorrow."

Given that she was queen, Penthesilea expected Melanippe's agreement to arrive swiftly. But rather, her sister frowned.

"I do not think we should interfere," she replied.

Penthesilea flinched if she had been slapped by the words.

"Not interfere? It is a battle. Interfering in battles is the thing we do. It is our very calling."

"Small battles. Small wars. Not ones this size. We have seen before that we are not invincible. This army is bigger than the army in Athens. Countless times bigger. Look at our numbers. If this war does not go the way of the Trojans, then this could be the end of us. We would never be able to regain our numbers."

A fierce heat rose within the queen.

"Are you truly serious? You would run from a fight? A fight that I am obliged to support? Without Priam, who knows where I would be? I would certainly not be here, within the walls of Themiscyra. You and I both know that."

"So we must all pay the price for what you have done?" Melanippe demanded. "This obligation is yours and yours alone. If you had not gone to Priam, then we would have continued as we were."

The heat had spread, burning through her torso.

"Was it not you who said I should go to Priam?"

"Yes, for your purification. To aid you. Not to damage what little remains of us. I know how this sounds, my sister, I do. And I wish I could say it another way, in all truth. But the fact remains that you promised you would ride into battle to aid Troy and Priam should he need it. You did not promise us. You did not promise the Amazons, and our women should not be held accountable for your bad decisions. We cannot win this fight. This will be Athens all over again, but this time, none of us will return. Surely you must see that?"

FIFTY-SIX

A FIERCE RAGE BURNED WITHIN HER, A FIERY HEAT, EXPLOSIVE and unquenchable. It throbbed and seared all the way down to her hands, which she flexed and clawed, her fingers twitching, as if the only way they might find comfort would be by pulling on a bow or swinging an ax. She had stormed away from Melanippe, astounded by her stubbornness. How many insults had she spewed, all in the supposedly reasonable voice of concern? Had she not implied that Penthesilea's presence in Pontus was unrequired? That the women would have done perfectly well without her? That her purification had brought nothing to the Amazons? She was their queen. Their rightful queen. Perhaps her years of ruling had gone to Melanippe's head. Did she think that, by having Penthesilea ride out alone to Troy's aid, she might resume the role of queen and fight only when necessary or preferably not at all? Did she not see that, under such a rule, the name *Amazon* and the fear that it invoked would slip away like silt on a riverbed? No, it could not be. She would not see that happen. She would gather all the women together. All the nomads, all those who still lived in Themiscyra. All those girls who had yet to draw their first blood and proclaim themselves true Amazons. She would call them all to her, and they would fight under her command.

She paced outside the citadel that night, knowing Cletes would lie awake without her by her side, yet unable to bring herself to come inside the walls within which her sister still slept. So instead, she took her bow and arrow out on the steppes, where an old hide hung on a wooden post as a target for the younger children. By daylight, the tears in the pelt were visible in their hundreds, reducing it to mere strips of leather. But at night it was just a dark shadow, lost in the darker shadows of the trees that swayed around it. The clear smell of night, cold and unrelenting. Without pausing for thought, the queen emptied an entire quiver into the hide, each a fraction higher than the last, knowing, even without looking, that she had drawn with her arrows a perfectly vertical line. The women would come with her to Troy.

By the time she retreated to her chamber, the moon was a fading coin, slowly descending in the wake of Selene's chariot. The stars misted into the bleaching sky. It would soon be morning, but she would not be sleeping.

"I take it your words with Melanippe did not go well," Cletes said, unable to stifle her yawn as she sat up in the bed.

Penthesilea dropped down beside her, running her tongue along her teeth as she attempted to restrain the words attempting to free themselves from her lips.

"She does not think it is right for me to call the Amazons to Troy's aid. She does not think it is to their benefit or obligation."

In the watery light, Cletes's dark eyes glimmered softly, trained solely on Penthesilea, although she waited a while before she spoke.

"You must understand her view on this matter," she said.

Penthesilea leaped to feet, the blood that had only recently cooled once again scalding and pumping with angry fervor.

"You cannot side with her! You think she is right?"

"Penthesilea, my love, I did not say that."

"You said she has a view."

"Because she does. And one that is valid. Our numbers are small. Dangerously so. She does not wish to see her father's and her sisters' legacies eradicated."

"And you believe that I do?"

"Of course I do not. And neither does she. But surely you see her fear? The battle is greater than Athens with more men against us and fewer Amazons. And in Athens we were fighting for a purpose. We were fighting for our queen. Our queen who had been stolen. We had been wronged. In Troy, it is not we that have been wronged."

Penthesilea snorted, but Cletes continued. "Consider, before Athens, when did we ever ride out with all of our women? Never, that is the truth of it. There would always be those who remained behind, those who defended Themiscyra and the children, and those too injured to fight."

"But there are none who need defending now," Penthesilea countered.

"Exactly."

The words rattled around in the empty space. Melanippe's disagreement was one thing, but Cletes? Penthesilea was queen. She was queen, and she wanted to do this. Surely that should be enough? Through the dim light, Cletes found her arm and brushed it gently with her fingers.

"I know that this is what you want, my love," she said. "I know that you owe Priam for the life he has returned to you. But you are queen, and you know that it is not only your wants that must be considered here. You have women. Women who look to you. Who rely on you to make the right decisions for them and their families."

She could still hear the throb of rushing blood, although its intensity had decreased, and a new sensation had formed in her gut. A churning, like the curdling of milk. This was what she wanted. This was what she needed. But they were right. It was not what the Amazons needed.

"What should I do?" she asked, returning to her seat beside Cletes. "How can I do this? I must go. I must help Troy."

"I know you must. And I am certain that there are women who will wish to aid you. So ask them. Gather them together, and ask them; do not command them. If they wish to come and fight with you, then thank them and rejoice in private. And if they do not, then you will offer them no ill will or animosity. You will understand that, too."

It was a fair solution, and one that Hippolyte herself had offered often during her reign. She had never forced a woman to fight, if they did not feel they were able to. Yet such knowledge did not ease the bile that churned within her.

"And if no women come with me?" she said.

"Then you and I will go into battle at Troy side by side," Cletes said, and placed a kiss upon her forehead.

"And what of Antianeira? What if we both go to Troy and do not return?"

"Then she will be the one to continue to tell our tales, just as we have taught her to do."

So it was decided, and Penthesilea sent word the next day. All the nomads and women of neighboring tribes were to return to the steppes to hear their queen speak. They were to bring their weapons, for she had a request.

When the day arrived, neither Penthesilea's heart nor feet would cease their skittish movements. Muttering to herself, she wrung out her hands as she trod back and forth.

"We leave tomorrow morning. It does not matter if we leave with fifty or with only two, we leave then."

Cletes nodded, allowing her partner the room she needed to stride. "As you wish, my love."

Whatever support and blessings Cletes offered to the queen, their impact had been reduced by the tension that had grown between her and Melanippe, the animosity so intense that they could not be within each other's sight for even a minute before the bickering began. When, finally, all the women had gathered, Penthesilea could not look her sister in the eye, for fear of what she might say.

The queen dressed in her full war attire. Seated on a chestnut mare, she fastened her zoster around her waist and slid her knives and swords into its length. She positioned her quiver so that it lay flush to her thigh and strapped her bow to her back and her ax to the side of her horse where she could reach for it if she needed it.

"Penthesilea, it is time," Cletes said.

A lurching sensation, both sadness and determination, flickered in the queen as she rode into that crumbling space that had once been their magnificent arena. Over a hundred women stood before her. Some of them were girls so young that, on foot, they would not yet have reached the flanks of the horses upon which they sat. Some were so old that their skin, loose and paper-thin, hung in folds down their faces and necks. Over a hundred women, where once there had been thousands. Over a hundred women that had come at her call. Penthesilea remained on the mare as she called out across to them.

"Amazons. Thank you for coming together. For coming to me. I suspect that many of you will know why you are here."

Murmurs drifted lightly on breeze, but she did not listen closely enough to pick out any words from them.

"As we are all aware, war rages in Troy. A war that has been raging for nearly ten years. The Grecians have camped out on long beaches outside the citadel, throwing all their might at the wall. They had attempted to starve the Trojans. They have killed their men and raped their women and priestesses in the hope that they will submit. But the Trojans have not submitted. Still they stand behind the great stone walls. And yet, in my heart, I feel that they require our help. That we are to be the decisive element that will allow Prince Hector and King Priam to claim victory over these invaders."

The women were silent, eyes boring into her, as if they knew she still had words left to give them.

"Some of you may know, but some of you may not, that I myself have an allegiance with King Priam. He aided me in a time when my life was darkness. When I could not see the light that shone upon me. At the time I was most in need of his aid, he offered it freely and willingly. I tell you, as a queen, as *your* queen, that he is a good man. The man who saved me was not greedy, not corrupt, not seeking betterment purely for his own ego. He was a family man. A king who thought of his citizens. And if his son Hector has turned into half the man that Priam was—" She heard the whispers on the wind like the rustling of leaves. "Yes, Hector is quite a warrior, you have heard that, too. But that does not mean he does not need our help. I am obliged. I am obliged to go to their aid and fight for them, as if I were fighting for your own lives. I cannot tell you to fight with me. I am your queen, but you are your own people. We live separated by distance but not by beliefs. So I ask you. I ask if there are any women here who would travel with me to Troy, ride, and face the Grecians with me. I ask if any will seek to defend a city that my father, Ares,

God of War, dotes upon. I cannot promise that you will return. I will never make that promise to you. But still I ask, humbly, are there women that will come and fight with me?"

Her question hung in the air, hovering like a breath of air crystallizing into water on a winter day. Horses tugged against the riders as looks were exchanged between the women. Several pairs of eyes cast down. Older women and younger women. Those who had never seen a fight and those who remembered all too vividly how close they had come to seeing the end of their lives in Athens. From the back of the arena, a single voice called out to her.

"I will ride with you, my queen." Cletes had dressed in her war clothes, her hat strapped to her head, boots laced up her thighs. She looked nearly twenty years younger, like the same girl she had fallen for all those decades ago, and despite the situation, Penthesilea could not help but feel a bloom of deepest love flourish within her.

"You have my sword." An older woman, Themodosa, stepped forward.

"And you have my bow." Amina, the next to speak, had been just a girl when they had ridden to Athens. Too young to fight, she had stayed behind with the other small children. And now she was a fully grown Amazon woman, ready to fight beside a queen who felt as if she had barely ruled her.

"Thank you," Penthesilea replied.

"I will ride with you, too." Evandre stepped forward on her horse. She had been injured in the first days at Athens. It had been only her second battle, but unlike so many, it was not her last. She had been strong, then. And she looked stronger now.

By the end more than thirty women had agreed to ride with her. Melanippe was not among them.

"There is no ill will," Penthesilea told her, finding the words truer than she would have anticipated. "I understand, my sister. You must keep our women here. You have a place, you belong here."

Melanippe lifted her head, tears shining in her eyes. "If you see our father, give him my blessings."

"I will."

The women moved amongst one another, offering hugs of farewell, gifting weapons they thought would be of use. Several young girls looked longingly at Penthesilea, including her own beloved Antianeira, wishing they could come, too. During her first rule, she would have allowed it. Allowed the girls the chance to test themselves and prove their worth. But not now. Not anymore.

"My queen, may I say something?"

As Penthesilea turned, she found herself addressed by Klonie. That same Klonie who had ridden with her to Athens all those years ago, when they had first set out in search of Hippolyte, and who had survived the battle with Theseus, too. And now she was still here, standing only a little less tall, wishing to return with her for what might prove their greatest battle.

"Of course. Please. You have something on your mind?"

At the queen's question, Klonie inhaled, warning Penthesilea that she was unlikely to find favor in what she was about to hear.

"The Grecians, they are on the shore? Lined along the length of the beach?"

"With their numbers so great, they are most likely to have filled it," Penthesilea replied.

Klonie nodded, taking a moment longer before she replied.

"Then we may find it difficult to penetrate their army. If we ride across land from Anatolia, we will arrive facing their greatest defense, closest to the citadel."

"What other option is there?"

She understood what Klonie was saying. If the Greek soldiers were arrayed close to the wall, they would have to use all their energy fighting through them to reach the gates of Troy, from where they could offer the most protection to Priam. But what other choice was there? The question had barely formed in her mind when Klonie offered her an answer.

"We could take a boat. That way, we could arrive behind the Grecian army, in their camps, and surprise them with an attack from there. We need not travel far on the ship, just from Hellespont. That way they would never suspect it was us, for Amazons have not been known to travel by water before."

Unease rippled through Penthesilea. Traveling by sea was not the Amazon way. The truth was it unnerved her. Their lives were on soil and earth, not on water. The sea was Poseidon's realm, and Poseidon was Theseus's father. That alone was enough to fill her with dread.

"I cannot…" was all she managed to say. "This battle will be hard enough. What if something goes wrong?"

"Such as?" Klonie countered. "It would only be a small vessel. I have made several such journeys over the years. I am certain that I will find a man who can take us to Troy. For a price."

"Small ships more easily succumb to the swells of the sea and are blown off course by the winds. No. I understand what you are saying, but no."

The women, who had now gathered around in a large cluster, fell silent, with Klonie's head bowing in disappointment.

"What if we divide?" Cletes said, bringing life back to the conversation Penthesilea assumed she had subdued. "What if you take half the women by land, and I take those who wish to travel by boat? It would be an attack from two sides then. Entirely unexpected."

When Cletes looked at Penthesilea in that moment, it was not as a woman looking at her queen, but as the dearest of friends and so much more. This was the way they had always looked and spoken to one another, and for that instant, not Klonie's nor Melanippe's nor anybody else's opinion mattered.

"You believe it will work?" Penthesilea asked.

"I do. I think it wise."

Penthesilea drew away from the women and closer to Cletes. Cletes had been right about calling the women together like this. She had been right about going to Priam to seek purification. Every good decision Penthesilea had made had almost always involved Cletes in the shadows. It would be arrogant to ignore such a coincidence, now more than ever.

"Then that is what we shall do," she said. "We will divide. Those who wish to ride to Troy on horseback with me, I will lead you. The rest, you will go with Klonie and Cletes. You will bring the food, too. And extra weapons." The women nodded, pleased by this arrangement. "Now, it is time for us to end this decade-long war."

FIFTY-SEVEN

ONLY TWELVE WOMEN RODE BEHIND PENTHESILEA, A STRONG wind at their backs. It was as if the gods themselves were willing them forward, hastening their journey. The sky was filled with coral clouds, fluorescent in the morning sun, without a hint of rain on the horizon. They rode silently; there was no need for words above the drumming of hooves and the gentle pulse of the sea. It was not until they had been riding for some time and a light sweat glowed on her horse's coat that Penthesilea realized she had not turned around to gather a final image of Themiscyra before it disappeared from view. She had not looked lovingly on her home or uttered a silent prayer to the gods to keep all who remained in its walls safe. But she would see it again. Her father would ensure it.

When they reached the Sea of Marmara, they rested their horses, checked their weapons, and ate. Several stalls had been set up at the side of the road, selling roasted chestnuts and fish, skewered and set over hot coals until their skin bubbled and blackened. They bought as much as they needed to abate their hunger, and a little more besides, before lying down to sleep and gather their strength. Cletes and the others would have left Pontus by now. They had stayed a little longer in Themiscyra, taking the time to assemble provisions and load their horses. Gods willing, they would arrive at almost the same time.

As the horses buried their noses in the long grass, and the women slept soundlessly, their fingers curled around their daggers, Penthesilea's attention became fixed on a group of men huddling together, their hands animated as they spoke amongst themselves. She had traveled far enough and seen enough of the world to know when men were talking of war, and the gasps emitting from this group only confirmed her suspicions. She pushed herself off the ground and moved across to them.

"You," she said, looking at the one who was speaking most animatedly. "You have news from Troy?"

He blanched, stepping back at the sight of the queen, only her eyes and lips visible beneath her helmet. For this fight, they had chosen their metal helmets. These were harder and less comfortable that their leather caps, but beneficial all the same.

The man stuttered, struggling over the same syllable several times before finding something coherent in his throat. "I—I…yes. Yes. There is news. They are saying that Hector has done it. He has killed the warrior Achilles. The Greeks cannot win without him. Now it will soon be over. It has to be."

A long, low whistle blew from Penthesilea's lips, as an image of young Hector rose to her mind. He had killed Achilles, arguably the greatest warrior the Greeks had ever known. He would become part of history, forever. There would be celebrations behind those walls tonight. Perhaps the ships were already leaving. She offered no thanks to the men, turning immediately and returning to her women.

"Come," she said. "Ready your horses. We should leave. We still have another day's ride ahead of us. When we arrive, we will camp on the mountains behind Troy. You can rest then, before we attack at first light."

The closer they came to Troy, the thicker the sense of anticipation in the air, the excitement radiating from each and every one of them, Penthesilea included. Yes, there were only twelve of them, but in truth, these were the strongest twelve women Penthesilea still had. These were the twelve she would have chosen to ride with her. Several of them were women she had grown up with, women whose thoughts she could anticipate and who could equally anticipate hers in the heat of battle. The younger ones had the same spirit and fervor that she saw in herself. Even tired and labored, these women could defeat hundreds upon hundreds of strong, able men fresh to the fight. The Greeks were unlikely to be that. Ten years at war would take its toll on anyone, the more so after the sickening news of Achille's defeat. They would slice through these men one by one. Their arrival would be the final event in the Trojan war.

Three days after leaving Pontus, and with an amber-tinged sky above them, the Amazons crested the final hill that brought Troy into view. The gasps from her women came in quick succession, and even the queen had to stifle a noise of astonishment. She had seen it before, of course, the gargantuan feat that was the citadel of Troy, but never could she have imagined the sight that lay upon the shore. Row upon row of triremes, like those Heracles had arrived in all those years ago, their number so great it was as if their sails had become a new horizon. As far as the eye could see stretching north and south, only ships, bobbing slowly up and down, rising and falling in the low tide as if the sea were breath and the ships the skin that rose and fell with it.

"I have never seen such a sight," Amina said beside her. "Have you? Have you ever seen such a sight?"

The young girl's voice trembled, but it was Thermodosa's older tone that replied.

"No, we have not. No one has."

There were no scouts here. No Greeks or Trojans, just hills and valleys. They slowed the horses, now, advancing at a walk so as to find the best lay of the land and sea, attempting to spy a weak spot from which they could cause most damage to the Grecian army.

As they drew closer, they became aware of an affray by the great gate of Troy.

"Are they fighting?" Polemusa asked, quickening her pace a fraction. The queen strained her eyes into the distance, but it was all too far away to know for certain. Shouts echoed off the citadel walls and rebounded out to sea, but they did not sound like the sounds of battle. She knew the sounds of battle well; she had run or ridden into such situations a thousand times before, albeit against a lesser foe. And always came the sonorous clang of metal as sword struck shield. Where was that sound now? No, this was something different. This was the sound of cheering.

"We must get closer," she called to the women. "We need to see what is happening there. If there is a battle beginning, we should strike now."

"What about camping out for the night? Waiting for the others?"

"We cannot give the Greeks time to rest and regroup. Cletes and the other women will join us when they arrive, if they are not already here. I am certain the wind has been favorable."

The anticipation had been replaced by a surge of energy, a powerful force that drove her onwards. Her horse's hooves drummed, harder and more rousing than any war dance a man could perform.

The women rode at her side. Only thirteen together, and yet they were an army.

They rode to a rocky outcrop, from where she could see the whole length of the beach. The men were gathered a short distance in front of the city gate, but as she had expected, it was not a battle. They were watching something. Dust spiraled upward, blurring the air. A stray horse, perhaps? One that someone was attempting to catch? Only a horse and chariot could raise that much dust, but why? A king's announcement perhaps?

"We need to get closer," she said again. "We need to know what is happening."

Beneath her feet were what was left of what had once been a narrow path, weathered by the crash of waves and the relentless changing of the tide. Now only part of it remained. Occasional steps, shining green with algae, jutted from the rock face. Strands of seaweed clung to rocks, their thick tresses reflecting the dull light. No horse could walk down such a path. Frustration boiled within her as she searched the landscape for an alternative route, but there was nothing clear. This path was too slippery, a certain disaster for some if not all of her women. And yet she was so close. So close to the tents of the Greeks, no doubt full of fat bearded kings tending to their gout.

"Wait here," Penthesilea said, and dropped from her horse.

Ax in hand, she jumped down onto the first ledge, where she landed surely enough, only to take her next step and have her foot slide on the slip of the algae. In less than a heartbeat she had righted herself, but now she was exposed. If any of the Grecians did happen to emerge from their tents and look up, they would see her there, climbing down the rock face, as helpless as she had ever been. Using the strength in her arms, she scrambled down again, balancing on her toes and employing her ax as an anchor to brace against the slippery stones. Slowly she descended, one rock, then another, until her feet reached the surer pebbles and sands of the beach.

The leather-clad tents were densely packed, and the sand flies hummed around her ankles as she walked, her footsteps muffled completely by the ground. Men were walking back to their tents, broad smiles and laughter on their faces. They were happy, cheering, talking of wine, and the last thing she wanted was to let them know she was there. She slipped backward, observing them from a fissure in the rock edge, and waited. And though she did not know what it was she waited for, she knew she would see it when it came.

Her opportunity struck a few minutes later when a man moved away the group and came toward her, where he began to relieve himself against one of the rocks. As he emptied his bladder, she slipped behind him and, pressing a knife against his throat, dragged him back and out of the sight of his comrades.

"If you scream now, I will end you," she said.

She felt the rise and fall of his throat, grinding against the edge of her blade, and his breath rasping as she constricted the airflow to his lungs. "Do you understand?"

His head bobbed in the tiniest of nods, and she reduced the pressure by a fraction. In a moment of panic, he lunged forward, but she tripped him with her foot. The man fell forward into the rocks, his arm blocking his head from serious impact, yet she caught him and twisted him around to face her, this time digging the knife in deep enough to draw blood.

"I can run this blade through your vocal cords before you even attempt to scream. So stay exactly where you are," she told him. His whole body was shaking, every muscle clenched in fear. It was a miracle the Greeks had not been beaten already if this was the caliber of their men.

"Tell me. What was that? The dust we saw. What was it?"

The man sputtered, an unintelligible sound followed by a heaving cough. Silencing him with an elbow to the stomach, she loosened the knife a fraction. Through his wheezes he continued to cough, but a single word came out. A name.

"Achilles," he said.

A flutter of confusion flicked in the queen. Achilles was still alive? It was not uncommon for rumors to become confused as they crossed land and sea. But the Sea of Marmara was not so far from here that the men she had spoken to should have made such a grave mistake.

"What was he doing?" she asked, accompanying the question with an increase of pressure. "Why were people watching? What was all the dust from?"

The man's wheezing had transformed into a shallow sob, and she felt her hand become damp as drops fell from his bearded face. Tears? Tears, when he was about to die in battle? He disgusted her.

"H…he killed Hector. He was dragging the body around, behind his chariot."

"What?" Penthesilea's dagger fell away in her hand, although the man was at least wise enough not to try to escape. "What do you mean? Did Hector get caught when they were fighting with chariots?" The idea made no sense to her. They were both warriors of the highest caliber. They would want to prove themselves by fighting on their own swift feet, swords and shields in their hands. No decent man fought on a chariot, unless it was for the purpose of entertainment.

The man was crying, his breaths staggered.

"He tied him to the chariot. Achilles tied him by his feet, and dragged him, for what he had done to Patroclus. For killing Achilles's cousin. For killing Patroclus."

The air seemed to freeze solid for a moment, although Penthesilea regained her poise in just one breath.

"This is war! Are you are telling me that Hector killed a man, and for that, Achilles dragged his body around from a chariot?"

The man nodded again.

Rage filled her. To drag a body around, to humiliate the vessel after the death, the very idea was simply unthinkable. And to do such a thing to a man such as Hector! That sweet little boy who had thought only of protecting his king and his people. No talk of fame. No talk of notoriety. The boy who had looked upon her gift of arrows as if it were more priceless than every gem in Corinth.

And Achilles had done this to him.

The man gulped, the color of his eyes intensified by the lens of tears that flooded them.

"That is all I know. That is all that happened. I swear to you. I swear to you."

Penthesilea nodded, not that the man could see. He was telling the truth, and he knew no more. With a flick of her wrist, she drew the blade across his throat and pushed him toward the stones where the blood stained the sand beneath him.

As she scaled the rocks, her mind felt a cold detachment from her body. Her women were where she had left them, their eyes looking out into the distance, learning the landscape, learning what they could about the terrain and the men they would fight there.

"What did you discover?" asked Amina, as Penthesilea mounted her horse. "What have you learned of our opponents?"

Penthesilea pulled on the reins of her horse and kicked it straight into a canter.

"I learned what I have been called here by the gods to do," Penthesilea replied. "I have been called here to kill Achilles."

FIFTY-EIGHT

THE EUPHORIA WAS LONG FORGOTTEN, EVAPORATED FROM THE women like morning mist in the first rays of the sun. What they were facing was no normal foe but an enemy whose mercilessness surpassed even human dignity. These were animals, tyrants, beasts who deserved to be slain and skinned like the Nemean lion. They lit no fire that night, for they could not risk drawing attention to themselves, and although the night was warm enough, humid and thick, Penthesilea found herself longing for the warmth of Cletes beside her. For her soft hand and gentle laugh.

She did not sleep. Instead, she rehearsed her movements, over and over again, envisioning all the manners in which she might kill Achilles. She was determined it would be she who would kill him, and she would ensure he suffered the same dishonor he had cast upon Hector. An arrow in the heart. A spear to the belly. Her ax sweeping through the tendons of his neck. It did not matter how, only that she did it. Achilles was not a hero. No hero defiled a corpse as he had, dragging Hector through the dirt, hauling his body over rocks and stones. She could only imagine how the coarse earth had ripped at his flesh and torn the skin from his bones. Even Theseus, the man she despised and whose death she dreamed of daily, would not have suffered such a fate at her hands. She could face ten thousand men tomorrow, but there was only one death she craved.

That morning they rose and, having found a less precipitous slope down to the beach, watched on as the battle resumed at early light. It was not an unusual position for them to take, lost in the chimes of spears, observing their opponents in fight as they studied their weaknesses and devised a manner to bring about their demise. Yet today, her eyes did not study the Grecians and the ways in which they fought. Instead, they scoured with ever-expanding frustration, seeking just one man.

"Should we not fight?" Thermodosa said. "I worry that the Trojans will be lost without Hector's command. Is that not what we are here for?"

And yet Penthesilea could barely hear her, so intense was the pounding in her ribs. With the same focus that a hawk, circling above long grasses, brings to bear on the smallest of voles, she scanned up and down the shore, searching through the blur of bodies. She saw the flashes of helmets as they reflected the sun, heard the smash of metal upon metal as one man fell to the ground upon another. She might never have laid eyes on Achilles, yet she knew, with absolute certainty, that the moment she laid eyes upon him, she would know him.

The battle wore on, and despite Thermodosa's concern, it was an even match. For every Trojan soldier Penthesilea saw fall, another Grecian met the same fate. It was no wonder the war had ground on for so many years if this was the manner in which they fought. Still, she waited until the heat of the midday sun painted ripples in the air. In less than a day, she had learned exactly what type of hero this great Achilles was. One that defiled honorable men, then, while his own men forged battle, lounged in the cool comfort of his tent, no doubt in the company of women he had taken as slaves. The thought of his name alone was enough to bring bile rising to the back of her throat.

"If I cannot come to him, he will have to come to me," she said, unable to stand his impertinence any long. Then, raising her sword, she signaled to the women to commence their attack.

The battle cry of thirteen women tore through the armies as if they were a hundred thousand. Their hooves thundered, their steeds snorting clouds of wet breath in the air, and one arrow then another flew from their bows.

"It is the Amazons!"

She heard the cry from somewhere. Greek or Trojan, it mattered not. All men paled in fear and shock as the women rode into the affray, slicing down the Grecians.

"Bring me Achilles!" Penthesilea cried, as she swept her ax through three breastplates with a single swing. "It is only Achilles I want. Bring him to me."

Men backed away, some diving into the sand, others crawling like crabs on their hands and knees in an attempt to avoid the length of her blade. She paid them no mind, reverting to her bow and bringing an end to all who tried to evade her. Men dropped to the ground by the dozens, her fellow Amazons' arrows as deadly as her own.

Once they had seen which side the Amazons were fighting for, the Trojan men, who had retreated toward the wall and were watching the spectacle in silent awe, now began to aid the women in their decimation, moving with a rhythm that told of their years of war together. They obeyed the instructions of the women without question or hesitation, grouping and regrouping on their command. Yet Penthesilea was blind to it all.

"I want Achilles," she cried again. "Bring me Achilles! I will show him the same respect he bestowed upon Prince Hector." Her muscles burned as she moved with a swiftness that she had not felt since her youth, her father's blood pumping within her. "Bring me Achilles!" she cried again, and then, from between the huddled figures of the terrorized Grecians, a parting formed, and a man stepped forward.

He was a man of such stature, she had not seen his like before. Colossal in size, greater even than the greatest of the Gargareans. His arms and legs bulged with muscles, the veins coiling around them like snakes. Each step he took shook the earth beneath his feet. The Trojans retreated, now, placing themselves behind a wall of mounted Amazons. A wall from which Penthesilea stepped forward. She knew from his stature alone who it was she faced.

And it was not the man she wanted.

"Ajax, son of Telamon." Penthesilea dropped to the ground, her shield and ax in hand. Her horse turned in a circle, churning up a ring of dust, and creating her own arena. "It is not you I plan to kill today. I seek only Achilles."

"Queen Penthesilea. I am afraid that will not be possible." He offered no other words as he lifted his bronze shield with one hand and swung his sword at her with the other. With so much weight behind each swing, the force with which he struck was immeasurable. Each strike rattled through her own shield, causing her very bones to tremble. And yet, no matter how he tried, he could do no more than strike her shield, except on those occasions where he swung too far, and struck the sand instead. There was no lightness to his feet, no finesse and skill in the way he prepared each strike. He was a man whose brute strength alone had ensured he would win every fight he entered into. Every fight except this one.

"Bring. Me. Achilles." Each word was punctuated by another smash of her ax until, with one final swing, she knocked the immense

warrior to the ground. Before he could right himself, she was straddling him. Lifting her ax high above her head, she swung it toward
his breastplate, stopping only as the two metals met. His eyes bulged
with fear as he stared up at her from the ground.

"I will kill you," she hissed. "Or you can fetch me Achilles."

The instant she had stepped over him, Ajax scrambled onto his
hands and knees and raced toward his men.

"Fetch Achilles!" he cried into the crowd. "Fetch Achilles!"

Amidst all the noise and chaos, Penthesilea closed her eyes
and breathed a lungful of air. A strong breeze blew in across the
sea, the scent of storm clear and strong in the cold crisp air. It
was the type of storm she remembered watching as it darkened
out at sea, long before it reached land. She and Hippolyte had
loved those storms as children. They had loved waiting for that
first light drizzle that spotted the skin, before the thunder and
lightning commenced.

In that moment, she could feel her sister there beside her. She
could feel Hippolyte, and Antiope, too. And Hector. There were
people who needed her to grant their vengeance, and she would
bestow it here and now.

The hushed whispers alerted her to the approaching figure, and,
opening her eyes, Penthesilea readied herself with her ax.

Though not as imposing as Ajax in stature, this man exuded
a different kind of strength. People parted around him, the space
forming as it always did when she or Hippolyte had arrived somewhere
new. His walk was closer to a swagger than a stride, and several blond
curls escaped from the bottom of his helmet. She grimaced at the
cocksure confidence that oozed from him. This man was the very
antithesis of Hector. This arrogance. It reminded her of one man
and one man only. At least she could rid the world of one of them.

"I do not believe we are acquainted?" Achilles said, swinging his sword in a round circle.

"I can rectify that."

Penthesilea made the first move. She chose a long strike, a difficult move from distance, something her opponents rarely anticipated, yet Achilles did. He saw her ax coming and dodged her with ease, causing her to tumble past. Immediately balancing herself, she spun around and struck again. Once again, he avoided her blow. She could feel her breath coming thick and fast as she lunged and struck again, and then again, her blows never landing, her opponent always just out of reach. The sand grazed her knees and elbows as Achilles twisted and turned, combining the force of her latest strike with his own evasion and knocking her down. With one push, she was on her feet again, swinging for him, and this time her ax clanged against his shield. But it was not enough. He did not seem to be tiring at all while her fight with Ajax had seen her use all her strength. Ajax had never come close to hitting her, but she had spent energy avoiding his clumsy blows, and still more bringing him down. And now, suddenly, she found herself on the defense, her attacks few and far between, and the smell of her own sweat more intense than she could ever recall. She shook her head, trying to cast it away, and Achilles took advantage of this momentary distraction to strike again. The edge of his blade sank into one of the plates on her arm. With a guttural yell, she twisted away, wrenching the metal apart.

A trickle of blood ran down toward her elbow. It was a nick, that was all. It would heal quickly. Yet even as these thoughts rolled through her, so did another. She could not help recalling that the only person who had ever drawn her blood was Hippolyte, and that action had been enough to distinguish her as queen.

Her heart pounding, she shuffled back in the sand, placing more

HANNAH LYNN

room between her and her opponent than she had ever needed in a fight before. Her ax, she thought now, was the wrong choice of weapon, for she would need to get closer to deal a fatal blow while he had now dropped his sword and plucked a spear from the sand. It glinted, showering the sand below them with a thousand reflections, constellations moving against a yellow sky.

How could she reach him? Hippolyte would know what to do in such a situation. This battle would already have been over if it had been her fighting Achilles.

Her mind drifted to her sister. To her smile and her eyes, which even in death had shown compassion. She would hold those eyes in her memory always, she knew. Even if she lived for a thousand years, they would be as clear to her as the image of her own hand. So fixed was the glimmer of Hippolyte's eyes in Penthesilea's mind that it took a moment for her to realize the glint she could now see was not her sister's smile but Achilles's spear, moving through the air toward her. The queen tilted her head, as if she had all the time in the world to consider the object hurtling in her direction. All the time to twist her body away.

And yet she did not. She simply frowned at its sparkling tip as it plunged into her chest.

EPILOGUE

DEATH ON THE BATTLEFIELD WAS THE ONLY HONORABLE
death for an Amazon, and it was such a gift that Penthesilea
received that day. On the yellow sands of Troy she lay,
Achille's spear through her chest, her heart growing fainter with every
beat until finally it was still. Some say that Achilles removed her helmet
and fell instantly in love with her. That he wept for the loss of his equal,
longing to spend just one more breath with her. But he felt no desire
for the queen; it was the gaze of utter peace that graced her face that
he longed for. The slightest of smiles on the warrior's lips, as if she had
slipped away serenely. As if she were exactly where she wished to be.

The twelve women who had traveled to Troy with Penthesilea
fought valiantly, their arrows and swords felling Grecians by the
hundred in the name of their queen. But it was not enough. The
enemy's numbers were too overwhelming. One by one, they fell,
warriors until the end.

And what of the remaining Amazons? Those like Melanippe,
who had stayed in Pontus, and those who had traveled with Cletes
on the ship that was bound for Troy?

Melanippe lived out her years on the steppes around Themiscyra, continuing to teach the ways of the Amazons to the nomads. She grew crops and hunted rabbits. No longer did she ride to war but found contentment in the simple life, camping under the stars and bathing in the rivers. As the years faded, the younger children grew to know her simply as Melanippe, another nomad, a woman of extraordinary age who could shoot an arrow or ride a horse with greater skill than any person they had ever met, and who could weave magical tales of the gods and the warrior queens and princesses. They did not know she was one of the princesses of whom she spoke. That she was the daughter of Ares. And that was the way she preferred it.

As for Cletes, her boat never reached the shores of Troy but was blown off course by a fierce wind that ravaged the sails and tossed and twisted the vessel until its ropes snapped and its masts splintered. One by one, the Amazons aboard were lost to Poseidon's swell. All except for Cletes.

Through some grace, she was not lost to the water but swept onto a distant shore, a place in which the Amazons were creatures of myth and legend. Knowing there was no way for her to ever reach home again, she etched out a life on those pale shores, never disclosing her true identity. After some years there, she married a king and became a fair and compassionate queen, always loyal and faithful to her husband.

But in her heart, there would only ever be one true love for her. Penthesilea, the Queen of Themiscyra.

READING GROUP GUIDE

1. Who are the queens of Themiscyra, and what are their roles in the Ancient Greek world? Were you familiar with their story? If so, how might the myths you've heard in the past differ from this retelling?

2. Describe the Amazon women and some of their customs. Did any of this surprise you? Were you familiar with this group of female warriors?

3. What is the relationship like between Hippolyte and Penthesilea? How does that change through the novel?

4. How does Theseus betray Hippolyte, and what is her reaction to his actions? How did you feel about their relationship throughout the novel? Discuss.

5. This is a retelling of Greek mythology. Why might the retelling of myths and legends be important?

6. What position is Hippolyte in when Penthesilea finds her in Athens, and what is Penthesilea's reaction to Hippolyte's choices? Did you see this coming?

7. What is Hippolyte's new life in Athens like? Did you think she was content? Why or why not?

8. Discuss the story Aegeus tells of the Minotaur in Crete. How does Theseus involve himself, and how does this event change the course of the story?

9. Why does Penthesilea leave Themiscyra and give the title of queen to her sister? Does she find what she is looking for in Troy?

10. Love, sacrifice, and revenge are vital themes throughout the story. Discuss the ways these ideas intertwine with one another. How might each of the character's decisions be impacted by all three themes?

11. The story concludes with Penthesilea joining the battles of the Trojan war. How does this story end for her, and how did that make you feel?

12. The story of the queens of Themiscyra might be read as a tragedy. Why is that?

A CONVERSATION
WITH THE AUTHOR

Why Hippolyte and Penthesilea? What about their story inspired you to retell it?

They are such incredible women, and I wholeheartedly believed that they deserved their own stories, not just some footnotes in another hero's history. The relationship between the sisters is also so complex, as is taking on the role of queen and the sacrifices that entails. There was just so much to explore.

The story has a large cast of characters. Did you have a favorite as you were writing?

Yes, I have to confess I loved Cletes. She was such a steadying character for Penthesilea, never demanding anything from her but pushing her forward in exactly the right way whenever she needed it.

What do you think is most important when writing a modern retelling?

I think it's so important to know which story you want to tell. There are so many out there with intertwined characters that you have to stay true to the vision you have. You also want to draw people into the lives and the worlds there, but it is a novel, not a text book, and finding that balance between sharing all these amazing facts you've learned about your characters whilst ensuring their story shines through is paramount.

What do you hope readers take away from this story?

I want people to see that women—and people as a whole—do not have to be defined by one characteristic. Hippolyte was a queen and a strong and powerful fighter. That didn't mean she couldn't fall victim to Theseus's emotional abuse. Penthesilea was the most formidable fighter and knew the perils of war, but that didn't stop her grief and turmoil after her sister died.

Where do you draw creative inspiration from when writing?

Anywhere and everywhere! Each time I write one of these books, I discover a new character that I want to explore further still. The list is never-ending.

What are you reading these days?

My TBR pile only ever seems to grow! At the moment, *Atalanta* is at the top of that list, but I also love to delve in and out of different genres too.

ACKNOWLEDGMENTS

I need to extend a heartfelt thanks to Adrienne Mayor. Although I have never met or conversed with her, her book *The Amazons* proved an invaluable reference throughout writing this *Queens of Themiscyra*. If she ever reads this, I apologize for some of the poetic license I applied to the lives of the nomadic people for narrative flow. I hope you understand.

To the team of people that made this story a reality, including Jenna and the team at Sourcebooks. Thank you for taking a chance on this story and me. To Emma, Carol, and Joel, thank you for all the help you gave me, not to mention Kath, Lucy, and Jane, whose unwavering support has been there for me book after book. I would be lost without you.

To my amazing readers. Thank you so much for coming on this journey with me. You will never know how much I appreciate you. Thank you for allowing me to do this job.

Lastly to Jake, my first reader, harshest critic, and long-suffering husband. The hours you spent with me helping this book be the best it could was no small feat, and I know that at times it took as much from you as it did from me. I am so grateful for how you helped make this vision come to life and for everything you do for me and our family every day. Thank you.

ABOUT THE AUTHOR

 Hannah Lynn is a multiaward-winning novelist. Publishing her first book, *Amendments*—a dark, dystopian speculative fiction novel—2015. Her second book, *The Afterlife of Walter Augustus*—a contemporary fiction novel with a supernatural twist—went on to win the 2018 Kindle Storyteller Award and the Independent Publishers Gold Medal for Best Adult Ebook.

Born in 1984, Hannah grew up in the Cotswolds, UK. After graduating from university, she spent fifteen years as a teacher of physics, first in the UK and then Thailand, Malaysia, Austria, and Jordan. It was during this time, inspired by the imaginations of the young people she taught, she began writing short stories for children and, later, adult fiction.

Now, settled back in the UK with her husband, daughter, and horde of cats, she spends her days writing romantic comedies and historical fiction. Her first historical fiction novel, *Athena's Child*, was also a 2020 Gold Medalist at the Independent Publishers Awards.